THE SINGHING DETECTIVE

THE SINGHING DETECTIVE

SERIES THREE
SUGAR AND SPICE

M C DUTTON

Matador
9 Priory Business Park,
Wistow Road, Kibworth Beauchamp,
Leicestershire. LE8 0RX
Tel: 0116 279 2299
Email: books@troubador.co.uk
Web: www.troubador.co.uk/matador
Twitter: @matadorbooks

ISBN 978 1788035 538

British Library Cataloguing in Publication Data.
A catalogue record for this book is available from the British Library.

Printed and bound by CPI Group (UK) Ltd, Croydon, CR0 4YY
Typeset in 11pt StempelGaramondRoman by Troubador Publishing Ltd, Leicester, UK

Matador is an imprint of Troubador Publishing Ltd

*To my wonderful children Helen & Ben, Richard
& Amanda and Andrew & Nansal and my darling
grandchildren Isabella, Kiera, Rebecca, Josh, Thomas,
Bradley, Max and Edie-Rose.*

Children are the hands by which we take hold of Heaven.
(Henry Ward Beecher 1813-1887)

PROLOGUE

He whimpered in the corner. He was too young to understand anything. At six years old all he knew was he wanted his mummy. They had hurt him and done things he didn't understand. Sometimes they were nearly nice, they hugged him and kissed him but not like his mummy, and then they did things he just knew weren't right and they hurt him badly.

There was one man who hit him and he was very frightened of him. The attacks had covered him in bruises and burn marks. Now traumatised and exhausted, he was past crying. He rolled himself into the smallest ball he could in the corner and hoped they would leave him alone. He wanted his mummy so badly. She would make it better and cuddle him and make him safe, warm and comfortable. He could imagine her smile and her smell. She always smelt warm and safe, and like Mummy.

Little Kevin Parsons, the middle child of Marie and Peter Parsons, died violently on Guy Fawkes Night, 5th November. As the skies lit with stars and the bright colours of exploding fireworks, Kevin's life was extinguished. The cameras had rolled and taken every intimate detail of the end of Kevin's life. Kevin had only been on Earth for six years but his cruel and wicked murder would ruin many lives for years to come. His body was found dumped and discarded amongst rubbish on a municipal tip in Essex. It was two workmen, shifting rubbish as usual, swapping jokes and football updates, who found Kevin. What they saw lived with them for many years.

Kevin never knew that there was a large-scale hunt going on for him. He had been missing for two weeks of utter misery and pain. His mother Marie and father Peter had been on the television pleading for his return. It was headline news. Strangers had helped search for him in the nearby woods. He never knew that his mother and father would never get over his death, and when his body was found, his mother would be sedated for a long time. After everyone else's life returned to normal she had taken to pill-popping and just sitting. Her husband started to come home later and later, until he never returned. Marie and Peter divorced and Kevin's brother Jamie and sister Emily never knew what it was like to have a normal mother who cared for them or a father who was around. Their lives were destroyed by the knowledge that not only had Kevin been kidnapped and murdered, but also that his little life had been full of indescribable pain, fear and vicious buggery. The autopsy showed he had been systematically raped, and the burn marks all over his little body showed he had been tortured. The police did their best to hide some of the details of the autopsy report from the parents, but the parents insisted and read too much. The report showed in graphic detail the full extent of the mutilation that had taken place. Even the professionals, used to the wickedness of society and hardened by most facts, shed many tears when reading how Kevin's body had been abused, used, ripped and torn by paedophiles. What parent could cope with that knowledge?

CHAPTER 1

This is Where it Starts

DS Jaswinder Singh, known as Jazz to his friends and enemies, had been idling around helping out where needed while Ash Kumar recovered. *At least Ash is alive,* was the best Jazz could come up with. He was still getting the catcalls of "OK, this one survived, but only by luck".

Ash was up for a commendation for his brave undercover work. Jazz had worked hard to get Ash to come back and work with him. He told Ash, in truth, that he needed his meticulous, anally retentive attention to paperwork. Jazz knew his shortfall; he hated anything to do with paperwork, but Ash loved it. They were both to realise they were a match made in heaven.

If Jazz thought he was going to get respect from Ash, he would be very disappointed. Ash knew who Jazz was and liked him. But he wasn't going to let him get away with anything he didn't agree with. His traumatic time being held as a prisoner, with the constant threat of being killed, had led to him having sessions with a counsellor, and through that he came to the conclusion that he, Ash Kumar, was a good officer who should be listened to.

In future, he would make sure that Jazz would not have everything his own way. Never again would he be so stupid as to take action without proper backup especially in a dangerous situation, but by the same token, he wasn't going to let Jazz lead him into anything life-threatening. *No siree*, he thought, he was going to be safe and sober and not stupid this time. He would keep control and have a quiet life.

This way of thinking was never going to last long. Working with Jazz was never going to be straightforward.

Ash arrived in the CID (Criminal Investigation Department) office to handshakes and "Well dones" from colleagues who had been far less generous when he had started over a year ago. He was enjoying the adulation. He could have told them that it was Jazz who engineered his release and saved his life. He could have told them that it was his own stupidity that got him into trouble in the first place, but he reckoned Jazz owed him this little bit of fame.

Jazz grimly watched the display in front of him and thought, *Bollocks to the lot of them*. He still had Ash on his team, which was a first! He nearly laughed at that, but remembered Tony Sepple and the near-smile died. Sepple's death still gave Jazz sharp pains in his chest when he thought of him.

The smile nearly appeared again when he thought that at least the treacherous bastard police sergeant Bob was now permanently disabled through beatings in prison, and that Bam Bam had gone down head first into the cheese grater (a wire mesh ten feet high from the ground across the central area of a prison to stop missiles being thrown down on to prisoners below), and was deservedly bloody dead. Some things work out well, and he was proud of that.

Ash and Jazz went off for a chat and to settle in. A cup of tea was in order, and they made their way to the canteen. The lovely Milly spotted Jazz as soon as he entered and she had a cup of tea ready for him. Ash might be the hero of the day, but he had to wait until Jazz was suitably comfortable and had answered all Milly's questions about what he needed. She insisted he had a bacon sandwich, which he declined, but after the third time he gave in and said a bacon sandwich would be wonderful.

Ash sat and waited until eventually he was told to come and collect his tea from the counter; Milly wasn't his slave, you know.

Ash whispered, "Bloody hell, things don't change, do they?"

Jazz laughed. At least the women in his life wanted to wait on him. Milly was his number one lady and Phyllis was his second in command.

Phyllis was a rather shy girl of about thirty years old. She would blush bright red whenever she saw Jazz. He only had to walk into the CJU (Criminal Justice

Unit) and Phyllis would scurry around to make him a cup of tea and find him one of those special biscuits kept hidden in a tin, away from stealing fingers. Food was not safe in a police station. Sweets, biscuits, crisps – if left on show, they would disappear. Police officers always worked on the hoof, and mealtimes were a luxury.

It was a bone of contention that those arrested and kept in cells were catered for regularly, given a menu and hot food on tap. They sat and waited whilst officers missed meals and rushed around getting whatever information was needed to effect a charge.

It was also a bone of contention that they had to wait on the bloody phone for the bloody CPS (Crown Prosecution Service) to read and make a decision on a charge, and in quite a few cases they would say there wasn't enough information for any charges. The regular mutterings would be that, years ago, when officers were allowed to be officers, they could arrest someone and charge them and that would be that. None of the fannying around they had to do now for the CPS, who didn't know their arse from their elbow. The CPS had a tough job, and an uneasy relationship with officers on the beat. Jazz was one of their main critics.

Paperwork not being his best subject was never a problem for Jazz. Phyllis had taken it upon herself to look after every case he had. She would type out the paperwork, put it in order, gather outstanding forms needed and present Jazz with a good working file on his case. She adored him, and a smile from him was all she needed in return. They took the mickey out of her in the office. As Jazz appeared a whoop would go up, and calls to Phyllis that her loverboy had arrived, as if she hadn't seen for herself. Her blushes got redder and Jazz's smile got bigger. He liked the fuss and attention from all the ladies in the CJU.

In passing, he popped in to say hi to Phyllis. He knew he would always get a beaming smile, and his words listened to and hung on. It was good for his ego. No one else did that in the CID office. He needed a boost to his ego today, with Ash the hero spread all over the station.

As usual he wanted to go to the IBO (Integrated Borough Operations) office to see what was coming in, but he couldn't. He was given the boring, arduous and decidedly uninteresting gang crimes to sort out. So far it had been the odd scuffle with knives, the taking of bikes and mobiles and the sniffing, smoking and swallowing of anything remotely illegal. Shit sticks, and it wouldn't be long before Jazz found himself in the middle of something not right in his town. The attacks on him were personal and from different directions. Someone wanted to cause him grief.

CHAPTER 2

Are You Sitting Comfortably?

He sat up straight on the ancient settee. The old springs inside groaned as he sat down. The heavy mosaic velour tapestry in a dull green dominated the room. Feeling decidedly uncomfortable, Jazz tried to balance the fine bone china cup and saucer on his knees as he tentatively bent forward to sip the hot tea and tried not to slurp. Mrs Edith Cameron beamed and looked on contentedly. In a manner that was reminiscent of the '40s, Edith Cameron, who was the wrong side of seventy, cocked her head and waited for appreciation of the tea she had lovingly prepared.

"Mr Singh, I am so glad you came today. I know you are going to be a great help." Her voice had a cultured tone that didn't quite take out the East End twang. She was certainly quite posh for the area.

DS Jaswinder Singh was trying to be refined and sit still in this grand old lady's home in Barking. It was a beautiful house overlooking the park. It had seen better days, like its owner, but it still had a grand look.

This very regal looking old lady got up to get Jazz the matching plateful of chocolate biscuits. As she came up to him the air around her moved and the fragrance of lavender wafted across. It was a nice smell, but as the sweetness of the lavender scent left him it was replaced by the bitterness of piss. Old ladies seemed to have waterworks problems, and he did his best not to notice. It would have mortified Mrs C if she thought she stunk of piss.

He accepted a chocolate biscuit and thanked her nicely. The pungent smell hit him harder as she got closer, but he had the good grace not to retch. He smiled, took the biscuit and just stopped himself dunking it in his tea. He knew that wasn't good manners. It was an uncomfortable meeting, but this was part of his new job.

Mrs C sat herself down in an armchair opposite him. She proceeded to tell him about the young boys she had seen outside her house with those jackets with hoods on. She had watched them through heavily netted windows. She saw one of them clearly when he took his hood off to put on a baseball cap. Yes, she said, she would recognise him if she saw a picture.

Barking Park had become a no-go area for youngsters wanting to play, ride their bikes or just meet friends. Now it was a mugger's paradise and bikes and mobiles were stolen from anyone who entered the park alone. This group had intimidated a lad of eight years old and taken his bike, his money and his mobile. Jazz wondered why any eight-year-old would have a mobile, but he knew that it was just old-fashioned to think like that. All kids had mobiles, and some had two or three of them. That he never understood! Why more than one? He would get someone to explain it to him one day.

So Mrs Edith Cameron was his prize witness for the moment. There was no CCTV in that part of Barking, so he would accompany Mrs C to the police station to look at some mugshots and see if she could recognise the lad. The baseball cap he had put on belonged to the eight-year-old they had just robbed, and Mrs Cameron described the bike they were pushing, which sounded the same as the one that had been stolen.

Although Mrs Cameron wanted to chat, Jazz pushed the conversation along and asked her to accompany him to the police station. She smiled, and, quite excitedly, got up to get her coat. The smell reached him again and he mentally noted to make sure to open the window of the police car.

He got to the custody suite and sat Mrs Cameron down in one of the rooms. He avoided the looks he was getting and the faces being pulled as Mrs Cameron walked by. She smiled at everyone, totally oblivious to the pervading smell that was encompassing everywhere she went. The custody room was small, so Jazz left the door open. Mrs Cameron thought he suffered from claustrophobia and sympathised with him. Jazz just nodded and got on with finding the computer with all the ID photos on it.

DCI Radley had decided that after the last fiasco

of the three murders (the Godfathers of London), Jazz was relegated to small-time cases. It wasn't that he hadn't solved all the murders; it was more that everything he touched seemed to create problems and potentially life-threatening situations. He accused Jazz of flying by the seat of his pants, and suggested that it was more by luck than judgement that the case had a satisfactory result. Jazz thought darkly that DCI Radley was never fucking pleased. He had solved more murders in his short time than all the other pissheads in the CID office.

Since the riots in the summer of 2011, the youth of Barking and Dagenham tried to recreate the carnage every year. This year a concerted effort of various gangs joined forces and used their mobile phones to strategically organise the rioting. The targets were always going to be the sports shops, and any shop that had electrical goods and jewellery.

The way it worked was that a fight was arranged on the other side of town near Beckton ski slopes. A small contingency of two gangs would cause mayhem and run amok. Police from surrounding areas would be called and Barking Police from Fresh Wharf would take to cars and vans and go to sort it out. At the same time, Dagenham Town Hall would have a small group of gang members fighting each other and throwing eggs and stones at the town hall. So the Dagenham and Romford Police would be sent there.

All was going to plan. The biggest group of gang members would be waiting in areas around Barking town centre on their mobile phones. When they got the message that said, *GO!*, they all, as one, raced to the Barking shops that had already been cherry-picked for robbing, overcame the staff and helped themselves to everything they wanted. They had the town almost to themselves because local police were elsewhere!

The coordination, which almost had a military precision to it, displayed in these undisciplined young people was very worrying. It took twelve hours to regain control of Barking town centre.

He had been told to work on the gang crimes in the Barking and Dagenham area, and that there would be no overtime. Overtime was banned. No money spare in the budget. This bugged Jazz, who worked hard and long and now wasn't going to get a pissing penny extra for it.

Mrs Cameron picked out a photo of the delightful little miscreant known to all the community officers on the Gascoigne Estate. Charlie Thorpe, a young lad of thirteen years old who relied on his brains and brawn to steal and intimidate. He hadn't been seen in school since he was ten years old. There were the usual social workers, school heads, mentors, probation officers, police, psychologists, psychiatrists – they had all had a go at doing something with Master Thorpe, but to him it was just a laugh. He wasn't going anywhere; the odd tag he had received, and of course a referral order to start with, made him feel invincible. He was a thieving bully who was never going to amount to anything. He was on the ladder for a life of criminality, not the poor underprivileged boy without a father that the army of bloody do-gooders portrayed him as. These people made Jazz's blood boil. Bloody social workers giving the likes of Thorpe any excuse for their criminal behaviour. Jazz knew of many boys from similar backgrounds who had done good.

There was going to be no pleasure in arresting this boy. He would be cocky and smirk, knowing the worst they could do was keep him overnight, but he knew his rights and demanded everything. His mother had given up on him and wouldn't go to the police station with him, so an appropriate adult would be contacted to sit in with him during his interview. He would demand regular breaks with food and drink. He was a minor, and he told all the officers he would report them if they didn't "treat him good".

Jazz gave this little shit to Ash, who would love to complete the paperwork and speak to the CPS just to get Thorpe a community service sentence that he was never going to attend.

CHAPTER 3

Old Lace, Old Grudges

Feeling a bit low (kiddie gangs always made him feel like that; there was no justice for victims or for him), Jazz sloped back to his desk to find a complaint from DCI Radley. That fucking man didn't leave him alone. Everyone else got on with their work but he was constantly jibing, pushing and wanting. OK, Jazz conceded, he had a bit more trouble than most officers but he also had far more fucking successes. He thought fiercely that the Met Police ought to make up their minds on whether they want results or candy-arsed sweetness to give the public.

He conceded he might not say the right things, like "Goodness me, sir, may I help you carry your stolen goods? Your back will hurt if you pick up that forty-two-inch colour TV you stole from an old lady's house." He asked himself again – was he in the right job? Sadly, the answer every time was yes. He loved it. While he could work the way he did and get away with it, he would, just to fuck them all off! That made him smile.

Phyllis was waiting for him at his desk. He smiled and wondered if he would get a cup of tea. She gave him some papers for the 'old lady flowers' case, as it was known. He thanked her. He had done the paperwork but it wasn't up to standard, and Phyllis took them away and put them in a clear order. He was grateful for her help, and told her that from now on Ash would be taking care of all his paperwork so her life was going to get easier.

He thought that would please her, but it didn't. She tried to hide her scowl. Then she smiled and said that she would always have tea ready for him anyway. He smiled back at her and told her she was wonderful. Warming to this compliment, she hesitantly suggested that perhaps they could celebrate his paperwork now being done by Ash, thus giving him more time. Jazz laughed and said that yes, it would be a celebration for both of them. Blushing redder than a blazing fire, she hesitantly added that perhaps they could meet for a drink after work to celebrate.

Jazz was already laughing, and continued by saying that he had better not – her husband might come after him and beat him up. Laughing, he added a dismissive, "As a brilliant ideas person, this is not one of your best." Phyllis nodded and left, and he giggled at the thought of her husband coming to take him on. He thought Phyllis was far too generous with her time, and he didn't want to take advantage any more than he had to. He liked her.

His stupidity was a big mistake, and it would come back to haunt him.

The complaint from DCI Radley was about the old lady flowers case. Jazz looked up as Ash called over to him. He was balancing papers and files and looked to be in a hurry. He shouted in passing that he was off to the charging centre to interview Charlie Thorpe. After his run-in with some other gang members and the trouble they had caused him with the Bird Man of Barking (Barry Bentall was the untouchable gang leader in Barking – no one messed with him), Ash relished interviewing and charging any gang member that came his way. He fiddled with the papers in his arms, carefully extricated a small file, and threw it on Jazz's desk.

"DCI Radley is pushing for an arrest in this case now," was all he said to Jazz. It was the old lady flowers case and Jazz was not going to charge anyone with this. Ash shrugged and said he would have to; the DCI needed a charge for his monthly figures and he was gunning for this to be done before the day was out.

Ash was in a hurry to get back to the charging room and Charlie Thorpe, but he left with Jazz's forceful "Bollocks to all of that" ringing in his ears.

Mrs Joyce Simpson, eighty-three years old and living in sheltered accommodation in Rainham Road, Dagenham, was a keen gardener. She had a very small front garden, which she kept in bloom for the summer.

Her pansies and begonias had been systematically pulled up. It was assumed it was local lads who, in passing, destroyed her garden. She had replanted three times and each time, the following week, they were all pulled out of the ground and left to shrivel up and die. Now Mrs Simpson was getting a bit frightened at the thought of lads coming in the night to pull up her plants. She thought they might come and hurt her next.

It was a community police problem to start with, but DCI Radley wanted to Jazz to investigate. Mrs Simpson was now threatening to talk to her nephew, who was on the local council, and she was also going to ring the local newspaper and tell them. Mrs Simpson was a feisty old lady and she had got the media-friendly DCI Radley worried. He had said to Jazz that as he was looking after gang crime, this was one he could easily deal with. He could tell by the look on Jazz's face that he was not best pleased, and pretty disgusted to have to deal with such a little, insignificant and demeaning case.

After receiving a long lecture on looking after the needs of the community, however small, Jazz sloped off to visit Mrs Simpson. His life seemed full of old ladies these days and he wasn't happy. The sheltered accommodation on Rainham Road was a neat little row of ground-level accommodation. Each had a tiny front garden, which some had grown flowers in and others had just left tidy with a wheelie bin, a bit of grass and a token potted plant.

Mrs Simpson had gone to the trouble of digging the

ground and had what looked like two flower beds. The flower beds were empty except for a few sticks in the ground and a lot of disturbed earth. Jazz wanted to get this over with and asked Mrs Simpson to confirm her complaint. She was having none of this and wouldn't be rushed. She told Jazz in an almost school teacher tone she would not discuss anything until he had a cup of tea and two Mr Kipling fondant cakes. Jazz sat containing his frustration while Mrs Simpson fussed around him ensuring he was sitting comfortably and drinking his tea. Eventually she sat with her tea and explained about her plants ending up lying on top of the earth, pulled out by their roots. She spent the next ten minutes informing him that today's youth had no respect and that she was frightened. Jazz established that she had planted various plants three times and each time they were pulled up by the next week. He noted that there were other plants in other gardens, maybe not as pretty or as many as in Mrs Simpson's, but they had not been touched.

He asked, as if in passing, how she got on with her neighbours. Apparently, Mrs Baker next door was a real cow and didn't speak to her. It was to do with her radio and television. Mrs Simpson had to have the sound up quite loud because her hearing wasn't very good, and Mrs Baker had complained and complained and reported her to the council, so they weren't talking.

Mrs Simpson, who up to now had seemed a sweet old lady, suddenly stared at Jazz, and with more venom than he thought she had the energy to exert, she spat, "She's a bloody old mare, that one. She is bullying me and no one cares – I can't help my hearing!"

Now into her stride and shifting her ample bottom in the chair to make herself comfortable, she went on to tell him how this feud had gone on since last year. They scored points off each other with Mrs Baker complaining to the council and Mrs Simpson telling the milkman, the neighbours and generally anyone who would listen that Mrs Baker was bullying her. Jazz got a really good picture of what was going on. It was time to visit Mrs Baker and get this sorted.

He knocked on Mrs Baker's door, trying to keep his patience in check. "First it's fucking gangs and now fucking grannies fighting."

He was made to have another cup of tea and another Mr Kipling fondant cake. Mrs Baker would have none of his excuses. "You are a young man and you need to keep your strength up," was Mrs Baker's excuse for pushing the cake and cup of tea onto his lap. If he never saw another pink icing-covered cake it would be too soon. He wondered if that was the only cake sold in this area. He was feeling quite queasy, but with Mrs Baker watching closely, he managed to swallow the last mouthful and washed it down with a gulp of tea.

They talked about Mrs Simpson and her flower beds. Mrs Baker said nothing and just sat with pursed lips. She watched Jazz closely, and only when he said that he had her on CCTV pulling the plants up did she confess. *Well, there was no CCTV that would have seen that, but she didn't need to know that,* thought Jazz. She was a feisty lady and said she wasn't going to apologise, but there was a hint of embarrassment at being caught out. Jazz agreed that if she promised not to do it again he would forget it. He insisted, though, that she bought a present of a box of plants for Mrs Simpson. He suggested she say that it was a peace offering. He warned her he would be coming by to check that she had done this. Now looking quite ashamed, Mrs Baker promised to do what he said and Jazz left, stating that no more would be said of this.

There was no way he was going to charge Mrs Baker. She was so old he thought the shock might kill her. He would explain to DCI Radley and hope he would see sense.

Actually, he suggested that arresting someone as old as Mrs Baker would make DCI Radley look heartless. Jazz painted a picture of this frail, little old lady being arrested and put in handcuffs. He suggested the press might make a meal out of that. After a very short consideration DCI Radley agreed with Jazz's decision and no more was said about his monthly figures.

"Oh, I have the touch, who's the daddy?" was the question put to a startled young PC as a smug Jazz sauntered out of the police station. He didn't want to go home to his room at Mrs Chodda's straight away. He had to pass the local Cranbrook pub, and he thought, *Why not?* He fancied a whisky for a change; he wanted to savour it in the ambience of an English pub.

Charlie behind the bar was a friendly sort of guy who smiled but didn't talk much, which suited Jazz. One look and he poured another drink for him, and Jazz was on his fourth double when he felt something big settle beside him. Before he turned to look he heard the grunt of someone making himself comfortable on a bar stool, and knew it was Boomer.

This wasn't usual, and Jazz asked, "What the fuck are you doing here? You don't come into pubs that often."

Boomer was not best pleased with this welcome, and in no uncertain terms he suggested Jazz did something anatomically impossible and pretty painful too. He ordered one of what Jazz was drinking from Charlie, who nodded and poured and left them to it. It was late, and both needed this relaxation time. Life in the Met had got pretty awful recently with all the new rules, forms and ideas. There was no overtime paid, but the work still had to be done. There were no ifs or buts; they had to get on and do the job. They sat supping whisky and just idly chatting, comfortable in each other's company. Neither were great friends with anyone else in the station, and Boomer was suspicious of most.

The pub was going to be busy later; there was a banner up, saying something about a stag do for Maurice going on that night.

Jazz studied it for a moment and then turned to Boomer and asked, "Weren't you married at some point, Boomer?"

Boomer rumbled an agreement and added, "Not as fucking often as you."

Jazz choked on his whisky and laughed. "That's fucking right, I never learned the first time, but what happened to you? After all, you're such a gentleman."

Boomer looked at him for a moment, and then saw the joke and laughed. "It lasted a few years but when we moved to the country she got involved with the hunting and shooting set, they were all toffee-nosed tosspots but she loved them. I was in London working and only home on days off, so she joined this group and very quickly went from a housewife to an arsehole and that was that."

Jazz nodded knowingly and they drank in comfortable silence. It was a nice moment that didn't happen very often.

Boomer left after an hour but Jazz lingered until closing time. A night of whisky, and then the fresh air hit him as he left the pub. He staggered in the direction of De Vere Gardens, not noticing traffic or time. The walk took twice as long as usual. It was only five minutes from the Cranbrook pub but it took half an hour to walk there and then another five minutes to put the key in the door. He staggered up the stairs and fell on his bed.

CHAPTER 4

Punjabi Tête-à-Tête

He woke the next morning with a crick in his neck and drool on his collar. The headache hit him as he tried to sit up. He vowed never to touch whisky again. He needed a shower and a change of clothes, but first, two paracetamol and a coffee. He left his room looking halfway decent. Detective Sergeant Jaswinder Singh was generally a natty dresser. His suits were always from Marks and Spencer, he wore a tie and was generally considered a sharp, handsome guy, by women at least. He was tall, slim and his shaved head gave him the look of a model. The hangovers were taking their toll; his eyes were darker and although this gave him an interesting look, they bordered on bloodshot.

He got to the police station a little late, but he thought suitably sober-looking. Boomer saw him walking slowly up the stairs in the station and tutted. Jazz was hung over again, and by the looks of him he had dressed with his eyes closed.

He led Jazz to the canteen and to the tender care of Milly, who poured him a very black coffee with three sugars. She had seen Jazz in this condition before and knew what was needed. She scolded him gently as she made him sit in the corner where he wouldn't be noticed too much, and then bustled around him setting his collar straight and tidying his jacket. She set the coffee down in front of him with a pile of serviettes to mop up the spills his shaking hands would cause. It usually took about half an hour before he began to look more normal and able to go to work. He thanked Milly and as he passed Boomer's office he nodded his appreciation, words were not necessary.

Sobered up now he was ready for the custody sergeant who was looking for him.

"Jazz, there's a domestic on Gascoigne Estate. An Asian husband is threatening to blow up the place and its in a block of flats. The Gov reckoned you would be able to talk to the guy and sort it out. He isn't talking to anyone and gets more and more angry when our officers talk through the door. He has a big dog in there as well and the officers are waiting for backup. You have to go there now and sort this out."

Aggrieved at the urgency and although sober, he needed a little time to collect his thoughts. "Am I the only bloody detective around to deal with this?" he asked.

The answer was succinct, "You are the only bloody Asian around here who speaks Punjabi Singh!"

Jazz thought, *Fair enough!* He shrugged his

shoulders, took the address and went off to get a lift to the Gascoigne Estate.

When he got there he knew which block of flats it was by the three police cars, police van and ambulance sitting outside. The officers had cordoned off the area in front of the flats and a small and interested group of people mingled close by. Jazz went up to one of the officers and showed his badge, he didn't need to do that, they knew him. He was introduced to the wife of Pinder, the man in the flat. She was crying and saying they had had a fight and he felt disrespected.

She had married him in India and it had only been six months since he arrived in England and he didn't like it here. She said he worked as a waiter in the local Indian Restaurant which was owned by her father's cousin and he hated the work. She said he was very depressed and wanted her to go back to India with him but she was born in England and didn't want to live in India. He spoke a bit of English but when upset, he reverted totally to Punjabi.

Her name was Tara and she was scared. Pinder had told her he was going to blow himself up in the flat. He didn't want to live here with a downtrodden job in a cold wet country. In his country his family had servants and he came from a good family. He lived in a shit home in a shit country and had a shit job. His wife disrespected him; his family in India would be ashamed. He wanted to die.

Jazz got the picture. He asked what number the flat was and was told it was number 24. He said he would go and talk to Pinder and see what he could do.

He walked up the stairs until he got to flat 24. He knocked on the door and said, "*Sat sri akal, Pinder.*" (Hello, Pinder.) He heard a grunt as a reply. Jazz then shouted through the door, "*Kee karda aya?*" (What are you doing?)

This opened a stream of conversation from Pinder, who said he had had enough. They talked in Punjabi and Jazz asked if he could come in and sit with him. Pinder sounded a bit drunk. After a few minutes the door was unlocked and opened and Jazz was allowed into the room. He looked around and saw a bottle of Chivas Regal half-empty on the table. A huge German Shepherd dog stood alert and growling by Pinder.

Pinder looked a mess. He was Sikh and had his turban on, but it wasn't straight. He hadn't shaved and he smelt of booze and sweat. He locked the door after Jazz entered and looked at him darkly.

"What do you want?" he asked.

Jazz quietly sat down at the table, and with an understanding smile, asked if he might have a peg with him (An alcoholic drink, small is 30ml and large 60ml is almost always called a peg in India.). Pinder got another glass and put it down heavily on the table. He wasn't moving very evenly and the drink had got the better of him.

"I am afraid of dogs, Pinder, would you mind putting your dog in another room?" asked Jazz. Actually, he loved dogs and German Shepherds were his favourite, but a protective dog of that size in the same room was not a good idea.

They sat and drank whilst Pinder told him how frustrated he felt being in England, and how his wife didn't respect him. It turned out he hadn't got any explosives in the flat; it was just the drink talking. Jazz asked if he was attending his local Gudwara (Sikh temple), and Pinder said he hadn't so far. He hadn't talked to anyone much since arriving in England. He couldn't talk to anyone at the restaurant because it was owned by his wife's family and he couldn't lose face.

After a chat and a bit of joking about, Pinder agreed to go to the police station quietly. He understood he could be charged and was compliant. It was decided that he would go to his local Gudwara and find someone to talk with. Jazz, satisfied now that Pinder was OK, called the officers waiting outside and said he was ready to go to the police station.

Two officers were let into the flat by Jazz and looked around. Jazz told them the dog was in another room and there were no explosives.

Jazz left with a pat on Pinder's back and a handshake, saying, "*Fir milaan ge.*" (See you again.) Pinder was calm and went quietly. Jazz asked that a Punjabi interpreter be made available at the police station.

As he left, Jazz sighed to himself. England wasn't paved with gold, as most Indians thought. It was bloody hard work, and always bloody cold too. He laughed at the thought. He loved England. It was his preferred place to live and he hoped Pinder would sort himself out and get on with his life. *Still*, he thought, *onwards and upwards. Shit happens!*

He went back to the police station and filled out the necessary paperwork. He hated fucking paperwork, he just wanted to do his job, not spend hours filling out forms. When he had finished, he gathered up the completed forms and handed them over to the custody sergeant. Someone else would take it over. He left grumbling that even though Ashiv did most of his paperwork he still had to do some; even a little felt too fucking much.

By now it was late afternoon and he reckoned he had earned a drink and home time. He had a few good swigs from his flask – as he told himself, he had bloody earned them today. He couldn't remember if he had eaten last night; he certainly hadn't had anything today, and he was hungry. He ordered a big pizza to be delivered by the time he got home. He stopped off at Sainsbury's for some top-up bottles of vodka and some peanuts. He liked to keep a couple of bottles of vodka for emergencies.

Mrs Chodda heard the key in the door and rushed to open it for Jazz. He didn't mind. He hadn't seen her for a few days, which was pretty normal by the standards of his normal working week, and today he felt like chatting. She tempted him with some of her samosas, and led him into her wonderfully busy kitchen. He saw the plastic bins in the corner. To the untrained eye they looked just like dustbins, but one contained her uncooked rice and the other her flour; she bought in bulk, which traditionally most Sikhs did. She had more saucepans than most restaurants and spoons and ladles all over the place.

He made his way to her wooden table in the middle of her huge kitchen. It was the most welcoming of tables, and he sat down comfortably. Mrs Chodda had a huge range to cook on – in fact it was a cooker with six gas burners, and on the other side of the kitchen was another stove with four burners; Indian cooking involved many dishes being cooked at the same time. Her kitchen was always warm and full of the aromas of curry, spices and oils. She always had a large pot of oil that was regularly used. He had watched her take a little of the oil from the pot to oil her chapattis or cook her samosas, or she would take some for her pakoras. She was a marvellous cook, and to watch her bustling about stirring and baking was to feel like a little boy again, watching his mother. He ate the samosas with the chilli dip she put before him with relish, and after the first four samosas, he was beginning to feel better and more relaxed.

He sat and told Mrs Chodda about the man in Barking saying how unhappy he was to be in England and married to an English-born Indian bride. She nodded sympathetically.

"He has to make peace with his life," she said profoundly. Jazz was impressed. She looked piercingly at Jazz and uttered the words of Sri Guru Granth

Sahib Ji: "Through devotional worship of the Lord, liberation and bliss are obtained."

Jazz wasn't sure if the words were meant for him or the Indian chap in Barking.

"Blood... erm... I mean goodness, Mrs Chodda, you are pretty good at remembering the sayings of the Guru."

She sat back and smiled, pleased with the compliment.

"I am at the *Gudwara* every day. I help cook the meals in the *Langar* (The eating area is known as the *Langar*), it is my *Sewa* (Every Sikh is expected to perform *Sewa*, a selfless serving of others in the community). As you know, even whilst cooking, we hear the words of the Guru through the tannoy. It keeps me at peace."

There was silence for a moment. Jazz didn't know how to respond to that; it was all a bit heavy for him. He asked instead if he could have another samosa. Mrs Chodda happily filled the plate again and told him to help himself.

There was something he wanted to ask Mrs Chodda, and he felt he needed to choose his words carefully. She tended to jump to conclusions so easily that he figured, ruefully, she would be a great contender for the next Olympic high-jump.

"So, Mrs Chodda, have you heard from your niece Amrit yet?"

He tried to sound airy, almost nonchalant, but she wasn't fooled. She looked at him and gave him one of those *I know what you are thinking* smiles which embarrassed and infuriated him. She understood him too well, and that was uncomfortable.

"Amrit is still in India. She should have come home a week or so ago but the family want her to stay for a bit longer." She noted the glum look that Jazz tried to hide.

"I expect they are looking for a fine husband for her over there," he offered, not at all happy at the thought.

Mrs Chodda smiled and said, "If you knew Amrit, you would know that you can't tell that girl what to do. She had one arranged marriage and she won't have another. Next time she said she would only marry for love, if at all. I personally don't think a good Indian man would want a divorced woman with a child."

She saw the look of disbelief on Jazz's face and added, "Oh, I know, I know, it is different here in England. But tradition is still tradition for some."

She looked pointedly at Jazz, knowing he wasn't a traditional Sikh at all. She got up from the table and busied herself at her stove. Jazz watched and was about to ask when Amrit was expected back when the doorbell rang. It must be his pizza. He made his excuses, picked up his carrier bag, clinking with two bottles of vodka, and thanked Mrs Chodda for her fabulous samosas. A night of pizza, cricket on the TV and a few drinks was his kind of night.

He needed a good night because it wasn't going to last. It was going to be quite some time before he would have another easy, relaxing night to enjoy.

CHAPTER 5

Bloody Gangs

There had been a fight outside Barking station. It had happened at midnight and there were eight youths in custody. Jazz got a call saying that one in particular was not known to the borough, and he was making no sense. Jazz was told to interview him.

He hated this part of his fucking job. Kids playing with knives, getting easy sentences from the courts, and him having to take all the crap they dished out. He was sick of being called a fucking pig by a snotty-nosed kid who was just asking for a good slap.

The fight had been nasty, with four gang members in hospital. One was on life support and not expected to survive. The repercussions of the fight were that a late-night bus driver who witnessed the event was so traumatised he was receiving treatment, and a station cleaner who had hidden in a photo booth in the station was scared shitless and refusing to leave her home. After SOCOs (scene of crime officers) had gone over the area looking for clues and specimens for analysis, the street cleaners were out cleaning up the blood so that the residents weren't shocked.

Police officers who had attended the carnage should have gone off duty hours ago. They were now dog tired after being on duty all night, sorting out the mess and getting the charges put on. It had taken ten officers to arrest the gang members and take statements. The officers had to stay on duty until all the paperwork was completed and then they could sign off.

Winston Boeke was recorded as nineteen years of age; a swaggering, skinny young man with a beautiful leather jacket and four iPhones found on his person. He was not local, and gave an address in Stoke Newington. Why he was with the Deville Gang, no one could find out. He had over fourteen hours still on the PACE clock (Police And Criminal Evidence Act – to detain a suspect for up to 24 hours) and the powers that be had decided that Jazz, as the detective working on gang crime, could talk to this young man and sort out who he was and why he was in Barking.

Resigned to interviewing this miscreant and feeling quite petulant, Jazz flicked open the wicket (the opening in the cell door to view the prisoner) to take a look at the piece of shit that had been part of a murderous fight last night.

Winston Boeke looked up and stared defiantly at the wicket. He knew he was being looked at, and was considering swaggering over and spitting into the wicket to teach them a lesson, but on second thoughts he just stared in disgust.

Jazz had seen all he needed to, and slammed the wicket shut. "Shit!" he said to the custody sergeant. "He's a fucking Blood, and that's gonna be a big problem."

Liam, the custody sergeant, looked quizzically at Jazz.

"Did you see that fucking big tattoo on his arm?"

The custody sergeant grunted and nodded, not knowing where this was going.

"Well, little Liam," said Jazz, with the sarcasm that meant he was disliked by most officers, "it's a five-pointed star with a 5 in the middle and the words 'death before dishonour' underneath. And he is wearing red, which tells me he is a Blood."

Now the custody sergeant was animated. "What the fuck is a Blood doing in Barking? We don't have them here."

Jazz nodded, and wondered this too.

The Bloods and Crips were gangs in London. They were originally the names of gangs in Los Angeles, America, but when it got tough out there they brought the idea over to England. They were very much drug-related gangs, *and for our sins*, thought Jazz, *it was easier for them to work in Britain*. Los Angeles had cleaned up their act and got a handle on the Bloods and Crips there. With cocaine and heroin coming into England by the shedful, they came to London to continue their lucrative money-earners. They brought with them all the violence and tight codes of the gangs that meant the Metropolitan Police had to organise special units to deal solely with Bloods and Crips. The gang wars and murders were not reported extensively in the press, so the public were not aware of how dangerous and controlling the gangs were in large parts of London. Drugs and murders were rife.

Walking back to the custody suite, Liam asked Jazz if he knew much about the Bloods gang. Jazz had studied facts about them. He told Liam he'd had a brush with them a few years ago when he was working on a case that had something to do with the Bloods gang.

"I hear they are a tough lot. Are they very different from Barking and Dagenham gangs?" asked Liam.

"They are a law unto themselves," Jazz said with a shake of his head.

Now he had started, he filled in the bits he knew about the Bloods gang. "Bloods and Crips started in America and are drug-related. The Bloods' sworn enemies are the Crips. The massive UK market for cocaine has led to the gangs launching a new front here. A quarter of the gangs in London have aligned themselves to Bloods or Crips. What we found was that gang activities became more organised. Small street crews were grouping together, copying the LA Bloods and Crips culture. Around 2010 our gang problem was as bad as LA's was in their bad days.

"They are worrying. I got to know them when I was in Manchester. The UK gangs copy the LA versions. They are made up of sets, and each set has its own leader. A leader is usually an older member with a big criminal background. The leader asserts himself through his reputation for violence, ruthlessness and his personality. The boys are usually between the ages of sixteen and twenty-two years, and are called soldiers. Now, these soldiers are bloody dangerous because of their willingness to use violence both to obtain the respect of gang members and to respond to any person who disrespects the set. They have all got a lot to prove to their peers and don't give a damn who gets maimed or killed in the process.

"They recruit mainly school-age youths from African communities. They offer something these young boys have never had: a sense of belonging, protection, respect and the trappings of gang life. There is the gold jewellery, cash and expensive sports clothes. When you join, you are a member for life. They are organised, their members are loyal and ruthless and they are into all crime, including a heavy emphasis on selling drugs. I don't want them here in my town."

Jazz looked at the custody sergeant and said, "The worst of it is, he will speak gang slang and I don't understanding a fucking word of it, and I am supposed to interview him. Shit!"

Before Liam could say anything, Jazz said he had to go out for an hour and would be back to interview this bastard. He asked for the interview room with the two-way mirror and an earpiece. Jazz left before he started to get all the reasons why he couldn't have any of it from Liam.

Jazz checked his watch; it was 11am and he knew exactly where he was heading. Barking Court, (now closed), looked over to McDonald's in the town centre. That's where Mad Pete would be about this time. Mad Pete never cooked anything, and over the years he had kept McDonald's, Chicken & Ribs and Youngs Chinese in Longbridge Road in business. McDonald's was his favourite, and he also conducted a bit of business in there. His young villains knew where to find him any morning after 11am.

Jazz looked through the window of McDonald's. It looked pretty empty at this time of day, but there Pete was with his face in a Big Breakfast. He knew it was Mad Pete, the long, lanky, greasy, shitty hair hanging over the table as he sat hunched forwards in his black full-length leather coat. Mad Pete fancied himself as Neo in *The Matrix*.

The thought of a McDonald's Big Breakfast made Jazz feel hungry. He opened the door and acknowledged Mad Pete with a hand up, but as he was about to pass by him, he stopped, and on second thoughts, Jazz sidled up to Mad Pete and whispered, "Fancy yourself as Neo, do you, in that coat? Well, stick an M in it; you smell more like Nemo." Jazz gave a theatrical loud sniff in the direction of Mad Pete's head. "Yeah, I smell fish, you arsehole."

Smirking, Jazz went to the counter to order a Big Breakfast and two coffees. In minutes he was sitting with Mad Pete. He had got him another coffee to tide him over. Neither said anything; just a nod between them and a look of disdain from Mad Pete whilst they got on with eating and drinking. The meals got cold quickly so there was no time to waste. They ate in a comfortable silence.

When finished, Jazz, not wasting any time on frivolous conversations of 'How are you?', got straight to the point.

"I need you to come back to the station with me as an interpreter."

Mad Pete choked on his coffee. "I ain't no interpreter, Mr Singh. I can barely speak me own language." Tickled at his own funny quip, Mad Pete rolled up with laughter.

Jazz, irritated, added, "You speak gang slang, and that's what I want you to interpret. I need you to come now and no more fannying about."

Mad Pete sat up straight and started to shake his head. "No, no, Mr Singh. I have my anonymity to protect. I am a hero to my young gangsters, I can't let them see me helping the filth – you understand that, don't you, Mr Singh?" he implored, very uneasy.

Jazz did know this. He didn't want to lose Mad Pete's anonymity either; it was very helpful to have him as his snout.

Mad Pete was starting to fidget and look around, worried. He was building up to a druggy fit and Jazz didn't want him spreading his panic all over McDonald's and drawing attention to them.

He leaned over the table, grabbed Mad Pete by the scruff of his filthy T-shirt and whispered menacingly,

"Seriously, did you order an adult-size portion of stupid and pay 50p extra to go large on that?" He let go of Mad Pete's T-shirt and with a look of disgust, wiped his sticky hands on a tissue. Mad Pete quietened down and listened.

"I have a Blood soldier in custody and I need to interview him. I won't understand a fucking word he says, but you will. I have arranged for you to be in a room next to the interview room, it's got a two-way mirror. I will wear an earpiece and you will listen to this Blood and tell me in Queen's English what the fucking hell he is saying, capisce?"

Mad Pete looked at him, incredulous. "What the fuck *is* capisce?"

"It means 'OK?', you stupid bastard!"

"Well, Mr Singh, I might not know one word, but you know nuffink about gang slang, so who is a stupid bastard now?" said an affronted Mad Pete.

Jazz was going to slap him round the head for his insolence, but saw the funny side and just giggled. On second thoughts, he gave him a stinging slap round the head anyway, just for the hell of it. Putting his hand over his ear to stop the pain, Mad Pete followed Jazz out of McDonald's and they walked to the car that took them to Fresh Wharf Patrol Station, where Winston Boeke and the other gang members were housed.

Fresh Wharf was a new patrol centre; a grey building that housed the many departments of the Metropolitan

Police. It was a high-tech, state-of-the-art building that looked like a warehouse to the untrained eye.

They went in the back way into the custody suite; newly opened with thirty pristine cells tastefully painted in prison green, which looked quite light and airy. Prison green was usually an oppressive colour, but in its newness, it felt quite pleasant. Each cell contained a bed that was bolted to the floor, a sink and a toilet. It wasn't pretty. CCTV cameras covered all the cells, so every inmate could be watched constantly from the bank of screens on the custody desk. There was no privacy afforded to the inmates, with the toilet in full view of the many CCTV cameras. It was clean, bright and so far there was no graffiti anywhere. It was never going to last. At least now the custody officers could see potential trouble as it was going to happen.

There had been, in the past, many occasions when inmates had wiped their excrement and piss over every wall, floor and bed. In the days before CCTV an inmate could cover a cell with their human waste before officers had spotted it. The new cells were easy to hose down, not like the good old days when a bucket and brush were needed.

Everyone that entered the custody suite area was not only on camera but also voice recorded, so Jazz quickly got Mad Pete organised and taken into the interview room adjoining where Winston Boeke would be sitting, waiting. The earpiece was ready for Jazz to put on, and they tested it out. Mad Pete enjoyed shouting into his microphone and seeing Jazz jump in shock. The giggling stopped when Jazz threatened to put him in a cell and leave him there to starve until he had eaten his fucking leather coat.

With twelve hours left on the PACE clock, it was time to get on with the interview of Winston Boeke. Jazz called Ash to come and sit with Mad Pete in the adjoining interview room and oversee what was going on there. PC Richard Wood was asked to sit in on the interview but told to keep his mouth shut; he had nothing to do with the interview system. His presence was all that was required. PC Wood nodded and walked in first.

Interview rooms were small and stark: a table and four chairs. The table was against the wall with a recorder attached to the wall by the table. The only relief on the grey walls was the thin red line that went round each of the four walls. This was the alarm. Any trouble and officers touched the red line, which set off alarm bells all over the police station. This was an emergency line and on hearing this everyone would drop what they were doing and race to the room to help an officer.

The red line was also to be seen on the walls in the custody area. Bringing criminals into the custody area from the vehicle yard outside could potentially be hazardous; a group of football hooligans trying to carry on their fight in the custody area, or a cuffed villain who suddenly got a bit of extra energy to break free of the officer holding him, would kick, barge and nut anyone close by. It only took a few prisoners to be gathered together in the custody area and a fight could kick off.

When all were seated, with a nod from Jazz, the interview was started. He turned on the tape and said in a bored monotone that Detective Sergeant Singh was here to interview Winston Boeke in regard to the fight outside Barking station. He informed the tape that PC Richard Wood was also present. Now he had got that over and done with, he looked up at Winston Boeke, who was lounging back on the wooden chair, staring right back at Jazz nonchalantly. The look of hatred was barely hidden behind the swagger of this skinny young man. Jazz wasn't looking forward to this at all.

"So, Winston Boeke, why were you outside Barking station last night?"

Winston looked at Jazz and a smirk peeled itself across his face. Looking at no one in particular, he said, "You smell bacon here? Oh, I see." With a flick of his fingers he added, "Snap! Here comes 5-0."

Jazz looked at this miscreant and guessed what he said.

An excited Mad Pete came through his earpiece. Snorting with laughter, he said, "He's calling you a pig, Mr Singh. He is taking the mickey out of you being a police officer."

Jazz nodded; he guessed that. He was on tape, so had to be careful what he said.

"Let's keep this proper, Winston. Just want to find out what happened yesterday and why you were there. You live a long way from Barking, so why were you in Barking and why were you part of the fight?"

Winston glared again; he didn't want to be here, and he had got caught up in something that wasn't anything to do with him. He was a Blood, and it was shit to be caught in Barking at some stupid little gang fight. As a Blood he had a reputation to maintain, and it wasn't going to happen here.

"I come here to see Charles, my boy, my son, and we is chilling."

Mad Pete translated that he had come to Barking to meet up with his best friend and have a good time.

Jazz wanted to know why they were outside Barking station, and why they had joined up with one of the gangs there. He asked if Winston was recruiting for Blood gangs in Barking.

Frustrated and wanting this messing around to stop, with eyes flashing Jazz said through gritted teeth, "I want answers, and I want them now." He thumped the table with his fist, and Winston jumped.

Winston calmed quickly and wanted to defuse the atmosphere. Posing like a big man, all laid-back and laughing, Winston took his time in replying.

"You got me bent, I ain't doing nuffink. We is looking for some candy."

Mad Pete translated that he wasn't here to recruit and was just looking for girls.

Enough was enough. Jazz tuned out Winston and just listened to Mad Pete; it was driving him mental having to listen to this kid talking nonsense. It worked better that way. Winston paled at the thought that he could be kept in custody in fucking Barking. The threat was enough for him to become cooperative.

It turned out, with much embarrassment, that Winston Boeke, the tough soldier of the Blood gang, was here to see his auntie. Now Jazz was close to laughing. This candy-arsed soldier in the Blood colour of red, with a motherfucking tattoo for all the world to see and gangsta slang, who all gangs recognised as tough Blood gangsta, was here to see his auntie and step-cousin. How tough was that? OK, he shouldn't have, but Jazz curled up and laughed hard.

"OK, Winston, let's see what we can do about protecting your street cred among the gangs in Barking, but in return I want details of what happened at Barking and what made you visit your auntie. Let's try and just speak the Queen's English, if you don't mind. I won't tell them you can speak it." Again Jazz curled up laughing. What a total dick this soldier was.

PC Wood said nothing, but the look on his face said it all. He felt as if he were in a madhouse. This wasn't the way to conduct an interview.

It turned out that Winston the Blood soldier didn't see the gang fight starting. He was busy chatting up a couple of girls with his cousin. He thought he was doing well but when he turned upon hearing the shouting behind him, he saw the young men that had been milling around chatting had suddenly switched from easy-going to full-on fighting. He saw two get shanked (stabbed) and grabbed his cousin and moved back into the shadows of Barking station. The police arrived very quickly and surrounded and grabbed everyone, including Winston.

Winston said he wasn't here to recruit for the Bloods. He added that the gangs in Barking and Dagenham were crap and he would never be married (joined) to them, or them married to the Bloods.

He shook his head and looked at Jazz. "I am burned," (insulted), "that you think I would want to be part of those gangs, or I would consider them for the Bloods."

Jazz asked again, with heavy sarcasm, "Why did you come to Dagenham to see your auntie? It doesn't sound like something a big brave Blood soldier would do."

All he got in reply was a two-fingered salute, and through gritted teeth, "SMD."

Jazz held his ear as a near-hysterical Mad Pete screamed with laughter. Jazz nodded to PC Wood to stay there and left the room.

When he got outside the room he took the earpiece out and raced next door, apoplectic with rage. He threw the door open and grabbed Mad Pete.

"You bastard, you could have turned me deaf by screaming into the microphone. Now calm down or I will put you in one of the cells and leave you there to rot."

Mad Pete calmed down quickly and cowered back into his chair.

"So what does SMD mean, and tell me without screaming with laughter."

Mad Pete didn't like to rile Mr Singh in this way; he always got hurt and he didn't want to get another smack. Ash, shocked at such violence coming into the room, was just finding his voice to interject when he caught the warning glare in Jazz's eyes and stayed seated and quiet.

"Now don't hit me, Mr Singh, it's not a nice thing he said to you," was the scared response from Mad Pete. Jazz could see he was panicking and calmed down, realising how tense he had got, and stroked and patted Mad Pete's lapels as a placatory gesture.

"OK, just tell me what he said and I will go back, no problem."

Mad Pete, serious now and not laughing, said, "He told you, 'Suck my dick'."

Jazz nodded and grimaced. "Oh, is that all?" He gave a warning look to Mad Pete and told him to keep his responses quiet and no shouting in his fucking ear. He went back to interview the little cocky bastard and find out what the hell he was doing in Barking and Dagenham.

The interview went on for another two hours with a comfort break in the middle. The story unfolded painfully slowly, but it transpired that Charles Osei was Winston's step-cousin and they had been quite close when they were children. Auntie Dionne had brought them both up. Winston's mother was in London and couldn't look after him when he was young. He went back to her when he turned thirteen years old. He was always fond of his Auntie Dionne, and he'd heard she was unwell and had recently had a 'woman's operation'. Winston didn't know what was actually wrong with her but with a bit of probing from Jazz it turned out to be her stomach and Jazz reckoned she'd had a hysterectomy or some such mysterious woman thing. So she was laid up in bed and hadn't been well for a while. Winston was just checking on how she was. He didn't need to add that Auntie Dionne was more of a mother to him than his real mother had ever been, or that he missed her.

It looked like Winston and Charles had been in the wrong place at the wrong time. Jazz would check the CCTV footage and make sure it had all happened as Winston said. Before he let him go, Jazz was going to check out Auntie Dionne Osei just to make sure that part of the story tallied up. He wanted to be sure that there was no Blood recruitment going on. Barking and Dagenham had enough problems without the thought that big and violent gangs like the Bloods and Crips might come to his town.

Auntie Dionne lived on Longbridge Road between Dagenham and Barking. Jazz told Winston he would be staying for a bit longer at Her Majesty's pleasure while he checked out his story with his Auntie Dionne. Winston was not a happy soul at the thought of more hours in a cell.

Jazz let Mad Pete go with a lot of argument; Mad Pete wanted to be paid for his skills. After a big argument, during which Jazz told him his skills were crap and he was lucky not to find himself in a cell for his cheek, he gave Mad Pete a £20 note and sent him packing.

Ash had never seen the pair of them working together and knew if he told anyone, he wouldn't be believed. It was surreal, but he had to admit, the job got done. Ash warned Jazz that he was heading for trouble in treating Mad Pete as someone the Met Police would use as an interpreter. Mad Pete wasn't on the official list of outside people used by the Met. Jazz laughed and told Ash that he hadn't asked the police for any money so it didn't matter. He didn't want to hear about confidentiality, or that Mad Pete was now privy to an interview. He dismissed Ash with the comment that he should do what he did best and get the interview typed up on an MG5 (Case summary form) in case there was a charge to be placed on Winston Boeke. He would be back later.

It was supposed to be a quick check with Auntie Dionne but Jazz, if he had known what he would be confronted with, would perhaps have walked off in the opposite direction. He was about to pull up a big stone that had hidden maggots of the vilest and foulest kind.

CHAPTER 6

Is This the Start of Something Big?

There were about eight hours left on the PACE clock before Winston Boeke had to be either charged or set free. Jazz wanted to get this sorted quickly, and get on with some real police work. He suffered anything to do with gangs, but kept an eye out for something juicier. He wanted a real criminal with real thought processes, not stupid little kids who thought they were tough because they could stab or shoot someone; there was no skill in that.

As he was about to leave Fresh Wharf he got a call from DCI Radley, who wanted to know about Winston Boeke and was concerned that a Blood soldier was in his neighbourhood.

Jazz growled to himself, "He bloody knows everything that goes on in this station." Trying to lighten up, he told DCI Radley what had been said in interview and where he was going. This met with with DCI Radley's approval; he wanted this sorted today. He asked if there was going to be a charge put on Winston Boeke and Jazz told him there wasn't anything so far, but if his story didn't pan out with his Auntie Dionne, then a charge would be fashioned to get him off the streets. This met with DCI Radley's approval, which made a change, thought Jazz.

Dionne Osei lived in a council house, and from the outside Jazz could see she had made it her own. The brightly coloured pots in the front garden and the pink net curtains adorning the windows certainly cheered up the street. He rang the bell and listened to a rendition of *Rule Britannia*, which seemed to go on forever. Eventually the door was opened by a woman who stood, bent over, in a bright pink dressing gown. She looked in pain. Jazz politely asked if she was Dionne Osei and the lady nodded. Jazz told her who he was and asked if he might come in, and perhaps she could then get herself comfortable. He could see how difficult it was for her to stand there. She grunted agreement and painfully turned around, and he followed her into her lounge, which had a bed in it. With a lot of grunts and groans, she got back into bed and laid back with a very long sigh into the welcoming pillows. Jazz watched this and didn't realise how tense he felt until she relaxed. He let out a sigh of relief and under his breath said, "Fuck this for a game of soldiers".

He asked if she needed anything and she asked him to put the kettle on and make a cup of tea, if he didn't mind. He didn't mind at all; glad to be doing something. This was a very tense house. He made two mugs of tea, and after finding out if sugar was needed and how much milk, he carried them into the lounge.

After a few minutes of sipping the tea, she asked what he wanted. He explained about Winston and her son Charles, who were in custody. That brought forth a tirade from Dionne, detailing her disbelief in the police, the system, the press, the neighbourhood. The boys, she told him, were innocent, lovely young boys who never did anything they shouldn't. Jazz wasn't going to argue the point. She didn't know what Winston did, that was for sure, and Charles, well, he had no criminal record and she could be right about him. He patiently explained that they seemed to have been in the wrong place at the wrong time.

She confirmed why Winston was there; he'd been to visit her because she wasn't well. She added that she couldn't do anything for herself at the moment and was totally reliant on Charles to help her, and Nekisha, her six-year-old daughter.

She explained that she had help from a neighbour, and she blushed a little, and coyly said, "I got me a wonderful man, who I think is sweet on me." Jazz smiled and said that was nice.

Quite animated now, she added that he was absolutely wonderful and when he visited he brought food and expensive ready meals from – and she whispered reverently – Marks and Spencer's. She stopped for a second to look for surprise and amazement in Jazz's face. He could see he should be impressed, and nodded knowingly. Satisfied by this look, she went on. Now looking coy and a tad embarrassed, she added that her man couldn't do enough for her.

"Even," she said, looking directly into Jazz's eyes and pausing for a nanosecond, "even taking Nekisha out for the day so I can rest." She smacked her lips in utter amazement that a man would do this for her. "You know," she said, now well into this conversation, "every weekend he comes and takes her out. Over the last few weekends he has taken her to his mother's house, and they keep her for the weekend. Sweettart, I can't tell you how wonderful it is not to have to worry about her and getting her meals. She get so bored here wiv me in bed. So honey, I sure still have it to attract such a wonderful man." She almost did a shimmy in the bed to prove the point that although she was seriously ill, she still had that va-va-voom of a sexy lady.

Why something went *kerching* in Jazz's brain, he didn't know. He asked himself many times – was he a bloody clever git or was he just a jaundiced bugger?

Trying to keep the mood the same, he asked where she had met this knight in white armour.

Dionne giggled. "I was in Morrisons shopping and he bumped into me by accident. He was so lovely and apologetic and asked if he could help me carry stuff to the pushchair where I put my bags of shopping."

Jazz nodded and smiled. He didn't want to make anything of it in Dionne's mind at this stage, so he asked if she had Nekisha with her at the time.

She looked at him, raised her head off the pillows and asked, "Why you need to know that?"

Jazz said dismissively, "Because I am in awe of women shopping, carrying bags and also having to look after little children. I couldn't do it. I think women are wonderful in how they manage."

Dionne lay back again contentedly. She smiled at his inferiority. "Of course, darling, I always have my Nekisha with me when I'm shopping. What sort of mother do you take me for? I would never leave her alone."

"So," Jazz continued, "what happened then?"

"Well, he walked home with me, pushing the pram with all the shopping in it. It was really lovely and I felt like a queen." She smiled contentedly. "He has been wonderful ever since."

Jazz looked around. "Where is Nekisha now? I'd love to say hello."

Dionne said she was with Peter, her lovely knight, and was coming home later that evening. Jazz nodded and again confirmed that Charles would be home soon, and Winston too.

Realising that in all the time he had been there, he hadn't asked this poor sick woman how she was feeling, Jazz asked the question. This opened the gateway to an angelic and brave hypochondriac. It would seem that Dionne was a slave to her illnesses, and she had many.

Then she mentioned her latest operation; she whispered, "*Hysterectomy,*" with raised eyebrows, then looked hard at Jazz and nodded knowingly. He raised his eyebrows in shock, which pleased her. Dramatically she gave him the horrific and actually incorrect details that she had lost everything in her middle area. She gently rubbed the whole of her stomach and saw with pleasure the look of shock on Jazz's face. In case he had forgotten she nodded at her stomach and told him again that hey had taken away everything and she had nearly died. There was the excruciating pain, and all the blood she had lost, but she didn't like to complain. She had to soldier on for her children's sake but it was stripping her of every ounce of energy. With that she sighed and flopped further back into the pillows with arms spread out, looking a little like Jesus on the cross. She was a magnificent martyr and Jazz loved the display, but had to stop himself laughing.

She saw his interest, and as she had his full attention she began to undo the buttons on her nightie. Jazz was just about to get up and move away, in shock and wondering what this femme fatale was about to do, when she uncovered an angry scar on her lower stomach. She pointed at it and looked up, assured he would be shocked.

In a whisper she said, "That took four hours." She was pleased with his look of surprise. Nodding now, she added, "I nearly died." He shook his head in astonishment. Now she pulled back the blanket and showed him her legs. Again in a mournful whisper, she said, "Varicose veins," and looked at him pitifully.

He looked at the blue mess on her legs and nodded. Before he could say anything, she thrust her arms at him. "Injections daily for months; iron." Again, Jazz nodded gravely and before she got anything else out he told her that she was a brave woman and he couldn't take any more. She liked that comment and added, "Well, darlin', you know how I feel."

With a friendly grin, Jazz told Dionne that he would like to visit again just to check how she was.

Her voice went up a few octaves as she screeched, "But darlin', I would love to see you again. How kind you are to me." With that she dramatically flopped on to the pillows again, and in a frail voice told him, "Now I need to rest, I am so tired after this conversation."

He got up to go, but before he left she raised a hand and pointed in the direction of the kitchen. In a pained and feeble voice she asked, "Sweetness, before you go, could you please bring me that tin of biscuits on the side there? The sugar helps give me a little energy to see me through."

Jazz went and got the tin, saying it was his pleasure to help. The bubbling smile was not far from his mouth, but contained for the moment.

As he was about to go out the door he turned, as if at a last-minute thought, and asked Dionne, "Oh, by the way, what is your knight's name again – Peter something?"

She said, "Honey, it's Peter Grimshaw, do you know him?"

Jazz paused for a second in thought and then said no, he didn't. With that he left, knowing he would go back later to see this Peter Grimshaw with Nekisha.

He got back to the station and immediately went and found Ash.

"Got an important job for you. Can you find out anything about a Peter Grimshaw? I know it's not much at the moment but see what comes up."

Ash wanted more information and grumbled that it wasn't enough, but Jazz had gone and he was left to get on with it.

The CCTV showed that what Winston Boeke and Charles Osei had said was true. They had their backs to the fighting, chatting up two girls. It showed quite clearly that they were not involved with the gang fighting, and the look of horror on Winston's and Charles' faces showed that the chaos came as a surprise to them. Jazz reckoned that Winston hadn't told his Blood set that he was leaving the area for a few days, and he wouldn't want to draw attention to himself in Barking in case the news got back to them. He had a reputation to protect, and being in Barking wasn't going to do him any favours.

It was agreed between the custody sergeant, Ash and Jazz that Boeke and Osei could be released. Before Boeke was released, Jazz had a final conversation with him. He told him he had visited Auntie Dionne and said how brave she was, coping with her hysterectomy. Boeke nodded; he thought she was wonderful. In the same vein, Jazz said how good it was that Peter Grimshaw was such a help to his auntie. Here Boeke grimaced. He didn't look exactly happy, and Jazz wondered why.

Winston Boeke, a Blood soldier, didn't want to stay in the interview room any longer than he had to. He didn't want a candy-assed chat with this pig. He wanted out, and needed to get back to his home. Questions about Peter Grimshaw were irrelevant, and he didn't like him anyway. His forty-odd-year-old auntie was going around with a man ten years her junior, and if that wasn't bad enough, he was white. What did a white man want with his auntie? It didn't make sense, and Winston wasn't happy about it. He didn't like the idea of a stranger looking after little Nekisha, but it was his auntie's call and she was very ill, so he put up with it. He wanted to go back to his Blood set; they had rules about things there and he knew what was what. His auntie had got very angry with him when he asked why she was with a honky, and he backed off. He figured she deserved some pleasure in her life; he just wished it had been with one of their own.

Before Jazz let Boeke go on his way, he asked for one of his mobile numbers to ring him on if he needed to. Boeke looked at this pig, and with a look of disgust, arrogantly told him to "SMD". Jazz, resigned and fed up with this lump of shit, resisted the urge to grab him, push him up against the wall and hit him. In a calm voice he said he might have concerns that might be

Boeke's as well. Of course the police had all of Boeke's mobile numbers on record, but as a courtesy, he wanted Boeke to tell him which one he could fucking ring him on and get a reply.

Boeke wanted to know why, and Jazz didn't want to tell him yet. He just said, "I am protecting your corner, just know that. If there is anything I think you could help me with or you should know, I will ring you."

Boeke was not happy. "I ain't no grass for the pigs. You can do what you like to me, I would never grass."

Fed up now, Jazz could hardly be bothered to explain anything, but he had to say something. "There may be something that could affect your family, your auntie. If so, I will tell you, that's all. I am on your side with this."

Boeke didn't believe any of it, but just in case he gave the number of his personal mobile. He had a mobile for personal stuff, a mobile for the Bloods, a mobile for the drug dealer and a mobile for his bitches. His life was very organised and he wanted it to stay that way.

CHAPTER 7

A-Hunting We Will Go

Jazz popped back at 8pm to Auntie Dionne's house. Charles Osei opened the door and his face dropped. Jazz put his hands up and assured him he wasn't there to speak to him or Winston. He was just checking Charles' mother was OK. He asked if he could come in. Charles was not happy but sullenly let DS Singh into the house.

Nekisha was there. She had just got into her pyjamas and was saying goodnight to her mother. The white man sitting in a chair in the corner and smiling had to be Peter Grimshaw. Jazz nodded to Dionne and said hello to Nekisha.

Nekisha shied away when he went near her, and Dionne soothingly said, "Don't mind her, Mr Singh, she is just tired." Now she beckoned to Nekisha to come to her, and she stroked her hair and kissed her and said she needed to go to bed otherwise she would be tired tomorrow. Nekisha nodded.

Peter Grimshaw got up to take Nekisha to bed.

He looked at Dionne and asked if it would be helpful if he tucked Nekisha in and read her a story. Dionne nodded, smiling. When they had gone upstairs, Dionne looked at Jazz through moist eyes and said how wonderful Peter was.

"He just loves my Nekisha. She is a beautiful child with lovely hair and such a cute face, but to have a man who isn't her father adore her so is lovely. I am a lucky woman, Mr Singh." She dabbed her eyes with one of the tissues strewn on her bed.

Jazz asked if Peter had far to come. He was certainly attentive, and he wondered if he lived around the corner.

Dionne, very proud and trying to be modest, said, "This man, this wonderful man lives in Essex. A long, long way from here, Mr Singh, yet he comes to see me every week, sometimes three times a week. That is devotion, Mr Singh, true devotion." She lay there with a tissue held to her face, looking angelic at the thought. Jazz had the distinct impression that this was a biblical moment. She lay like an angel, and Peter Grimshaw was her disciple who came to bow before her. This lady should have been a dramatic actress; if she were on a stage she would have flounced. It was fascinating to watch.

At the moment, though, Jazz's concern was for Nekisha, and to find out who this Peter Grimshaw was. Grimshaw came down the stairs within five minutes. Jazz knew he shouldn't jump to conclusions, but he wondered if knowing he was a detective had made Peter Grimshaw cut his visit upstairs with

Nekisha short. He hoped so. Jazz was going to find out a bit more about this fellow. He smiled and said how Dionne had been singing his praises regarding how helpful and kind he had been.

Peter smiled and looked at Dionne and said, "You are worth it, my dear."

Jazz thought that was a strange endearment for a thirty-odd-year-old. "I hear you live in Essex, which part? I know parts of Essex, lovely county."

Peter agreed it was lovely, and said he lived near Southend.

"That's strange, I was near Southend not that long ago. Do you know Piddlesham – oh, sorry, I mean Paglesham, lovely place by the water?"

Peter again smiled and said he knew Paglesham very well.

"Do you sail, Peter? It seems everyone near there has a boat of some sort."

Peter was now feeling a bit stressed at all the questions, and Jazz saw that. He laughed and said, "Sorry, Peter, it's the policeman in me – everything sounds like a question and I don't mean to sound like that. Dionne is such a lovely lady I just had to see how she was tonight. She was telling me about your first meeting and it sounded very romantic."

Peter smiled and agreed it was romantic, and then Dionne smiled too. Jazz thought they looked all loved up, but he wasn't feeling it. There was something not right and he wanted to find out what that was. He said his goodbyes and left.

On the way out he telephoned Ash. He wanted him to refine his search of Peter Grimshaw to the Southend area and possibly Paglesham. When Ash answered the phone he asked why the fuck was he being rung at this unearthly time when he was at home with his wife eating his dinner. Jazz said it was only 9pm, and wondered what all the fuss was about. Nevertheless, he said he would see Ash tomorrow in the office and wished him a good night.

Before he got far he turned back and looked at the cars outside Dionne's house. It was a main road but Jazz reckoned Peter Grimshaw's car was the one parked outside the house. It was a two-year-old Mercedes, not one of the big flashy ones but a neat silver car, plush inside but discreet outside. He took down the number plate and text it to Ash. He wasn't going to ring him again. *Let's see who this knight in shining armour truly is*, thought Jazz. Jazz was fond of Dionne, a wishful femme fatale, and he wanted to protect Nekisha. He hoped he was wrong, that he had become jaundiced as a policeman. Everyone has an angle. Doesn't anyone do anything to be nice any more? Sadly, he didn't think so. He would love to be proved wrong.

Time to go home, have some fish and chips and a few drinks. With that lovely thought, Jazz made his way home via the fish and chip shop.

CHAPTER 8

Face-Off

Jazz was grabbed as he went through the door of Ilford Police Station.

"You've got a right one in custody to deal with," was all he was told by the custody sergeant as he rushed off for his breakfast.

Jazz made his way to the custody suite and picked up the paperwork. He gave a summary glance through the wicket at the offender. It was all standard stuff at this stage. The noise of the wicket opening made the man look up from the bench in the cell. Jazz stepped back in shock. The man's face was obscenely disfigured. He had no nose, no lips and the numerous scars on his face were oozing something obnoxious. He shut the wicket quickly and realised as he took in a deep gulp of air that he had held his breath at the sight.

His name was Chris Hudd. According to the report from the doctor on duty, Chris Hudd had a parasitic ailment that was being treated by the hospital. It was not infectious and was, in part, due to his use of drugs.

He was a crackhead and was, unbelievably, thirty-two years of age. He looked much older.

Jazz sat down to read the report. Apparently a woman had parked her car in Ilford. She had bought a thirty-two-inch television and left it in the back of the car. She said she had seen a disfigured bloke matching Chris Hudd's description looking at the car. When she came back an hour later, the car window was smashed and surprise, surprise, the television was gone.

Police tracked Hudd to a boarding house that catered for homeless single people round the back of Ilford High Road. They asked to see the CCTV footage as the camera was in the foyer, and saw Hudd come in with a television-sized cardboard box. No television was found in his room. He had been arrested that morning and brought to Ilford Police Station.

Normal procedure would be an identity parade for the woman to identify Hudd as the person she saw. Jazz sat back and thought, *Where the fuck am I going to find half a dozen men with no nose, no lips and bloody disgusting scars?!* Of course it wasn't going to happen. He would have to interview Hudd regardless and see what he said.

Ash was told where Jazz was and went down to the custody suite to find him. Jazz told him to check out cell number 6.

Ash came back quickly, and all he could say was, "Jeez." He looked at Jazz and asked what he was going to do. Ash knew the standard procedure would be an identity parade.

Both Ash and Jazz sat in the interview room, waiting for Hudd to be brought in and questioned. Jazz told Ash to keep shtum and leave it to him. When Hudd was seated, the usual procedure was conducted in a monotone for the tape. After naming everyone in the room and setting the time as 10am, the interview began.

Jazz established that Hudd was a crackhead and knew he would be getting desperate soon, and acknowledged the doctor would be returning soon to take a look at him. Hudd nodded. He was gasping for a cigarette but that wasn't allowed either. Jazz said he would get this over with as quickly as possible, and if Hudd cooperated, then he would be made more comfortable soon. He felt sorry for the poor bugger.

"Did you know the thirty-two-inch television was bought for Tommy, who is in hospital? Little Tommy is having a really bad time and this TV was bought to make his poor life a little better. So tell me, where is the TV now?"

Hudd looked almost sorry. Jazz pushed it further. "Tommy has nothing but pain in his life and he was looking forward to having his own TV to take his mind off all the stuff being done to him. You must know a bit how he feels with a face like yours, and he is only a little kid."

That did it; Hudd cracked and sobbed.

"I took the TV out of that woman's car and took it

to Cash Converters. I am sorry, I needed to get some money for my stuff." Hudd was now quite distraught.

Jazz got him a cup of tea and wondered how he was going to drink it without lips. He asked Ash to take down his statement and get him to sign it.

Later, Ash found Jazz outside having a cigarette. "So, how awful that a little boy lost his TV. How did you know that? It's not in the paperwork I have read."

Jazz looked at him and said, "I made it up. There is no Tommy in hospital. I was never going to get an ID parade with his face. The CCTV showed him carrying in an empty box he said he found outside. Later CCTV saw him carry a black plastic bag with something in it out of the building, but we don't know it was the TV for sure. He stole it and we couldn't prove it. I needed him to confess, and luckily he has a bit of a heart. Enough said!"

Ash was about to remonstrate that it wasn't right to do that, but stopped and just laughed. "You are just a lying bastard, DS Singh."

Jazz smiled. "Yep, that's right, that's me. Need that information, Ash – see you in ten minutes upstairs?"

Ash shouted, "OK," as he watched Jazz striding off.

Jazz felt good. A charge in place; a great way to start the day. He should have made the most of it; the day was going to go downhill fast.

CHAPTER 9

This Could Be the Start of Something Big

Ash had been delving into AWARE (the Met Police computer system) and making enquiries on Peter Grimshaw. He never knew there were so many bloody Peter Grimshaws in London and Essex. But what was very interesting was that the Mercedes didn't belong to a Peter Grimshaw, it belonged to a Michael Simmonds who lived in Hockley. He felt that tingle up the spine that told him this was going to be an interesting case.

In the CID office, Jazz sat at his desk. The other detectives crowded around the other desks in the room and grumbled about fucking hot-desking. One looked at Jazz and asked contemptuously why the fuck he had a desk of his own.

Before Jazz could answer, Ash walked in and busily answered, "Because we do real detective work and get results, that's why." With a triumphant smile at the room, he thumped a pile of files on to Jazz's desk. With a theatrical loudness he announced, "This is the information you required. We have work to do, DS Singh." Then Ash sat down and whispered, "I think that put them in their place."

Jazz wasn't sure whether to laugh or cry. This little bastard had stuck up for him, which was a first. On the other hand, his impression of a tough detective wanted a bit of work. But in that moment, he loved this guy.

The thrill of the chase was on. At this moment neither knew what was going to happen. Ash was waiting for information to be faxed to him on Michael Simmonds, together with his driving licence, which should have a picture on it. What he had at present was information that said Michael Simmonds was a gardener who worked for a high-profile businessman in Paglesham.

"Not bloody Paglesham again!" was the response from Jazz.

Ash took no notice and continued that he had a lot of information on David Bateman, who was the businessman in Paglesham.

Excitedly, Ash took a deep breath and started. "OK, David Bateman is a millionaire. Comes from a wealthy family but did something wonderful with stocks and shares back in the '80s when others were not so feisty. He bought a big place in Paglesham at end of that decade and turned it into a palace, with the stables converted into self-contained accommodation. It is just off the Paglesham Road, but surrounded by fields so no one lives close by."

Jazz sensed there was more as the excitement in Ash's voice got higher and faster.

"But in 1974 he was sentenced to two years in Chelmsford Prison for kiddie-fiddling. There was no register then of sex offenders, that didn't come until the Sex Offenders Act 1997. So when he came out he got on with his life. He has been a pillar of the community ever since."

Jazz was having none of it. "A paedophile is always a paedophile. What makes him a pillar of the community?"

Ash flicked through his file and found what he was looking for. "He is a born-again Christian, Jazz. It's well-documented, and he is something big with the church in Canewdon, giving money to support it and its charities. Well-liked and respected in the Rochford area of Essex." Tapping the file and shaking his head, Ash continued. "By the looks of it, you are gonna be in big trouble if you mess with him, he is near sainthood according to this."

"Bollocks to that," was Jazz's response.

Jazz thought and said they needed to see a picture of Michael Simmonds to see if he was Peter Grimshaw for starters, and then a plan of action was required. Ash nodded, excited at the thought of working with Jazz on this.

"You have to talk this through with DCI Radley, you know," was Ash's next comment.

Jazz nodded and just uttered, "In time, in time. Let's see what we get first."

Ash went off to the fax machine to see if Michael Simmonds' driving licence had come through yet. Jazz left for the custody suite, leaving a list of instructions for Ash to get more information on Michael Simmonds and David Bateman.

His parting shot to Ash was, "There's something wrong in my town and we are gonna put it right."

Ash thought sarcastically that Jazz sounded like a Wild West sheriff, but he had to admit, there was a sense of excitement in the air and he was going to get as much information as he could off the system.

It was going to be the rock-solid gold information that would take them off-piste and into unchartered areas of evil.

CHAPTER 10

Another One Bites the Dust!

The custody suite was busy today. There were prisoners and witnesses to be interviewed and it was all hands to the pump. There were at least six detectives working in the interview rooms. Last night must have been a particularly busy night.

There had been a change of shift and Shirley was working as the custody sergeant. Jazz liked Shirley. She took a joke, and when she laughed her enormous boobs seemed to take on a life of their own and move independently of the rest of her. It was fascinating to watch. Shirley had a temper and a mouth on her. There had been many male prisoners who had commented on her boobs and got a sharp mouthful of abuse back. Her put-downs were legendary; most went over the heads of prisoners but the officers around enjoyed the joke. She was near the end of her career at forty-five years old. Shirley wasn't very tall and had a roly-poly figure and bleached-blonde curls that appeared just above the custody desk, but when she was in full flow, no one would misbehave in her custody suite. She couldn't run fast, but my God! Her arms and wrists were muscular and strong, and she could put a prisoner in a tight armlock that had grown men crying if she was pushed too far.

Feisty Shirley and respectful Jazz understood each other and got on well. He never overstepped the mark with her, and she looked after him.

"I have got a strange one for you, Jazz," she said. "I have a biter in custody and I need you to interview the brother, who was a witness. Officers are having a lot of trouble getting the family to understand what we are saying. They are British, so don't know what the problem is. Will you have a go with him?"

Jazz took the file of papers and had a look at what had happened. The family were the Carters and the brother was Alfie. Allegedly Johnny Carter was an aggressive, violent person with a record of GBH. He had a few drinks and got into a fight with a friend of Alfie's who had come round for the evening for drinks and some wacky baccy.

The friend was called Malcolm Low, and he was in hospital with an ear missing and his nose nearly bitten off. He had bite marks on his face and his eye socket was under review, his neck had been bitten hard and an artery severed, which nearly led to his death. Malcolm was being interviewed in his hospital bed by another police officer.

"Bloody hell, Shirley! This one is dangerous. Is he locked up in one of the cells?"

Shirley said, "Not bloody likely, he is too dangerous. He is being held in a secure mental home in Essex until his court trial. He is gonna be an IPP." (Imprisonment for public protection.)

Jazz took the file to the room where Alfie, the biter's brother, was waiting to give his statement. He introduced himself and sat down opposite Alfie, and proceeded with the usual explanation of why Alfie was here and how he was giving a statement of the events of the previous night etc.

Alfie sat straight-faced with no eye contact or sign of understanding. Jazz stopped, looked and asked Alfie if he understood why he was here. Again, no response.

"Is your name Alfie Carter?" asked Jazz, and he waited for a response.

Alfie fidgeted in his chair, looked at Jazz and uttered, "Fucking why am I in this bastard place?"

"Because you are giving a fucking statement on your tosspot of a brother."

Alfie smiled and said, "OK, why didn't you fucking say so?"

Jazz thought for a moment. He had spoken to people like Alfie before. It was utterly weird but they couldn't have a conversation unless it was full of expletives. They just didn't understand straight English. This was going to be a full and rich statement of liberally sprinkled swearing and facts that would be quite interesting when read out in a court of law with all its pomposity.

Alfie gave his statement. "We were pissing around, taking shit and sucking beer. We were fucked! Johnny got arsey with Malcolm. They were going fucking mad. Johnny is a bastard when fucked. He soddin' bit Malcolm's fucking ear off, and then the bastard bit a fucking lump out of his neck and the blood was going fucking everywhere. I nearly shit myself. Malcolm was bloody screaming and fucking crying."

It took Jazz about an hour to write out the statement and get Alfie to sign it. He tried to put in some semblance of English that the courts could understand.

He explained to Shirley that the family were unable to understand a normal conversation; it had to be full of swear words for them to understand. She said she would tell the other officers who were having trouble with the sister and mother.

He'd done his bit in custody and now Jazz was keen to get back to Ash and continue with finding out who Peter Grimshaw was.

CHAPTER 11

The Plot Thickens

Ash was still getting information and told Jazz to give him another hour. In the meantime, Jazz jumped in a vacant police car and took off to see Dionne on the pretext of finding out how she was. He wanted to know if Grimshaw was around.

"Darling, you are so kind to visit little me. I am coping with the pain, thank you," was the coy answer from Dionne to Jazz's polite enquiry.

He was trying to think how to bring Peter Grimshaw into the conversation when Dionne asked, "Did you hear, Mr Singh? Peter only had a window smashed in his lovely car last night. Some little toerag stole his satnav and some music discs he keeps in there. I was so mad – the man is wonderful and this happens to him. The area has gone right downhill, Mr Singh. Have you caught them yet?"

Jazz said he would make enquiries. He asked politely if Peter was around today so he could ask what was stolen. Dionne said he wasn't coming back until next weekend. He had to work. She looked at Jazz and nodded knowingly.

"I have a boyfriend who works, I am a lucky girl."

Jazz raised his eyebrows and tried to look impressed.

He explained it was a passing visit and he had to get back to the station. Dionne felt honoured that he'd visited little her, and with a beaming smile she thanked him for popping by. Secretly she thought that her sexual magnetism had obviously snared this handsome police officer. She thought she should be careful how she looked at these men; she was obviously a babe magnet. She lay back on her pillow with a self-satisfaction that made her preen her hair a little in case another man called to enquire about her health.

Jazz got in the car and rang Ash and asked him to check if an incident had been recorded involving a car being broken into. Ash had the registration of the Mercedes, so could check. He came back within a minute and said it hadn't been reported according to the records at Ilford, Barking and Dagenham nicks. Jazz thought that very interesting. Ash added that he had the photo of Michael Simmonds if Jazz wanted to get back to the station and take a look. He didn't need an invitation; Jazz put on the blue light and got back to Ilford in record time.

As he got out of the car Jazz's mobile rang. It was Mad Pete in a very agitated state.

"Mr Singh, I need to see you quick. I've got

something you need to see, it's bloody diabolical and I ain't keeping it long." Mad Pete wouldn't say anything more and Jazz said he would get round to him in two hours. Mad Pete moaned that was too long, but quietened down when Jazz said he would bring McDonald's with him and he couldn't come before, but promised he wouldn't be later than two hours.

There was a spring in his step. Life was getting better and better. Jazz liked it when there was stuff going on. He could smell trouble and he could smell success. On the basis of success, he took his hip flask out of his pocket and had a good swig of vodka. He felt bloody good.

Ash had got his information together. First he showed Jazz a picture of Michael Simmonds. Jazz looked at it hard. It was obviously Peter Grimshaw. He sat back and thought. Michael Simmonds worked for David Bateman, a paedophile. Simmonds worked as Bateman's gardener. He didn't look like a gardener, and his hands, as far as Jazz could remember, didn't look like they did manual work.

Something was very wrong. *Simmonds has his car broken into and he doesn't report it to the police. Unheard of – unless, of course, you have something to hide. He has made friends with a little girl and he works for a paedophile. One and one always makes two.* This was serious.

He had an address for Simmonds and an address for Bateman. Ash had looked at the electoral roll for both. Simmonds lived alone in a very nice house, better than a gardener would have been able to afford, but Bateman had two men living in the converted stables. Ash had found out that the two men worked for Bateman on his land and helped in the house. Jazz thought they were very lucky to be able to live so close to the house in such lovely accommodation. He wondered if he was looking for trouble or just being bloody brilliant.

In answer to a question, Ash confirmed that neither Simmonds nor the two men living in the stables had a criminal record. Only Bateman had a criminal record, and that was a long time ago.

Now was the time to talk to DCI Radley, so he knew what Jazz was investigating. He would see him in the morning. It was getting late in the afternoon and he had to be at Mad Pete's flat soon. Although Mad Pete got agitated easily, it was unusual for him to ring and ask to see Jazz. It was usually the other way around.

Jazz looked at Ash and said, "Well done for the work. It's getting late and I am off to see Mad Pete. See you in the morning."

It was their favourite; Big Macs, large fries and coffees from McDonald's. The block of flats smelled of rotten greens, which seemed strange because Jazz reckoned no one ever cooked anything in these flats, let alone greens. The grubby blue door was Mad Pete's. It took several minutes for all the locks to be opened. Jazz shouted that the McDonald's was getting cold.

"Alright, alright, Mr Singh, I am nearly there," shouted the panicky-sounding Mad Pete. Jazz wondered what had spooked him this time.

When he opened the door Mad Pete looked around urgently to make sure no one else was on the landing and gestured impatiently for Jazz to come in.

Jazz moved the bits of paper strewn across the settee and sat down. "Don't you ever tidy this pigsty up?" asked Jazz as he handed Mad Pete his Big Mac and fries. Just as he was getting stuck into his big mac, Jazz looked up and for a moment it looked like Mad Pete wasn't going to eat his Big Mac, which would have been a first.

"Look, if you don't get something inside you, Pete, you will be fit for nothing. You are a long streak of piss as it is, you need food!"

Pete nodded and tucked into the Big Mac with manners a pig would be ashamed of. They ate them quickly. It was not good when the burgers and fries got too cold. The coffee was still piping hot. It didn't take long to finish the food, and afterwards both lit up cigarettes and finished their coffees. Relaxed and quiet, Jazz asked what had upset Pete.

Tense and looking around as if wanting a way out, Mad Pete whined, "Mr Singh, I do a little business in the area, you know that..." He stopped and looked for agreement from Jazz, who kept quiet and tried to look interested.

'A little business' was fencing stolen goods. Jazz didn't think it was the time to argue that Mad Pete was a thieving bastard and should be arrested, so he nodded and let him continue.

"Well, Mr Singh, this morning some lads brought stuff to me they got last night, nothing much but amongst some CDs was a DVD, and I played it. Mr Singh, it is fucking awful and I feel sick, and if there is one thing I can't stand it's kiddie-fiddlers, and Mr Singh, it made me sick to watch it." At this point Mad Pete had got himself extremely agitated, and shouted, "You gotta do sumthink with this, Mr Singh, it ain't right."

Jazz had never seen Mad Pete so distraught. Even the DVD which showed a man being tortured in water and then being run down, drowned and buried by a barge didn't upset him like this, and that was truly sickening.

"So, are you going to show me what it is, Pete?" Jazz asked soothingly. Mad Pete was on the verge of a druggy fit, and that would waste a lot of time. Jazz had just wanted to go home and relax and have a few drinks before he went to sleep, but now he was alert and ready to see what had made Mad Pete so upset. He had mentioned kiddie-fiddling. Was that a coincidence?

The DVD was played and for the next thirty minutes Jazz and Mad Pete looked at a bit of hell on earth.

The little boy in the film had been drugged. He was awake but very calm. Jazz counted six men who had had buggered him. He presumed the filming wasn't in real time. He couldn't see their faces; the camera seemed to concentrate on the little boy, who looked well under ten years of age. Things were done that Jazz didn't think were possible with a small child, and that caused the boy to cry out in pain. Jazz and Mad Pete instinctively grabbed each other's hands out of solidarity and comfort at such a sight.

The end was too much, even for the supposedly hardened detective, who watched the little boy being slowly strangled. It lasted for minutes and caused Mad Pete to cry out and Jazz to wipe away the tears that were streaming down his face.

Both were unable to recover for quite a few minutes. It was heart-stoppingly awful. Jazz had seen some stuff in his time, but this? This was beyond all sanity and humanity. He wasn't going to sleep tonight. The boy's face would haunt him for a long time.

In a whisper (loud talking was not possible), Jazz asked Mad Pete where the DVD had come from. Mad Pete, crying and snot dribbling from his nose, said he wished he had never seen it. He didn't know where it came from.

Jazz's voice quivered with emotion as he whispered, "I don't care at the moment who stole this. I don't care who they are. I just want to know *where* they stole it. I've got to get this person if it's the last thing I ever do."

Mad Pete nodded far too many times. "Mr Singh, I will get that information tomorrow for you." With his eyes flashing and venom in his voice, he added, "I wanna see the bastards caught and given a right good kicking too."

Jazz took the DVD and thanked Mad Pete for contacting him. It all sounded polite and correct but neither felt good about this. Jazz left and went to Ilford Police Station.

En route, he phoned Ash. "Yeah, yeah, I know it's late, Ash, sorry but this is important. For the love of God, will you shut up and listen?" He was sick of listening to Ash moaning when there was something so vile and rotten in his town that needed burning out. Ash convinced Jazz that he needed some sleep and tomorrow they would both be fresh to look into this, and they would get results. They would get the bastards who did this.

After Jazz had recorded the DVD as evidence on his AWARE system and bagged it and locked it in his cupboard for the night, he went home. It was late now and he hoped that after a few drinks he could erase the little boy's face from his mind and get some sleep.

Mrs Chodda was up and opened her kitchen door to say something, but she caught the look on Jazz's face and just wished him goodnight as he went up the stairs to finish that bottle of vodka he had in his cupboard.

The next morning Jazz woke with a thick head, a dry mouth and tired from a lack of sleep. He couldn't get the boy's face out of his head. A shower helped, and by the time he had shaved and dressed he knew what he was going to do. He was on a mission to find out who the boy was and get his killers.

It occurred to him that Simmonds had had his car broken into, and Dionne had said he'd lost a satnav as well as the CDs. Would that be far too much of a coincidence? Nah, he thought. He was going to get the bastards, all of them. First things first, he needed to see DCI Radley. Gone were the days when he would've acted in a cavalier way. This was far too important and urgent to keep to himself.

CHAPTER 12

Clarion Call

Ilford Police Station was a hive of activity. There had been a football match the night before and today the custody suite was full of drunken hooligans that were just sobering up. Their briefs and family and friends had arrived, and all wanting to see them. Jazz skirted round the lot of them as they talked, shouted and milled around the police entrance. He made straight for his desk in the CID office on the first floor.

Ash was already at work. "Jazz, just to let you know, Bateman hasn't had his DNA taken. He was jailed before 1997 when the Sex Offenders Act became law and DNA was taken as a matter of course. He hasn't been in trouble since, so no chance to get his DNA."

Jazz frowned at this bit of information, but at the moment it wasn't relevant. It would be very important later.

He rang Mad Pete for the information on where

the thieves had got the DVD. Mad Pete was asleep and wasn't happy to be woken at 9am.

"Do me a favour, Mr Singh – no one gets up at 9am. I will let you know after 11am, when hopefully I can raise one of them."

Jazz accepted that, but wanted Mad Pete to write down the names of the CDs of music that were given to him. He wanted to check with Dionne if she knew of them.

He told Ash that they were going to talk to DCI Radley, and that he would take the DVD to show him and Ash.

Jazz warned them both that it was harrowing, but nothing could prepare them for what they were about to watch.

The jigsaw puzzle was laid out in front of a stunned DCI Radley and a tearful Ash. They had watched the DVD first. It took Ash several hours to regain control; the tears kept coming. The little boy was about the same age as his son, and it was too much for him to cope with. Jazz, now resolute and angry, wanted to make sure DCI Radley knew where they were going with this. He was going to get the murdering bastards. DCI Radley sat quietly and nodded at everything Jazz told him.

After what felt like a long silence, with Jazz watching and waiting for DCI Radley to speak, DCI Radley spoke in measured tones. He wanted, very badly, whoever was responsible for this poor boy's demise and treatment to be brought to justice. He spoke in polite terms because at this moment he couldn't bring himself to use the words that best described what he saw.

The argument was about to begin.

"I think this is too big for you to work alone, Jazz. This is for the Emerald team, who are far more experienced than you in dealing with paedophiles."

"Give me a couple of days, Sir, and we will find out who the young boy is. We don't want to spook this group. I have an inroad, and with Ash's help, and he is bloody good, Sir, we will get this started. Give me two days and then I'll hand it all over to the Emerald team. I want this gang of scumbags caught, and I think they will be hard to catch. Nothing has touched them yet, otherwise they wouldn't still be working and grooming Nekisha. I hear Nekisha is safe until next weekend, so we have time. He will be back for her then. In the meantime, we will interview Nekisha using officers skilled in this area."

DC Radley, filtering all the information being thrown at him, asked Jazz, "Are you sure Nekisha is being groomed by a paedophile group and do we know the group?" Jazz, anxious to get started and desperate for DC Radley to give him the go-ahead, stated, "We know that Simmonds lied about his name and I am pretty sure the DVD was in his car when it was broken into. We'll know in an hour." Jazz was in full flow, and finished with a plea: "Please, Sir, we are hot, we are in there, let us try and get some information that links the names we have. Bateman has got away with murder, literally I reckon, and Simmonds has helped him."

DCI Radley made him promise to keep him informed of every step he took. He wanted to know what Jazz's grass had found out. He agreed that DI Tom Black and his team could help for the time being, it was a murder after all, but after a moment of thought DCI Radley added that at least one member of Emerald was to be included immediately too.

Jazz nodded in agreement and added, "Sir, Bateman is outside of the Metropolitan Police region, but if he is implicated with Simmonds then they crossed into our area so they are ours to take."

DCI Radley could see that.

As Jazz was about to close the door, DCI Radley called to him. "By the way, you had better contact Essex Police too. We will be treading all over their territory and it would be good manners to talk to them. So to recap, at least one member of Emerald must be involved now, if not more, and you must talk with Essex Police, is that clear?"

Jazz nodded. He wanted to get away before the sodding cleaning woman and the fucking Red Arrows, together with every pissing marching band in the country, were included in this too. Any more people involved and confidentiality would be out the window. Still, his major worry was that too many officers would clog up the investigation.

He had agreed he would report back to DCI

Radley in two hours after he had spoken to his contact, who was finding out where the DVD was stolen from, and any update with Emerald. Lots to do, but first he found Ash in the canteen.

A cup of tea was needed for Ash, who was still in a tearful state. Jazz made the excuse of going to the toilet and took a long swig of vodka from his hip flask. God, he needed that! The lovely Milly brought tea and a freebie rock cake each. From the look of them she thought they needed something nice to eat.

Looking at each of them with concern, she asked gently, "Are you OK, dears?" They shook their heads and said they couldn't talk about it yet. She fussed for a few moments, making sure the mugs of tea and rock cakes were positioned comfortably in front of them, and then left them to chastise officers who were grumbling at the counter, waiting for their tea.

The first thing Jazz wanted Ash to do was find out who the little boy in the DVD was. "You are the king of computers, Ash, you will find him in no time. Then organise a meeting with Emerald. I am going to ring Mad Pete in a while to see if we can put Simmonds in the frame for this."

Ash went off to get on his computer and find the little boy. He was called Kevin Parsons. He disappeared in 2011 and his body was found in a municipal dump in Essex five weeks later. He lived in Hoddesdon, Hertfordshire with his mother and father, who were now separated. His body had been mutilated and what had been done to him had caused irreparable damage to his internal organs. The cause of death was coldly articulated on the computer as strangulation, not the slow asphyxiation shown on the video. Ash was still emotional.

Jazz called Emerald and spoke to DI Paula Rudd. DI Rudd was in her late thirties and had seen and heard more about child pornography than a young woman should. Jazz had met her in the past and her eyes looked haunted. She also had a mouth on her and took no lip from anyone. She was a tough cookie. She was joining the team for this case.

It was still not quite 11am, so Jazz went to find Boomer. It was first thing in the morning but Boomer was in full flow.

"I'm fucking bored, bored, bored!" he told Jazz. There was nothing much happening and his team were mopping up various cases. The DVD was played for Boomer and his reaction was quiet (for Boomer), but heartfelt and emotional. He so wanted to be part of this investigation. He was invited to the meeting, which was to be held at twelve noon.

Jazz had got his team together. It was gone 11am and now time to ring Mad Pete. Mad Pete had spoken to the lads who broke into the car and confirmed that the DVD came out of a car in Longbridge Road, a Mercedes, and they took the satnav as well.

In answer to a question, Mad Pete replied incredulously, "No, they fucking won't come forward and confirm they broke into the car. Are you mad, Mr Singh?"

Jazz nodded, and with a rueful smile said, "It was worth a try."

"I have got something you will want though, Mr Singh," Mad Pete coyly offered, and triumphantly added, "I've got the satnav they took, and we both know what that means, don't we?."

Jeez, thought Jazz, *Mad Pete is never this helpful*; it had got to him too. Jazz excitedly told him to move his bony arse and get to the station within the next half-hour with the satnav. The satnav would confirm the owner. 'Home' on a satnav, as all good criminals know, takes you to the car owner's home. Many house burglaries followed the theft of satnavs.

This was going well, and in passing to the meeting room, Jazz stuck his head around DCI Radley's office door to update him. He had never been so on the ball, so organised; he was riding high, things were moving and he was going to get the murdering bastards. A trip to the gents' for a quick swig of the clear liquid from his trusty hip flask and he was ready.

CHAPTER 13

Ring a Ring o' Roses

DIs Boomer and Paula were mouthy, loud and fearless, and contrary to opinions in the station that they would clash, they seemed to get on together. Ash put the pictures of Simmonds and Bateman and little Kevin Parsons on the boards in front of them, and said he was waiting for a picture of Nekisha.

A plan of action was worked out. DI Paula Rudd started. She had the old file on Simmonds. This was not a Met job. It was an Essex job, but she got the file off the AWARE system. Paula had access to anything to do with paedophiles throughout the country.

David Bateman was convicted of sex with an eight-year-old girl back in 1976; he got five years and was out in three years. It was the only offence he'd ever been convicted of, and he'd been a paragon of virtue and lawfulness since.

"Fucking rubbish. A paedophile is always a paedophile, they can't and won't change," Jazz shouted, exasperated and annoyed now. "We have a paedophile ring out there that not only subject young children to vile sexual practices, but also murder them. Snuff movies are the vilest fucking murderous, shittiest..." He raised his hands, exasperated, running out of words to describe it.

Paula, who had seen and heard most things to do with paedophilia, was not moved by his outburst. "Calm down, Jazz, I am quoting what I know. If you Google David Bateman you will get his profile, his businesses and his charities." She had run off pages of information on David Bateman, and as she handed out copies she said, "His profiles will tell you everything he wants you to know about him. Surprisingly, there is no mention of his prison record in anything you Google, but he can afford people who'll ensure this doesn't get out. If he is part of this, then let's get the fucking bastard." Paula looked up expectantly, and saw fervent agreement from everyone.

Just as Jazz was about to answer her, his mobile rang. He listened and made excuses to leave, saying he would be a few minutes as it was important.

Mad Pete was waiting round the corner in McDonald's as arranged. The meeting was quick, with staccato conversation, but Jazz grabbed the satnav and Mad Pete got himself a Big Mac meal with the tenner Jazz handed him, and waited there as instructed.

Jazz was back within ten minutes. Out of breath (he had to give up the fags, he told himself), he put the satnav on meeting room table. The battery was still full and an address came up under 'home'.

Triumphantly and theatrically, Jazz asked Ash to tell him Simmonds' address. He told everyone present that the home address on the satnav stolen from a Mercedes in Longbridge Road last night, together with CDs and the DVD of Kevin Parsons' death, was Minerva Cottage, Paglesham.

There was silence as Ash looked up the address and told them it wasn't the address Simmonds had registered with the DVLA or the electoral register.

Crestfallen, Jazz asked, "What the fuck's going on?"

What needed to be looked at was the connection between Simmonds and Bateman, both with Paglesham addresses. It was a coincidence that was too big to be ignored.

Jazz asked Ash to look at the Paglesham address and let him know ASAP if Simmonds lived there. It didn't need saying, but Jazz vehemently stated, "We needed to get the bastards."

It was argued by all present that they needed the thieves to confirm that the DVD was one of the stolen items. Simmonds would deny it. Simmonds didn't have any record at all. A plan of action was formulated.

Paula Rudd and Jazz would go to visit Dionne and Nekisha, Paula to interview Nekisha and Jazz to calm down Dionne and see what she could tell him. More information was needed on Simmonds. If he was grooming Nekisha, he could have previous in some form or another. Ash would go through every record and see what he could find on Simmonds.

Bateman was a different kettle of fish, and Jazz and Boomer would look at him. Jazz had an idea and it was too far off the scale to share with everyone. Boomer was the only person he would discuss it with.

All would come back tomorrow with updates. It was going to get dangerous, and Jazz and Ash would pay.

It was 2pm and everyone went for a late lunch. Jazz and Paula grabbed a sandwich together and talked about visiting Dionne. Jazz rang her and said he would be round this afternoon if she was in.

Dionne was flattered – the man couldn't keep away! But in her sexiest voice she said, "Sure, honey, I look forward to seeing you."

Jazz raised his eyebrows and grimaced as he thought, *She ain't gonna be pleased to see me after we start talking.*

Paula and Jazz spent another hour just chatting and getting together their plan of action. The chat was flirty but Paula stopped it before it went further, he was known as a loose cannon and she didn't need that. Jazz asked if she had to let someone know when she got home tonight. She knew what he was asking and told him bluntly that she wasn't seeing anyone, and wasn't interested in anyone she worked with either. Jazz shrugged, a bit put out. He had got used to women thinking he was gorgeous; his flirting was only meant playfully, so her put-down was unexpected. He liked her and thought she was feisty. With a smile, he got her another cup of coffee.

Each knew what the other was doing at Dionne's. It was now 3.30pm and time to go. Nekisha would be home from school any minute. Jazz said he would meet Paula by the police car they had appropriated; he wanted a cigarette, he told her, but he also wanted a drink too. His flask was getting low, but he carried two now so he had enough for the rest of the afternoon.

It took fifteen minutes to get to Dionne's. The traffic on Longbridge Road was building up but parking was no problem. Paula had her doll with her in her bag, and Jazz had his thoughts on how to talk to Dionne fully sorted and was ready to deal with the tears that would come.

Dionne opened the door and was surprised to see a woman with DS Singh. Her surprise turned to confusion and then denial, and in the end she exploded with anger.

First of all they explained that her knight, Peter Grimshaw, was in fact Michael Simmonds. She said they had got it wrong, and they showed her a picture with his real name. Then Jazz, as delicately as possible, explained their concern regarding his interest in Nekisha. Now Dionne was outraged, furious, and wanted them to go.

DI Paula Rudd, used to dealing with distraught and disbelieving parents, took over. It wasn't the time for messing around, so quite clearly DI Rudd asked, "Let me just have a very easy and safe conversation with Nekisha. I am very experienced in talking to young children and I know what to look for. We will get this sorted now, and if we are wrong we'll apologise and leave you in peace, but if we are right, I know you'll want this sorted out now."

Dionne, mute from shock and shaking, nodded her agreement. Paula went off to find Nekisha in her bedroom and spend a little time chatting with her. Jazz stayed with Dionne. He offered to make her a cup of tea.

Paula went upstairs with her bag and knocked on Nekisha's bedroom door. After knocking twice and calling her name, Paula tentatively opened the door, not wanting to frighten her.

"I am Paula, Nekisha, can I come in?" she said quietly and respectfully.

Nekisha was sitting in her bed wrapped in her duvet, her head just poking out of the top, every part of her hidden inside the bulky protector. She shied back against the headboard and looked silently at Paula with doe eyes that appeared wary.

Paula smiled carefully, not wanting to scare this child any more than she was already. "Look," she said, holding up her warrant card, "I am a police officer, here to help, not to hurt."

Nekisha's eyes darted from Paula to the card and back to Paula. She nodded hesitantly but still wouldn't talk.

"Can I sit down at the end of your bed?" asked Paula quietly. She added quickly, "I would just like to chat with you. Mummy said that was OK, and she is downstairs talking with a nice police officer and having a cup of tea. Would you like a drink or anything?" she asked Nekisha.

Nekisha shook her head, and by now Paula had sat down. She was used to dealing with traumatised children who didn't want to talk and knew it could take a few hours to get through to Nekisha.

The first thing she did when she sat down was to get out a beautifully dressed black doll called Nekisha. Nekisha looked surprised.

Paula nodded and smiled. "I know, what a coincidence that this beautiful dolly has your name. I think she looks a little like you. She has a curl at the front of her hair just like yours, what do you think?"

Nekisha was interested and sat up a little bit and nodded. No smile yet, but she looked intently at the dolly. Paula fussed over the dolly Nekisha, straightening her little woollen jacket and patting her hair.

"Would you like to hold her?" asked Paula, and Nekisha brought out a hand from inside the duvet and took hold of the dolly held out to her. This was a six-year-old child, so talking about dollies was good. Paula told her how dolly Nekisha was loved by her mummy, and how she liked her hair brushed, and Nekisha listened and nodded. It was at this point that Nekisha said she would like a drink and a biscuit, so Paula smiled and left to go to the kitchen. It was going well.

Jazz looked up as Paula came down the stairs, and

he tapped Dionne kindly on the arm to say he wouldn't be a second and followed Paula into the kitchen. In answer to his urgent question whispered into her ear, she told him that it was far too soon to have got anywhere, and said it would be at least another hour before she could start making any sort of progress.

Jazz moaned that it was taking so long, and in response Paula fiercely whispered back, "Go fuck yourself, Singh, I know what I am doing."

Shocked at her rough response, he held up his hands and said, as placatory as he could, "OK, OK, just asking. I'll carry on talking to Dionne. She ain't a happy woman."

Paula had got a drink and found the biscuits, and with a grimace at Jazz she told him, "That's your problem, Singh – I've got my own." With that she was out of the kitchen and halfway up the stairs before he could think of a retort

Dionne was very unhappy. At present she was recalling the birth of Nekisha, and Jazz was trying to keep his cup of tea down in the face of all the messy, lurid, painful and pretty disgusting details. *What was afterbirth and placenta all about?* he asked himself

Dionne understood that DI Paula Rudd, or Paula, as Jazz said she liked to be called, was just gently finding out if there was any reason to be concerned about Nekisha's contact with Simmonds, as it now seemed he was called. Jazz had explained to a very tearful and accusing Dionne that it was a precaution, and that he felt sure she would like to know that Nekisha was OK and nothing untoward had happened. That settled, Jazz had asked about Dionne's life, to keep her occupied and to find out the history of where they came from.

Dionne, as she told Jazz to call her, was not in a vampish mood. The tearful and sombre side of her made Jazz think she was a really caring mother and auntie. She talked about Winston and how she had brought him up. Apparently the men in her life had been a bit wild but she had brought a homeliness to her children's lives, and although she considered herself a desirable woman, she was a mother first. She spent the next hour convincing Jazz that after Mother Teresa, she was the nearest to sainthood in this lifetime Or was that just Jazz getting a bit jaundiced? He was anxious to find out what they were dealing with, and hoped Paula was getting somewhere with Nekisha.

The drink and biscuit went down well and Nekisha seemed a little more at ease. As she was still under the duvet, Paula spent time encouraging her to sit on the side of the bed and talk with her. After an hour of getting to know each other and playing with the dolly Nekisha, it looked like the time spent in making Nekisha feel comfortable was paying off. She got out of bed and unwrapped herself from the duvet to show Paula a picture she had drawn. It was a very dark picture with a dark house, something Paula recognised as not a happy picture.

Nekisha went to the bathroom, and in her absence

Paula looked quickly at the bed. She took off the sheet and noted the mattress was stained in a manner that suggested the bed had been wet on a number of occasions. She sniffed the stained patch and it smelled of urine. Another sign noted.

When Nekisha came back into the room Paula had the dolly in her arms. She gently started asking questions. Nekisha was reticent at first but when given the dolly, proceeded to show Paula where her body had been touched by other people. This gentle and experienced officer heard things she would rather have not heard from a young child.

Paula came down the stairs and the expression on her face told Jazz the news was going to be awful. Paula looked at Jazz and then at Dionne, who could also tell the news was not good. She started to cry, and Jazz grabbed one of the tissues on the bed and gave it to her.

DI Paula Rudd went into work mode. She told Dionne and Jazz that there was cause for concern, that Nekisha had been groomed and it appeared there may have been some sexual touching. Now she was going to ring the Richmond Centre, a place, she explained, where a child and mother could stay in a pleasant environment and doctors would examine Nekisha and the full extent of her molestation would be known.

Dionne was inconsolable and wanted Nekisha to come straight downstairs to her. The two of them were left to cuddle each other whilst Paula got on the phone and asked for a place to be made available now. She said they would be leaving within the next ten minutes. Paula helped them pack a suitcase for their stay and Nekisha, quiet and scared, sat by her mother and waited.

Jazz was going back to the station and Paula would take Dionne and Nekisha to the Richmond Centre, a big old house set in large gardens near Loughton. Another police car had been called for and would be arriving any minute. There was no time to waste. They had a paedophile ring, Jazz was sure of that, to put away.

Jazz knew they had a bit of time. Simmonds had been visiting Dionne nearly every day, but strangely he was working this week and could only come at the weekend. Jazz reckoned their meeting had rattled Simmonds and he was keeping away. He would be ringing towards the end of the week, just to see how the land lay. They needed to get their facts together and move fast.

It was 7.30pm and Ash would have gone home by now, so Jazz decided to pay a visit to Sainsbury's and get another bottle or two of his tipple. His flasks were practically empty now; one last swig and he got in the car and took off. It was going to be a pizza tonight. He rang from the car and ordered it so that when he got home he would have a quiet evening of eating and drinking. The look on Nekisha's face made him shudder, but anger would take over and he would go on the rampage. Tomorrow would be the start of something nasty.

CHAPTER 14

Snakes and Ladders

Jazz was up early. Nekisha was on his mind, as was
Dionne. The meeting with the team was scheduled for
10am to play catch-up. Jazz needed to speak with DI
Tom Black, or Boomer as he was known to anyone
who worked within shouting distance of him. He had
a cunning plan.

OK, he admitted, he had drunk a tad more than he
should have last night, but he was tired so fell asleep
before he got truly pissed. He brushed his teeth to
clear the furry animals that were living in his mouth.
The shower cleared his head and by the time he was
walking towards Ilford Police Station he was thinking
clearly and almost had a spring in his step. He felt his
two inner pockets in his jacket and was reassured that
the full flasks were there.

It was time to sort out Bateman and Simmonds.
Jazz went straight to Boomer's office. DIs had their
own offices, so privacy was certain as Jazz unravelled
his brilliant plan.

Boomer growled a no. He was laughing, but still said no. Jazz started again.

"Look, it's worth a try. We don't want to alert or scare off Simmonds and Bateman, they will just get flushed down the toilet and we will lose them in the sewers."

"I know they are shit, but stop this and talk straight, Singh!" was the growl from Boomer.

"OK, we send in Mad Pete. He can go there asking for a job in the gardens. He looks so bloody awful no one is going to think he is a plant."

Boomer laughed at that. "A plant?!"

"OK, wrong word, but you know what I mean," said Jazz, now a full and enthusiastic member of the Mad Pete Society. "He can find stuff out for us. It's a brilliant plan." Jazz, seeing interest, added, "Mad Pete is a rat and he can scurry into the darkest corners without being seen. He will be our Exocet missile, or rather, our dirty bomb." Jazz laughed at this.

Boomer thought again – it had an interesting ring to it the second time around. "But will Mad Pete agree to do this? He's a bloody fucking nutter."

"That's the only turd in the swimming pool. He doesn't know yet," was the sheepish reply. "But he will do it, I guarantee it!" Jazz knew the cowardly Mad Pete, but he also knew he would do it for the right price.

Boomer wasn't that convinced; he thought the morning meeting would show a way forward that was easier, and for a change, legal. They both laughed at that. Boomer added that there were officers who were good at going undercover and were far more reliable than a fucking druggy with a massive personal hygiene problem. Jazz had to agree that made sense, but he would bide his time.

That was the last time they would get any peace in this case. Things had been happening behind the scenes, and as Jazz made his way to his office he was apprehended by a police sergeant and a police officer. Without saying anything, they grabbed Jazz and took him to DCI Radley's office. This was the most novel way he had been summoned to his boss' office, he thought, but he was in for a bigger shock.

If DCI Radley had been a cartoon figure you would have seen steam coming out of his ears. He stopped short of pacing up and down as Jazz was brought into his office. Before Jazz could say anything and as he was about to draw breath to ask the question, DCI Radley started shouting loud enough for everyone in the vicinity to hear him.

"I trusted you to do a job! I know you are a fucking idiot, but a criminal, never! You have caused me a huge amount of trouble and I'm just about keeping the fucking press away for the time being!"

Jazz was shocked, totally mystified and scared. The look, the words – what the hell had he done? DCI Radley calmed down; he didn't really believe it, and looking at Jazz's face, almost felt sorry for him.

"Look, if there is something you want to tell me

before we start, if you want to confess, it will go better for you," was the best Radley could come up with. He saw Jazz ponder, and then shake his head. With a sigh, he motioned for Jazz to sit down.

"What's going on, Sir? I haven't done anything I can think of. What is this all about?"

"Your computer has been compromised. On a tip-off from the press, of all bloody places, I was told a computer in the CID office had been used for illegal purposes. All computers have been searched by our IT people and your computer was found to contain illegal images. It had pornographic images of children, women, and all were the highest category at level five." Radley pulled a face, disgusted at what he had looked at.

Jazz jumped up, shocked. "What the fuck?! I have never, ever, Sir. I just wouldn't... I can't – wouldn't – stand for... I hate such things." He spluttered, lost for words. After a few seconds he whispered, almost to himself, "Someone must have used my computer, but why?"

Radley asked, "So who knows your password, DS Singh?"

Jazz thought. No one would have his password, why would they? He shook his head. He sat quietly, thinking; he had to push all the muddle out of his head and think clearly. *Think, man, think*! he told himself.

Of course, the right question came to him. "Sir, did IT log what time the images were on my computer? They should be able to check."

DCI Radley cursed inwardly – of course, he should have thought of that. He opened his office door and called for the IT person to be found and sent to his office, with a very irritated, "*Now.*" Because the press had been involved, and because of the seriousness of what was found on Jazz's computer, IT had sent someone to Ilford Police Station to help with any questions on processes and searches. The Metropolitan Police's AWARE system, and all computer enquiries and faults, were logged to a centrally-based department in London stuffed full of computer geeks.

They both sat in silence and waited the five minutes until Stewart Dingle entered the office. Stewart was the mastermind of computer systems in the Metropolitan Police Force; he knew everything about computing but very little about people. It had been said that if you had an outgoing personality and got on with people on a social level, you would not be a good IT engineer, and Stewart proved this beyond doubt.

He was a skinny man, about twenty-six years old, obviously single and planning to stay that way, judging by the carelessly but not cheaply dressed bearded person in front of them. Stewart hovered in front of Radley and Jazz, looking mildly embarrassed to be there. Slightly bent forward and nodding his head, he preferred a limp handshake as a gesture of welcome.

"So you know all about these computers, do you... er, Stewart, isn't it?" asked Radley. Stewart nodded. "So tell me in a few words how you found the site and images that came from DS Singh's computer," he added. "We need to know when these images were called up, the time and date, and how easy it would be to access these sites – in fact anything that would help us piece together who might have done this."

Stewart was now in his comfort zone. He took out his papers and asked if he could use DCI Radley's computer to access the information, which of course he was granted permission to do.

"Will this take long?" asked Radley. He was anxious to get this cleared up soon. Jazz looked at his watch; he had about one hour before his meeting and he wanted to be there very badly. This was all feeling very wrong, and the timing was suspicious.

"Well, Sir, to explain how this works is utterly fascinating. Combinatory logic eliminates the need for variables in mathematical logic. It was introduced by Moses Schönfinkel and Haskell Curry – we have moved on but they are awesomely great. But their work has more recently been used in computer science as a theoretical model of computation, and also as a basis for the design of functional programming languages. It is based on combinators."

He came up for breath and looked at Radley and Jazz. He wasn't bothered that they both looked glassy-eyed at the information, and continued. "In practice, digital computation aids simulation of natural processes including those that are naturally described by analogue models of computation, for example, artificial neural networks."

He came up for breath again, and Radley shouted,

"Enough!" He realised he sounded a little abrupt, and DCI Radley smiled and thanked Stewart for his illuminated explanation of what computers do and asked if he would kindly just tell them what they asked, which was what time and date the images appeared on Jazz's computer.

Stewart nodded, and with a few faster-than-lightning taps on the computer, brought up the information. It could be clearly seen, between a lot of what looked like gobbledygook, that the sites in question were called up and the pictures looked at between 4pm and 5pm the previous day. Stewart confirmed that the right password had been put in to access Jazz's computer, and it was confirmed that the data was accessed from his computer and not a remote computer. Stewart was thanked and asked to wait outside until further notice.

"I have proof I was not in the station during this hour, Sir. I was with DI Paula Rudd, who was interviewing Nekisha. Someone was in this office and used my computer and password. There has to be someone around who saw who that was. Why call the press, Sir? Because they wanted to cause trouble for me and the case I am working on – it's too much of a coincidence. How the hell would a paedophile ring get access to a police station and use one of our computers, and know my password? There is something rotten in this station, Sir."

Jazz tried not to show it, but he was seriously rattled. Not one to think before jumping into any fire, he had been burned a few times, but this was different. He had only just started this investigation and already someone was trying to discredit him.

DCI Radley was very perturbed. He didn't know who to trust. Jazz obviously wasn't the culprit, but he gave him a warning that he was doing something that pissed off someone and he needed to be careful and watch who he was working with. He told him he didn't need to remind him of past events.

It was agreed nothing would be said to anyone outside of that room, with the exception of Jazz's team. He could tell them and warn them to be careful, but this was confidential information for as long as DCI Radley worked on finding out who had been in the CID office yesterday between 4pm and 5pm. Radley told Jazz that Ash was accounted for; he had already checked him out. He'd spent the afternoon in the ops room looking up information and went home straight from there. Jazz was sent on his way and told to report back by 5pm tonight and give an update. Ilford Police Station was not a secure or happy place.

Jazz made his way to Boomer's office. DI Tom Black was quieter than normal and obviously very busy. Jazz was told to wait, so he went to the canteen for a coffee. He had half an hour before his meeting and he needed to clear his head and think. With only ten minutes before their meeting with Paula and Ash, Boomer found Jazz and got himself a quick coffee. Milly was very amenable today.

"OK, let's go with your idea for using the druggy

scumbag of yours. All my men are gonna be tied up with a machete murder for quite some time," whispered Boomer urgently.

"Need any help with the machete murder?" asked Jazz, oblivious for the moment to all the troubles brewing in his case. He just hated to miss a good murder hunt.

"God, no, Jazz, all taken care of. Think it's bloody terrorists in East Ham, and we will be busy for a while before the terrorist squad take over later," Boomer added begrudgingly. "This meeting starts soon, let's see what info comes out of it."

Jazz kept quiet. He would tell them all together what was happening and see if they had any ideas to put forward.

The case board now had a picture of Nekisha on it, and one of Dionne as well. Two more children's faces were on the board now too, and Jazz waited to see what that was about. Paula, Ash, Boomer and Jazz were there to report and decide how to move forward. It was a sombre group, and Paula started.

"I have just come back from the Richmond Centre. The tests on Nekisha have started and we don't have all the information yet. What I can tell you is she has been groomed for the past two months and she has not been raped or buggered. We got there just in time to save her that. There has been sexual touching and possibly some sort of invasive touching, but we can rule out rape or buggery. By the sounds of it there could have been more than one man involved in her grooming. More information will be available by the end of the day. She is a child, and her use of language is limited in these circumstances."

Paula looked up after giving the information in a matter-of-fact and professional manner, and was surprised to see horror on their faces. Her team were used to such obscenities; although never at ease, they accepted verdicts and got on with the job in hand to arrest paedophiles. It had been a long time since she had seen such horror in a meeting with police officers.

Jazz asked, "How is Dionne, the mother? Has she been able to add any other information?"

Paula told him that Dionne was beside herself and not able at the moment to contribute anything further to their information on Simmonds. Dionne was not coping well with what had happened to Nekisha, but Paula said that later today she would interview Dionne again.

Ash got his notes out. "The Hockley address for Simmonds has been investigated and no one lives there. It looks a nice house but the curtains are closed. Officers who went to the house were under strict instructions not to try and gain entry. I presume at the moment we are operating a covert operation?"

Jazz thought that sounded pretty good, and smiled to himself. Ash was getting into this.

Ash continued. "The address on the satnav in Paglesham was quietly checked out last night by local police who drove by. The address is part of the stables on Bateman's property that have been turned into three separate bungalow dwellings. The police were aware of Simmonds in the area. He has a small yacht he moors in Paglesham."

Jazz interrupted with a woeful cry of, "Not that bloody boatyard again near the poxy Plough & Sail pub?!"

Boomer just laughed. It had been a painful experience for them both to be duped the year before by that sly bastard Gary Nunn; slippery as a handful of eels in a bucket of snot. Needing to find a barge for a case they were working on, they hired Gary Nunn, a local boatman. He made them pay a few hundred pounds and took them on an hour's boat journey that they could have walked in five minutes. The thought of it still rankled. Jazz hadn't given up on the idea of putting him in his poxy boat and setting fire to it and giving him a fucking Viking funeral.

Ash asked for hush so he could get on with giving his information. "So," he shouted, hoping it would quieten Jazz and Boomer, "locals say that Simmonds lives in one of the converted stables and works as a sort of personal assistant-cum-gardener-cum-chauffeur to Mr Bateman, and has done for quite a few years."

Ash added that the information came from the local community police, who knew most of the people in the village so no one local was asked these questions. He confirmed that he'd asked the police to keep it all quiet so Bateman and Simmonds didn't get to hear about the enquiries.

He added, with a sense of triumph, "The

community police did say that Simmonds is highly respected in the village and surrounding areas. He is a very pious man and enjoys helping the local church, and he often goes on sabbaticals and could be quite reclusive. It was said that he regularly spends days in religious contemplation, and is often joined by monks from a monastery in Norfolk."

"Bloody hell, Ash, that's a bloody good bit of information. Well done, my son," came a sincere congratulation first from Jazz, then followed by a cry that was almost a cheer from the others. They were cooking with gas. "Monks from a monastery, my arse!" added Jazz as he looked at Boomer.

Ash hadn't finished; there was more. "Checking through AWARE and RTAs," (road traffic accidents) "etc., Simmonds and Bateman haven't got anything on them, not even a parking ticket or a speeding ticket. Apart from his earlier criminal record, Bateman has been whiter than white. Oh, and by the way, he has no DNA on record anywhere. His offence was way before DNA was taken automatically so we have no way of linking him to the cases shown on the board."

They all looked up at the board and saw a smiley school photo of Kevin Parsons.

Before they asked, Ash said the other two pictures of equally innocent and happy, smiling children were of Paul Jones, eight years old from Norfolk, and Belinda Moore, nine years old from Suffolk. The two children had been missing for over a year. Each disappeared within six months of the other. There were no leads, and the children came from good loving families.

Jazz asked why they were on the board. Ash said triumphantly, "Because each child came from a single-mother family, and at the time of the disappearance the mothers had a boyfriend who was very attentive to the children. The description of the boyfriend is similar in each case: same height, colouring, and actually not dissimilar to our Simmonds." With an added flourish he added, "It has a *modus operandi* to it."

Again, there were cheers for Ash. *My God, he has done well*, thought Jazz. It wasn't appropriate, but he thought, *I am the dog's bollocks for finding Ash.* For a moment he felt quite self-satisfied, until he thought of the children involved and the filth that was out there. Steely now, he told those present that they were going to put away the scum who had done this.

"For starters, Ash, get the picture of Simmonds sent to Norfolk and Suffolk constabularies and get the two mothers to see if they recognise Simmonds as their boyfriend."

Boomer cleared his throat, and almost apologetically, said, "After Paula and Ash's sterling work, I am afraid I don't have much to say yet. Essex Police want to know why we are snooping on their ground, so Jazz and I need to organise that. We need their cooperation and it's only good manners to talk to them. Jazz and I will discuss the next step forward when we have looked through the information Ash has collected. It will involve finding out what Bateman and Simmonds really do in that house."

Now it was Jazz's turn to address them all. He ensured the door to the office was closed, much to the consternation of those present.

"I was hauled into DCI Radley's office this morning. My computer had been compromised and was found to have illegal and pornographic pictures of children and women on there. The press tipped off DCI Radley. Someone had my password to access my computer system and they used my computer. It was accessed yesterday between 4pm and 5pm. It is noted that all of us here were not in the vicinity of the CID room and my computer. We have someone who is able to access our building and computer without being challenged.

"We are on a case that is shaping up to be a potentially huge paedophile ring, and then this happens. I think it's too much of a coincidence. We are getting close and we are all in danger of being compromised, or worse. This is another reason why I think it could be a big case. We have rattled someone and they have the balls and ability to walk into the lion's den and cause mayhem. Everyone," Jazz looked around at the faces before him, "everyone be accountable for your time and your work. Keep it logged and report in regularly. I don't want any of you to be compromised."

They all shifted in their seats, uncomfortable with what they had heard and with so many questions to ask.

Boomer broke the silence. "Does that mean I've got to work like that, for God's sake?!"

Jazz laughed, and told him of course, just like he himself always did. With that Boomer spluttered in his seat and Ash looked on in surprise. Before anyone could say anything else, Jazz, sombre now, reminded them that he didn't want to lose another officer on his shift.

There was a heavy five-second silence, which Jazz shattered by telling everyone to, "Bugger off and do what you've gotta do. Back here tomorrow for a debrief, 11am again."

Just as they were all about to leave, Jazz called Ash back. "On second thoughts, Ash, would you personally take the picture to the mothers and see what they say? I trust you more than the county police to do this properly."

Ash nodded and left. Jazz followed Boomer, and in an urgent whisper asked for a place where they could talk about what they would do next.

CHAPTER 15

Undercover

The first thing they had to do, Jazz and Boomer decided after getting a coffee from the canteen and a 999 all-day breakfast, was to visit Paglesham and the local police. They needed to know what they were dealing with.

"I don't want to bump into that bastard," was all Jazz said on the subject of Gary Nunn. They couldn't go to the Plough & Sail; they didn't want to be seen. It was a small village and if anyone farted it was on the news, or so Boomer reckoned. The local police were important; Jazz and Boomer needed to get their permission for treading all over their patch. It was a courtesy more than anything else but this was going to be a delicate operation and an upset and belligerent local police force would not be helpful. They borrowed the police BMW, much to the annoyance of the drug squad who wanted to use it later.

It took them just under an hour with the blue light flashing to get to Rochford town centre. The police station was a quaint old building with a *Dixon of Dock Green* blue light outside. It was a classic old police station and Boomer felt moved to take a photo of it on his iPhone.

"It's not gonna be here much longer with all the cutbacks, and its like will never be seen again. I will say just two words: Fresh Wharf!" was Boomer's response to Jazz's call for 'David Bailey' to hurry up. Fresh Wharf was the new grey industrial police patrol centre they worked in now, and Jazz just nodded, understanding exactly what he meant.

The police station was minimally staffed with someone on the front desk and the two community police officers sitting out the back waiting for Jazz and Boomer as instructed. Apparently they had a civilian who did some sort of paperwork part-time but other than that the cells and interview rooms were all at Southend Police Station. Their welcome was by no means rousing. The look of distrust and annoyance from the two community officers at having to wait for them did not make the meeting a happy one.

Jazz didn't have time for bullshit so he pulled rank and told them to be kind enough to get everyone a cup of tea and a biscuit. They said all refreshments came from the café across the road, so Jazz offered a £10 note and said he would wait. In the meantime, he asked if they had any files on Simmonds or Bateman. The answer was a swift no. Mr Bateman was a pillar of the community and Simmonds worked for him, and they were honest citizens. That was a disappointment but Jazz badgered them for something on these men.

In the end, they found some information on Bateman in the local parish council news and Rochford Gazette. They rummaged for the copies, gave them to Jazz and Boomer and then the two of them left to get the tea. Jazz shouted after them not to forget the guy on the front desk. They nodded as they left the station.

It made boring reading. It looked like Bateman chucked his money at any charity in the Rochford area. They would not get any help from local organisations, that was for sure. Bateman was, indeed, a saint to them.

The tea was drunk and a chat with the two police officers confirmed the man's sainthood. Both officers lived locally in Rochford and were well aware of Bateman and Simmonds. They told them of all the good works Bateman paid for in the area. He had declined any requests to sit on committees or join the parish council. Everyone thought him a modest recluse who helped any ailing charities in the borough, but his main project over the years had been with the church in Canewdon. They thought he had spent on average over half a million pounds on restoration work and charities each year. By the time they told the story of the little old lady who was facing hard times in Ashingdon, and how he had paid for her home to be decorated and stuff, Jazz and Boomer were seriously pissed off. This was not what they wanted to hear.

The officers were off duty in two hours so it was decided that they would all drive past where Bateman lived to orientate themselves. Jazz and Boomer joined the officers in their local police car; they didn't want to attract attention to themselves. It was imperative, the officers were told, not to mention their visit. They asked what it was all about and Jazz told them they were not able to discuss anything at the moment. The two officers were not happy with such a covert operation on someone they admired, but it was their job and they understood. Jazz knew this was going to be a Metropolitan Police operation and the details would be kept to themselves. DCI Radley would talk to the DCI in Southend to ensure they were informed and protocols and courtesy were observed.

It took about fifteen minutes to get to the mansion on the lone road to Paglesham, which ended after four miles with the boatyard and the river. It was an isolated place, with farmland for as far as you could see. The mansion was on a remote part of the long road, way before the boatyard, which was surrounded by pretty country cottages sprinkled with landed gentry-type properties and finished off by a typical flower-bedecked country pub: the Plough & Sail.

Under instruction, the little Panda car drove past slowly, and Jazz and Boomer took a good look. It was a huge mansion and they could see the stables in the large gravel courtyard, which had been converted into cottages. There was nothing else around the whole area, just farmland. The mansion was white and cream with big white pillars that guarded the entrance. By the size of it and the number of windows, Jazz reckoned it must have had at least seven bedrooms, and big ones at that. The cottages were built in what looked like that pretty grey stone you see in the country. All was quiet and they couldn't see anyone around. They drove a few miles further up the road and turned round and came back for another look. The gardens were long with thick but perfectly groomed hedges bordering the road; they seemed to go on for a mile. You couldn't see anything inside to get a feel of the gardens. The nearest house was a mile or so further down the road. A perfect place to come and go, and no one would know.

Back at Rochford Police Station Jazz thanked the two officers for their help and they left on the note that nothing must be said of their visit here or their interest in Bateman. Jazz and Boomer said nothing to each other until they got in their car and started their journey back to the real world.

"Bloody strange place is Paglesham," was the comment that broke the silence.

Boomer looked at Jazz and suggested he just wasn't used to the countryside. "It sure ain't Barking, that's for sure," was the reply from Boomer.

"Perfect place to take children and not be seen. We need to sit down and work out what we want Mad Pete to do," Jazz said.

Boomer agreed. They both felt uneasy. The mansion and surrounding lands had an oppressive feeling to them. The mansion seemed to exude a sense of evil that had now grabbed them. They tried to shake off the feeling, not able at this moment to share it with each other. It was stupid; it was a bloody house and nothing else. They couldn't allow their feelings to interfere with down-to-earth police work.

Back at Fresh Wharf the day shift had gone off duty. Boomer checked his office and all his CID officers had left for the day.

"Bloody people, turn my back and they sod off early."

Jazz suggested it might be good because they could sit down in peace and quiet and work out what he was going to ask Mad Pete to do. He intended to go and find him this evening. Time was of the essence. Simmonds would be contacting Dionne later in the week and Jazz didn't want him rattled.

Through gritted teeth Jazz said, "We are going to get those murderous bastards, so let's get down to it."

Later, Jazz called Mad Pete and said he wanted to talk to him. Mad Pete started moaning about being busy, needing to see someone about a dog. But Jazz told him to shut up and said he would be round in twenty minutes. He added he would bring him a Big Mac and fries.

Mad Pete asked, pushing his luck, "Does that include a McFlurry?"

Cheeky bugger, Jazz thought, but wanting to keep him sweet, said, "Of course."

This made Mad Pete worried. A nice Mr Singh was a scary thing – he wanted something and that was going to be painful; it always was.

In a panic, Mad Pete saw the signs and needed to get out of his place pronto. He didn't want to do anything. He liked his life as it was and Mr Singh messed things up for him. It was a good idea for him to disappear for a bit, but there was stuff to gather up and he needed to be quick about it. There were some tasty mobiles on offer and he had some buyers who would give him a good price for them. He didn't want to miss out on that deal. He grabbed his phone, some money to pay cash for the stolen mobiles he was getting and some smack for later. He shook his head in disgust at his panic – of course, he needed to take all of his stash of smack; he could sell some easily, he was never going to miss a chance.

Everything he needed had been thrown into bags, and with a last look around in case he had forgotten anything, Mad Pete was ready to leave. He figured he had about ten minutes to get out of the building before Mr Singh arrived.

As Mad Pete opened the door to rush out, he bumped straight into a figure, stopping his getaway. There stood Jazz, smiling, with hands full of two McDonald's bags.

"I come bearing gifts, Pete. Where the fuck are you going?"

Mad Pete shrunk back into his room. "Mr Singh, you said you would be twenty minutes," he stammered.

"I know you, toerag, I thought you would try and scuttle away. Now why would you want to do that when I have brought you a McFlurry as well?" said the malevolently smooth Jazz.

"I, er, I had to see a man about some merchandise. I would have come back," offered a scared Mad Pete.

"'Course you would have. I believe you. Now sit down and eat this stuff, the Macs will get cold and the McFlurry will get warm." Jazz wasn't going to upset Mad Pete; he needed him on his side.

The meal was finished and cigarettes were lit, and coffees, which had mysteriously stayed hot, were sipped. Both were deep in thought, brooding on what was to come.

"Pete, you did a good job giving me that DVD and the satnav. I have been working hard on the case and it looks like it could be quite interesting. Think we know who is involved." Jazz didn't want to say at this stage that it was potentially a fucking big monster of a case.

Mad Pete was interested. He didn't like what he had seen on the DVD.

"Our big problem is, the person we want to look at has the locals setting him up for sainthood. He has no police record of interfering with children since before the Dark Ages. We have no reason to go near him and we don't want to alert him. He is as rich as fucking royalty and as untouchable as bloody Barry Bentall the Bird Man of Barking to his fucking friends." Jazz looked at Mad Pete and saw he still had his interest.

"What we need is someone who would never under any circumstances be confused with the police. Someone clever, cunning, and who has the ability to melt into the background. We need a little fucking ferret to get some information out."

Scared now, Mad Pete saw what was happening and protested. "Not me, Mr Singh." Incredulous at being even considered for such a thing, he added, "How could you even think of it, Mr Singh? I ain't got any training, and if he did kill that poor kid, he's bloody dangerous to be around." Now Mad Pete was seriously worried, and beginning to get very agitated "I ain't doing it. You can't make me. It's got to be against the law." He calmed down for a second, then asked, "What did you want me to do anyway?"

At Jazz's suggestion of having a smoke to calm himself, Mad Pete rolled a spliff and after a couple of drags, a quiet calmness allowed Jazz to think it through a bit more. He could see Mad Pete's eyes darting and his hunched shoulders were almost touching his knees. He nervously puffed on the spliff. Jazz was asking a lot, and he wondered if he should reconsider putting Pete in that sort of potential danger.

"OK, I hear what you are saying, Pete," was the placatory answer from Jazz. "I want to tell you what I think you could do and what I hope you can do. It is, at the end of the day, down to you. I won't force you to do anything you don't want to do." Not totally true, but Jazz thought it sounded good. With Mad Pete still hunched and looking to the side of him at Jazz, he continued to smoke the spliff and waited.

"OK." Jazz took a deep breath; this wasn't going to be easy. "If we sent a police officer in undercover I suspect he would be sniffed out pretty quickly. You, on the other hand, are a fucking filthy toerag that no one would think was a police officer – more likely in trouble with the police, so not a threat."

Mad Pete was hurt, remonstrated. "That's not nice, Mr Singh."

"Look, Pete, this is your undercover alias, it's just that you fit it rather well," said Jazz, uncharacteristically diplomatic. He needed Mad Pete to buy into this. Mad Pete accepted this, pulled a face and nodded.

"What I want you to do is what you are an expert at. Just nose around and try and find out any information you can. There are people who visit the guy's mansion regularly and a list of their names would be good. The police think they are monks from a monastery in Norfolk, but I think they are paedophiles who get together regularly. You are fucking brilliant at getting information and finding things. Look what you did with the Bird Man of Barking, and how you knew what the Holy Trinity were up to. You knew more than anyone and no one ever suspected you were doing it. Mad Pete! You are the 007 of the East End, the Nemo of Barking." Jazz, worn out by thinking up such praise, sat back and looked at Mad Pete.

He wasn't stupid, he knew when he was being bullshitted, but it sounded good. 'Nemo of Barking' had a ring he kinda liked.

"I don't want you to do anything that puts you in danger. Just do what you normally do, and ferret around as you do things, that's all. I was going to suggest you go as a car cleaner-cum-gardener. It would give you access to the house and garden. I know cleaning may not be your strong point but I figure you will only be there for a short while. Your story could be that you were in the area visiting a girlfriend in Ashingdon and she threw you out. Say you have no money and are looking for work, and you heard Mr Bateman is looking for staff and is known to help people who've fallen on bad times in the community. Reinforce that you will work for your money and don't mind what you do."

"Why should I do it, Mr Singh? I don't wanna work for some toff. I don't do that," moaned Mad Pete.

"Well, I need your help, Pete," was the honest answer. Jazz added, "I so want to get the murderous bastards that killed Kevin Parsons and buggered him. They have already started on a little girl, Pete, she has been groomed and we reckon she was to be the next victim. There may be more and we have gotta stop him."

Mad Pete was quite emotional at the thought of that little boy on the film. He took a deep breath and said, "I will do it, Mr Singh. What's in it for me first, though?"

"You would be on my payroll, Pete, so I will give you £200 and you stay there for a couple of days. Is it a done deal?"

"OK, Mr Singh, I will give it a go. I have thought of something. I think that poor kid had been given something to keep him calm, maybe scopolamine (Scopolamine leaves victim in a state of compliancy, where their mind is totally controlled so they can be raped and remember nothing at all), maybe some brown (Brown is a street form of heroin used, sometimes by clubbers, as a chill-out drug. A small dose gives the user a feeling of warmth and well-being. Bigger doses can make you sleepy and very relaxed) or even GHB (GHB (gamma-hydroxybutyrate) gives the user feelings of euphoria, reduced inhibitions and drowsiness). I could let it slip I can get stuff. Might be useful to them, and I could earn myself some money as well."

Jazz thought, *Bloody hell, what is this man into?*, but he had to agree it might be useful. Jazz confirmed the name of the millionaire paedophile as Mr Bateman, and that Mr Simmonds was his right-hand man. They talked for a while and agreed that tomorrow morning Mad Pete would be dropped along the Paglesham Road to walk up to the house. He would be given a microphone to wear and Boomer and Jazz would monitor him. Jazz reckoned he should get there way before 9.30am, when Bateman might still be around. Mad Pete could appeal to him for a job. An earpiece would also be given to him so any instructions to get out quick could be passed to Mad Pete immediately.

Jazz had had the conversation all his own way so far, and Mad Pete would have none of it. It was his life, for fuck's sake, he told Jazz. Now he set down his rules and became quite assertive, compared to the miserable, whining bastard he usually was.

"I ain't wearing no microphone, I ain't wearing

no ear thingy. If they catch me with it I am dead. I have worked for a few fucked-off, shoot-you-soon-as-look-at-you men over the years, and I know how to stay in the shadows. Your fucking *Hawaii Five-O* surveillance is likely to get me killed, Mr Singh."

Mad Pete was scared but determined to give it a go. Kevin Parsons, the poor lad on the DVD, had got to him as well. Besides, he could see a bit of business here too. *There's money to be made with these paedos and that ain't no bad thing*, he told himself.

Jazz was a bit taken aback by Mad Pete, and a little worried. He was a fucking arsehole most of the time but he was *his* fucking arsehole, and it would be a bloody nuisance if he got wasted – well, that's what he told himself.

"OK, Pete, but you keep in contact. Ring when you can and when it's safe. I will text if it's an emergency and you need to get the fuck out. *Capisce*?"

"*Capisce*? Why are you going all French on me, Mr Singh?" was the only response Jazz was going to get from Mad Pete.

As Jazz left, saying he would be round at 7.30am to pick him up to go to Paglesham, he told Mad Pete, "Before you start moaning, just shut the fuck up! Normal people get up at that time. We will pick up a McD's en route so you will be fed and watered. And by the way, numb-nuts, *capisce* isn't French, you stupid bastard, it's Greek, like Latin, an old word. You stick with me, kid, I will educate you." With a laugh, Jazz left and got on his mobile as he walked to the car.

Boomer was waiting and met Jazz in the Cranbrook pub. They went over the plan for tomorrow. Boomer was disappointed Mad Pete wouldn't wear a wire or earpiece, but reckoned Mad Pete might be right and they wanted to keep him as safe as they could. There would be hell to pay if DCI Radley found out what they were doing and using a civilian too, although Jazz reckoned Mad Pete had never been civilised, so wasn't a civilian.

They had a few drinks and both were hungry and ordered some bar food. Jazz went for southern fried chicken and chips in a basket. Boomer was going to ask for soup in a basket for a laugh, but changed his mind when the gorgeous barmaid asked him what he wanted. With a smile he told her about a few fantasies he would enjoy and was very lucky not to have his face slapped and be thrown out of the pub. They both giggled as she walked away.

It was nearly closing time when Jazz and Boomer made their way home, with a reminder to meet early the next morning. Jazz was a tad tipsy from ordering quadruple vodkas and putting in a little lemonade. In response to Boomer's look of amazement, he said that each measure was pissing puny and a quadruple was equivalent to any poured in normal households. Boomer shrugged his shoulders and caught a knowing look from the barman that said this was normal for Jazz. They would meet at Ilford Police Station at 6.45am and use one of the undercover police cars.

Boomer was waiting as Jazz arrived. Again, he

could see it had been a heavy night for DS Jaswinder Singh. Although shaved and showered and dressed in a smart, tailored, dark blue suit, the trappings didn't hide the deep, dark shadows under his eyes and a haunting look of painful fatigue.

"Bloody hell, Jazz, you look like shit."

"Ta very, sir. Can we get the fuck outta here? Time is going and we need to get back for that meeting," was Jazz's response. The sharp morning wind made him shiver, and feeling cold and not at his best, he needed a coffee.

They were at the police garage early, which gave them an enviable choice of vehicles. They took a pretty nippy BMW 5 that was usually the first to be booked every morning. It would be the second time they pissed off the drug squad, who thought all the elite undercover cars were their exclusive property. It was nearly 7am and they needed to get to Mad Pete's and get him up. Jazz was under no illusion that he would be sitting there in his best clothes with a small suitcase packed. He laughed at the thought.

They knocked for what felt like half an hour, but in reality was about fifteen minutes. Mad Pete must have been psychic; he opened the door as Boomer was just about to kick it in, or perhaps he heard him shout, "If you don't answer this fucking door in seconds I am gonna fucking break it down and make soddin' earrings out of your bollocks, you slimy prick!"

Two neighbours' doors were cautiously opened a fraction, but when they saw Boomer wasn't talking to them, they closed their doors quickly and scurried back to bed. Mad Pete was not happy; he moaned that it wasn't fair to get him up so early. They watched him get his coat and wallet and phone and a bit of smack to last him a few days. He shuffled behind Jazz and Boomer to the door, pushing his long, greasy hair out of his face.

They picked up McDonald's breakfasts and coffees for three. It was just coming up to 8am, McDonald's was open on the A13 and they were the first customers. They ate their food en route with Boomer driving one-handed along most of the A13 with either a coffee or a McBreakfast in his hand. He put the blue light on just for effect; it moved the traffic out of the way and got them to the Sadlers Farm turn-off in record time.

As they got on to the Paglesham Road they turned into a lay-by to have a last-minute chat. Mad Pete seemed fine. He said that he was used to making himself useful to people who were under the radar. He didn't see a problem. Jazz said they would wait until 9.30am in case he had the door closed in his face.

Mad Pete said, "They won't close the door in my face. I know their type, they will want me."

It was now 8.50am and they had got there in really good time. They drove a bit closer and Mad Pete just had to walk around the next bend and there was the house. Without looking back, he took off. Boomer took the car back to the lay-by and they waited. A few cigarettes later and with no phone call, they checked the time and it was just past 9.30am.

"Well, it seems he played a blinder," said an amazed Jazz.

Boomer reckoned, "His fucking T-shirt got stuck to the door and they couldn't get rid of him; a bit like shit on your shoes."

Jazz laughed and added, "One thing's for sure: if he hadn't got in, he would have rung for a lift. With all this fucking grass around, Mad Pete would be confused, he wouldn't know where the fuck he was in a place full of green stuff that he couldn't smoke."

Humour over, Boomer gunned the car and set off at speed to Ilford. They were heading back to even more trouble, but no one had phoned them to give them a warning of what was going to happen.

CHAPTER 16

What the Hell is Going On?

They got back to Ilford Police Station in good time. They had half an hour before the meeting with Ash and Paula. They got out of the police garage and gave back the keys in record time. The drug squad would lynch them, and they giggled as they walked quickly into the body of the police station, where everyone was milling around and working with a sense of urgency that looked pretty impressive to the untrained eye.

Jazz made his way up the stairs to the CID office and his desk to see if Ash was around. He found Ash in a state of mute panic, and the computer guy was back.

"It's all gone, it's not possible, but it's all gone," was all Jazz could get out of Ash.

"What's going on, Stewart?" Jazz remembered the IT guy from yesterday. Ash wasn't making any sense and he hoped this guy would tell him.

"DC Kumar's computer has been compromised and he has lost a file. It was the Bateman and Simmonds file. I am just looking to see if I can retrieve it. It's not possible to lose everything, all files are automatically saved to servers in London, but it is not there. Someone has gone in and destroyed the file. It was done on your computer again, DS Singh, not a remote computer. Your password was used to gain access. They have to have a signature on the system and I am trying to find the file and retrieve it."

"Jazz, it has everything I know about the paedophile case on there. It's all gone and the hard copy can't be found." Ash was distraught.

Again, Jazz's computer and password had been compromised. It didn't make sense. There was no CCTV in any of the offices, so no way of finding out who could have done this.

Jazz went to DCI Radley's office to inform him. He would tell him that it looked like they were being made fools of, and at the top of the list of suspects were Bateman and Simmonds. How were they able to do this? If it was them (and who else could it possibly be?). It seemed to stack up; porno on his computer and only the Bateman and Simmonds file missing. If that was the case then they would know they had been rumbled and know everything that was happening and that was a worry.

No one but Boomer and Jazz knew about Mad Pete, though, and Jazz would ensure it stayed that way. Mad Pete was a worry gnawing away at him. He was a prick, he conceded, but Mad Pete was *his* prick. He pulled a face at such a thought. Moving on now, he had other things to worry about, and facing DCI Radley was his next one.

DCI Radley was not a happy man. He had the chief superintendent on his back. A lockdown was being instigated and Jazz was told confidentially that the person or persons involved would be caught. Radley would say no more, but he told Jazz to continue as normal.

Just as he was about to leave, thinking he had got off quite easily, DCI Radley told him that he wondered why it was always Jazz, never anyone else, that caused the biggest problems at Ilford Police Station. He asked what it was about him that attracted bloody problems.

Jazz answered cheekily, "I suppose I am just lucky." With speed he left DCI Radley, avoiding the steely look that said 'suspension from the job'.

It was past 11am, and telling himself to bloody keep his mouth shut and show a bit of respect in future when talking to DCI Radley, Jazz made his way to the meeting room.

At least their case board with its pictures of the victims had not been touched. The room was locked after they finished, so no one had been able to access it.

With DI Paula Rudd and DI Tom Black waiting, Jazz and Ash came in, a little flustered and fidgety.

"What's up?" was Boomer's question.

Jazz and Ash sat down, and with a deep breath Jazz told them of the latest compromise. "We have lost all the information – the file has been erased on the computer system; something that was supposed to be impossible to do. I don't know who is doing this – DCI Radley has put his best men on it, but the only people who could possibly be interested in deleting their file has to be Bateman and Simmonds. How the fuck are they getting into the station? Or are we missing something here?" The frustration in the room was palatable.

Ash was anxious to give everyone his information. He had been to interview the mothers of Paul Jones, the eight-year-old from Norfolk, and Belinda Moore, the nine-year-old from Suffolk. It had taken him until late last night to see both mothers.

Ms Jones, or Amy, as she told Ash to call her, had looked at the pictures and recognised Simmonds. Apparently she had been at the shops and he had bumped into her and sent all her shopping flying. He had helped her pick it up and take it to the car. From then on he became a fixture on an almost daily basis, but he never stayed the night. She said he was quite old-fashioned and didn't think it correct with a small child in the house. She did say that she was beginning to get fed up with him; not romantic enough. But he bought her lots of nice things for the home and helped with Paul, who had become quite belligerent and stand-offish with her. She said that Arthur – and that was the name he used, Arthur Bells – said Paul needed more male company, and took him off for weekends to his farm in Suffolk. Apparently he disappeared just before Paul did, and she just thought that it was her fault. She was so distraught and upset when Paul disappeared she forgot about 'Arthur' for quite a while, and then just thought it was over. On being asked, she said she had never heard from him again.

It was a similar story with Ms Moore, who liked to be called Ms Moore. This time it was a woman and a man who befriended her. She recognised Simmonds as the man. They told her they were a married couple called Jimmy and Sheila Baker. They became good friends and brought presents for Belinda and nice things for Ms Moore. She said they couldn't have children of their own and just loved Belinda. They disappeared before Belinda disappeared, so she never thought of them again. They said they were going abroad.

"So," said Jazz, "there is a woman involved in this as well. Did Mrs Moore give a description of her?"

Ash said he asked her and all she could remember was a blonde woman about forty-five years old or so, a bit rough but very nice. Not slim but not fat either, about the same height as Ms Moore, and she was five feet five inches tall. Ash looked at the database. The description was so general that he found lots of women who answered to that description. He reckoned he needed a bit more information.

"Well done, Ash, you have done a fantastic job. Was that information on the computer?" asked Jazz.

"'Fraid so," was Ash's reply.

Paula wanted to update everyone. She told them that Nekisha talked of a woman looking after her, and she was blonde. A selection of pictures would be shown to Nekisha and to Ms Jones and Ms Moore to see if they tallied up.

"Further, Nekisha has talked about a big house and little houses close by. It would seem that Simmonds hardly saw her when she was in the big house – it was more the lady and another man. Pictures of Bateman were shown to her and she recognised him. She spent time with him, and he cuddled her and took photos of her and gradually he got more intimate. He penetrated her digitally on the last visit we have since found out."

A shocked Jazz said that he had seen Nekisha when she was returned after that visit, and she'd seemed fine. "How could that be?" he asked.

Paula smiled, a cold and resigned smile. "He had been grooming her for quite a while. She wasn't fine. She learned to accept and it became normal – that's what grooming is all about," she added. "He told her that it was normal and that her mummy would be in big trouble if she didn't behave, stuff like that."

"The bastard!" was all Jazz could think to say.

"Dionne is a problem, though," Paula added. "She is totally hysterical and we are having to organise counselling for her. She will not be well enough to return home with Nekisha for a while. Luckily, they are in a good place and there are family apartments so they get to have a home together while they are being counselled. Nekisha is seeing a counsellor already. Hopefully, this will help." It was depressing to hear, but Paula added, "Luckily we got to Nekisha before she was raped. That would have done some internal damage and I am not sure if she would have returned home after that. Based on the video of Kevin Parsons, it looks like she could have been gang-raped and then filmed as a snuff video. It is all a strong possibility, so good work and well done, we have saved her from that."

All nodded; that was good to know.

Neither Jazz nor Boomer talked about Mad Pete being at Simmonds' home. They both decided that this piece of information would remain secret until the infiltrator was found. For now Ash would get those photos and show them to Ms Jones and Ms Moore, and to Nekisha.

Time was ticking on and this needed sorting by the weekend, or an excuse would be needed as to why Dionne was somewhere else. Simmonds might still contact her but if, as it was starting to seem, they knew about the investigation, Dionne would probably not be contacted.

It was decided they would all meet again tomorrow but at the end of the day, and 4pm was suggested. It gave Ash a chance to check if any of the women whose pictures the police had on file were familiar to the mothers and Nekisha. Jazz also hoped that by tomorrow they might have a lead from Mad Pete. The investigation was all bits of information but there was not enough to get Simmonds. It all felt like a mess, and it was about to get messier.

As Jazz left Boomer's office after a brief discussion on Mad Pete, he was pulled to one side by a sergeant sent by DCI Radley.

"You've got a case to look at by tomorrow, Jazz, the details are on your desk. Mr Radley wants this dealt with ASAP."

In response to grumbles of "I know I am Superman but fuck me, I am on a big case", the sergeant just shrugged and said he was following orders.

Jazz went to his desk and looked at the file. Whilst going through it, he got a phone call from Mad Pete.

"Mr Singh, I am out in the road, having a walk to the pub to take a look around. I spoke to Mr Simmonds and he has taken me on. They've got a room above the garage I can stay in. It's well good, Mr Singh." Mad Pete sounded confident, which Jazz didn't expect.

"So you are in, are you?" asked an incredulous Jazz. He had to admit that Mad Pete was good at what he did, and he didn't sound frightened.

"It's all good here. I am doing a bit of gardening but they need my talents in getting them drugs. I will be very useful to them," said a very self-satisfied Mad Pete. Jazz got a strong impression that Mad Pete was doing what he normally did and had made himself indispensible to the scumbags. He needed to keep him focused and working for him.

"I hope you know you are working for me, Pete. I don't want you going off and just helping them. Remember, they are fucking scumbags. Just remember that video. I need any information you can find.

You are a fucking Hoover for scummy information. Hoover away and do it soon, or there will be trouble."

"I have to be careful, Mr Singh. I will get you some information as soon as I can. I am working hard for you here, you know," Pete added in a hurt voice.

"OK, I'm sorry, Pete, you are doing a fucking fabulous job and well done for getting in there. Let me know as soon as you get anything. By the way, is anyone looking startled or skittish about anything?"

Mad Pete, suspicious now, said "No, why Mr Singh? No one knows who I am do they?" Jazz confirmed he was as safe as houses; no one would believe a lowlife like him would be anything other than what he was: a fucking scumbag. Mad Pete, relieved, thanked Jazz for saying that.

Mad Pete was not being totally honest. He had got himself well ingratiated with a few men working at Bateman's home. He knew they were as bent as a nine-bob note. He was going to make a lot of money here, and that suited him well. A few trips to the East End to get stuff for them would be very profitable. He felt that he was on home territory. Mr Singh could wait a while for whatever he thought he could find. He liked it here; it was like being on holiday.

It was agreed Mad Pete would see Jazz soon when he came to the East End to get drug supplies for Simmonds and Bateman. He promised to keep in contact if he had anything of interest to tell him before then. Jazz should have listened to his instincts about Mad Pete. He felt uneasy about something he couldn't quite put his finger on.

CHAPTER 17

You Know it Makes Sense

Jazz made his way to the building society in the High Street. The file he was given said there had been five bag-snatches in Barking within the last week, and all were elderly women who had just come out of the building society. It was obvious to Jazz what had happened but he went along to just check it out.

It was now 2pm and the building society was fairly busy for this time of day, with four women queuing for the cashier, a man at the cash dispenser and two people, a man and a woman, sitting on the chairs near the entrance. There was only one cashier counter open; they obviously didn't expect many people at this time of day.

The reception desk was unmanned for the moment, but then in a flurry of skirt and high heels, Marlene appeared and introduced herself to Jazz, and asked with a smile if she could help him. Jazz smiled and asked to speak to the manager. He didn't want to announce himself to all present as a police officer, so he added that his department had made the appointment. He gave his card, which had his name and rank on it, to Marlene. To her credit, Marlene just looked and walked to the manager's office to inform him Mr Singh was here to see him.

While he waited, Jazz looked around at this bright and sunny space. It was modern, with the obligatory queuing rail and the bank of cashier windows. If he'd had time, he might have read the many offers that were posted on what looked like every available wall space. There were percentages off this, and percentage profits on that. He noted that all doors to access staff or staff-only rooms were securely closed and it would take sticks of dynamite to gain illicit entry to anything beyond the waiting area.

Now the waiting area was a different kettle of fish. Jazz sat and picked up a building society magazine to look like he was reading it. A man had come in and was waiting in the queue. He was on his mobile. The man and woman sitting down seemed to be waiting for something but Jazz didn't know what. He watched as one of the women at the cashier window was putting quite a bit of money into her bag. She was sensible; she made sure it was in her bag and zipped up before she left. The man with the mobile seemed to change his mind, and after a few minutes he left the building society too. Trying to look nonchalant, Jazz put the magazine down and left, following the man with the mobile phone. Whilst following he got on his mobile and rang IBO and said that an old lady was walking down the High Street with one of those wheelie shopper bag things, and would local PCs please go there immediately and keep an eye out for her? He said he suspected a bag-snatch was going to happen.

The man in the leather jacket was walking determinedly towards the Gascoigne Estate and was not aware of Jazz following him. He turned off the main road and headed towards a block of garages. They were industrial garages with a side door into them. The man slipped in without looking around. Listening at the door, Jazz heard what sounded like Romanian being spoken. He didn't understand a word but had heard the accent and language many times in the custody suite.

He called IBO and asked if the police had gone to the town centre and found the old lady. The answer was yes, and she was in the process of being robbed. Apparently she was a feisty old lady and held on to her bag, but in the end they pushed her over and got the bag. The police had got there in time to run after the two men who had robbed her. They were young officers and it didn't take much for them to catch and apprehend them. The thieves were being taken to Fresh Wharf as they spoke. The old lady, Mrs Partridge, was being taken to Queen's Hospital for a check-up but she didn't seem too bad.

Jazz asked IBO to ensure the two men's mobiles were seized. He knew they would be, but he wanted to check if they had been rung within the last ten minutes, and the number that had rung them. He needed to get the leather-coated man's mobile and then – ta-dah! If they linked up, he'd have them bang to rights.

He asked for backup and for a police van and a few useful officers to assist him in arresting the man he had seen in the building society. He absolutely knew it was him who tipped off the two thugs out in Barking High Street who robbed Mrs Partridge. Proving it would come later. He needed help because he'd heard a few voices in the garage.

The van and six officers arrived. Jazz was impressed with the turnout. A few burly officers were mixed in amongst the six, and they looked as if they'd be pretty useful if things turned ugly. After scouting around, a back exit was spotted.

A call of, "Police – open up!" was shouted out and they all burst into the garage. As expected, the four men inside bolted for the back door and were barred by four officers waiting there. It was all over in minutes and all were arrested, cuffed and put in the police van. Mobile phones were taken and bagged.

Jazz looked around the garage. It didn't have a car in here, but it did have rows of cable hanging on hooks. It looked like there was enough cable to stretch from Land's End to John o'Groats. He recognised some of it. Cable theft was a preferred business these days; there was money in cables, in the form of copper. Strip the outer off and lovely expensive copper could be found inside. He recognised the type of cable used only by BT and Virgin, and he thought some might be cable from train tracks. He looked in disgust. There was a fucking fortune here, all stolen over some time. He reckoned they'd found it just in time. The thieves must have been about to sell it on. He wondered if they stole it or whether they fenced it. Interviews would find that out.

He passed the case to DI John Thomas, and yes, his nickname was Dick. He had been dealing with stolen metal; it was big business. Jazz had enough on his hands at the moment. He would wait for his pat on the back and look forward to it later. He gave a wry smile to himself. *When hell freezes over*, he thought. That Dick wouldn't give him credit for anything.

Now he made his way back to the building society. It was late and they would be closed, but he phoned ahead and said he wanted to talk to the manager now.

Jeremy Brown was the manager's name. He was a smart looking, slim blond six-footer with a firm handshake. Jazz wondered if he was getting old. Building society managers were looking so young these days. Jeremy was actually thirty-five years old, and life had been kind to him.

The niceties were said quite quickly, and Jazz explained who he was and why he was here, and that many street robberies were attacks on elderly women who had left the building society after drawing out money. Politely, Jazz explained it was his job to assess risk and see if the building society could do anything to help their customers stay safe when they left the building.

That said, Jazz proceeded to tell Brown exactly what they were doing wrong.

He pointed to the chairs by the entrance. "You can sit down and watch easily who is drawing out money at the cashier window. You can see a wad of notes being pushed through by the cashier and picked up by a customer. Old ladies often have shaky hands and it takes them time to put their money into their purses. Ample time to see how much money they have withdrawn. So, get rid of the chairs. If someone is disabled, bring them a chair to sit on if they need it, you have a receptionist they can ask."

The manager nodded and could see the sense in that.

"Also, we have just arrested a man who was in here today on his mobile phone. We suspect he phoned through to his accomplices that Mrs Partridge had left the building with a nice bit of money in her purse. He is Romanian and could say what he liked – no one in here would understand him. She was in fact robbed after leaving here today, but we caught the accomplices and the man in here on the phone. I would suggest you do not allow mobile phones to be used inside the building society."

Jazz was on form, and very politely he added, "Perhaps I could suggest that if someone is withdrawing a large amount of money, especially an elderly person, why not put the money in a envelope for them? Then no one can see how much is in the envelope and it is easier for an elderly person to put it in their bag."

The manager nodded again. He wondered why he had never thought of that, but he assured Jazz this would all be dealt with tomorrow morning. With a very grateful shake of his hand and a pat on the back, Jazz left feeling he had done something good today. It was worth a drink, and he felt for his flask. He needed a celebratory swig.

He took himself off to a quiet area off the main road and enjoyed a long slow swig, feeling the liquid heat up his mouth as he swirled it round with his tongue. He gulped the liquid down and immediately relaxed and felt that wonderfully good feeling he only got with vodka. Tomorrow things wouldn't be so good, and he would need his drink to help him through. For now he headed back to the station to write up his report. Ash couldn't do it for him; he was busy with photographs.

By 8pm he was ready to go home. He picked up two bottles of vodka, fish and chips and a headache. It had been a very busy day and he felt like shit. Mrs Chodda opened the door before he could get his key out and reminded him that he had been asked to join her for supper. He gave her his boyish smile and apologies. He showed her his fish and chips and said he had to work late. She could see he was tired, and she also saw the clinking bag with two bottles of vodka in it. Her disappointment could not be hidden and she asked that next time he must phone her if he couldn't attend. She would cook for him another night. He heard female voices in the kitchen and knew he was supposed to be introduced to them.

He was tired; he was full of crap and concerns and

ideas on what to do next with the Simmonds/Bateman case. He just needed some peace and quiet, something he couldn't remember happening for quite a while. But Mrs Chodda was a good woman and he didn't want to upset her. With a sigh and a heavy heart, he said he would put his food upstairs and just come down to sample her pakoras for a while if that was alright. Mrs Chodda beamed and said that if he could come for just five minutes that would be wonderful.

The five minutes turned into twenty minutes. The young lady was far too young for him. She seemed incredibly shy, naïve, and actually boring. She answered with "yes" and "no" or a tittering giggle if she didn't have an answer. Now her mother, who accompanied her, was full of talk. The family history could have gone on for hours but it seemed that they were a high-caste family and practically royalty. Jazz nodded out of politeness but was aching to get away. His throat was scratchy and he needed a drink; his belly was empty and he wanted his fish and chips. Even Mrs Chodda's pakoras couldn't stem the hunger. He just wanted to sit down and relax.

He got up, and with a flourish of "wonderful", and "so glad", and "a pleasure to meet you", he made his excuse of an important case to work on and left to microwave his fish and chips.

Mrs Chodda gave the other woman a smug look: *Well, I told you how important he was.* Jazz didn't feel it was very well-mannered to have left so early, but in the scheme of things, he just didn't care – a drink was more important, and he poured a large one. He knew Mrs Chodda would cover his back. She had taken to boasting about how important he was to the Metropolitan Police Force, and how busy he was. She told all the adoring mothers that he was a Sikh warrior in the Metropolitan Police Station, and that he solved the hardest of crimes. He smiled, imagining the nods of wonder this would cause. If only they knew how sordid and seedy most of his work was, they wouldn't be so impressed, he thought.

Just for a moment, he wanted to be fucking Morse, or Frost or Columbo – those detectives didn't have to deal with sodding building society thefts and crappy jobs like that, and didn't have to keep landladies happy by being looked at by ambitious mothers. All he wanted to do was concentrate on the Bateman/ Simmonds case and get them arrested. Was that too much to fucking ask, he wondered, angry at all the piddly jobs and distractions that took him from what was a deadly and filthy case. He wanted to arrest them and see them all go down for years.

He finished his drink quickly and poured another. The fish and chips tasted better on the second tumbler of vodka and orange.

CHAPTER 18

Things to Do and Places to Go

Another morning, another hangover. He had been told in the past that you don't get a hangover from drinking vodka. *Well that was a piece of piss,* he told himself. He felt like shit. After a shower he picked a pretty natty grey suit with a pink shirt and tie. By the time he had dressed, finished a piece of fish left over from last night and drunk a coffee he was feeling a bit more normal. He looked in the mirror and admired the view.

"You are a handsome devil, Jaswinder Singh," he told his reflection. A sharp suit and a classy shirt. He had a trim, slim physique and stood six feet tall. He could have been a model if he had gone down that route; having no hair accentuated his big eyes and chiselled cheekbones and made him look strikingly handsome. Some at work had, in the past, put up pictures of *Austin Powers'* Dr Evil and put Jazz's name underneath, but he was far more handsome than that.

He was dressed to kill and couldn't remember why

he was dressing this well today. It might be because he had to see DCI Radley to update him. The man was keeping a very close eye on him and his work. Jazz didn't care. A bit of praise wouldn't go amiss. Then it came to him. He was due in court today. *Bloody 'ell*, he thought – he needed to keep up with all of his cases.

He was due in court at 10am for the case of Michael Stokes. Michael intended to plead not guilty and there was no question about this – he absolutely was guilty. He had been in a fight in a petrol station. The victim had upset him in some way and he had turned on him and hit him so hard he fell to the floor, and Stokes then proceeded to kick seven bells out of him. The victim had his front teeth kicked out. The kicking caused his nose, jaw and three ribs to be broken. He was bruised all over and in a sorry state; in hospital for a few days. There was no reason for the attack – it was Stokes in a bad mood. He was known to the police. He had run off after the attack but the victim recognised him from a line-up, which Stokes now contested.

Jazz had asked the petrol station for their CCTV, which would have shown the attack. The petrol station refused to give the recording, making all sorts of excuses. Enough was enough and with the court case drawing closer, Jazz did what he had to do to get that CCTV copy. He told the petrol station he was closing them down for forensic analysis, and that they would be closed for at least a week. He assured them that he didn't want the scene of the crime compromised and he thought it would only be a week, but who knows, if the SOCOs were busy it could be longer. It was untrue and he had no power to do that, but it worked. Reluctantly the CCTV film was found and given to Jazz. It showed Stokes clearly, and he was taking it with him this morning to amaze the court and settle this case once and for all. He wanted Stokes to go down for a long time for what he did. Stokes had a history, so the judge should give him at least five years.

He got to Snaresbrook early. It was a GBH with intent so went straight to the Crown Court. Jazz showed the CPS lawyer the video and the judge was made aware of the evidence. It was shown in court as soon as the proceedings got started. The jury had been sworn in and after the initial formal proceedings and plea were sorted out, the video was the first thing shown to the court. A change of plea was swiftly asked for and Stokes now pleaded guilty. He had no choice.

Great, thought Jazz, *all done and dusted*. It was all over in an hour and Stokes would come back for sentencing in a week. Jazz shook hands with the CPS lawyer. Most CPS lawyers liked working with Jazz; they all knew he went above and beyond the call of duty to get evidence for convictions, which made their work easier. He left with a commendation from the judge ringing in his ears for getting the evidence presented in time for the court trial. It was a good start to the day, and Jazz walked with a renewed spring in his step. Someone appreciated him for once, he thought.

By 11.30am Jazz was on his way back to Ilford Police Station, another case with a guilty verdict meaning he had less to deal with. He had about twenty ongoing cases at present, most waiting for court appearances. For the moment, he wanted to concentrate on Operation Kevin, named after the video of Kevin Parsons. He so wanted to get Simmonds and especially Bateman, who had evaded the police for far too long. He was in no doubt whatsoever that Bateman, a convicted paedophile who had supposedly found God, was still a practising paedophile. Proving it was going to be the hard part.

He got to Ilford Police Station in time for his appointment with DCI Radley. It would seem Radley wanted to know every little piddly thing Jazz did. It was as if he didn't trust him. Jazz laughed at that thought. Of course he didn't trust him. His last few cases had caused mayhem; two police officers had been killed on Jazz's watch and his last case had endangered the life of Ashiv Kumar. Even so, he thought petulantly, there was no need to pull him in every day to report on when he had wiped his arse and said "please" and "thank you" to the public out there.

The meeting went well. Radley was still looking into Jazz's computer being compromised. The computer boffins reckoned in time they would come up with some sort of signature to tell them who had accessed Jazz's computer. In the meantime, unbeknown to the police station personnel, a hidden camera had been installed showing anyone entering the CID office, and more to the point, trained on Jazz's computer. Radley cautioned him that there were only three people in the station who knew of this, and suggested Jazz might want to remember that when he was at his desk, a camera would be permanently trained on him and to watch what he bloody got up to. Jazz smiled at this. He had no intention of spending too much time at his desk.

They talked about yesterday and the building society risk assessment and what was in place there. The garage near the Gascoigne Estate had produced a small fortune in copper. Jazz got a well-done for uncovering the Romanian gang. Also, the mobile phones were checked and the tip-off was proved by the numbers rung.

Jazz updated Radley on Bateman but at present there wasn't too much to tell him, except that today's meeting should bring in some new information to work on and they had plans afoot. At this DCI Radley frowned. Jazz quickly said that it was all up for discussion with his team, not solely his idea, which sat better with DCI Radley.

He left Radley's office thinking the day couldn't get any better. Even the tight-arsed DCI had given him a well-done. He should have known. It was always the way; he got praised in preparation for a very long, dark fall. But for now he only knew he deserved a celebratory swig of vodka from his flask and one of the lovely Milly's 999 all-day breakfasts for lunch.

Jazz caught up with Boomer, who was telling some officer to, "Fuck off and get some work done." He waited until the officer left and sat down to discuss what was going to happen at Dionne's house this weekend. If, by chance, Simmonds contacted the house as he was supposed to do, something needed to be in place to put him off the scent.

Between them they concocted the story that Dionne had gone to her cousin's home in Hastings by the sea for recuperation because she was feeling unwell. She had taken Nekisha with her. A friend, Natalie, had moved in to look after the house and Charles. 'Natalie' would be PC Yvonne Anderson, who was quite excited to work undercover. Someone would have to talk to Charles and explain what was going on. He would be very confused. It occurred to Jazz that no one had sat down with him and explained what had happened. His mother's version would have been very emotional and may have lacked sufficient facts for Charles to understand. Jazz said he would make a point of seeing Charles later.

The meeting at 4pm confirmed that upon being shown the photos, the mothers in Suffolk and Norfolk recognised Betty Lemus as the woman they met with Simmonds. Paula also confirmed that Betty Lemus was picked out as the woman who looked after Nekisha. Nekisha said she was very kind to her, but she also confirmed she undressed her and put her in a room naked, where a man with a little mask came in and touched her. It turned out to be a bandit-type mask but Nekisha had said it was glittery and blue and wasn't frightening. A picture of Bateman was shown to her but she couldn't recognise him. All thought the chances were that it was Bateman who liked to keep himself unrecognisable whilst Nekisha was going home. Glumly, the idea was put forward that when and if Nekisha was going to be raped and murdered, the mask would have come off.

Jazz felt the heat rising at the back of his neck and spreading over his head. He wanted Bateman and Simmonds so badly. Simmonds they could arrest, but Jazz wanted the whole lot. Bateman wasn't going to get away with this. His house was used, his so-called staff were involved – they were all going down, he would make sure of that.

Before they disbanded Jazz told them that PC Yvonne Anderson was going to play the role of a friend of Dionne, and would be house-sitting and looking after Charles. If Simmonds rang she would tell the story of Dionne needing a break to recuperate. PC Anderson would alert Jazz if a call came through. He also said he was off to talk to Charles about what had happened and try and keep him calm. Paula said Dionne had talked to him and he had visited her at the centre.

Ash was going to delve even further into anything on Simmonds and Bateman, but didn't hold out much hope. Paula said she would check out all the child porn sites to see if Simmonds or Bateman had been online. She had many contacts in the chat rooms too, and would report back. Ash added that he was looking at

Bateman's previous offence to see if he could see any names associated with him at the time that might be in the frame today.

Boomer thought it was all good stuff and wished them well. It was decided to meet again at 4pm tomorrow; it being Friday, there could be some movement on Simmonds, who would be ringing Dionne to get Nekisha for the weekend. PC Anderson was in place tonight and would stay there until further notice.

The talk with Charles Osei didn't go as well as Jazz expected. He was fuming. He knew a bit, in fact he knew a lot about what was happening from his mother Dionne, and this was the first opportunity he had to blast off at someone. Jazz hadn't thought it was going to be a picnic but he was surprised at the venom he got. Charles was beside himself with anger and rage and he hated all white men. He wrongly accused paedophiles always being fucking white supremacists who hated black people. He ranted that there were no black paedophiles. Jazz figured this wasn't the time to tell him he was wrong. He needed to get rid of his rage. Charles then started on the police. He hated the police, who didn't give a flying fuck about black girls.

Jazz answered, "That's why I am here, because I do care, and so do all of my team who are working hard to catch these people."

All he got in response was fists held up at him and Charles screaming, "Too late, you're too late."

Jazz had had enough of his rage. He gave him his time to get it off his chest and now he had to listen. He told him simply that Nekisha was alive, she had been groomed and touched inappropriately but not raped, and certainly not gang-raped and strangled like a little white boy they had seen on a snuff video. He said Charles should be rejoicing that the police had sussed this all out as early as possible and Nekisha was safe and getting counselling. Charles was told that there were a lot of police officers working hard to catch these men and they wouldn't stop until they were caught. Charles paced up and down for a bit and then just plonked himself down in a chair and sobbed like a baby. He was inconsolable for quite some time, and then, embarrassed, got up and took himself off to the bathroom.

The knock at the door was PC Yvonne Anderson. It was agreed she would stay every evening until 10pm and then go home to return the next morning. Simmonds had always rung in the evening and never after (10pm) Dionne had told him she was asleep by (9.30pm) because of her health.

When Charles came back, he seemed calmer. Jazz introduced him to Yvonne and said she would be staying here with him, and that she must answer the phone as she would be giving the story that Dionne and Nekisha were staying with relatives by the sea. Charles was told in a strong, clear and measured way that under no circumstances was he to say anything to anyone. If Simmonds rang they didn't want him spooked.

Charles became animated again. "Why the fuck have you got to be nice to Simmonds? Arrest the fucker now."

Jazz explained. "Look, there are more people involved than just Simmonds and we want to catch all the murderous fuckers. If you want to help Nekisha and your mother, then just carry on as normal." Jazz raised his hands and said, "I know, I know, that's not easy but we need you to play your part. Simmonds knows you. Put my number in your mobile and ring me if you need me, or if anyone contacts you. Do you want to stay with anyone local, Charles? You don't have to stay here."

Charles mumbled that he would go to his friend Joseph's around the corner. He didn't want to stay in the house alone and had been staying at Joseph's most nights.

This agreed, Jazz felt able to leave. A key was found for PC Anderson to let herself in and out. Jazz noted that in plain clothes of jeans and a neat T-shirt, she looked pretty fit and very different from when she wore the standard Met uniform with ill-fitting trousers, which wasn't very attractive on women. She noted the appreciative smile. He was pretty gorgeous, but everyone knew he worked so far off-piste he often got lost or lost others. In a split second she decided he was best left alone. She didn't return the smile, she just nodded an acknowledgement and turned to make a cup of tea and settle down and watch TV.

It was about 7pm and Jazz decided to go home via the *Gurdwara*. He hoped Deepak was there. Deepak always made him feel welcome and useful. He knew when there was something on Jazz's mind and gave him time. Just to sit with the man, not saying anything, made Jazz feel better and strangely helped him in his own decision-making.

Deepak was there, full of wisdom as usual. A cup of stewed tea from the big urn by the kitchen, and a corner was found. They sat on the floor on the carpet provided for those eating and drinking in the *Gurdwara*.

After sitting for some time in comfortable silence, just sipping their tea, Deepak looked up and smiled at Jazz. All he said was, *"Pride in social status is empty; pride in personal glory is useless.* Sri Guru Granth Sahib Ji."

Jazz marvelled at how he knew just the right thing to say. Why Deepak picked that particular saying, and just how appropriate it was to him, Jazz just didn't know. He wondered if he was perhaps too full of bitterness and thought it could be partly based on being fucking unappreciated. He needed to listen to the words of the Guru. His glory and success were his property, not down to some fucking arsehole at the nick with stars on his epaulette telling him he was wonderful. This didn't translate to Deepak; he didn't need to explain anything to this good man. Jazz just smiled and nodded, looking down at the floor. With a sigh he thought, *So much to do, so much to understand and so little time.*

He left Deepak and the *Gurdwara* feeling lighter and stronger and made his way home. A drink en route would help, and once outside the *Gurdwara* he felt for his flask of vodka. Tonight was pizza night and he rang Pizza Express and ordered ahead. He picked it up as he passed on the way home.

He got into his room without being stopped by Mrs Chodda and plonked down heavily on his bed. The TV remote was there and he scoured the programmes until he came across some cricket in Australia. With the pizza still hot, and a vodka and orange close by, he kicked off his shoes, hung up his good suit and lay back for a relaxing evening in his boxer shorts and socks – *not sexy*, he thought with a giggle.

His mobile phone rang at 9.30pm. It was PC Anderson. She told him that Peter Grimshaw, aka Simmonds, had just rung to speak to Dionne about Nekisha. Sounding curt at first, Simmonds quickly made an excuse, saying he was worried about Dionne because he had been phoning earlier and there was no reply. He said he was sorry not to have spoken to her before she left. PC Anderson thought he sounded pissed off. He said he would ring next week when they were supposed to be back.

Jazz thanked Yvonne – he said he preferred to call her that. He added that 'PC Anderson' sounded very formal and she was on his team for the moment, and everyone was on first-name terms. She smiled at this, still thinking he was trying to chat her up. The slightly slurred words made her realise he was well on his way to being drunk. They said goodnight and she confirmed she would be back at the house tomorrow morning in case Simmonds rang again.

When he had put the phone down, Jazz sat still thinking. Fuelled by drink but still able to think straight, he couldn't fathom what was going on. If his computer had been compromised by Simmonds and Bateman they would have known the police were involved, yet they were still working on Dionne to get at Nekisha. It didn't make sense. They should have been backtracking quickly and clearing up any signs that showed contact with Nekisha. Bateman was whiter than white according to everyone and he wouldn't risk compromising himself by continuing. He was far too clever for that. What the hell was going on?

Today had been full-on and Jazz hadn't spoken to Mad Pete for a while. He needed to know what he had found out. He needed answers that made sense. Tomorrow would be busy.

CHAPTER 19

Chaos and Confusion

Surprisingly, Jazz woke and felt good. He almost jumped out of bed and got ready for work. There were things to do and places to be. Today he was going to find out what that slimeball of an excuse for a human being had found out. Mad Pete would be in trouble if he had forgotten he was there to help Jazz, and not to make himself some money by supplying drugs.

A shower, a shave and a shit and after a swig of Fanta from the fridge he was ready. With a spring in his step and a clean shirt on his back he got to Ilford Police Station by 8.30am.

He went straight to DCI Radley's office. Radley was already at his desk and working. He looked crispy-clean in a white starched shirt with his hair immaculately in place, his police jacket correctly hung on a coat hanger to the left of him on the coat stand. With his black-rimmed glasses and that quite cool, well-built physique and chiselled face, DCI Radley could have been mistaken for Clark Kent.

Jazz thought, *Superman? Only in Radley's dreams.* The idea of pristine DCI Radley in his OCD office of cleanliness and tidiness wearing his Y-fronts over his trousers made Jazz giggle.

DCI Radley looked up as he heard Jazz coughing as he tried not to laugh. He looked inquisitive; he hadn't asked Jazz to come and see him.

"Sir, PC Anderson rang last night to say Simmonds rang wanting to talk to Dionne, and he accepted the story of Dionne staying with her sister to recuperate with Nekisha. But Sir, if they compromised my computer, they wouldn't have continued to try to get at Nekisha. Someone else must have compromised my computer. Who the hell else is getting at me?"

DCI Radley permitted himself a little joke. "Jazz, those who don't want to get at you wouldn't fill a fag paper." He laughed at making such a merry quip.

Jazz didn't think that was very funny. He left the thought with DCI Radley, who was still having Jazz's computer monitored but so far no one had approached it. It all felt wrong and he didn't know who to trust. Talking of trust, he needed to hear from Mad Pete. He tried ringing him but got no answer.

He passed by Boomer's office and told him about Simmonds ringing and Yvonne giving him the story about Dionne and Nekisha staying with a relative by the sea, which he seemed to buy. He talked to Boomer about his worries that if Simmonds and Bateman were responsible for compromising his computer, why the fuck would they still be contacting Dionne?

Boomer couldn't answer; all he could come up with was, "Who says paedophiles are fucking clever? They could be fucking stupid."

Jazz shrugged his shoulders, not agreeing or disagreeing, but he did add, "How come Bateman, a known paedophile, is now treated like Jesus in his area and the police have nothing on him? It shows he *is* fucking devious and fucking clever."

Both agreed something was not right. Jazz sent a text message to Mad Pete. They had a code in case anyone saw Mad Pete's phone. *Jilly needs some stuff urgently – can you help?* It was a crap message but Mad Pete would know what it meant. He wasn't replying in a hurry.

Just as Jazz was about to go to his desk, Ash rushed up to him and took him to one side. "Guv, just got news in. The house, supposedly Simmonds' house, has gone up in flames. The fire brigade were called in the early hours of this morning."

Jazz called Boomer, and with a "What the fuck is going on?" they went to find a spare police car in the compound. Ash was told to come along as well; this needed sorting. They took off to Hockley, an hour away.

The fire brigade was still there. They got hold of someone in authority, who was looking at the now-sodden house sending plumes of steam up into the air. They were told that an accelerant had been splashed throughout the ground floor. No one had been in the property. Jazz spoke to the small crowd of people hanging around watching the spectacle. According to the neighbours, no one had lived there permanently for years. Someone came and collected post every now and then. This was definitely an arson case, but who did it?

Jazz, Boomer and Ash sat in the police car. They had got the BMW again. They talked through what they had heard and seen and what to make of it. The questions were: had Simmonds fired his own house to obliterate any evidence? What evidence, they didn't know. Had someone else done this, and if so, who had he upset? Was there an argument within the paedophile group? They hoped so.

Jazz left Boomer and Ash to fight out who had the nearest answer. He sat quietly, thinking. This didn't make sense.

Jazz got out of the car as Boomer was telling Ash to, "Fuck off and get a life." Jazz thought, *Ah, team enthusiasm, nice to see them both getting on.*

He walked a little way from the car and sat and thought some more. Then it came to him. An angry Charles Osei, wanting to know what the police were doing for his sister Nekisha, feeling let down by everyone and frustrated at not being able to do anything to help his sister. *What is he going to do? He's going to phone his cousin; a bad-ass fucking Blood soldier, put it all together and you have trouble.* He got on the phone to Winston Boeke, Dionne's nephew. Boeke had given him a number to ring if there was any news, and now was the time to ask the questions.

"Yeah, man, what you asking?" was Boeke's cautious response to Jazz's cheery hello when he answered the phone. They talked around each other for a bit, but soon Jazz had had enough.

"Why did you torch Simmonds' house in Hockley?"

Boeke, not fazed, answered, "Fuck off, man, and don't be giving me this shit."

"He wasn't living there, Boeke. He just used the house for post. It was a waste of your expertise."

"Where the fuck does he live? He's a paedo and he touched my little sister and he ain't gonna live." With a nanosecond's pause, Boeke added, "Allegedly, of course."

Jazz nearly smiled at this. "You are a fucking nuisance and she aint your sister. I should send in the heavy squad to arrest you."

Boeke, angry now, said, "She is my little sister in my heart. I love that girl. You can't say I started that fire just you prove it! There is nothing you can find that puts me and the fire in the same place. I have fifty people who will say I was here in London."

Jazz knew that, and worn out by the interference, said, "OK, OK. Man, you could have caused me a lot of problems. We are after these paedos, but you have just warned them that someone is on to them."

Boeke answered unhappily, "Aww, man, don't give me none of that. I can't hack it. He should've been warm and toasted in his bed last night, the fucking bastard!" With a frustrated sigh he asked, "Is there anything you want me to do for you, man? I wanna help. My family are my respect and I gotta do right by them. This man is dead by me."

Jazz said, "For a start, stop helping, but if I need anything you will be the first I contact. Don't talk like that, otherwise I will have you banged up before you can say, 'Oops – pardon me, officer!' We are gonna get them, leave it to us. I've now got to get the fire brigade to lie about the cause of the fire."

With that he flipped his mobile off and walked with purpose, muttering about "Fucking macho men sticking their oar in and causing me more work", to the man in charge, who was busy talking to his firemen.

Jazz explained the dilemma and luckily Fred, the senior fireman present, was the watch manager, and he agreed to put in writing that the fire was started by an electrical fault. The watch manager looked after small teams but attended this fire because it threatened at one point to spread into the adjoining houses. His teams worked hard to put the fire out and the neighbours were safe.

They were waiting for the owner to arrive. Apparently he was working away and they had a number for him through the electricity board. For now Fred would tell the owner, Mr Simmonds, that it was an electrical fault. Fred said he had the authority to hold his report for a week, and after a week he would write a report with the correct reason. He asked if Jazz had any idea who started the fire. Jazz shook his head and said he hadn't. He added that Essex Police would sort this out (although under his breath, he added, "No chance").

With a bright smile, Jazz thanked Fred for his help and shook his hand. He was grateful for a week's grace to sort this bloody mess out. It was getting complicated. He wanted out of the area quickly. Simmonds was bound to arrive at some point and Jazz didn't want to be there. He got back in the car and they headed for London.

The conversation was muted. All were thinking. They needed to do something, but what was their next move? They had Simmonds in the frame, along with Betty Lemus and Bateman by association, but they would get him on something, along with the others. It was looking to be a huge case. If they were honest, it was too big for them to handle, but Jazz, with the bit between his teeth, would get Bateman as well before the week was out. He promised little Kevin he would get those who abused and killed him. The memory of the video tortured Jazz. He was a big, tough detective but this vile, horrific fucking filth that had ruined and exterminated the life of an innocent little boy had floored him. He was never going to let anyone know that, but he would get his killer.

Sitting in the car, Boomer broke the silence by saying that they had their hopes pinned on Mad Pete for the moment. Ash perked up at this and asked what was going on.

"Oh, fuck! Boomer, you big mouth! We were not

telling high-and-mighty here." Jazz nodded in Ash's direction.

Ash, resigned to hearing something unprofessional and inappropriate, asked what they had done. They told him Mad Pete was undercover at Bateman's pile in Paglesham. They just hadn't heard from him for a while.

Ash quoted large sections of the police manual stating why they should not have used a civilian as an undercover agent, and why they shouldn't have used anyone without permission. He quoted sections of the manual, which Jazz reckoned he made up, stating they could be hung, drawn and quartered for what they had done. After a five-minute rant Ash quietened down and just looked at Jazz for an answer.

Boomer started – he just laughed, slapped Ash across the back and said, "You crack me up, little Ash. You will make a fine detective one day."

Ash, angry at such frivolousness, replied, "I am going to get the fucking sack for associating with you two."

It was Jazz's turn to laugh, and he good-naturedly ruffled Ash's hair. "You will keep us on the straight and narrow, Ash. We will do better next time."

With that Boomer and Jazz shared a high five and laughed until they passed the Billericay turn-off on the way back to Ilford.

They parked the car and just missed the drug squad, who were looking for their booked BMW police car. They were shouting at someone, asking,

"Who the fuck took our car?" Boomer, Jazz and Ash giggled at getting one over on the very precious drug squad team. They sloped off quickly into the busy concourse inside Ilford Police Station, looking as if butter wouldn't melt in their mouths.

They all took different directions: Boomer to his office, Ash to his computer and desk, and Jazz sat for a moment in a quiet corner, thinking. He asked himself again: why hadn't he heard from Mad Pete yet?

He sat and felt for his three trusty flasks, one inside pocket, left side and right side, and one in an outside pocket. He took one out and took a well-earned, hefty swig, which he rolled a little in his mouth before gulping it down. The second swig was not quite so big, but like foreplay, very deliciously hot and smooth and full of anticipation, with building excitement. The third swig was as smooth as velvet and as fabulous as a climax. He sat and savoured for more moments than he should have. With his eyes closed and smiling, those near him wondered what the fuck he was doing. God! He needed that.

With a sigh, he knew he needed to get a grip. This case was a mess and getting nowhere fast. Jazz left the police station and made his way to Barking, calling at all the places he knew of that were haunts of Mad Pete. He had been seen the day before buying drugs. It looked like he was buying good stuff and had lots of money with him. No one had seen him today.

It was a worry. Now the house in Hockley had

been torched, Nekisha was not available and Jazz still wasn't sure who had compromised his computer – it didn't sit together. Something was wrong and if he hadn't heard from Mad Pete by the end of today, Jazz was going to have to do something drastic. Had Mad Pete been found out? Jazz was responsible for him, and although he was a filthy wanker, he was his wanker.

The four o'clock meeting started without Jazz. He arrived a few minutes late but it didn't look like he had missed much.

Jazz just wanted to summarise for everyone present what had been happening. He talked of the fire at Hockley, his computer being compromised and Nekisha not being available. He said he was worried that if Simmonds or Bateman put this together, then they could back off rapidly. He wanted to move this forward as quickly as possible. Paula had looked on all the known sites, but found no sign of Simmonds or Bateman. She saw the look of disappointment around the table. She was a drama queen. Now she had their disappointment, she added a huge 'but'. As one, they all looked up expectantly. She smiled.

"We have access to some new sites that you can't access through any search engines. These are paedophiles who speak to each other. Our office have set up a user name as a paedophile. It has taken a long time to be accepted but now we have street cred. We found Simmonds and Bateman contacting these people and accessing pictures and information. The pictures and information they were accessing were criminal, and on the scale of one to ten they were accessing pictures rated as number one, which is the worst kind of child pornography. They don't use their real names but the computer tags are theirs. There is a lot going on and we are still searching. We have found the random paedophiles they contact, and now we have their computer tag, we are looking to see if there is a group they work with. Just need another day to get that information."

Everyone was full of admiration. The work Paula had done was immensely useful. They now had Bateman as an active paedophile.

Jazz just had to say it, with a triumphant, "I told you so! Once a paedophile, always a paedophile."

Everyone agreed with him. Jazz was known for his unorthodox way of working, but also his natural 'copper's nose' for things.

It was agreed that they were going for the whole group and would let this run a little longer. The snuff movies were what they wanted and Jazz added that he badly wanted Bateman and Simmonds and anyone else involved.

Ash and Boomer had nothing new to bring today. Paula was the star and it was hoped they were getting close. At some point, Jazz said, they wanted Bateman's DNA. Now there was the right to approach all paedophiles convicted before the legislation date of 1997 and legally ask for their DNA. Jazz said he didn't want to do that at the moment. He said they were already on dodgy ground with all that had happened lately. He didn't want to alert Bateman or Simmonds to any interest in them at present.

They all disbanded to get on with what they were doing. Jazz said to meet tomorrow at 4pm for a catch-up. All agreed and left. Jazz called Boomer back, and when the room was empty he told Boomer about his problem with Mad Pete.

"The bastard is making money with Bateman and Simmonds and I reckon he is not answering my calls or messages because he is having a bloody good time making money out of them. He is a little slimy toerag of the first order. I need to get his attention. He is our way into Bateman's house." He looked at Boomer for help.

Boomer wasn't much help. He suggested waiting outside Bateman's house and "jumping the fucker when he comes outside".

Jazz said he would think on it. Too much had happened and he didn't want to alert Bateman and Simmonds any more. That was about to change. Trouble and danger always had Jazz's name on them, and they were calling him again.

CHAPTER 20

Here We Go Again

Jazz made his way home. An early night, a few drinks to look forward to and collecting cod and chips from the chippy on the way home sounded like a good night to him. He was going to think about what to do about Mad Pete. He sent another message to Mad Pete, adding that he was desperate. Anyone looking at the message would think he was desperate for drugs, but Mad Pete would know there'd be trouble if he didn't reply.

Mrs Chodda popped her head around the kitchen door as Jazz entered. *Oh no, please don't invite me in,* thought Jazz. He smiled and Mrs Chodda just said good evening and hoped he was having a nice night. He nodded his thanks and took himself up the stairs at a decent speed, not wanting to disrespect Mrs Chodda. He closed his door and sighed with relief. The evening was now his.

First a drink – he had put his vodka and orange in the fridge so it was nice and cold when he took the first sip. He ate the fish and chips out of the paper using his fingers; it tasted good that way. The second large vodka and orange helped the chips go down and the third was his after-drink. By now he was feeling full and glowing. He closed his eyes for a moment; lying there on his bed with screwed-up chip paper on the floor and a nice drink beside him, life felt relaxed and good. That feeling wasn't going to last, was it?

In a vodka-fuelled stupor he heard a noise, an irritating noise that kept on and on and bloody on. He opened his eyes, realising he had fallen asleep. It was his phone, but he couldn't find the damn thing! He hunted in his pockets, on the bed and then got up and looked on the table where he had put his wallet, police badge, his handcuffs, watch and change; it was a mess, but where the bloody hell was his phone?

He found it under some bits of paper and answered urgently.

It was midnight, according to his phone, and a whining voice whispered, "I am fucked, Mr Singh. Something terrible is happening here and I want out. I am scared, Mr Singh, it wasn't my fault. I didn't know not to go in there, I was just looking out for you." It was Mad Pete, and he was terrified and crying now. "You have got to help me, Mr Singh. Send in the big squad with guns and get me out of here. I am going to be a dead man soon." He started to cry again.

Jazz was instantly wide awake; the vodka-fuelled stupor disappeared quicker than a fart in a wind tunnel. He sat up, rigid, thinking fast and hard.

"What the fuck is going on, Pete?" whispered Jazz. "Where are you now?"

"I'm outside, down the road, away from the house. If they know I have come out here to ring you I will be killed, stabbed, even tortured, Mr Singh. Get me out of here," cried Mad Pete, sobbing again.

"OK, OK, let's calm down for a second here. If you are outside and down the road, no one can hear you and you are safe for the moment. Now, sit down on the roadside somewhere and talk to me."

Mad Pete had had the foresight to bring with him some stuff to inject, and on Jazz's instructions he got on with it and after a little while was much calmer. He lit a cigarette and sat back.

Jazz, not known for his patience, bided his time. He knew Mad Pete well and after about ten minutes he reckoned he'd be settled and the heroin would have taken hold, so he started with his questions.

There was a lot of whining, a lot of blaming Jazz for everything that was happening, which Jazz let go. It transpired Pete had been accepted by the two men working for Bateman and Simmonds. They did odd jobs for them and were highly trusted. They were in their mid-forties so no spring chickens, but their loyalty to Bateman especially was unbreakable. Their names were Jim and Derek and they were built like two brick shithouses.

Mad Pete added, "I wouldn't fuck with them, Mr Singh, they are huge." They lived in two of the converted stable cottages in the forecourt of the big house. Mad Pete was allowed the use of a third cottage next to them. In total there were five cottages, with two of them at right angles and the big house on the opposite side, almost making a square of the forecourt. He wasn't allowed anywhere near the other two cottages.

Jim and Derek liked Mad Pete. They said they were looking for someone to help them get certain requirements, which Mad Pete understood to be drugs, and he told them he was their man.

Excitedly, Mad Pete added, "They wanted good stuff, Mr Singh. I could make a fucking fortune from them." He realised what he was saying, calmed down and returned to what was happening.

"I came back to Barking and got them some good shit. They gave me wedges of money and when I got back they were excited and pleased that I could get everything so easily. They are fucking idiots, Mr Singh, no idea about getting good contacts. I saved them a fucking fortune and made myself a nice wedge too." He heard Mr Singh tut, and made quickly made excuses. "But I was working for you, Mr Singh. It had to look fucking bloody brilliant on my part to gain their trust, and I did. They knew they were on to a good thing with me."

Jazz just said, "OK, I see," and let Mad Pete continue.

"So, I got introduced to Mr Simmonds and Mr Bateman on the second day. I was called into the big house and an office in there. They were very civil and hoped I would work well for them. They seemed very nice, Mr Singh. I was beginning to think you had got it wrong about them."

Jazz listened and raised his eyebrows, but didn't say anything. He had Mad Pete in full flow and he knew there was a lot more to come.

"I was there to help with the garden and run errands for them on account of me being younger. I liked it here, Mr Singh. I got this lovely little cottage with one bedroom and a dinky little bathroom. I liked Jim and Derek. They said they wanted more of the good shit I had got them. They said they needed a constant supply. I was on a winner, Mr Singh." He paused for a moment and added, ingratiating himself, "I was doing it for you, Mr Singh."

Jazz didn't think for one moment that was true. He reckoned the ungrateful slimeball was on a good earner and was going to continue supplying them for as long as he could. The bastard deserved a slap. No wonder he wasn't returning Jazz's calls – he was on holiday out there in the countryside, earning more money than he was used to.

"So I made two trips to Barking this week and got a lot of shit for them. Enormous amount, and I wondered why they needed so much so quickly. Well, I found out why, Mr Singh."

Jazz was now very attentive. "Go on, Pete, what's happening there?"

This comment made Mad Pete very jumpy, and he started snivelling again and got himself worked up towards a druggy fit. Jazz couldn't have that happen; he would get no sense out of him if it did.

"OK, OK, calm down, it's going to be alright, Pete. I am here to help you," soothed the dulcet tones oozed through the phone from Jazz. Mad Pete nodded on hearing this and lit another cigarette to calm himself down a bit.

"So, I was having a great time, Mr Singh. The lads were great to be around and they wanted more things. They wanted cameras – not the hand things, but big fucking video cameras. They said they didn't want a paper trail from buying them, and could I get some for them? Well, Mr Singh, I can get most things as you know, and I said yes. I got some top-end cameras and video recording equipment. I didn't think, Mr Singh, what they wanted it for, I didn't ask. I never ask anyone, too much information."

Jazz, cross by now, said without thinking, "You stupid prick! You were there to find out stuff for me. You should have asked."

"I didn't need to ask, Mr Singh, I saw where they were put. I ain't happy, Mr Singh." Mad Pete started snivelling again. "Things are happening, Mr Singh, something big is gonna happen soon and I don't wanna be around it or part of it."

Trying to keep his temper, Jazz asked, "What the fuck is going on, Pete, for Christ's sake?! Tell me!"

"Don't have a go at me, Mr Singh, I am in deep shock. I ain't good, I feel ill and I am fucking shit-scared. You gotta be nice to me. I ain't holding it together very well."

Jeez, thought Jazz, this was like watching paint dry. So much promise, so much happening and fuck all being told to him.

"Sorry, Pete, you take your fucking time." After a slight pause, Jazz added, "Just tell it as you feel comfortable."

"So, Mr Singh. I saw the cameras I got them going into one of the cottages. I was a bit curious and went and took a look. You'll never guess what, Mr Singh – although it looks like two cottages they are one cottage and there are just two rooms in it. The big room had full-length mirrors on the walls. It scared the fuck out of me, seeing myself like that. The cameras were being put up on the walls and it looked like a couple would be handheld by the way they were lined up. Nothing is connected yet but the lads, Jim and Derek, are doing that, I think. Jim is a bit of an electrician so it's most probably him."

Jazz wondered what that meant – it sounded pervy to him. "Was there any furniture in the room?" he asked.

Mad Pete said, "No, but I think something might be brought in tomorrow. I overheard a conversation one of the lads was having – it was Jim on the phone, talking to a shop, I think, and arranging a delivery tomorrow. I don't know what, though. There was big lights in the room too, so something was gonna be filmed there and I don't feel good about that, Mr Singh. Something ain't right."

Too true, thought Jazz. *A lot seems to be being prepared for something.* He needed to ask Mad Pete something.

"Pete, have you heard anything about a group of people coming to the house soon?"

"Yeah," said Pete, amazed that Mr Singh knew that. "How did you know, Mr Singh? I saw a list of people by the telephone, don't know if it's them or not. I sort of borrowed it. It had twelve names on it, I didn't know nuffink about any of them. I figured all the shit I bought them might be for a party. But if it's a party, I ain't sure what type of party it is." Mad Pete started to whine again.

Jazz licked his lips and asked very carefully, "Pete, have you got that list on you, by any chance?"

"Yeah, Mr Singh, it's in my pocket."

Jazz jerked his arm in the air and whispered, "*Yeeessss.* Pete, can you read out the names to me, please?"

"It's fucking dark here, Mr Singh, how the fuck am I gonna read anything?"

Jazz, excited and annoyed at the same time, tried to be calm. "Pete, you have a super-duper bollocking phone with more apps on it than a fucking full-size computer at NASA, you must have the torchlight app on it."

"Oh yes, Mr Singh, I have. Very clever of you," whispered a giggling Mad Pete.

Jazz dived around, looking for a working pen and a clean piece of paper. *Where the fuck is anything when you want it?* he asked himself. Eventually he found an A5 envelope, which he tore open so he could write on the inside, and a small blue pen from Argos that he accidentally took.

Together they worked on the list, ensuring Jazz got the names written correctly. There were twelve names. It seemed to take ages, and when he checked the time it was half past one in the morning. Mad Pete had stretched everything out for an hour and a half and they still hadn't reached the punchline of why he thought he was going to be killed.

Still trying to keep Mad Pete calm, Jazz tried to phrase the next question carefully. Mad Pete, although at a reasonable level of sanity, was bubbling with anxiety underneath, and this, from Jazz's experience, could erupt at any moment.

"So, Pete, you now have the list and you cleverly hid it. You have seen the cottage and overheard the telephone conversation about a delivery. You are a clever bastard!"

Mad Pete got all modest for a second. "Well, you know, Mr Singh, I just do what I do."

"So what happened next, Pete?"

"It was dinner time, Mr Singh, and we all eat in the kitchen with the woman there."

Jazz perked up. "What's her name?"

Mad Pete tried to think; he was feeling a bit fuzzy at the moment. It was late and he'd taken a fair dose of heroin. "Was something like Betty Lettuce, or something like that. She is very strange, Mr Singh, all smiles but I don't trust her, the eyes are cold. I notice things like that."

"Does Betty Lemus sound about right to you, Pete?"

"Yeah, yeah, Mr Singh, that's it. Think she is a housekeeper there. She cooks a bit and eats with us."

"Sounds comfortable there, Pete," Jazz said affably. "So what did you do after you had eaten?"

"I went on a rummage. That's when I took a look at the two cottages knocked into one. The lads had settled down with a good whisky and some shit and seemed very comfortable, and the woman had gone into the rooms upstairs in the big house. I think she had a room in the house. Never saw no one else so went for a fag outside and took a look."

Jazz could tell he was stalling again. He wondered what the fuck he was going to tell him, if he ever got around to it. Jazz murmured encouragement.

"When I was in the big room in the cottage I heard a noise, Mr Singh. It scared me." Mad Pete was getting agitated now. The *oooh* noise was rumbling in the background, which could explode into almost screaming if Mad Pete got into a full-blown druggy fit. "They is gonna kill me, I am a dead man, I don't wanna die, I don't wanna die."

Jazz had to stop him before he got much further into this. All would be lost and he would be useless. The whole of Paglesham would hear him when he was in a fit.

"Pete, Pete, calm down. You are OK. I will look

after you, you know that. I am going to get you out. Now tell me, what was the noise? Just say it calmly, you are away from the house so you are safe, very safe." Jazz hoped that sounded soothing enough. He wanted to shake the bastard and get him to just fucking tell him what was going on.

"Mr Singh, I heard a kiddie sort of crying and moaning in that other room in the cottage. I think they have got a kiddie in there. I shouldn't have been there, they are murdering scum, Mr Singh, and they will kill me and torture me and cut my knob off, and tear my nipples off." Mad Pete was getting carried away in his fear.

Jeez, thought Jazz, *what the fuck am I to do?* First he had to get control of Mad Pete. "OK, Pete, stop there. Now just think and get calm. No one knows you were in that cottage. You are a devious rat and good at getting into places, so you are safe there. They obviously trust you because you have got their drugs and stuff for them, so safe there too. No one knows what you know. *Capisce?*"

"Gawd, Mr Singh, what's *capisce* again?"

Jazz could have laughed at that, but he was calming Mad Pete down and didn't think it appropriate. He continued, in a soothing way, "Pete, *capisce* means 'Do you understand?' Now I know you do understand. I know how good you are at working in a dangerous area. You worked for all those gangs with no troubles, so this is the same. I want you to go back to your cottage and go to bed. Tomorrow I will sort something out for you. Don't worry."

Jazz desperately wanted to ask more questions about the kiddie in the other room, but knew he would lose Mad Pete. Did Mad Pete hear a child or did he hear a cat or something? You just never knew when Mad Pete was on the shit. Jazz had heard enough, and there were things that needed doing.

Mad Pete seemed placated and agreed to go back to his cottage. Jazz suggested he could say that he had taken some good shit and wanted to see the stars, or something like that, if anyone saw him leave. He would look drugged-up enough to be realistic, Jazz thought. Mad Pete mumbled an agreement and turned off his phone.

Jazz sat for a while, thinking. So much to take in and so much to do, but it was – he looked at his watch – now 2.30 in the morning. He would never get anything done at this early hour. He knew exactly what he was going to do and he would need all the help he could get from his team. He set his alarm for six in the morning and tried to sleep. Tomorrow was going to be a very busy day with an early start.

CHAPTER 21

Into the Valley of Death

That annoying noise woke him from a very deep sleep.
It was like a burrowing insect in his ear, it grated and
hurt his nerve ends as Jazz tried to put a pillow over
his head to get rid of the awful sound. He moaned
and eventually woke properly and realised it was his
alarm. Everything flooded back and he sat up quickly.
It was six in the morning and he needed to be at
Ilford Police Station by nearly seven. He got up and
showered quickly. He liked long showers, letting the
water warm, relax and cleanse him, but today it had to
be quick. No suit today; it was going to be jeans and
a T-shirt.

When dressed he grabbed a Fanta out of the fridge
and a nearly rock-hard piece of pizza he was saving for
something or other, and left the house. He checked his
pockets – flasks in place and filled from last night, and
that all-important list safe in his inside pocket. He had
grabbed his ID, wallet and keys.

He was halfway to the police station when he

finished the piece of pizza. No taste but a bit of protein, he reckoned. The Fanta had been drunk pretty quickly and he tossed the can into a litter bin outside a shop as he passed by.

He got to Ilford Police Station just before seven. He had rung Boomer on the way in and was meeting him at 7.30am. Paula was up. Jazz gave her the names over the phone. She was alert and keen and took them down and said she was on her way to the police station and would get them in the system as soon as she arrived. Ash was a different kettle of fish. He had been up half the night with one of his kids who had an earache. He started to moan about it being so early but Jazz quickly relayed some of his conversation with Mad Pete to him, and Ash gasped at the thought of a child being kept and abused, and said swiftly that he would be in at 8am.

Jazz toyed with the idea of letting DCI Radley know what he intended to do and dismissed the thought instantly. He didn't need Radley's lengthy, politically correct version of policing. There was a child to rescue. He needed to move now – no time for meetings, discussions, liaising with Essex Police et-bloody-cetera. Jazz was going to do it his way.

He got on the phone to Rochford Police and spoke to one of the community officers. They moaned that they were busy but Jazz knew they were not. Eventually they agreed to Jazz's request to go immediately to Paglesham Road and wait in the lay-by near the witches' house. It could be seen from the road, just sitting there brooding inside a copse of trees and wild bushes, and Jazz was convinced dark deeds had happened there. It made him shiver, and he remembered the story of the Canewdon witches not far away and that gave him the heebie-jeebies. Paglesham had this effect on him.

Time was getting on. He had the Essex Police organised; now he had to get Boomer on his side and they had no time to waste on plans of action, for goodness' sake. He would do what he always did: leap with eyes closed into a situation with no idea of what the hell he was going to do or what the fuck he was going to walk into. It usually worked OK, he told himself.

As arranged, Boomer arrived and called Jazz to the police garage. He had got the BMW again. A very nifty car and sweet to drive. Jazz had got a wire; a new thing he didn't know how to use, but he took it to Boomer, who was far more used to dealing with surveillance.

Milly ran up to him with bacon sandwiches and coffee for both of them. She was stunningly wonderful for a seventy-something-year-old, and seemed quite sprightly and smiley around Jazz. It was her busy time but she left the canteen to find Jazz and make sure he had something to eat. Jazz gave her a kiss on the cheek and told her it would bring him luck. Then they were off.

The journey along the A13, chuck a left at Sadlers Farm and through to Paglesham, was done in record time. The blue light flashing helped. Boomer drove and he was enjoying himself. His huge presence behind the wheel looked awkward but he managed a few nifty moves along the way. It took an hour to reach Paglesham Road and in that time Jazz filled Boomer in on everything he had talked about with Mad Pete.

Jazz had a plan, and it wasn't until they stopped in the layby in Paglesham Road and said goodbye and thank you to the community officers waiting there that he would talk to Boomer about it. Jazz needed the community officers to go. He didn't want anyone in the house to see police officers waiting in Paglesham Road. Jazz and Boomer were in plain clothes and the BMW didn't have police markings on it, so they could just sit there. Apparently, so the community officers told Jazz, birdwatchers were known to stop there and watch birds. Why any sane person would do that Jazz had no idea, but for today they could say they were birdwatchers. Boomer had field glasses with him, which was a good thing. Now they were settled with everything in place, Jazz filled Boomer in on what he intended to do.

Boomer asked, "So why the fuck are we waiting here?"

"We are waiting for a van or lorry. This road is five miles long but it is a dead end, so everything coming in or going out has to pass by here. There can't be many that come down here, it's a deadend road finishing at either the church end or the boatyard end. We will stop any van or lorry until we find out which one of them is delivering to the mansion, and then I join the van team as a Mr Shifter, and when I am in the mansion or cottage I can have a nosy around."

He looked at Boomer for approval and got a look that said, *Are you fucking mad?* Jazz pulled out of his pocket some wires and a small earpiece, and a box of sorts.

He handed them to Boomer, saying, "Here, take it, I am not stupid. I grabbed one of these things I found in the surveillance room. You can listen to everything that goes on. Better than Bam Bam's house, this stuff is new and looks good shit." He saw Boomer's nonplussed look and asked, "You know how this works, don't you?"

Boomer shrugged his shoulders and carefully touched the wires and connectors that made up the listening device as if it was a lump of shit he wanted to get rid of quickly. "I have never had to put one of these fuckers together, one of the lads does that. I don't know how it works."

Jazz sighed again; he had to stop making decisions without engaging his brain. "How fucking hard can it be?" he said as he grabbed the bits and pieces from Boomer.

They sat for half an hour working it out, and actually it wasn't difficult, thank God! It seemed to have been designed for idiots to use. Jazz put in the earpiece, which had a small microphone in it as well so he could whisper instructions to Boomer and Boomer could hear everything going on in the room. Boomer tested out whether Jazz could hear him talking, and that worked. After a few arguments, Boomer realised he must keep his voice very quiet when speaking otherwise he would deafen Jazz and alert everyone around him to their conversation. Tested now, Boomer reckoned the device had a pretty good distance of a mile or so. Jazz wasn't sure. He wanted him to get a bit closer to the house if he could, when the time was right.

Jazz said the first thing he needed to do was find out if there was a child being kept in the other room in the mirrored cottage Mad Pete looked around last night. He asked Boomer to listen out for a signal word of danger and to come and get him if he used it. The word, Jazz said, was 'help'.

Boomer looked at Jazz and said, "Help? That's not very fucking original, is it?" They both giggled.

Jazz realised that perhaps he hadn't thought this through very well. They had no backup for the child, if there was one in the cottage.

"Boomer, when I have gone, can you get Paula to be around here if she has found out the information on those names on the list? It would be good to know who they are and if she has found out anything of interest. You could contact me when I am in the house, but if I say, 'Stop' then stop talking because I need to concentrate on something or someone in the house. Does that make sense?"

Boomer agreed. It was getting fucking complicated. He would get Paula to join him if necessary, but not Ash. "I don't want Ash here, Jazz, he is a fucking politically-correct-and-all-that-bollocks police observer and we will get nothing done with him around."

Jazz agreed, but added, "Ash is gonna contact you with the names of any children missing in the surrounding areas. I need to know that too."

They still had some coffee from the lovely Milly, so they sat back and waited, and waited some more. A Tesco van went by, a posh Waitrose van went by, lots of small vans to do with boatyard services, or so it said on the side of the vans, and quite a number of cars went in and out. They watched a couple of cyclists pedalling like there was no tomorrow down Paglesham Road, but no van went to the mansion. Having stopped so many of them and knowing how people gossip, it wouldn't be long before someone told someone in the mansion that men were asking about them. Jazz hoped the delivery did come today because tomorrow would be too late. He needed to get into the cottage today to see if a child was being kept there.

They sat in the car, not only waiting for a lorry delivering to the mansion but also waiting to hear from Ash and Paula. Ash should ring as soon as he found out any details of any child reported missing in the surrounding areas. It was a big job, cross-referencing many police forces from Essex, Norfolk, Suffolk, Hertfordshire and London. Paula, meanwhile, was looking up the list of names Jazz had got from Mad Pete and finding out what she could about each one of them. Time was getting on and Jazz badly wanted some information. Today was the day to get Bateman and Simmonds, and every bit of ammunition was needed to get them. Jazz knew that Bateman was too clever to be caught easily. The bastard would have covered his tracks magnificently, but come hell or high water he, Jaswinder Singh, would get the fuckers for Kevin, if it was the last thing he ever did.

It was 12.30pm when a furniture van turned into Paglesham Road and was just building a little speed when the two men in front spotted, about one hundred yards in front of them, a man waving a police sign at them. The men pulled up, wondering what this was about. One thought it could be a check on road tax and insurance, but this was surely too quiet a road for that. As they stopped, they asked what was the matter. Each noted that the officers were not in police uniform, but they flashed their badges to confirm who they were.

In answer to Jazz's question, the driver said that yes, they were going to the mansion in Paglesham Road. They were delivering a bed. One of the men was in his fifties, Jazz reckoned, and the other one was a cocky-looking twenty-odd-year-old. A quick assessment of them both made Jazz decide to go with the older man and leave the younger one with Boomer. He didn't want to say in front of them both, but he told Boomer that the younger one would give the game away. He would never be able to act normal. He would either do a John Wayne impression and try and look hard, or try and show Jazz up as a laugh.

The situation was explained to the older one. Jazz would come with him as his helper and the other guy would wait here for his return. He tried to ask questions, to find out what was going on, but Jazz said that it was not his concern and he was to do what he usually did on a delivery and then go. Jazz would do whatever he was going to do. He would, he said, help him put the bed in place first. This didn't sit well with the older guy, but he accepted he was doing his duty for Queen and country. Jazz thought that sounded a bit steep, but the older man bought it so that was alright. He didn't want to tell the guy too much because he would get scared and he needed him to act naturally.

There were a few things to get settled before they took off to the mansion in the Beadells Boudoir Bedroom Furniture van. Jazz said he would find it hard not to giggle if asked who they were. The older man agreed it was a candy-arsed name but they paid his wages. He said it was a round bed they were delivering and carrying it would be tricky, and Jazz was to do whatever he said. Jazz agreed and pulled out of his pocket a flat cap and put it on his head, pulling the peak down, covering his face a little. Boomer started to laugh but Jazz reminded him that Simmonds had seen him and his bald bonce was pretty noticeable, and if Boomer thought he was going to wear a wig, he had another think coming!

Boomer told him he would be listening and to be fucking careful. Jazz, impatient by now, agreed quickly and told Roger, the older delivery man, that they had better get on their way. Jazz was to be called John for the time being, and that is what he would answer to. With a cheery wave to Boomer, who wasn't at all sure he liked what was about to happen, they set off for the three-mile journey to the mansion.

They had only got a mile up the road when Boomer spoke into Jazz's earpiece and told him to stop; he had some news. They pulled over – Boomer had heard from Ash.

"It ain't good, Jazz." Boomer sounded quiet, for him. "A six-year-old boy is missing in Hitchin, Hertfordshire. He was on his way home from school but he never reached home. His mother is a single parent and works, so he was to let himself in and she'd get home about an hour after he did. No one saw anything. The mother mentioned she had been seeing a wonderful man who adored her, but he worked long hours and could only come at the weekend. Ash showed her a picture of Simmonds and guess what?" Boomer answered his own question. "It was Simmonds. There is nothing to tie Simmonds to the boy being missing, but you, me and that fucking saint Ash know it was him. You've gotta find that boy, Jazz. His name is Archie, Archie Prentice."

Jazz nodded, and not wanting Roger the driver to comprehend anything, he suggested that perhaps Boomer might wish to speak to his friends in his area of work and ask if they wanted to come to the party.

"Tell them to bring presents with them."

Boomer confirmed he was asking for his team to

be alerted and to get themselves down here as quick as fuck, and to be armed. Jazz agreed that sounded very nice.

Boomer had been given a huge headache. This wasn't America. Getting guns wasn't easy; there were stacks of forms and reasons to be stated in order to get a gun and a few rounds. That was why Boomer always kept his own gun, just in case. It was his property; not exactly legal by Metropolitan Police standards, but up to now he hadn't had to use it. He reckoned today might be the day he needed it. He would wangle something. He got on to his team and organised them to come down. It might be a wild goose chase but it was better to be safe than sorry. He laughed to himself at such a sensible comment. Nothing he had ever been involved in with Jazz was safe, and he had always been sorry.

With a jovial cry from Jazz of, "OK, Roger the Dodger! Let's get on with this delivery", Roger, not entirely stupid, wondered what the hell was going on, but he knew better than to say anything. He wanted no trouble at all. He would make the delivery and get the hell out of it and leave this strange, mad and very un-policeman-like man to do whatever he was going to do.

They arrived at the gates to the mansion quite quickly and Jazz pulled his cap down a little to hide his face. Roger was feeling a bit chatty and said to Jazz, "Hey, look at that mark on the gates. This is a big van and every time I come here, I don't know why, but I seem to scrape that post."

Something went *ping* in Jazz's head. He looked at Roger as he spoke into the entryphone by the side of the gates and waited for his opportunity to ask. There wasn't much time to say anything, as the gates would be opening soon.

Quickly, Jazz asked, "Roger, how many times have you been here and what were you delivering?"

Roger thought for a moment, and Jazz pushed him to hurry up.

"I reckon," he mused, looking up at the sky, "in the two years I have worked for the company, I have been here three times."

Jazz needed more – what had he delivered?

Roger answered, "Oh, always the same bed, the big round bed, yes, identical. Strange, isn't it, that they change it so often? That's why I remember it, I deliver lots in this area but never that amount of beds to the same house."

Jazz urgently whispered to Boomer – did he get that?

Boomer grunted, "Yes."

Jazz said quickly, "Get Ash to contact the company and get dates, then check where those dates fall in relation to – "

Boomer finished the sentence "In relation to the boys."

Jazz answered quickly, "Spot on. Gotta go, gotta go."

Jazz knew he was pushing his luck talking on the surveillance device because suddenly there was a tap on the window. Jazz looked up and saw a monster of a man standing there, dressed in dungarees and a checked shirt with sleeves rolled up, showing muscle-bound arms the size of most men's thighs, and waiting for them to come in.

The house was enormous. A pretty modern mansion, but with six big windows facing the courtyard on the first floor. He could see the cottages – they looked newly restored, three to the left side of the house and what looked like two to the right, but Jazz knew that those had been made into one. It looked quite empty in the courtyard. He hoped he could slip in unnoticed.

Here we go, thought Jazz. Apart from finding the little boy, if he was there, he wasn't quite sure what the hell he was going to do or how he was going to do it. He felt a little excited and a little scared. The adrenaline was flowing and he needed to keep calm.

CHAPTER 22

Feet First and Brains Second

The guy walked ahead and waved the van in. He motioned a circle, which they took to mean he wanted the van to turn round so the back was facing the double cottage. He went up to the driver's window and nodded.

"Alright, mate? Can you put the bed by that cottage door?" He pointed to the double cottage. "Just leave it there, we will sort it out and get the unpacking done, no worries."

Roger nodded and got out of the van. Jazz got out too, and again pulled down his cap. He nodded to the big guy who was watching, and he nodded back. The big guy watched intently as Jazz and Roger got the huge double bed out. It was enormous and the base and mattress were really thick and heavy and difficult to move.

Roger, not happy with the useless git he had to work with, kept saying, "To me, to me, now turn left – no, no, left, you pillock! Gently does it. You go down backwards – don't drop it, idiot! That's it, now gently put down." Then he turned to the big guy and said, "You just can't get the staff these days, can you?"

The big guy laughed. Roger knew Jazz wanted some time to move away, so he asked the big guy if he might, perhaps, have a glass of water, as it was really hot work. Reluctantly, the big guy said for them to stay put, get back in the van and he would bring a glass of water for him.

Jazz was really impressed. "Cheers, Roger, you are my main man. Brilliant thinking, Batman!" He slipped away.

Roger wasn't impressed. He wanted Jazz as far away from him as possible. When the big guy returned with his water he told him that Jazz was sulking in the back of the van for being told he was a useless tosser. The big guy laughed at that and Roger gulped the water, thanked him, gave the glass back and gunned the van and reversed out. He was relieved to be on Paglesham Road, heading back to pick up his guy and get back to the store's yard.

When he got back and picked up his lad, he had a quick debrief with Boomer, although there wasn't much he could tell him. The main thing was that he had left John (Jazz) skulking somewhere in the mansion's grounds. Boomer thanked them both and they went on their way. Boomer had heard everything through the microphone secreted in the earpiece, and he whispered to Jazz that he was to tell him where he was when he could. At least the surveillance equipment was working, which made a change. Now Boomer would just have to wait. He lit a cigarette and waited for his lads to arrive.

Paula rang him and went through the list of names. It would appear they all were men working in government, banking and the church. All had good positions in these areas. Boomer reckoned they had been protected for quite some time. Paula said there was no known information on any of them in the paedophile network. None were known on the websites, not even on sites that could not be accessed through search engines like Google. Paula said they appeared whiter than white. She was on her way to Paglesham. It was going to get very crowded in that small parking area.

Boomer related this information to Jazz in succinct, clear words. All on the list were not known in any area as paedophiles.

He got a very quiet "OK" back from Jazz. Thankfully the bloody earpiece was working. The range was pretty good and that might be because the land was flat and there was nothing in the way between where he was and the house where Jazz was. Boomer wasn't happy; this was a dangerous situation with only a flimsy earpiece as Jazz's safety net.

Well, it was easy to hide away behind the two cottages and Jazz found a nice little niche in some bushes that couldn't be seen from the courtyard. He stayed there until two big guys had put the bed inside, faffed about and then left.

While he waited he looked around. He couldn't see any CCTV cameras anywhere, which surprised him. On second thoughts, he reckoned they didn't need it, and perhaps they didn't want too many cameras watching what they were doing. He looked around – this area was overgrown with bushes and a couple of trees. He found a suitable little space resting his back against a tree with the bushes in front hiding him – perfect.

Relaxed for the moment, he took the opportunity to have a little drink from his flask. It was lunchtime anyway, he told himself. He wouldn't drink too much. There were things to do and he wanted to find the boy. He looked at the double cottage and sighed – he hoped the boy was in there. A quick in-and-out and arrest the lot of them would suit him fine. *But*, he thought, *it ain't gonna happen*. When was anything that easy? Never! He had another swig from his flask; he needed it.

When he heard the door close and the footsteps of two pairs of feet crunching heavily across the courtyard, he got up carefully and moved forward cautiously until he could just see them enter the mansion.

He whispered, "Boomer, I am going to try and get into the double cottage through the back door." Boomer acknowledged he had heard him.

The back door was, luckily, unlocked. Out in the

middle of nowhere he supposed everyone felt safe. *They would have it bolted, alarmed and with CCTV everywhere if they were in East London*, he thought ruefully. He could feel his heart thumping loudly as he eased his way into the huge room. Just as Mad Pete had said, it was wall-to-wall mirrors. It was fucking frightening to see himself in every direction. There was nowhere to hide in this room. The bed had been placed against the middle of the back wall, and he looked up and saw the ceiling had mirrors too.

There was something very uncomfortable and unpleasant about the room. Then he saw what it was that was spooking him. On the floor near the wall to either side of the bed was a low post, and attached to these were chains and manacles. The floor was carpeted in a thick and expensive pile. The sort of carpet you could almost bounce on, it was so thick and tight. There were cameras set up in each corner, and just as Jazz was about to panic he saw they were not plugged in. Movable cameras? He could see why they would want that; better pictures of the action.

The feeling of discomfort grew stronger. It was strange, and Jazz had never felt like this before. This cottage had seen some vile and wicked actions, he reckoned; he could feel it in the walls. He wondered if this was what had spooked Mad Pete. There wasn't another room; the whole ground floor was one big studio.

Disappointed and at a loss as to what to do, he stood and considered what to do next. He whispered to Boomer, describing what the room looked like, and as he looked around he saw a wooden door, a bit like the ones you have as your six-foot garden gate, with one of those lift-up latches to open it. He lifted the latch, and when the door opened he saw stairs. Feeling elated, he quietly climbed the stairs, making sure he closed the wooden door behind him. Someone might come back to the cottage. He wondered whether he had shut the back door and for a moment he wasn't sure, but yes, he had, so downstairs looked as it should.

The staircase was winding and tight. He climbed slowly and carefully. He couldn't hear anything. At the top it opened on to a small hallway. He could see two doors off the dark hallway and crept towards one of the doors, and as he walked the old wooden floor creaked. He held his breath, stopped and listened, but nothing stirred. In that moment, reality kicked in and he realised he was trespassing on private property. If caught, the best that could happen was he could be arrested, and the worst could be that they would finish him off. They were murderers and paedophiles, so unlikely to offer him a cup of tea and a telling-off. It wasn't a hot day but suddenly he felt wet with sweat. He wiped the stinging droplets from his eyes. Blinking hard, he told himself to buck up and get on with it. He had a little boy to find. This helped.

He tried the first door and this turned out to be a small bathroom with a toilet. He carefully closed the door and went to the next one. He opened it carefully and put his head cautiously around the door.

He spotted the unmade bed and bits and pieces that seemed to make up a child's room. He sidled into the room, which was nearly as big as the ground floor. He quietly closed the door and looked around. There was no child in here. But it was obviously a child's room, and by the look of it, it had been used recently. He found most of the toys that were out were boys' toys. In a toy box he found lots of dolls and things that girls would play with, but those on the floor and on the bed were all boys' toys. Some pyjamas were on the bed and they seemed to be for a boy – the age on the tag said *8–10 years*, which could fit a child of Archie's age.

Was he putting two and two together and making five, he asked himself? You can always make the crap fit. He needed to be objective. Then he picked up a crayon drawing, and written in the corner was the name Archie. *Bugger*, thought Jazz, *it has to be true*. But where was Archie? He wasn't here. He relayed this to Boomer, who told him to get the hell out and they would think again. Jazz was in the compound and had no intention of leaving without finding out if Archie was anywhere in the buildings, and what was happening with the list.

Jazz rang Mad Pete, who thankfully answered. He was outside having a fag, and was alone.

"Where are you?" whispered Jazz

"I'm having a fag in the garden, Mr Singh. Mr Singh, don't ring me, it's too dangerous for me. You will get me killed. I thought you were gonna come and get me out of here?" Mad Pete was beginning to panic.

"Calm down, Pete, I am here now." Jazz hoped that would make him feel safer, but it had the opposite effect.

"Oh my God! Mr Singh, you are gonna get me killed. Where are you? No, don't tell me, I don't wanna know. Just don't do anything that will get me killed, please," pleaded Mad Pete, who was getting more and more agitated.

"Fucking calm down, Pete. I am not going to get you into trouble. I just need you to do something for me. It's not much to ask, you just need to use your immense skills."

Mad Pete didn't like the sound of such praise, it usually meant trouble. He was seriously scared. Everything had been cushy for him here. They liked him and appreciated his skills in getting drugs and equipment easily. This was a very different place for him; he liked it. He had even had a wash. Now he had Mr Singh on his back and he knew he would have to do what he asked, and it would be dangerous. If he could have run he would have, but out in the middle of all this land and with no buses, he had nowhere to go.

Resigned to his fate for the moment, although he would always keep his options open to finding a way to save his skin, he said, "What do you want me to do, Mr Singh?"

Jazz told Mad Pete he was in the double cottage at the moment, and upstairs. He said he must have heard the boy that they now thought to be Archie Prentice, a six-year-old who was going to be very scared and wanting to go home. No one knew what had been done to him yet.

"Oh no, Mr Singh, don't say such things. I don't like it," whined Mad Pete.

"So, Pete, it looks like he was in this room at some point, but he ain't here now. I need you to look in the mansion to see if he is there. Can you do that now and let me know as soon as possible?"

Mad Pete started to moan and panic about not being able to do that, and how Mr Singh was going to get him killed and how he couldn't just go into the mansion because he wasn't an indoor person. Jazz cut him short.

"Look, Pete, stop pissing around. If that little lad is in there we need to get him out and make him safe. Now you know that makes sense. I don't want you to rescue him or do anything dangerous. Just tell me if he is in the house and where he is, *capisce*?"

"That bloody word again, Mr Singh – *capisce*? It's not fucking English!"

"Just do it, Pete, and ring me immediately. Any news on that list you gave me?"

Mad Pete thought for a second. "Oh yes, Mr Singh. They are all coming to the mansion tonight for a party. Oh fuck! Do you think that's to do with the boy?"

"I so fucking do, Pete. We have got to move quickly. Something not nice is gonna happen if we don't stop it. Now go. You will think of something, you are good at that."

Just as Jazz was going to flick the mobile off, he saw

he was down to only a few bars of power. He forgot to charge it. "Shit, Pete, don't be long, my fucking phone is gonna let me down soon."

"Jeez! OK, Mr Singh. I'll do it now but you ain't fair and you ain't giving me much time."

Jazz told him to shut up and get on with it, and then made his way quickly but quietly out of the cottage and back to the bushes. He closed all the doors and made sure it didn't look like anyone had been in there. His timing was immaculate; the two heavies came out of the mansion and back towards the cottage. They were carrying some chairs and a small table. He watched them as they joked with each other and chatted about a pint later in the Plough & Sail. They made a couple of trips for more chairs and then they were gone.

Jazz took the opportunity of another swig from his flask. He needed something to keep him focused. It tasted smooth and gave an exquisite kick to his brain cells. He was certain it helped him think.

He whispered to Boomer what was happening and how he was waiting for Mad Pete. Boomer had heard everything and grunted his acknowledgement. He grumbled that to have a mobile with hardly any power was bloody stupid. He reminded Jazz to put it on silent.

"You don't want the fucking thing to ring while you're hiding, do you, fuck-face?" He did say that the surveillance system had been crystal-clear but every now and then it hiccuped, so he hoped it would all be over soon, before it crashed.

This was not what Jazz wanted to hear. Under his breath he urged Mad Pete to, "Come on, come on, tell me what I need to know."

Sitting in the bushes, desperate for a cigarette and having another swig from his flask, Jazz had time on his hands as he waited. He had come rushing in like the cavalry; he had Boomer's team coming to Paglesham all tooled up, and Paula too. All this commotion and now he didn't know what he was going to do next. It all felt stupid, and looking up at the sky, it was threatening to fucking rain at any time. All that adrenaline had got up and gone. Jazz sat, thinking. He had to get into the big house somehow.

This was fucking stupid. Boomer had allowed that arsehole of a detective to go into a dangerous situation without proper backup and without any proper authority. *What's new?* he thought, but it didn't make it right. They were murderers of children, so what made Jazz think they wouldn't murder him if they caught him? He felt uneasy with no one to call on immediately to help if necessary. He hoped his lads would get here quickly.

He got out of the car for some air, stretched and looked around. The road went through an area of fields full of corn ripening. Despite the odd roof in the distance, the farmland seemed to have taken over Paglesham. He saw a pheasant run out of the cornfield into the road. He liked pheasants, beautiful birds with multicoloured plumage; he had shot many and eaten them. He wished he had his shotgun with him; he could have bagged a few, and the place seemed full of rabbits too. He liked the countryside; it felt normal and proper. Still, he wasn't here for a shoot – *well, not yet anyway*, he thought grimly.

The car phone rang – it was Paula. There was more news he needed to tell Jazz. Paula had gone through the list and found out some interesting information. With Jazz hiding in a bush waiting for something to happen, Boomer relayed what Paula had found out and it made for riveting listening.

"Jazz, I am whispering although I know you are arse-deep in mud behind the cottage. James Bond you ain't, my man." At that Boomer laughed and had to get some control on the giggles that wouldn't subside.

Jazz had to smile: *arse-deep in mud*. He took a look to make sure he wasn't sitting in a muddy spot.

"So, the list contains some very interesting characters who are whiter than white, you know that, but Paula has just heard from one of her team and it's a doozy! One of the guys on the list has shown his petticoat. He's a judge and he has proven connections with Simmonds. It looked tenuous at first but they have hacked into a new site and it shows their connection is a strong one. It would appear they have spoken recently on what they thought was a secure internet site. The language was vaguely coded but Paula said her team knew the language they used and were able to unscramble the conversations. They were talking about children and abusive situations."

Jazz grunted; he had heard everything Boomer had said.

Boomer continued. "I am throwing this in as a wild card but it would appear that Bateman is whiter than white because Simmonds does everything. He must pay that bloody fucker a huge amount of dosh to get him to do all the dirty work."

Again Jazz grunted a response. He was thinking. "Is there any way of finding out if they are all coming to this party tonight, here at the mansion?" he asked. Then, with disgust, Jazz added, "Those names on the list, a potential child held here, and I wonder if Nekisha might well have been involved too if we hadn't saved her. It sounds like they are going to have a child fest."

Boomer acknowledged what he heard by saying, "Fucking bastards! I am on it now, over and sodding out."

He got on to Paula immediately. She said she would get the office to work on it as a matter of urgency. She hoped she might have something to tell him when she arrived. She was on her way to Paglesham. Boomer wasn't normally a fan of women at work but Paula was the dog's nuts at what she did and now she had Boomer's sacred approval.

When he had finished talking to Paula he called up his lads and asked, "Where the fuck are you all, and did you get a decent car and tooled up?"

They confirmed they had just got the guns after a lot of meaningful discussions. Boomer laughed at this. His lads knew his way of working and although they were considered a cocky, loud-mouthed bunch by other teams in the station, they were given the respect they were due for getting the job done.

DCI Radley would be burning the mobile phone wires later, Boomer was told. He was gunning for the whole team now. He let them have guns after a long process of discussions, but he was not a happy bunny.

The team would be with Boomer in about an hour. *What fucking good lads are they?* thought a very impressed Boomer. His last comment before he let them go was, "Don't forget to bring me a Big Mac and fries. I am in the middle of fucking nowhere and we might not eat for the rest of the day. A coffee would help too."

With a "Yes, guv" they signed off and prepared to go to Paglesham.

Boomer quickly made a call to the office. He got hold of a duty sergeant he worked well with and had a quick chat. He wanted someone else to know what the fuck was going on at Paglesham in case they crashed the party later. When everything seemed to be in place, he needed to get back to Jazz.

He picked up the surveillance microphone and told him, "The lads are on their way and so is Paula. The lads have guns and will be ready to assist when necessary. Are you still arse-deep in mud?"

Jazz squirmed, uncomfortable now in this patch of dampness near the mansion. "I am losing the use of my legs here but OK for the moment. Will text Mad Pete in a minute to find out where the fuck he is. I need to get moving soon."

Boomer acknowledged with, "OK, but don't do anything stupid – well, not just yet anyway. Let the lads get here first. Oh, by the way – a Waitrose van has just passed me. Wonder if it's for you or someone in the village? Stay where you are just in case."

It didn't take long before the Waitrose van appeared by the gates and the driver pressed the intercom to be allowed in. Jazz saw this and stood up. He thanked the gods for their help. He knew what he was going to do.

He waited until the Waitrose van was parked in the courtyard and the driver was talking to one of the heavies who came out. The driver followed the heavy into the house, and this was Jazz's opportunity to run up to the back of the van. He opened the doors and got inside and prepared himself.

The driver was alone now. He opened the back doors to the van and nearly jumped out of his skin when he saw Jazz, who was flashing his detective badge and motioning him to be quiet. Jazz whispered to the frightened man that he needed his help to get him into the house, and then the man was to forget him and just do the delivery and go.

The man nodded his head far too much and was obviously scared, but a little interested too. "Do you want to help carry boxes to the kitchen?"

Jazz nodded and said he would like to act as his helper, and his name was John. The man said OK, and that John could call him Guv. Jazz almost laughed but this was going well so far. Just as they were talking the heavy came up to the van doors and asked what was happening.

Guv, now into this, said, "John, I told you I wanted those boxes over there." He pointed to a stack of boxes on the right-hand side of the van, tied down with ropes so they didn't move. "Be careful when you carry them, it's expensive champagne in there."

Jazz nodded and said, "Yes, Guv."

The heavy nodded, not recognising Jazz, who had taken his hat off, and said he would wait in the kitchen for them. When he had gone, Guv told Jazz how many boxes needed to go in. Guv looked at his list and said there were six boxes of champagne, two boxes of assorted other drink, and four boxes of food. It took them both about fifteen minutes to get the boxes into a storeroom adjoining the kitchen. Jazz kept his head down but the heavy didn't seem interested in what they were doing. He stayed in the kitchen.

Jazz asked Guv to say that John had gone back to the van to lock up when the heavy came into the storeroom and checked the boxes against the invoice. Jazz had seen a downstairs utility room next to the storeroom, and he hid himself in there. When it went quiet and Guv had gone back to the Waitrose van and the heavy had closed the storeroom and left, Jazz breathed deeply. He hadn't realised that he had barely breathed while listening to Guv and the heavy leave.

OK, he was inside the mansion, but what the fuck was he to do now, he wondered? He whispered to Boomer, "I am in the mansion."

Boomer acknowledged with a grunt and replied, "You bloody idiot. You were told to wait. Be careful in there, and don't forget to say 'help' if you need me to come in."

It occurred to Jazz that if he needed help, Boomer was too far away to be much good, but he wasn't going to need help, was he? No, he was going to find little Archie.

Before he left the utility room, he rang Mad Pete. He didn't get a reply so he was going to have to go it alone.

The little hallway that led off to the storeroom and the utility room seemed to be full of doors. One looked like a back door; another, he thought, led to the kitchen. He could hear muffled voices coming from the kitchen. He wondered if it was the two heavies, but he also caught a woman's voice. There was the door they came in through from the hall, and another door which was unknown. He gently opened it, thinking it might be a cupboard, but it was a cellar door; he could see steps leading down. This was a maze of a house, and for the moment he wondered what to do. He heard scraping of chairs in the kitchen, and feet – whoever was in there was on the move. He stood on the top step of the cellar stairs and pulled the door closed.

Sure enough, the kitchen door opened and he heard the two heavies spill out, talking and laughing and, he thought, heading for the front door. The woman shouted from the hallway and seemed to follow the men. It sounded like they all went out the front door, and he waited for a few minutes and heard nothing.

This was all worrying; he felt like a climber hanging on the edge of a precipice – anything could happen and everything was dangerous. He looked at his watch: it was now 3pm and time was getting on. Jazz again had no idea where he was or where he could go safely, but he needed to find Archie soon. He needed to remember he was doing this for Kevin too, and any other kiddies that had been in Bateman's grasp.

He opened the cellar door slightly and peered around it; all seemed still and quiet. He headed towards the kitchen. He figured the help was outside and whoever owned this fancy mansion wouldn't step into the kitchen – they would pull one of those bell thingies he had seen on those programmes on the television, calling for staff to come and answer them. The kitchen was a huge room. It had the biggest, thickest farmhouse table Jazz had ever seen in the middle. Although the mansion was a fairly new house, it was built in a traditional style and the kitchen was bigger than the top floor of Mrs Chodda's house.

With no time, he needed to find somewhere to hide if someone came in. There was a walk-in larder that would do, but he hoped to get further than the kitchen – he wanted to get upstairs and look around. He whispered to Boomer where he was, and tried calling Mad Pete again from the walk-in larder. The fucker was still not answering. Jazz was building to a state of frustration, anger and sheer fear. He had to get a grip.

The cavalry arrived. Six of Boomer's team of detectives in two cars. Close behind was Paula, and *Yea gods! She's brought bloody Ash with her*, thought Boomer.

First of all he welcomed his lads. He took a look at them and got the three who were wearing jeans and T-shirts to go to the Plough & Sail, get a beer and sit and wait. He told them to make one beer last; he didn't want them worse for wear if something happened and they were needed urgently. The story Boomer wanted them to have was that they were looking around for a boat to hire at the weekend for a fishing trip. He warned them to look out for shitface Gary, who was known to be as slippery as a handful of eels in a bucket of snot. He didn't tell them that Gary had got the better of him and Jazz last time they were here. He said he wanted them ready and if he rang they should move themselves quicker than fucking lightning. No one was to know they were police.

There started an argument – the other three detectives thought it unfair that they were not chosen to sit in the Plough & Sail and drink beer; they could do that just as well.

Boomer looked at them. "You are wearing suits, you numb-nuts – who the fuck is going to think you want to go fishing?" He added, "I need to thin you lot out. If any of the guests," and he said this with disgust, "start to arrive and they see all of us here, they will suspect something. There will be drinks all round when this is over. Now bugger off and do some work!"

The three officers got in the car and pulled faces at the other three detectives, who were scowling at them.

"Bloody kids, the lot of them," was Boomer's response to Paula's look of disbelief, "but they are bloody good at what they do, they are my boys."

Paula nodded at this. She knew they were all little Boomers – *And God help the lot of us*, she thought.

The other three officers were told to take the car further down the road and park in the lane near the sewage works. They looked surly and disgusted with their lot, but off they went. Boomer said the same to them: to be ready for his instructions. He shouted his thanks as they left for the McDonald's and coffee they'd brought him. He laughed with pride.

"Them boys are just great!"

Now that was settled, Boomer turned and looked at Ash. "Now, why the fuck are you here?"

Ash raised his eyebrows at such a warm welcome and started to fiddle with the file in his hand. Boomer raised his hands impatiently. "No, no, don't do that, Ash, just fucking tell me. I don't want it read word for word. Just say it, man!"

It was not how Ash liked to work; he liked to quote and show the evidence to back up his thoughts. "Well, actually, I needed to leave the station today. Something odd and very worrying has happened again."

Boomer pushed his face forward and nodded, egging him on. Ash was a little flustered at the size of this man in front of him, pushing him to get on with it.

"My paperwork for this case has all been stolen. I

permit myself a hard copy of the whole case file, it's easier to refer to when out and about. I know it should stay on the computer only so there is no paperwork, but that is not my way. Anyway, I came in this morning and my locked drawer had been opened and all the paperwork taken. The CCTV in the room didn't pick up anything. It's trained on Jazz's computer and desk, not mine."

Boomer listened and screwed up his face in disbelief. "Who the fuck has done that?" he asked.

They discussed when the drawer was locked and Ash told Boomer that because of what was happening he had copied the file and kept it at his home. He knew that was against police policy but these were difficult times. Boomer looked again at Saint Ash, hardly believing he would go against police policy. He laughed and slapped Ash on the back, telling him there was hope for him yet.

Ash added that the file had been erased from the AWARE system too. DCI Radley had got the IT man in again, and this time it wasn't erased from Jazz's computer; it was another hot-desk computer. It had to be someone who knew how the system worked. Not many would know how to erase anything on the AWARE system. Once put on AWARE, it was set in stone. It just couldn't be anyone associated with Bateman. To get in and out of Ilford Police Station wasn't easy if you didn't have the right pass, and you had to know how the system worked. Someone knew there was CCTV trained on Jazz's computer, otherwise they would surely have used his computer again.

Boomer looked at Paula. "Is anyone on that list anything to do with the police and police stations?"

It was a good point, and Paula looked at the list and said apart from two lawyers, who worked privately but may have accessed a police station as a brief for a prisoner, there was no one else. Boomer asked her to check out the two lawyers. It seemed a long shot. They wouldn't know the AWARE system, would they?

Ash continued. "Anyway, I thought it best to leave the station and come here with the only paperwork we have on this case. It's your backup and proof of what has been happening. You might need something because when DCI Radley has sorted out the computer breach he is gonna be gunning for you and Jazz."

Ash had his own agenda for the day. "I want to take a car and go to the bed place. I couldn't get any help on the phone so I reckon it'll be easier if I go there now. It's in Southend, which isn't far away, and then I will come back. Every bit of information will be helpful."

"Also, I have something else. I got the traffic police to check their cameras and Simmonds' number plate. I wanted to place him in the vicinity of the missing boys. It all tallies up. His car travelled to Hertfordshire, Suffolk and I reckon we have enough evidence to say he was in the areas when the boys disappeared."

Boomer patted Ash on the back; he was earning his money.

"We are gonna get these bastards, it's all stacking up well," was Boomer's triumphant response.

While Paula got on the car phone to the station

about the two lawyers, Ash asked why, judging by all the evidence stacking up and the possibility of a child being held in the house, they hadn't all gone in and just got a search warrant for Archie.

Boomer told him that there was more to it. They had no evidence at all that Archie was in there for a search warrant to be issued. Jazz had found evidence of toys and clothes in the cottage that showed Archie was there but Jazz had illegally entered the property. He added that he and Jazz didn't want to spook any of them yet; there was more going on. While they were looking for Archie, there was the list of twelve respected and high-up officials who were expected to arrive tonight for a meeting to consider too. Boomer said that it was more than just a question of getting Archie; it was about finding a highly influential and clever paedophile ring, and what else they had been involved in. To date they couldn't touch Bateman or the twelve, but tonight they should get them all.

So, Ash asked, where was Jazz, and how was this being handled? The explanation that he had got himself hidden in the house didn't go down too well, and after a ten-minute harangue about police procedures being breached, Ash said he was worried. There was something not right in all of this. If Bateman and Simmonds had any idea about the investigation, Jazz would be in mortal danger. Bateman had protected himself all these years and was considered a saint in Paglesham and the surrounding areas; he wasn't about

222

to lose that to some interfering, off-the-wall detective from London.

Ash took off in Paula's car to get the information about the beds and delivery dates. He was mad as hell and wouldn't take any nonsense from the shop. He said he would be back in an hour to see what was happening with Jazz.

Thanks to Ash's talk about the possibility that Bateman and Simmonds could know about the police interest, Boomer was getting a bit worried about what was happening with Jazz in the mansion. If the police system had been compromised they would know everything the police were doing. It was all in the paperwork; addresses and the list of names had been put on the AWARE system. It was a confidential, secure system, for God's sake, thought Boomer, but he got on to the surveillance system and whispered to Jazz to be very careful in case they had been rumbled.

He added, "Don't forget to say 'help' if you get into trouble. My lads are here and we will get there in a flash."

Just as Boomer said that, the surveillance system crashed.

CHAPTER 23

Risks and Revelations

Jazz heard the blank silence that meant the earpiece was no longer working. Thank God for his phone, he thought, and checked it. It looked like it was about to expire, with hardly any charge showing. *Damn and bugger,* was the best he could think of. He had to get on and leave the comparative safety of the walk-in larder and get himself upstairs. He couldn't hear anything, and hoped the people were in the cottage across the way, looking at the bed. He left the larder, picked up a tea towel and walked purposefully out of the kitchen into the hall. No one was around, and he went up the stairs quietly but quickly. If anyone saw him, he would say he was the kitchen help and see where that got him. He was an idiot, he knew that, but he had to get upstairs and he was no James Bond.

The landing of the upper floor had many doors off it, and he was spoilt for choice. There was another staircase he saw off the landing, and he presumed it led to the attic rooms. It would seem sensible to hide a boy up there, especially if you had delivery people putting stuff near the kitchen. It would be quieter up there.

He didn't wait to think it through; he headed for the next staircase to the attic rooms. Time was getting on, and he couldn't hang around for much longer. The stairs creaked as he climbed them. Why stairs always creaked, he didn't know, and he was feeling a bit spooked at being so far into the house and not knowing where anyone was. If anyone came out of the rooms they would see him straight away; there was nowhere to hide at present.

At the top of the stairs there were, once again, doors everywhere. He had the choice of four doors, and with no idea what was behind any one of them, he opened the first one. He was bloody lucky; he peered into the room, which was darkened by drawn curtains, and he saw the outline of a young lad lying on the bed. He tiptoed in and up to the bed and shook the boy; he didn't stir at all. He felt urgently for a pulse on his neck and found a strong one. Jazz exhaled heavily. The boy was alive. Looking at him, he could see he was heavily sedated. He expected they wanted him quiet and relaxed until they needed him to be awake. The thought made him feel sick. He had a very good idea what they intended to do with him.

Frustrated now, he needed to tell someone. He spoke quietly, hoping against hope that the earpiece was working again, but he got no response. He took his mobile phone out and tried to ring Boomer, but the screen stayed black: it had run out of power. He nearly threw the mobile at the wall in temper, but controlled himself. He needed to find Mad Pete to help him.

He left the boy – he was sure it was Archie; *same age and who else could it be?* He asked himself. He crept along the corridor and listened through the next door, and heard what sounded like Mad Pete's cough, quiet but thick and deep, and it always made Jazz feel sick when he heard it. He opened the next door slightly to peer in.

The figure in the room turned and stared at him in shock. It was Mad Pete. Just as Jazz was going to whisper, *Where the bloody hell have you been?*, he saw another figure beside Mad Pete.

Quickly going into humble mode, Jazz mumbled, "Sorry, Sir, the lady told me to come and collect some glasses. Is this the right room, Sir?"

Mad Pete stood open-mouthed, and the other figure moved forward into Jazz's clear line of sight. It was Bateman.

"I don't know who you are, but 'the lady' hasn't employed anyone to help in the house to my knowledge, so I presume you are a ne'er-do-well in my home." With that Bateman got on the phone and just said, "Here, now."

Within minutes the heavies bounded up the stairs and before Jazz could think clearly on what to do next, they had grabbed him. One of the heavies recognised Jazz as the helper from Waitrose; the other said no, he was the helper from the bed company. Now they knew he was there to cause trouble, but what trouble?

Jazz whispered, "Help," in the desperate hope that the surveillance equipment might begin to work again, but there was still the heavy silence in his ear.

Bateman made another call and in a short time Simmonds entered the room and immediately recognised Jazz. The heavies tied Jazz up and gagged him, and angry now at being shown up as rubbish security, gave him a few swift punches to his face. His eye swelled almost immediately and the blood trickling from his nose and mouth collected on the gag across his mouth, turning the dirty piece of material bright red. They left him on the floor and went to discuss what the fuck they were going to do with him. Now they knew he was with the police, they wanted to know if anyone else knew he was here, and who he had brought with him. Jazz felt that sickening, heavy weight in his stomach. He was done for and no one knew he was in trouble, except Mad Pete, and that depressed him even further.

Bateman and Simmonds left Mad Pete to go off and talk together on what was happening and what they should do. Mad Pete, when they had left, returned to see Jazz. He was now in quite a state and worried for his own safety.

"Mr Singh, what the fuck are you doing here? They will kill you."

Jazz made noises and jerked enough for Mad Pete to know he was saying he had to untie his hands and legs.

Panicking now, Mad Pete whined, "I can't let you go, Mr Singh, they will kill me and that's not fair."

The muffled noises from Jazz were getting quite loud and urgent, and his jerking around grew frantic. Mad Pete could see Jazz was mad as hell.

"I'm sorry, Mr Singh, I've gotta go." And he left.

Jazz, now tired and worn out with the jerking around, quietened down and lay still. He was thinking on what to do next. The surveillance wasn't working, so Boomer hadn't heard any of this; he was fucked.

Mad Pete returned with Simmonds in a short while. They looked like bosom buddies, thought Jazz, depressed. Mad Pete went up to Jazz and kicked him in the stomach, which hurt like hell.

"Yes, Mr Simmonds, I can tell you he is Detective Sergeant Singh from Barking nick. He is a bloody pain in the neck and hated not only by the likes of me, but his police officers too. It would give me great pleasure to top him. He has messed up many little transactions I have undertaken in London. He is the bloody bane of my life – I hoped by coming here I could get away from him and work in peace and quiet, Mr Simmonds."

Mad Pete looked quite excited, and was obviously enjoying this. He gave Jazz another swift kick for good measure. It caught him in the chest and Jazz gasped for breath, feeling like he would never breathe again. It took a minute or so for him to breathe normally once more.

Jazz wondered what the fuck he was going on about. Simmonds asked a good question: "So is your being here why we have Singh messing around here?"

Mad Pete hadn't thought of that, but replied, quite

quickly, "Could be, Mr Simmonds, could be. There is no love lost between us. He has screwed me many times. But what I can tell you, Mr Simmonds, is he is most probably here alone. No one will work with the fucker, he is off the wall and has a reputation for getting officers killed. I bet no one knows where he is – go on, ask him, Mr Simmonds." Mad Pete was insistent.

Simmonds ripped off the gag, and for good measure kicked Jazz in the arm and asked the question.

Jazz, hurting, mad as hell, shouted, with spittle coming out of his mouth, "I have the fucking whole of bloody Barking nick waiting outside to get you, arsehole! There will be vans, cars and tanks, officers with shooters outside, waiting to get you all."

Simmonds' forehead creased in thought for a moment; then quickly changed to lines of laughter. "You are the arsehole, Singh, if you think I haven't checked outside – there is no one and nothing out there. I have your mobile and it's dead, you stupid tosser! So obviously no one knows you are here. You are dead meat, Singh."

Jazz enjoyed the double bluff but his whole body felt limp with concern – what the fuck was going to happen? Mad Pete, looking as if he was enjoying himself, asked if he could top Mr Singh because it would make him feel good, but Simmonds said no. Smiling again, Simmonds looked at Jazz and said to him and Mad Pete that Singh would be dealt with and buried somewhere no one would ever find him. With that, Simmonds told Mad Pete to come and help him prepare something.

When the door closed Jazz wondered if Mad Pete was just getting his own back on Jazz for all the years of control he'd had over him, or whether he was playing a good game and trying to help him. Jazz reckoned he was too stupid to be that clever and he was going to help get him killed. Mad Pete was a miserable little flea-infested rat of the first order. He would do anything to save his miserable, skinny, stinking, bony arse. The thought was bloody depressingly useless, and it filled him with no hope for him or poor Archie next door. Jazz started to wriggle and squirm violently with an energy that only the thought of imminent death could conjure up.

CHAPTER 24

What a Mess

The three officers arrived at the Plough & Sail and were to be undercover until called on the radio by Boomer. The pub was old and a typically pretty little country place, with baskets of flowers outside hanging from the stone walls and tables with umbrellas for visitors to sit and sup and enjoy the fresh air and tranquillity of Paglesham village. Most locals stayed inside whatever the weather. They darkly hoped that *them there city folks* would keep out of their hair and sit in the sun outside.

The inside of the pub was small, and the height felt challenging but you were alright if you were no more than six feet, four inches tall. Most locals were not that tall. It was full of old wood, and knick-knacks of pipes and pots from an age when these things were used and valued. The old wooden bar had seen better days but it was polished with pride, and although gnarled and pitted with years of use, it shined with beeswax polish.

The three officers found a vacant table and sat

down. They looked around at the smattering of men of all shapes and sizes, but most had seen fifty years and more. They were given a look and then the men returned to their dominoes, or talking and supping of beer. One man seemed quite interested in them. He gave them a smile and a nod, and their returned smile and nod seemed to be the invitation he needed to scrape back his chair and come over to their table.

He introduced himself as Gary, and he observed that they were new to this area. They had been warned about Gary, so listened cautiously as he chatted away about Paglesham, and on hearing they were looking for a fishing boat to hire, talked about his boat being available.

Gary knew they were not fishermen; they hadn't a clue about fishing. They didn't know the terminology of rods and reels. He knew who they were. It was something about their demeanour, their way of talking, and how they looked around, clocking each and every person in the pub. Gary had sat himself down at their table and he leaned forward and whispered that he knew they were TBL. They decided he knew too much and asked him to keep it to himself, explaining that they were undercover. He made the 'O' sign with his mouth and nodded conspiratorially.

One said, quite jovially, "So, 'TBL' is the thin blue line, meaning we are police, is that what you meant?"

Gary shook his head and said, "No." Again he leaned forward and whispered, "It means the thick blue line – you are a load of tossers if you think you can walk into my pub and not be spotted. All police are thick and you ain't getting the better of anyone here."

The trio were not best pleased and wanted to take him outside and teach him some manners, but they couldn't draw attention to themselves. They were not a happy bunch. Gary, pleased with the effect he'd had on them, suggested, congenial now, that they might like to try a pint of Wallasea Wench.

"It's a tasty beer that will give you a good kick in the bollocks, but be careful, you townies couldn't cope with more than two."

They all decided that Gary was a fucking bugger and they would watch him. Needless to say, they all tried a Wallasea Wench and spent a pleasant few hours trying to make it last. Walkers crisps did very well that day. The table was covered with empty cheese & onion and salt & vinegar packets.

The bloody surveillance shit wasn't working and now Boomer didn't know what to do next. He wasn't happy he couldn't contact Jazz or hear what was going on.

DC Ash Kumar returned from the bed shop quite quickly. He had sorted out all the purchases. He told Boomer that six beds had been ordered over the past two years from Beadells Boudoir Beds. Apparently they were the same round beds, from their luxurious selection. No bedding was bought at the same time. Most purchasers of beds also bought their exclusive linen and satin bedding, but Mr Bateman never did.

The beds were very expensive so Mr Bateman was a special customer for them. On being asked, the bed shop confirmed that they didn't take the old beds away; apparently Mr Bateman had got rid of them.

Ash asked the question, "It's a big house, so many beds would be needed, surely?" He was told that they were always delivered to the door of the same cottage in the big driveway. Ash added, "Apparently the drivers always thought it funny that they didn't ever take the bed into the cottage. Drivers gossip a lot, I am told," he added ruefully.

Boomer listened and gravely asked, "Why did they change the beds so often?" He answered his own question: "Because they got damaged and soiled and had to be replaced." The thought made him feel sick, and Ash paled.

"Have you heard from Jazz?" asked Ash.

Boomer, embarrassed and annoyed with himself, told him, "The fucking surveillance stuff has gone off and I can't get in touch with him. What's the point of fucking surveillance if it runs out of battery? Fucking stupid!"

Ash took the box and wires off the dashboard and looked at it. "Guv, it's rechargeable. You just stick the end in the cigarette lighter and it charges."

The relief on Boomer's face was unbelievable; he seemed to have lost ten years of worry.

"It's gonna take a while to charge up, but if you had kept it in there all the time with the engine running it wouldn't have run out."

Boomer asked, "How long before it works again?"

Ash didn't have a clue. It seemed that Jazz had been out of contact for over an hour and the last time they'd heard from him, he was in the house.

"Bloody dangerous position to be in," said Ash. "I have an idea – I am going to the house to find out."

CHAPTER 25

A Knight to the Rescue

Ash was fed up and riled beyond belief at the stupidity of a DI and a DS. He fervently wished he had a higher rank so he could kick their arses all over the Met and demote them. Muttering about how he didn't want to get himself into trouble again, and how he just wanted to do things properly but these fucking stupid, gung-ho police officers had ruined his day, he took himself off to the mansion.

He used the undercover car. Ash had brought with him many sheets of information on Beadells Boudoir Beds and the portfolio of beds, linens and headboards they had available. He wanted to look officious. Boomer would have told him for nothing that Ash couldn't look like anything but a fucking officious tart if he tried, but didn't have the chance.

He pressed the button under the entry speaker on the gates and asked to come in. He had got out of the car and stood, with his hair slicked down, in a grey suit that looked very smart, and he was holding a portfolio with *Beadells Boudoir Beds* written all over it. He smiled into the entry box, knowing it would have a camera on it, and hoped he looked friendly and businesslike. He could see the courtyard through the gates and it looked empty and very quiet. He tried not to allow the fear that was creeping up from his bowels into his chest to reach his face. He wasn't a bloody actor, for Christ's sake, he told himself.

"I am the manager from Beadells Boudoir Beds, sir," was the cheery response from Ash to the surly question of, "What do you want?"

Ash was surprised at the gruff question and thought that would not be normal for such a prestigious mansion. Still, he continued in a cheery way, "Sir, I am here to check the bed you have received today is correct and not the dysfunctional bed we had in storage. I am very concerned that customers as respected and valued as your good selves have the correct bed from our L'amour range."

Ash hoped that sounded convincing. It must have, because the electric gates opened and he quickly got back in his car and drove into the courtyard. By now he was sweating a little and could feel the start of a stress headache, but he had to see if there was anything he could do for Jazz.

One of the heavies came out of the house and lumbered up to Ash, who got out of the car quite smartly, holding his Beadells Boudoir Beds paperwork tightly to his chest, as if for protection. The crunching sound of the gravel as the heavy walked across the courtyard in what looked like enormous Dr Marten kick-ass boots was very frightening, but Ash held in there and was breathing deeply but calmly. This guy must have been nearly seven foot tall and as wide as a brick shithouse. The look on his face was not happy as he peered down at the five feet, eight inches Ash. The shadow the man created made Ash feel freezing cold on this hot day.

Craning his neck to speak to this monster, Ash tried to maintain a smile, which kept quivering and disappearing into his chin.

"I am most anxious to talk with Mr Bateman regarding the delivery today. Mr Bateman is a valued customer and I wish to ensure that my men have delivered the correct bed." Ash hoped this sounded good.

The heavy told Ash to wait while he spoke to someone in the house. Ash wanted to go to the toilet desperately. All this anxiety had caused his bowels to loosen and he was feeling uncomfortable. He walked towards the front door and hoped the ape of a man would come out soon. In fact, he got close to the front door, hoping that when he came back he could dash in to a toilet. They were bound to have one downstairs, he thought.

No one came, and he felt like he had been standing there for at least five minutes and his bowels were getting worse. Now scared of shitting himself, Ash knocked on the door and timidly called out, "Hello?" but he got no reply. He looked inside the door to the hallway to see if he could see a toilet. Why the hell did he think someone would put the word *toilet* on a door in a private house? He hadn't thought that one through. He was getting more desperate and began clenching his bum and pulling in his stomach, now in that pain that only a toilet would relieve.

He called louder, "Hello?" but still no reply. Now in a panic, he had to find a toilet. There was nothing for it; he had to go in and try one of the doors. Everyone who was well off had a cloakroom toilet off the hall, didn't they, he thought. He proceeded to try the doors.

The second door led to a small hallway that looked like it led to somewhere. His eyes darted from door to door within the small hallway, looking for what could be a toilet; he was panicking now. Then he saw an open door at the end showing a bit of a tiled wall and he thought, *please God it could have a toilet behind it.* His legs had turned to jelly and the sweat was pouring off his forehead. He rushed to the room and saw it – oh, wonderful, heaven: a beautiful toilet. Undoing his belt and taking down his trousers gave his bowels an immediate expectation of release, and he just about had the time to sit down before all hell let loose. *Oh my God,* the joy and relief were immense, and he knew in that instant that this was the most satisfying moment ever. He sat for a while, trying to feel normal. His whole body shook with the pent-up tension this had caused. Time was of the essence and Ash reckoned if he was quick, he could go to the toilet and get outside again before anyone noticed. It was never going to happen, was it?

Feeling good and back to normal, Ash washed his hands and got ready to sprint back to the front door. As he opened the toilet door he saw the heavy go outside, looking for him. He stayed where he was for the moment, not sure what to do for the best. The panic that had subsided was now mustering every part of his body for an onslaught. *Oh my God*, he thought, *what do I do?* He should have just owned up and gone outside, but panic makes the sensible parts of the brain go into hibernation. Instead he decided to stay in the house and see if he could find Jazz. Between Jazz and himself, they could deal with anything, he reckoned stupidly. Besides, the heavy was a huge mountain of a man and he didn't want to get on the wrong side of him.

The heavy returned quickly and went up the stairs, calling out to someone called Jim. At this point Ash should have made a dash for the front door and got into his car, but oh no, the stupid part of his brain that was working on the fight-or-flight impulse had decided to fight. Ash, a natural born pen-pusher, had no idea about fighting. In the few seconds of indecision about where he should go, he heard the thumping of two men running down the stairs and then watched through the crack in the toilet door as they ran outside.

In that instant Ash made his way, quietly and quickly, along the hall and up the stairs. Where he was going he hadn't a clue, and what he would do if he was confronted by anyone he hadn't thought about.

The stairs went on forever. On the first floor it felt unsafe, too close to the front door. Then the stairs went up again to the attic. He thought he might be safer up there and would have time to think. Ash was sweating profusely in his panic, and for someone with anal attention to detail on paperwork, he hadn't a clue what to do first or where to go.

On the attic landing he could see a few doors, and now he hesitated, trying to decide which one to open first. Almost shaking now at the enormity of what he was doing, he went to the door behind which Archie was sleeping. Ash was so lucky to have reached this room. If he had known that Simmonds, Bateman and the woman were circling the area he wouldn't have tried such a stupidly daft approach. But now he was here, he closed the door quietly, walked up to the little boy on the bed and felt for a pulse. Archie was sleeping and his pulse was strong.

The feeling of elation at finding Archie was magnificent. Such a lovely little boy, innocent and peaceful looking, like his son; Ash shed a tear of relief. But now he had to do something to help Archie and himself to get away. Should he look for Jazz, or stay put and get Boomer and his team to come and rescue Archie and himself? So far none of his decisions had been based on sense or reason and it wasn't about to change now.

Ash needed to find Jazz, he decided. With Jazz

they could sort this out and get away with Archie. Ash's confidence in Jazz was high and unrealistic. Now on the super highway of stupidity, Ash left Archie sleeping and went to look in the other rooms on this landing. He couldn't hear anything; there was no sound of voices. The two heavies were busy outside, looking inside and behind the cottages, trying to find Ash, and they hadn't realised he might have come into the house.

Ash crept silently on to the landing and tried the handle of the next room's door. He opened the door slowly and peered into an empty room. He went inside just in case, but except for a double bed and a fitted wardrobe it was empty. He didn't want to stay in there; it had a coldness and an unused feel to it. The bed was perfunctory, not comfortable, and the room smelled musty and unused. In a confused panic, his brain darted from one idea to another and landed with the thought that Archie was here on the attic landing, so it seemed reasonable that if Jazz had been captured he would be on this landing too. Why he suddenly felt so confident, he didn't know. The fear had disappeared and Ash felt safe. His stupidity knew no bounds.

He went to the door to come out, but had the good grace to peer through the crack in the open door before going on to the landing. As he did, he heard shuffling and muffled sounds coming from the room next to this one. He waited, holding his breath and wondering what to do, when up the stairs ran the two heavies and there appeared to be a scuffle as they dragged someone out of the room. Ash kept as still as he could. His eyes grew bigger as he watched in terror. The person being grabbed turned and seemed to look directly at him, and he saw Jazz.

Dear God, he thought. Jazz had been roughed up and was bleeding from his nose and mouth, but was still energetic enough to kick and struggle, causing the two heavies to sweat as they tried to keep him still. Jazz saw him, Ash knew he did, and Ash almost thought he saw a little smile of acknowledgement.

"You will never be able to hide my body in that bloody river, I will be found, you bastards!" Jazz shouted.

The heavies had had enough, and one of them hit Jazz so hard on the chin he collapsed, unconscious. In a few moments they had all disappeared down the stairs and by the sounds of the footsteps, they were rushing somewhere.

Ash closed the door, went to the window and phoned Boomer and told him where Archie was. He watched as Jazz was thrown into a Land Rover, and it looked like Simmonds and Bateman got in the front and drove off at speed. They didn't go through the gates in the courtyard; instead they headed down a track by the house and he presumed they were going across the fields to the river. Ash relayed this all to Boomer, who told him to stay put and hide himself as best he could.

The two heavies returned to the house, and Ash immediately paled at the thought that they would be looking for him. Ash urgently asked Boomer to get him out of there. There was nowhere to hide in the bedroom. He looked under the bed and decided his best bet was to lie down on the floor and hope the bed would hide him if anyone looked into the room. He knew if they found him they would be seriously pissed off, and judging by how Jazz looked, they didn't mess around. His bowels growled again, but this time there was nothing left to cause him problems.

He lay waiting, not knowing if Boomer would get there in time to save him from the thugs. He could hear shouting downstairs, and doors being slammed and feet running around. It wouldn't be long before they reached the top of the house and found him.

Ash, muttering his mantra of, "Don't let me die, please don't let me die," lay as still as he could, hardly daring to breathe. He had been in this situation before, and that feeling of hopelessness he'd thought he would never experience again overcame him. He tried to keep his body still as he lay shaking in fear.

CHAPTER 26

Chasing a Wet Dream

Jazz's head banged on the floor of the Land Rover, and this jolted him into consciousness. He heard the door slam shut and the Land Rover bounced as two people got into the front seats. He could hear the panic in their voices.

He recognised Simmonds' voice, and judging by the way he was talking to the other guy as if he was important, Jazz reckoned he must be Bateman. They gunned the Land Rover and the tyres screeched and threw up stones in the courtyard as they turned the vehicle and took off across bumpy terrain. Jazz tried to look up but could only see sky and the odd overhanging branch.

Bateman was screaming instructions and asking questions, and Simmonds was patiently trying to answer them. Jazz thought Bateman was driving, but he wasn't sure. Bateman was not a happy bunny, he thought. Jazz tried to wriggle out of the ropes tying his hands, but he just made them tighter. They had cut the ropes tying his legs so he could walk out of the attic room; that was a mistake on their part, he thought cockily.

The questions and answers were going on while the journey took its bumpy toll. They were going to get to the private jetty for *Wet Dream*, Bateman's yacht. Simmonds confirmed it was full of fuel; it would take minutes to untie her and get her moving and they should be out of sight of Paglesham pretty quickly. They would go from Paglesham Pool to River Roach, then around Potton Island and join up with the Middleway waterway. Bateman, sounding hysterical, said that would take too long, that they had to get rid of him quickly. Someone would be looking for him soon.

Simmonds, the placator, said that it would take no more than an hour to get around Potton Island and down Middleway waterway where they could dump the body. It was deep there and no one used that waterway very much. Soothingly, he told Bateman that they would be back in time for their guests so for now, he should just concentrate on keeping the Land Rover upright and get to the jetty. The sarcasm was not wasted on Jazz. The Land Rover was being driven with a careless panic that felt to him like it was going to turn over soon.

Lying there, Jazz wriggled around, looking for something sharp. Perhaps he could try and cut through the ropes. *These things happen in films*, he told himself. Of course there was nothing in the pristinely clean and clear back of the Land Rover. After what seemed like an age of being tossed around as the Land Rover bumped and banged across what felt like rough terrain, they stopped and the engine was turned off. Urgently, Simmonds and Bateman got out of the car and Simmonds opened the back and got Jazz out. Bateman was already on the jetty and getting into the yacht. He shouted to Simmonds to hurry up.

Simmonds slipped a rope around Jazz's neck and pulled it tight. With his arms tied behind his back and feeling throttled by the rope, Jazz stumbled and ran to keep up with Simmonds. He was yanked onto the yacht and kicked down the steep steps into the small cabin. Simmonds had let go of the rope around his neck and the kick meant Jazz landed on the floor of the cabin, his head hitting it with a thud that shook his whole body. Although it was quite dark down in the cabin, Jazz could see a small settee built in, and a table and chairs in the corner. The galley was near the entrance to the cabin and he looked around, stunned but desperate for something he could grab to hit Simmonds with, or something to get the ropes off his arms. Now Jazz was angry and determined: the fuckers were not going to kill him. The cabin door was slammed shut.

Simmonds helped Bateman cast off, and after turning the engine a few times, it caught and the yacht moved forward slowly. Bateman turned the yacht around in Paglesham Pool and set the helm towards the River Roach and Potton Island. Bateman, not the best of sailors, was hysterical and not concentrating, and the yacht veered dangerously towards the shallows of the banks that made Paglesham Pool a narrow waterway to sail down. Simmonds screamed at Bateman to watch what the fuck he was doing if he wanted to get out of here. Under normal circumstances Bateman would never be spoken to in that tone, but these were exceptional times and he just wanted some help to get out of this bloody mess.

Bateman was known as the man in charge: calm – scheming, some might say – and always controlling. Today, none of those things could be said about him. His hands shook with tension; his head turned from this way to that in a panic. He looked to check he wasn't being followed; he looked ahead in case there were any boats in his way.

He was talking to himself, saying, "Oh my God, what will I do, what will I do?"

Simmonds, always his assistant, felt like the master at the moment, and was sickened by this man panicking and acting stupidly. He wanted to ask how they were going to kill Singh. Should they drown him? Stab him? They couldn't shoot him (no guns), so should they strangle him? But with Bateman so hysterical, this wasn't the time to ask. Simmonds reckoned he would just do it himself nearer Potton Island. He didn't want a dead body in the yacht for long, just in case anyone came by them. He noted Bateman was quite hysterical; wrestling stupidly with the steering as he turned the wheel this way and that, making the yacht zigzag across the Paglesham Pool, but *thank God* he stayed within the narrow waterway and looked fairly safe.

Simmonds took himself off to check on Singh and make sure the fucker wasn't doing anything he shouldn't. He opened the cabin door and went down the steep steps into the cabin. It was late in the afternoon and the light was fading, making the cabin darker. Simmonds strained to see where he was, and then he spotted Singh lying on the floor by the table. The bastard had wriggled over to the table. He needed to sort him out. In three strides he was upon Jazz and gave him a swift kick in his back. He heard the grunt of pain and knew he was conscious.

Jazz, his eyes smarting with the pain of the kick, pulled himself together. He had a plan.

"Oi, Simmonds, I need a piss badly and that kick in the back didn't help none."

Simmonds, in no mood to be bothered about this fucking nuisance, told him to wet himself; it didn't matter, he would be topped soon enough.

Jazz asked him, "Really? Apart from messing up this beautiful cabin," he wondered if the sarcasm was noticeable, "if I piss myself, some of it will be on the floor and maybe on the furniture, and my piss contains my DNA. Just remember, when I go missing the police will go to town to find one of their own – we always do. Everything will be looked at and even a trace of my piss will have enough DNA to send you to prison for the rest of your fucking life. Now, if you were sensible, you would let me go to the toilet."

Simmonds was silent for a moment in thought, then begrudgingly said, "OK, I will help you up and take you to the toilet, you bloody nuisance."

Jazz smiled and thanked him. When they got to the toilet Jazz asked sweetly if Simmonds cared to hold his todger whilst he peed into the bowl. Simmonds, angry now, told him to fuck himself. Jazz, now being very placatory, suggested that Simmonds undo the ropes tying his hands behind him, and before Simmonds could say that would be stupid, Jazz suggested he could put the rope around his neck and just pull if he tried to get cheeky. Simmonds grimaced, then thought and agreed it sounded a good idea.

Stupid fucker, thought Jazz.

Simmonds found some rope – it was a yacht; it had lots of bits of rope lying around. Once it was tied around Jazz's neck, he undid the rope around his hands.

"OK, go on," Simmonds encouraged as Jazz brought his hands forward to undo his trousers to have a pee. Simmonds stood behind Jazz, holding the rope tight around his neck.

It took a few seconds but Jazz stepped back into Simmonds, bringing his head back with such force that he heard Simmonds' nose crack. Simmonds screamed and fell over backwards, pulling Jazz with him by the tight rope around his neck. Jazz gasped – the rope had tightened and he couldn't breathe. Once on the floor, Simmonds, stunned for the moment and in pain, had let got of the rope and Jazz scrabbled to loosen it and take it off over his head.

Simmonds struggled for a few moments with breathing as he choked on the blood pouring down the back of his throat from his nose and broken teeth. Soon he panicked: Jazz was free and could get away. He tried to get up and scrabbled to get hold of Jazz. But Jazz, after coughing and choking his way back to breathing normally, was now fully in control, and he kicked Simmonds on the chin and knocked him out. He picked up the rope, tied Simmonds up and left him on the floor.

He gave him a final kick for good measure and whispered, "Bastard!" then headed quietly up to the deck to get Bateman.

CHAPTER 27

Now for the Big Guns

Boomer had paced up and down for the last hour, wondering why the fucking hell he had allowed that bloody idiot to go to the manor house looking for Jazz. He had spoken to his lads; the ones in the pub were having a good time and told him about their meeting with Gary and how they wanted to kick his head in. Boomer laughed; he knew exactly how they felt. He warned them to keep a low profile and be ready. Something was going down and he needed them alert.

He called up his men by the sewage works. He tried to keep a straight face when they complained of the smell and how their clothes were starting to smell of shit too. He told them, too, to be ready for his call. He didn't know yet what was going on but shortly he would be in contact with Jazz again, once the fucking surveillance contraption had recharged.

Paula sat in the car and waited for her instructions. Boomer was a pain in the neck and she was glad he was outside walking around. He had paced the little bit of field for so long she reckoned he had dug a ditch, and with a bit of luck he would disappear soon. How many times could he tell his team to fuck off, she wondered? Hearing that Ash had gone off undercover to see what was happening at the manor house was very worrying indeed; she knew Ash was no James Bond, but she hoped something would raise its ugly head soon and allow them to enter the mansion.

Paula had looked up any information she could get on the twelve going to the mansion tonight, but there was nothing to suggest they knew their way around Ilford Police Station. This all felt very wrong to her. Their work was compromised in the police station and files had disappeared, and now there were two officers undercover in the house of potential murderers. To cap it all, the idiots were there without surveillance equipment working, so there was no backup to aid them. *Gee*, she thought, *working with this lot is stressful.*

Paula, watching Boomer, saw him stop pacing to answer his phone. She could see it was important from the look on his face.

He came to the car in a rush and said, "Archie is in the house on the top floor." Before Paula could say anything he was calling his team – first the ones waiting near the sewage farm, as they were closer. All he said was, "Go, go, go. Ash in distress on top floor. Archie on top floor, drugged. Two civilians guarding the house as far as we know."

Again, Paula tried interrupt but Boomer, in full swing

ignored her and rang his lads waiting in the Plough & Sail pub and repeated that they should go now and rescue Ash and Archie, and then wait for him to arrive.

Now he turned to Paula and said he was off to help Jazz. He would give her a lift to the house but she was on her own for the time being; his team would be there when they got there. As he drove at breakneck speed along Paglesham Road he said Archie was on the top floor and sedated and Paula was to take him somewhere safe. By the time he said that, they had arrived at the mansion and he almost pushed her out of the car. He took off in a flurry of dust from the tyres, which screeched at their treatment.

Boomer was living on nerves at present. He saw his lads at the mansion, and he knew they would sort it all out. Paula would get Archie and take care of him. He wanted the twelve paedophiles who were due to arrive later, but for now his thoughts were solely on Jazz and getting him back safely. There would be only one way of doing that.

He screeched to a halt outside the Plough & Sail, just missing one of the tables and chairs arranged prettily outside the pub.

"Bloody things," was all he could say as he threw a chair out of his way upon getting out of the car. With a few grunts and groans he tossed more chairs aside en route to the pub and threw open the pub door. His size was holding him back; as a big guy he moved with the fluidity of a pregnant bear.

Breathless, Boomer had burst into the Plough & Sail pub, and with the light behind him everyone looked up and saw, standing there in dark shadow, a hulk of a man. It all went very quiet.

Standing there, agitated, his eyes darting from one table to another, Boomer could see the surprise on everyone's face as they looked up at his dramatic entrance. It was a quiet pub and not used to such commotion.

Quickly Boomer spied the person he was after, and in a voice more suited to a place the size of Wembley Stadium he shouted, "Oi, Billy Big Bollocks, I need your help now, it's an emergency."

Gary knew he meant him, and started to respond with the sarcasm he was good at.

"Don't start, bastard," warned Boomer.

In a rush and in almost one breath, he urgently said, "We have a paedophile trying to get away down the river and he has my detective sergeant with him. We have got to help him, otherwise he's a dead man. That bloody Eddie Willoughby at Essex Police Marine Unit based in Burnham can't help. Too busy being tarts in London with terrorist bollocks. You are the best I've got, and that's bloody depressing."

Boomer took a deep breath and carried on. "There is gonna be another murder if we don't get going. He has already murdered one child and we have got to stop him."

Gary got up a tad too slowly for Boomer.

"Move your bloody self. They have a head start and

your lump of shit won't move very fast. It's Bateman's boat, and it's bound to be a bloody good one at that."

Gary by now was moving faster, and as he passed in front of Boomer, Gary told him in no uncertain terms that his little darlin' was better than a *Wet Dream* any day. Boomer looked at him and wondered for a second what the fuck that had to do with anything.

They were walking fast now, and Gary said he needed a lift to Shuttlewood Boatyard down the bumpy road. Boomer knew what he meant and got back in the car and drove over them at breakneck speed, making the car jump most of them and putting the suspension under great pressure. As they flew down the road Gary had to explain that *Wet Dream* was the name of Bateman's yacht. It was fast, but Bateman was, in Gary's words, a bloody yachtie who thought he knew how to sail but hadn't a fucking clue.

With the fierce passion of hatred, Gary said, through clenched, uneven teeth, "I can catch him, no problem. I hate nonces, bloody paedos, I hate them."

When they reached the sea wall Gary jumped out and ran down the floating pontoon to his boat. Boomer tried to keep up with him but Gary, by now on his boat and shouting down the pontoon, told him to get back to what he needed to do, he would handle it. Boomer told him Bateman was a killer, and Gary laughed.

"I can take on any nonce. My little darlin' will sort him out. I will get the RNLI out to help. No problem. Now bugger off."

Before Boomer reached the boat, Gary had gunned it and taken off at a speed she didn't look capable of. Boomer, bent double and breathing heavily, raised his head from nearly between his knees and watched as Gary sped down the River Crouch towards Bateman's yacht, which could be seen in the near distance.

When he could breathe again, Boomer turned back and headed as fast as he could to the car. There was a lot going on at the house and he needed to check what was happening. He would call the RNLI helicopter himself and get them to help board Bateman's yacht. He hoped that bugger Jazz was alright. He didn't like leaving him, but he had no choice.

"Bloody boats," was all he could mutter as he drove at breakneck speed with siren blazing to the mansion.

The piddly, windy country roads were so frustrating. For such a quiet place he had three cars riding in the middle of the road to contend with, a stupid woman on a horse who gave him the finger for passing at speed, and a cyclist who had earphones on and didn't hear the siren or the horn, or for that matter the verbal pornographic filth Boomer was shouting at the fat-arsed woman cycling in the middle of the road on a bend so he couldn't overtake quickly or safely enough. His stress levels were far too high for an overweight, unfit man who would never see forty-eight again. For the umpteenth time, he thought he would jack it all in and just become a hunting-and-shooting man in Dorset. But for now he had some vile fuckers to catch and put away.

CHAPTER 28

Help and Hospitality

Ash lay still on the floor by the bed. If they came into the room they would have to walk over to the window and look to their left to see him. He told himself they wouldn't do that. He was sweating and his breathing was louder than he wanted as he heard them walking up the stairs and getting closer to him. He could hear them shouting to each other, and they were not happy.

They had a big event tonight with important people attending and a bloody little bastard had escaped them and could cause lots of trouble. They now had guns. They were not messing around. They had been told in no uncertain terms by Simmonds that the mansion had to be the safest place in England for their guests, and it was their job to ensure that happened.

For years, everything had gone like clockwork. The terrible twins, as they were known to those in the house, actually had names of Jim and Derek. Their job was to blend into the background and be bodyguards who were seen but not heard. There had not been many occasions when their services were needed, but when a mess had to be cleared up they were thorough, quick and loyal to Bateman and Simmonds. They had other jobs that kept them busy, such as taking on the roles of chauffeurs and butlers when guests arrived. They had been found by chance, working as bouncers in an East London pub. Bored, unappreciated and so underused. Life in the countryside had many advantages, and plenty of time off too. The money was good and they spent it back in the East End haunts. They knew what Simmonds and Bateman were about but it didn't bother them; it was a job.

Bateman and his paedophile ring had been in practice for many years. The exclusive group of high-powered people were well looked after and safe and secure with Bateman. The spin-off for Bateman was the power it gave him in business. He had some of the highest-placed people in the country with contacts that you just couldn't buy. He had made his millions years ago with good insider-dealing advice from his 'friends'. It had worked very well for everyone and the terrible twins made all the guests feel safe once they were inside the mansion.

To say the terrible twins were aggrieved would be an understatement. As bodyguards, the two of them had a good reputation to uphold, and now it was in tatters with Singh and now this little man, whom they presumed had something to do with Singh. It was too much of a coincidence. They were told that when he was found, they were to take him in a car and dispose of him somewhere near the marshes on Wallasea Island. No one would go there; it was a wildlife reserve and if the body was hidden in the marshes, it wouldn't be found. It was a dirty job, and they liked clean lines in their work. They had two hours to find him and dispose of him, so their stress levels were rising as they went higher up the stairs. It was going to be messy.

Ash, a wreck by now, listened intently as they came up to the top of the house and he heard the creaking of the stairs and knew they were on his landing. His head throbbed with pain as the panic told him to *Run, run, run*. He knew he had to stay put. He wished he had got into the wardrobe, perhaps that would have been safer, but it was too late now. Alternatively, he thought, perhaps he should have been in the room with Archie. He could have been on the floor by the bed with him. They might not have come in if they saw Archie on the bed. His mind was spinning with ideas of what he should have done. But here he was, lying here waiting to be found by two of the biggest men he had ever seen. They could just stamp on him, like an ant, and extinguish his life. Now he was getting silly and he told himself to behave and stop thinking. He needed to concentrate on stopping his body shaking and the heavy, panicky breathing needed to quieten down, otherwise they would hear him.

The tension was now as high as it could get, and he heard the door handle being turned and the door open. It felt as if his heart would stop and he would die of fright. A foot came into the room; it sounded hollow, there was no carpet on the floor, just floorboards, and the footfall sounded like a giant stepping into the room. Oh, to wake up in his bed at home – this was a nightmare.

A voice, heightened with surprise, shock and panic, shouted, "Jim, come here now." The footsteps quickly left the room and the door was closed. Ash, giddy with panic, sweating with relief and shaking with exhaustion, didn't know what was happening but he was so grateful for whatever it was that took that man out of the bedroom.

He listened to the shouting going on in the bedroom next door. It was the room where Archie lay, and Ash listened intently to what was going on. He could hear doors being slammed; a chair sounded as if it was thrown and footsteps ran manically back and forth. He hoped Archie was alright.

Then he heard, "Where the fuck is he? The bloody kid couldn't move, he was supposed to be out for the count for a further two hours, according to Mr Bateman."

One of them swore again and told the other, "Go check the other bedrooms. He couldn't have got very far if he woke up."

Then a second later, something occurred to one of them: "Perhaps the bloke we're looking for has got him!" Venomously, he added, "He's a dead fucker when we find him." That was when the door opened again, and Ash knew he was done for.

CHAPTER 29

The Chase is on

This was not how he worked. Bateman was usually in full control. He was a control freak but that's how he got things done, and that's how he had, for so many years, stayed out of any trouble. Everything he did was orderly, in place and worked perfectly. He had made his life profitable and oh, so enjoyable. There had been many youngsters passed through his home and he had such fun, excitement and sexual pleasure with them, and never once had there been a hint of anything untoward to the outside world. He was very proud and satisfied with his magnificent abilities to keep himself and his friends safe from prying eyes. But now he was panicking; something he was not used to feeling, and he didn't like it one bit.

Bateman was at the helm of the yacht with the engine running at its top speed of eight knots. The engine was straining as the yacht cut through the waves at a speed that was not practical or recommended in these waters. He was having trouble controlling the steering. The yacht wasn't happy with the speed and Bateman, unused to such sailing, was having difficulty handling her. They zigzagged like an old drunk down the river.

Although making a monumental mess of sailing, Bateman started to feel safe. With the wind in his hair and the open waters, it felt like freedom. Who the hell could get to him now? Suddenly, he almost laughed. The panicky feeling left him. He was going to win. He would get this Singh man out of his hair. This bloody bastard had caused so much trouble, and Bateman wanted him hurt badly and then killed. Simmonds was good. He paid him well and he had never let him down. Bateman knew that Singh would be killed and hidden away from prying eyes. Nothing could come back on him. As Simmonds said, they would be back at the house in time for the guests arriving and a lovely evening was planned.

The evening had been planned for many months. It was a shame they didn't have Nekisha as well. He had promised his guests a double tonight, it would have been fabulous; one girl and one boy, it just couldn't be better, but they had lost the girl for now. When the girl was back with them, they intended to have another double; he had promised his guests this would happen this year.

The little boy was quite a new discovery. He was only just being groomed, but for tonight's purpose that wouldn't matter. There was something totally delicious about a young boy, and to feel him and use him was exquisite. To feel the life leave his little body was something orgasmic, precious and rare. Tonight he would enjoy the experience, and he shuddered in sexual anticipation.

Bateman's attention was on trying to control the steering and thinking of the evening ahead. The wind had come up and was blowing hard, making the water choppy. He didn't hear what was going on behind him.

Jazz crept up behind Bateman, grabbed his hair and yanked hard and sharp, pulling his head back. As Bateman turned, he was greeted with a hard and swift punch to his nose. He howled in pain and let go of the wheel. As they struggled and fought the yacht wheel turned crazily. Bateman struggled free from Jazz's grip to grab the wheel, but the speed of it whipped his hands, breaking his fingers, and he screamed in pain.

Bateman saw the yacht lurching recklessly at speed towards the sandbank to his left. It was low tide and he needed to keep in the middle channel where the water was a suitable depth. He pushed past Jazz, who stood for a moment, knowing something bad was happening, but what, he had no idea. Bateman, unable to steer, tried to rush past Jazz, screaming in pain and panic, to the back of the yacht. He intended to throw himself overboard. When the yacht hit the sandbank at speed, all hell would be let loose.

Jazz wasn't having any of that and shouted, "Oh no you don't, you motherfucking little bastard, you ain't going nowhere," and he stuck his foot out as Bateman tried to pass him.

Bateman's stumble and lurch towards the side of the yacht coincided with the yacht hitting the immovable sandbank. Jazz was thrown into the cockpit and Bateman fell heavily against the side of the yacht, the force almost pushing him over the side. The shock of the impact rippled through the yacht and felt like an earthquake. They both hung on to whatever they could until it began to settle. Jazz, lying on his back looking up at the mast swaying giddily and wondering when the world was going to stop shuddering, heard the loud crack of the mast as it snapped off the spreaders. The noise, groaning at first, then ripping, was stone-cold terrifyingly heart-stopping. As if in slow motion Jazz watched in horror as the razor-sharp broken mast fell, with the determined precision of an arrow, towards Bateman and impaled itself in his stomach. The velocity of the impact carried Bateman over the side into the murky, sandy water. In seconds, the water surrounding Bateman turned red.

Jazz watched Bateman flailing helplessly for a moment. Their eyes met and Jazz saw for a second the utter despair and horror in Bateman's eyes, and then there was stillness.

Gary's boat had reached Jazz, and with an athletic jump, Gary was in the boat and looking over the side with Jazz.

"Is he dead?" asked Gary.

"Give it a moment," said Jazz, looking intently at where Bateman lay, just under the water, with the odd bubble coming from his mouth and hitting the surface.

After a minute Jazz looked round at Gary and said with a nod, "Yeah, the flailing has stopped and he has been under now a few minutes. I reckon he is dead."

"Good, I'll call the RNLI helicopter to come and 'rescue' him. Fucking paedo, impaling is good justice."

Jazz nodded and slapped Gary on his back. "Thanks for coming out. I don't have my wallet, so can't pay you."

Gary, surprisingly emotional, said, "This is for free, we don't want nonces in Paglesham."

Jazz then realised he still had Simmonds in the cabin, and asked Gary to come with him to make sure he was tied up securely.

With relish, Gary said, "My pleasure – show me where the bastard is. He won't move when I have finished with him."

The RNLI helicopter was on its way. Jazz and Gary sat in the back of the yacht, waiting. It was peaceful as they bobbed up and down. The tide was coming in and the water level had risen, covering more of Bateman's body. The only way you knew he was there was the mast sticking out of the water at an angle.

The birds, disturbed by the commotion, were now back to their usual sitting on the water, the seals that had left in a hurry came back, and Jazz, unused to such sights, saw them bob up and take a look at these two men waiting, exhausted but jubilant, for the helicopter. Gary felt about his person and in a deep pocket found the flask he kept on him for emergencies.

"I think we need a swig of this, don't you, mister?" said Gary.

Jazz took the flask and raised it in salute to Gary, saying, "I hate fucking boats."

Gary laughed good-naturedly. "You bloody townspeople, you haven't got a bloody clue."

Jazz tried to laugh at that, but his head hurt. He took another swig instead.

Relaxed and almost enjoying the bobbing about on this yacht, Jazz asked with interest, "So what happened here? And how the fuck did you think you could be John Wayne and rescue me by yourself, you bloody old codger?"

Gary sat back, arms spread, holding the side of the yacht in an expansive way, and smacked his lips in thought. "Well, to start with, this 'ere yacht is an expensive bitch but she ain't as good as my little darlin'. She's a Beneteau Oceanis, a little beauty if you know what you are doing. She would set you back at least £200,000. Got a nice sail on her and a fair engine, can sleep six people and all mod cons on her. That nonce thought himself a yachtie but he couldn't piss straight in a bucket. He was all la-di-dah and no knickers. You have to know how to handle her, and then she would treat you right. The nonce used her for la-di-dah drinkie-poos and took her out for a little zigzag up the river, he hadn't a clue how to handle her. Never seen him sail her straight. Never seen her with her sail up, he just used the engine. Too fucking stupid to know how to sail her properly.

"If you want to get the best out of your boat you have to stroke her, get to know her good points and bring her on, not put your foot down and be a wham-bam-thank-you-ma'am! Me and my little darlin' know each other and get on well. I look after her and she has never let me down."

Jazz again wondered why everything to do with boats and boating people seemed to be so sexual. It made him smile.

"So, is your boat called *Little Darlin'* then?" asked a relaxed Jazz.

"Nah, she is called *Jolly Roger.*"

That tickled Jazz, and he creased up with laughter. Gary didn't see the funny side of the name and looked quizzical. Coughing with laughter now, Jazz didn't want to explain little darling having a jolly roger! He had warmed to Gary; he was a good guy.

"Anyhows, I knew my little darlin' would get to her quickly, I knows the river and the currents. I also knows we were coming up to sandbanks, so if she hadn't run aground I would have given her a nudge that way. I know my waterways – he didn't."

Jazz asked, "So why, if this is such a fucking expensive yacht, did the whatchamacallit tall thing break? That isn't good, is it, for an expensive boat?"

Gary sighed, thinking, *Bloody townies know nothing.* "You can't go aground with any yacht at speed and nothing happen. The *mast*, not the 'tall bloody thing', is bolted together with the spreaders." With heavy sarcasm Gary added, "Oh, and for your info, spreaders are the pointy-out things for holding the wires to stabilise the *mast.*" Gary emphasised the word, and it was beginning to make Jazz giggle. "Anyhows, if you stop at speed and get grounded the *mast* is going to shake under a lot of tension and it will break at its weakest point, on the spreaders. You know, that break would have been razor-sharp. Slice straight through you. Well, looking at the nonce it did just that. Good justice!"

For a moment Gary thought and then he added, "So me coming here is like John Wayne, you say? Well, I likes that – I will tell the fellas in the pub tonight. That will make 'em laugh."

Jazz looked at Gary and thought him a bloody good fellow. In an unusual display of affection, he put his arm around Gary and slapped him on his back.

"You are a fucking stupid old sod, Gary Piss-Taker."

Gary smiled and nodded in agreement. It was a good end to the day. Simmonds, judging by the stillness and quiet below, was still out for the count after Gary had given him a resounding left hook to the chin. He would be dealt with later. Bateman was no longer a problem.

Jazz looked up and raised the flask and said, with a conviction that was a tad emotional, "Here's to you, Kevin – we got the bastard. Now you rest in peace, little fella."

They both sat back against the side of the boat, smiling, at peace, waiting for the helicopter. The water was gently lapping against the side of the yacht and it rocked in a very relaxed, almost hypnotic way. The flask was big but nearly empty now; one last swig each and it would be empty. It left them both with a warm glow, and when the helicopter arrived the co-pilot, seeing them both sprawled and leaning up against the inside of the boat, thought they were both concussed until he got closer and smelled the booze.

Used to rescuing yacht men who had fallen off their boats or grounded themselves, the RNLI pilot had never before seen a dead man speared by his mast in the water. He called to base that he would need more help in recovering the man from the sandbank. His co-pilot abseiled down on to the boat to find out what the hell had happened.

CHAPTER 30

The Melee Begins

Boomer's team had scaled and opened the gates to the mansion and were busily and quietly going off in different directions. Two of them took cottages to search; four of them headed for the mansion. Paula had arrived, and after being unceremoniously thrown out of the car by Boomer she made her way to the mansion. She got her CS gas canister out of its case and had it ready in her hand. She followed the four that were going into the mansion. There was no shout of 'Police!' – they didn't want to alert anyone to their presence. There was a child and a stupid fucking officer in there somewhere and they had to rescue them.

Once inside the hallway they heard the commotion going on upstairs. They could hear doors slamming and furniture being thrown around. Quietly but quickly they made their way up the stairs. Each had a standard police asp* (An asp is a police-issue truncheon made of carbon steel that is ten inches long when closed and twenty-one inches opened) secreted on their person. It was their good training that made them all automatically withdraw their asps in readiness, and with a sharp movement extend the small, solid piece of metal into a truncheon-like weapon capable, if used with force, of breaking an arm. They all looked for the moment as if they were holding lightsabers.

There were guns in their holsters inside their jackets as well, but they hoped they would not be needed. Apart from anything else, if a gun was fired it would take a fucking night of paperwork to explain it and no one wanted that.

It took no time to get to the top of the stairs and Boomer's team split into two groups of two, one taking one door and the other taking the other. Both rooms had someone in them, judging by the stamping around and the screams.

Paula carried her Met Police CS spray in her hand like a security blanket. The men were well ahead of her and up the stairs. She could hear the melee of shouting, stamping and swearing. It had been a long time since she had been on this type of raid. Looking around the ground floor, she heard a noise behind the door to her right – it sounded like a pan dropping on the floor. She supposed it could be the kitchen and headed in that direction. Paula was a strong and fearless detective but in this instance she wondered if she was just downright stupid. She didn't know what or who was behind the door, and with no apparent backup, she opened the kitchen door and looked inside.

Standing almost straight ahead of her was the blonde woman Paula recognised as the woman she had seen pictured with Simmonds.

"Betty Lemus, I presume?" was the sarcastic call from Paula. She hoped it hid the shock and fear she felt at the sight of the biggest carving knife she had ever seen in Lemus' hands.

Ash held his breath and closed his eyes – perhaps he wouldn't be found, he hoped.

Jim strode urgently into the room; the panic could be heard in his fast and loud breathing. It didn't take long before he saw Ash lying prone on the floor, so still that Jim wondered for a moment if he was dead. In seconds he was towering over him and yanked him to his feet. Ash, very much alive and scared, looked into the goon's face and gulped. With a menace that made the hairs on Ash's head stand up, the goon almost spat the words in his face.

"Where the fuck is the boy?"

"Don't know, I don't know," replied Ash, too scared at this point to think very rationally.

"I am going to beat you to a bloody pulp unless you tell me, you stinking little bastard," was the response from the goon. Just to emphasise his point, he punched Ash hard in the stomach and kneed him in his groin. He threw him, hard, back on to the floor and Ash lay there curled up, gasping for breath and holding his privates. As he rocked in pain on the floor, he thought hard about what the fuck he was going to do.

Just before a heavy kick to his head came his way, Ash held up his hands in a placatory fashion and said, "Alright, alright, I will tell you. I put the boy somewhere downstairs, but I am confused. I will show you, I will take you there."

With that the goon grabbed him by the collar, yanked him up to his feet and pushed him so hard he nearly fell down again.

"Get a bloody move on, bastard, and show me where the boy is."

It bought Ash a few more minutes. He was thinking hard on what to do next when the door opened again and in rushed two of Boomer's team. His relief turned his legs to jelly and he went back to the bed and sat down. He watched as Boomer's men got the goon, who answered to the name of Jim, cuffed and firmly held. His rights were recited to him as they led him away.

One of Boomer's men tapped Ash on the shoulder to check he was alright. Ash nodded and said, "Yes, yes, I'm fine, just get these bastards put away."

Ash needed a few moments to catch his breath and clear his head. He sat on the bed for a moment and just laughed. What a relief – he was safe. But now he wanted to help find Archie. Archie was about his son's age and the thought of anything happening to him was sickeningly awful. He needed to find Archie.

He heard the noise going on in the next room. There was shouting and swearing and an almighty scuffle and finally one of Boomer's men shouted that they had got a suspect called Derek in handcuffs. Ash heard his rights being read to him as he was marched away. It was confirmed that no one had found the boy.

The bedrooms on the two floors were searched to no avail. Jim and Derek were frogmarched roughly down the stairs to the police cars outside. A call was made to Boomer to say the two goons were in custody but there was no sign of the boy, Archie. Two officers took Jim and Derek at high speed to the local police station in Southend. It was a few miles away but with the blue light flashing they reckoned they could get there in ten minutes. They needed to get back.

It was a very exciting time for Boomer's men. They didn't usually have such a great stake-out. The two who were off to Southend wanted to get back for the next round. Boomer had rung ahead to Southend Police Station and asked for his prisoners to be kept there until their undercover raid was complete. He advised there could be more prisoners later. Southend Police Station was not happy. They got quite full most nights after drinking revellers caused fights and problems, but with a bit of arm-twisting from Boomer they agreed they would accommodate them for a few hours, but not all night. This suited Boomer. He arranged for four police vans to be made available from Barking and waiting at Southend Police Station within the next three hours. There was going to be trouble because of this tomorrow, but today he needed help. He would deal with all the bollocking tomorrow.

"Well hello, Betty, fancy meeting you here," was Paula's response to the grunt she got from the woman standing there with the biggest carving knife she had ever seen in her hand.

Betty Lemus was now feeling much more confident. She saw this slightly-built woman who was obviously a policewoman, but for the moment alone with no backup. She heard the police go up the stairs, and could hear the noise going on up there. She wanted to get away. Bateman and Simmonds had left her here and she wasn't happy.

With a smile Lemus looked at the woman in front of her, and with a relaxed confidence that was chilling, told her quietly, "Get out of my fucking way or I will use it." With sudden movements she jabbed the carving knife in Paula's direction. "I would enjoy sticking a pig." Lemus almost laughed at her comment, and twisted the carving knife in the air in a gutting motion.

Paula was tougher than she looked and told Lemus she was going to arrest her, and if she wanted to make her life easier, she should put the knife down now!

Lemus laughed and looked Paula up and down with contempt. "I could take you on with one hand tied behind my back, you stupid bitch."

Paula again advised her that she was under arrest. Lemus moved forward menacingly and told Paula to get out of her fucking way. Lemus knew she had very little time before the police came down the stairs and she wasn't playing with words any more.

"You either get out of my way, bitch, or I stick you with the knife. I don't care one way or the other."

Paula had had enough of all the banter, and again told Lemus she was under arrest and to stand still. Taking no notice, Lemus walked forward again and Paula shrugged her shoulders and said, "Now you have seriously pissed me off."

She brought up the CS gas canister, which had been cupped in her hand by her side, and sprayed it directly on to Lemus' face. The effect was dramatic. With a scream Lemus fell to the floor, gasping for breath. With eyes closed and streaming, she couldn't move. Paula opened the door to allow air into the room. She didn't want to get any of the spray in her face. After a few moments she cuffed Lemus and dragged her outside into the fresh air. Lemus pleaded for water for her eyes, but Paula said no, the air would clear the spray in a few moments, and water would only cause crystals and make it worse.

Boomer's men came down the stairs with the two goons Jim and Derek and saw Paula with Lemus. Lemus was bundled into the car and taken to Southend Police Station as well. So far, three caught and more to come.

Ash came down the stairs and Paula was glad to see him and gave him a hug, something she didn't usually do but he looked worse for wear. Ash looked determined and wanted to get on with some work. He was off to find Archie, and said he wanted to help in the search.

It had felt a good day so far until Paula heard that they couldn't find Archie. She and Ash helped with the search of the cottages. There was no sign of him. Ash saw the room full of mirrors and the bed with manacles by it and gulped. This was too much to bear. He was going to find Archie and make him safe. Every cupboard was searched and the grounds around the house were scoured. He wasn't anywhere to be found.

By the time Boomer arrived at the mansion he'd been advised that there were three in custody and no sign of Archie. He saw Ash, patted him on the back and almost gave him a man-hug. He was relieved and really glad he was OK. He could see he had been roughed up and suggested he clean himself up in case he was needed when the twelve guests arrived. He looked at his watch – it was going on 7pm and he thought the twelve would arrive sometime after 8pm, so time was of the essence.

For a start he said Paula would be the housekeeper for the moment if anyone arrived. They were expecting a woman to be there. Two of his men would be Jim and Derek. He asked Ash to clean up and become a helper in the house when the twelve arrived. The rest would help to search the farm and garden. The mansion was a large property with a few sheds on the land. The boy had to be somewhere close.

Boomer received a call that said Gary was taking Jazz and Simmonds to Paglesham on his boat, and a member of the RNLI would accompany them. Gary had a car there that would bring them to the mansion. They would be there in about half an hour. It was a relief to hear that Jazz was alright apart from a cut to the head. The RNLI man said he thought they had been drinking when he arrived at the boat, and Boomer just laughed. He wanted Jazz back here for later and to help find Archie.

He was proud of his boys, and they were all geared up and raring to go. They had spent all day just waiting and were like coiled springs. Now they were working, the energy levels in the mansion could have powered Paglesham village. Paula made some tea in the kitchen. The team looking for Archie were sent off searching and the two remaining were gasping for a cuppa and a fag.

Boomer, at last, could relax a bit. Jazz and Ash were safe, there were three in custody, Bateman was dead and Simmonds in cuffs. He almost rubbed his hands together with delight. A good day so far. The boy couldn't be far away and if the woman or the two men didn't know where he was then they hadn't got him. It occurred to him that Mad Pete was also not around. He would ask Jazz if he knew where he was.

The remaining undercover cars were put somewhere safe. There was a garage, and two were put in there. One was left outside in the yard facing the gates in case it was needed quickly. Boomer took a look at the cottage with the bed and the mirrors and saw the manacles and the cameras. His stomach turned and he was so very glad they had got the bastards. The twelve bastards coming later would be another success. It was a good day.

He wanted the house to look relatively calm and normal. Paula stayed in the kitchen with Ash. He made sure everyone was contactable if needed and they were; no more buggered surveillance stuff. He felt content for the moment. Soon it was going to get busy, but for now a cup of tea and anything he could lay his hands on to eat in the kitchen would do.

CHAPTER 31

The Round-Up

Jazz told the RNLI guy that they had a prisoner below. Gary said he would help him get Simmonds up the stairs. To go down into the cabin was a steep climb.

"I hate fucking boats!" Jazz growled as he negotiated the steps like a drunken tart.

Gary had nimbly climbed down them and looked up with disdain at this stupid townie hanging on for dear life to the steps as he gingerly put the next foot down.

Gary's cry of, "Come on, you nancy boy, we haven't got all day," encouraged Jazz to get a move on. With gritted teeth, he vowed he would stuff a bleeding cod fillet down Gary's gob when they got on dry land. The tide was quite high now and the boat was bobbing around, and Jazz moaned that he didn't like that at all and was beginning to feel sick again.

Gary, fed up with the moaning, snapped, "Change the bloody record, mister. We heard that one before. This is a boat, get over it!"

They went into the cabin and found Simmonds, who was awake now. He started to try and kick them, and was making a lot of noise. Gary offered to chin him again but Jazz said they needed him to climb up the stairs with them. Simmonds refused to move until Jazz said the boat was sinking and if they didn't get off in ten minutes he would drown. It concentrated Simmonds' mind and he reluctantly allowed himself to be pushed up the stairs on to the deck. It was hard work with his hands tied behind his back but Jazz would take no chances with him.

"Move yourself, bastard, otherwise I will kick you up those stairs. Any trouble from you and make no mistake, it would be an honour and a pleasure to cut your balls off, and don't think I wouldn't do it, you fucking paedophile."

Gary approved of the sentiment, and just added with disgust, "Nonce!"

It took a while to get Simmonds up the stairs, and the struggle was helped by Gary roping Simmonds and pulling him up. Jazz came up last and climbed the stairs like a one-legged monkey on a greasy pole. Exhausted now and feeling sick, the fresh air helped. There was so much going on and he needed to get back to the mansion. He mentally pulled himself together – going from nothing happening to everything happening at once was a shock to the system, and he hoped Boomer had control of the situation at the mansion.

There was no getting away from it, Gary was a good sailor and knew these waters. The wind had whipped the water up and the tide was running in the opposite direction. They chugged through the choppy water and it looked quite difficult to keep the boat straight, but Gary knew what he was doing. The RNLI man was full of praise for Gary's skills and related to Jazz how good he was. To Jazz it was just bobbing up and down, and he felt more and more sick.

Simmonds could see how distracted he was and made a move to push Jazz towards the side of the boat, and he presumed, over the side. Jazz, sick but not stupid, countered the move and chinned Simmonds, who fell backwards, out for the count.

Gary caught sight of the action and shouted, "What a poof."

Jazz laughed. Against his better judgement, he was liking Gary more and more. He was anxious to get back to the mansion and see what had gone down. He knew it was going to be a long night.

They docked on the floating pontoon at Paglesham. Jazz grabbed Simmonds and the RNLI man helped him drag him out of the boat and along the pontoon. Simmonds had come round now and started to struggle a little. Although not quite with it, he knew he didn't want to go with Jazz. Between the three of them they managed to get Simmonds into the car with threats of a kick in the bollocks if he didn't behave. The RNLI man had a report to fill out, and after taking a few details said he would contact Jazz at Barking Police Station tomorrow. He was heading back to help with moving Bateman and the embedded mast. It was getting late and they didn't want to lose the light.

They left him at the boatyard where a colleague was picking him up. With nods of thanks they took off sedately along the bumpy road.

Jazz looked at the time and, seeing how late it was, urgently told Gary to, "Get a move on, God knows what's going down at the mansion."

Gary put his foot down and the car flew across the dips and holes in the bumpy road and skidded right on to Paglesham Road. He drove at breakneck speed down the winding country road to the mansion.

They arrived breathless, anxious and ready for anything. The mansion looked quiet and calm and after locking Simmonds in the car, Jazz and Gary crept quietly into the house. They went straight to the kitchen and Jazz saw a couple of Boomer's men drinking what looked like afternoon tea. They all looked up as Jazz burst into the kitchen and Boomer, who was on the phone again, put a finger to his mouth, telling Jazz to be quiet.

It all looked normal and Jazz, hyped up with enough adrenaline to fuel the Olympic team and now feeling deflated, asked, "What the fuck is going on here?"

Boomer, off the phone now, looked over to Jazz. He was pleased to see him walking and talking, and expressed his delight. "You fucking bastard, I should get you bollocked out the police force for buggering off like that and giving me a pissing awful surveillance device that was knackered. You could have been killed, you silly sod!"

Jazz laughed at this tirade. "I love you too, darling," came the cocky retort, which annoyed Boomer and he growled a warning. He didn't want that kind of talk, especially in front of his men.

Gary stood silently beside Jazz and watched. Today would give him something interesting to talk about in the pub, and this peculiar piss-pair were pure gold as well. It was all going to get him a good few drinks bought for him over the next week.

First of all, Simmonds was being taken to Southend Police Station to wait with the others. He was surly and refusing to answer any questions. He was asked if they were going to make a snuff movie tonight, but he wouldn't answer. They didn't bother at the moment to ask anything more; the visitors would be arriving soon.

Simmonds looked at Boomer and said he had no right to arrest him – he had done nothing wrong, it was Bateman who did everything. After Boomer stopped laughing he told Simmonds to save his fairy stories.

Simmonds changed tack. He didn't want to go anywhere. He complained bitterly and loudly about his treatment by Jazz and Gary. He said he would report them to the police authority. He told Boomer that he had been knocked out, kicked in the bollocks, hit around the head and was in a very ill and shaken state.

Boomer looked at Simmonds with mild interest

in what he was saying. He nodded gravely at the various injuries explained to him, and after a suitable time he announced to Simmonds, "If you're looking for sympathy, matey, the only place you'll find it is between 'shit' and 'syphilis' in the dictionary, so shut it, you bastard!"

Jazz smiled; a typical Boomerism. Boomer had now had enough of Simmonds, and he looked around for one of his team and shouted loudly, "Oi, bastards, I have another bit of filth for you to take to Southend Police Station. Put down your fags and get him there ASAP. I need you back here quickly for the next phase, so chop-chop."

In a flash Simmonds was taken out of the room to the car, still moaning and arguing. In the distance Jazz heard him being told to shut the fuck up, and a grunt from Simmonds suggested he'd got a slap for being a nuisance.

Boomer quickly brought Jazz up to speed and told him he had missed all the excitement. He added that Paula had got Lemus and his boys had got the two goons, and they were all waiting at Southend Police Station for transport to Barking. But the boy, Archie, was nowhere to be found. Mad Pete was also missing. Boomer said he had his men out looking for the boy and Mad Pete.

Jazz turned to Gary and asked, "Can you think of anywhere within walking distance where someone could hide away?" He added that he knew Mad Pete, and he wouldn't hide anywhere on Bateman's property because he could be found; he would go somewhere close by but away from the house.

Gary had a think and suggested that there was, across the road in a field, a three-sided shed with straw in it for horses to use. He added, "If I wanted to hide, it's the nearest place to go away from here, and there are bales of straw to hide behind. You can see it from the road and the field is easy to get into."

Jazz asked which direction, and was told, "Left at the gates and look to your right as you walk down the road." Before Gary could say, 'Good luck' Jazz was out of the door. Time was of the essence; the twelve could be arriving any time within the next ten minutes and although Boomer had made the mansion look normal, Archie needed to be found and taken to safety. As for Mad Pete, well, Jazz would sort him out later.

He ran along the road looking between the hedges for this shed thingy in a field. He came to a gate between the hedgerows and saw it. It was about one hundred yards into the field. Jazz climbed the gate, noting mud on the rungs – so someone else had climbed it. He ran and stumbled across the field, ricking his ankle in a dip in the ground. Limping now, he got to the shed, and stood still. A whimper broke the silence; it was a child's whimper.

"Pete, are you here? It's me," Jazz called. There was a rustling amongst some loose straw that had obviously come from a couple of broken bales that sat on a stack of them.

"Mr Singh, thank Gawd," came the worried reply. Mad Pete sat up, and in his arms he had Archie.

Jazz looked at Archie and smiled and said, "Hello, little fella." Archie began to cry and held on tight to Mad Pete.

"He's sort of bonded with me, Mr Singh." Mad Pete smiled as he patted Archie's back to calm him down. Jazz could see that Mad Pete had bonded with Archie too, which was pretty strange. Mad Pete didn't bond with anyone.

After a pause, Mad Pete said he had to get the boy away. "I couldn't allow what was going to happen to happen, Mr Singh, it ain't right." He looked at Jazz and nodded. "I knew you would find us, Mr Singh, I told Archie that, didn't I, Archie?" He gave Archie a little hug to confirm that.

Jazz was quite touched by this. "Anything else I should know, Pete?" he asked. He could tell Mad Pete had something to say.

"Yes, Mr Singh. Look in the office room next to the big room. He has got some stuff in there. I sort of looked the other day. There is a secret compartment in the wall. I can't remember where now, I got spooked with what I saw and had to get out. There are some nasty DVDs stacked in that cupboard, judging by the titles I saw." His eyes warned he couldn't say more because Archie was there.

"Look," Jazz whispered, not wanting to frighten Archie, "we have to get away quickly. We are expecting the twelve to arrive very soon. I will check out what you said, Pete." After an embarrassed pause, not quite sure how to say it, he added, "Good job, Pete, well done." Jazz raised his hand and hesitantly and awkwardly patted Mad Pete on his back in recognition of his heroism. Mad Pete looked at him as if he was off his head; Mr Singh never said anything nice like that, but he nodded his thanks and looked away.

Jazz rummaged in his pockets, looking for the mobile Boomer had given him. He called Boomer and asked for a car to be by the gate to take Archie and Mad Pete somewhere safe. Boomer didn't want any more of his men to be away from the mansion. He said he didn't know what trouble they would have when the twelve arrived. It was agreed that Ash would take Archie and Mad Pete to Southend Police Station and they would wait there until the twelve had arrived and been arrested. Mad Pete carried Archie, who clung so tightly to him that he had to loosen Archie's arms around his neck in order to breathe.

The conversation during the walk to the car was a bit of a moan. Mad Pete said he didn't want to go to a police station, that being with the filth wasn't much of a reward for saving Archie, and he wanted somewhere comfortable. Jazz gave Mad Pete a bit of a slap for calling the police filth. He promised that he would personally ring ahead and say what a hero Mad Pete was, and that they were to feed them both and look after them. Jazz, knowing Mad Pete's stomach, reminded him that Southend was the seaside and they would have the best fish and chips. He assured Mad Pete that Southend Police Station was the Ritz of stations and he would have wonderful accommodation. A bit of a lie, but for the moment the name of the game was to get Mad Pete and Archie somewhere safe. He did ring ahead and ask that they be fed and explained that Mad Pete was a hero, so it wasn't all lies.

The car was waiting by the gate and Ash told Jazz, "No worries, will get them to Southend and get them some food and rest, then I'm coming back."

Jazz was going to argue, but actually he was glad Ash was coming back; he needed him to cover his back. If they arrested twelve paedophiles, they would need Ash's organising ability to get them ferried to Fresh Wharf for charging. Within moments, they were off and Jazz sighed with relief. Boomer could call his men back to the house.

The two who had taken Simmonds to Southend Police Station were now back and all were in the spacious kitchen, talking tactics.

It all felt surreal. The atmosphere was electric. Boomer's men knew they were going to arrest twelve men who individually outranked all of them put together. They were excited at such a coup, and scared as hell in case they got it wrong. Boomer and Jazz could feel the tension, so a plan of action was formulated to avoid any uncertainties when the time came.

CHAPTER 32

Disciples of Death

Jazz asked urgently, "Who knows where the intercom is for opening the gates and talking to the visitors?"

Boomer said, "One of my men is on it and waiting for the first to arrive."

It was a relief to work with such switched-on detectives, and Jazz replied, "Fucking brilliant."

Boomer nodded at such an accolade and said, "Paula, as the housekeeper, will open the door and show the first person into the lounge, where I will be with two of my men. We will arrest the fuckers and my men will take them upstairs and lock them in one of the bedrooms. One of my boys will watch over the paedophiles kept up there."

Paula nodded, knowing what she was to do, and Boomer's men nodded too.

Jazz was impressed. "Fucking brilliant, you'll all get a knighthood for this." They all laughed, not sure on that one.

It was agreed the visitors would be gagged and

cuffed. They checked how many sets of cuffs they had. Between them they had fifteen sets, far more than they should have had, but this was Boomer's team and Jazz, so Metropolitan Police standard issue didn't apply. They found some masking tape in one of the utility rooms off the kitchen, and some rope that might come in handy. They were ready for what was to come.

Boomer asked if Jazz had heard from DCI Radley. Jazz's phone was out of power, so he didn't know. Boomer said he had about six missed calls and a couple of messages from him that he hadn't read yet. They both knew they were in for a barrel-load of trouble.

"Hopefully this peace offering of arresting twelve paedophiles plus Simmonds and Lemus and the two heavies might help," Jazz ruefully exclaimed. Boomer grunted derisively at this comment. Neither thought they would get away with less than a total bollocking.

It was gone 8pm and the tension was thick, they could all taste it. Boomer's team were itching to get going, and like hounds before a hunt, they were boisterous, loud and brash, and had to be quietened down. Paula wondered if she should have gone with Archie to the police station but Jazz said he was superglued to Mad Pete and her help would be needed later.

Boomer looked again for something to eat; it was late and they hadn't had much for hours. He found food for the evening in the big fridges and helped himself to a few chicken legs. His men, seeing this, dived for the fridge too and he had to shout at them to stand easy in case they got a call from the gates. Jazz loved Boomer's team and the banter between them was good. He had a couple of chicken legs too. Paula watched this circus going on and wondered how anything bloody happened correctly with this team. She reckoned it was sheer luck they actually did anything right.

It was 8.30pm when the intercom buzzed. All immediately fell silent as Boomer's man, in a professional but friendly manner, asked who was calling. It was the first paedophile, and he had brought his chum with him. They were ticked off the list. Another two of Boomer's men ran to the lounge. They wanted no problems, so two men would take each paedophile. Four of them waited in the room with Boomer. Paula was asked to open the door and lead them to the dining room. Jazz told the man opening the gates to ensure they were closed as soon as they got into the yard. He didn't want anyone getting spooked and driving off. It all felt tense.

The two men came to the door and Paula opened it, graciously and with a smile. Their attire shocked her, but she managed to maintain the smile. They were wearing cloaks and cowls and looked like monks. As they came into the house, they seemed to know what they were doing and without any comment or acknowledgement they made their way to an anteroom off the kitchen. Paula watched, wondering what was going on, but realised they were doing what they normally did when they came to the mansion. It would seem that anteroom was where they disrobed.

From a flash of the cape as they came back into the hall, she could see they were naked under their cloaks. It was all done in a way that was standard and natural, like washing your hands after going to the toilet. They had done this many times, Paula could tell. When they were ready, they nodded to Paula and she took them to the lounge. They looked at each other; this was obviously not usual, and they seemed a little reticent for a moment. Paula noted this and gave a big smile and said Mr Bateman had an exquisite surprise for them in the lounge. They smiled at each other, visibly relaxed and followed her into the lounge.

Jazz listened and again thought that Paula was an ace detective, thinking on her feet; she was good. A noise made him turn around – it was the back door to the kitchen being closed. *God*, he thought, he had forgotten all about Gary in the rush. Gary had made himself a cup of tea and had been sitting on the step outside the back door having a cigarette. Now he was ready to leave. This caused a dilemma for Jazz: he didn't want anything to interfere with the twelve arriving, and Gary leaving by the front door might alert or spook them; that couldn't happen.

"Gary, my man, I am afraid it's too late to leave just yet. If you look in the fridge you can get something to eat and there might be a tinnie in there too for you to have while you wait."

The other detectives, who were sitting there checking their guns and cuffs in readiness, looked up at Gary and nodded, indicating that he could join them at the table. Well, Gary figured, he would have free drinks for a month when he told all his cronies in the pub about this. He was happy to stay.

Jazz opened the kitchen door with four of Boomer's men pushing behind him. The shouting was loud and chaotic. The two men in their cloaks were handcuffed and being led upstairs to the top floor where they would wait for the others to arrive. They didn't go quietly and one was raising quite a stink, accusing them of treason and telling them how he would tell the Prime Minister, whom he knew very well, and the commissioner for police, who was his best friend. They were led away politely but the officers were taking no crap from them and they were frogmarched at speed up the stairs. The masking tape would be put on up there.

The intercom went again: the next car had arrived. Two more of Boomer's men left the kitchen and went into the lounge. The other two stayed upstairs with their charges in case they made a noise. Jazz took the opportunity of running to the room on the ground floor that looked like an office. He put the light on and looked around – yes, an office with filing cabinets and a computer. He closed the door quickly; the front door was about to be opened to the next visitor. It was all very well arresting men who turned up in cloaks and cowls and took their clothes off, but it wasn't enough to charge them with anything. *Jeez*, thought Jazz, *all these bollocking top-drawer men and no concrete evidence to charge them with anything.* Prancing around in the nude and looking like a bleeding monk was not illegal. It could all go Pete Tong, he thought glumly, and he couldn't have that. With more high-powered murderous paedophiles arriving, it was paramount that evidence was found to incriminate them all. *No pressure there then*, thought Jazz ruefully.

Jazz reckoned that with the security in the house, it was likely Bateman kept information around and felt safe in the knowledge that he couldn't and wouldn't get broken into. Mad Pete was a grade-one rat and if there was anything to find, he would have found it. Based on what Mad Pete said, Jazz knew there was something here, and he was going to find it.

Paula took a deep breath. She realised she was as scared as hell, but as she opened the door the reassuring smile appeared on her face.

The next visitor came in alone. He was full of importance and barely acknowledged Paula. He too knew the form and made his way to the anteroom and hung up his clothes. When naked, he put on his cloak and came back to the hall and waited for Paula to take him to the usual place. Again, Paula said Mr Bateman had something exquisite to show him. The man raised an eyebrow and followed her into the lounge. It was difficult for Paula to see who these people were, but their names were told to the intercom detective and he was ticking them off. With the cloaks and cowls over their heads, Paula could see nothing that would allow her to know who they were. She wondered if they kept their identity a secret from each other, and that was how it worked. Two of them came together, so some knew each other. Tomorrow was going to be very interesting when they were all unmasked and their lives were scrutinised.

But this man was more in command, and was having none of the arresting jargon from Boomer. He argued and fought and told Boomer that he knew his history and would ensure he was drummed out of the Metropolitan Police with no pension and in total disgrace. Boomer told him that it had been tried before and if he wanted to, he should have a go at it, but he said that better fuckers than him had tried.

For the time being, he told this man he was arrested and would do as he was told. Just for good measure, Boomer, seriously pissed off now, gave him a kick up the backside and told him to go with the kind officers upstairs. He pulled the cowl off his head. There would be no disguises here, he told him. The prisoner's face looked familiar, and when he was taken upstairs, Boomer checked with the intercom detective. This paedophile ran a well-known newspaper and was known as a good Catholic. Boomer rubbed his hands together; he was going to love parading this one around the town and seeing what the press made of that.

They had only three in custody, but something gnawed at Boomer. They had some pretty top-drawer men coming here. Could they make all the charges stick? God, he hoped so – these men of authority had been part of or assisted in the assault of children and their subsequent murder. He had to get them. He wondered where that fucker Jazz had got to. He went into the kitchen and Gary, seeing Boomer making noises, said Jazz was investigating something. Before Boomer could ask more, the intercom bleeped again.

Boomer looked to Paula and she nodded. The intercom detective did his job and Boomer made his way quickly to the lounge. His two officers came down the stairs and joined him, ready. They had become a slick unit and each knew what was expected, and they got in position and waited. They were nervous and excited by this undercover job, but the tension was palatable too. This was the dog's bollocks of cases to be involved in; it beat Barking on a Saturday night, that was for sure.

Boomer didn't want to tell his men that each and every one of the paedophiles would, if they managed to get out of the charges, make sure their bollocks were roasted and their careers buried. They didn't need to know that now, he told himself. He shoved his hands in his pockets so his men didn't see them shaking.

It was very possible that they could all end up being kicked out of the police force. He loved his boys and he wondered if he had led them into a wasps' nest. Never a truer word said. If he had known what was going to happen, he would have got his boys out of this hellhole.

CHAPTER 33

A Good Reception

Jazz opened the filing cabinets that ranged along one wall. There was nothing worth looking at in them. It looked like paperwork for businesses Bateman owned or was involved in. On the face of it, they all looked legitimate and Jazz knew Bateman was a millionaire so all of this was possible. Someone would take a closer look at everything in these filing cabinets in the next few days, but he needed something to keep the twelve men in custody.

He stopped for a moment and stood in the middle of the room. There had to be something of interest here. Bateman couldn't run a large and very secretive paedophile ring with so many prestigious names without something being recorded. All those invited tonight had to be listed somewhere. How did he get them, and how did they meet and get to know one other? There had to be a link somewhere. Every one of the twelve was distinguished in his own field, but the areas were diverse, from judges to church people to high-ranking civil servants. All worked in different areas. Something joined them together, and Jazz needed to find what that was.

The cars were coming in thick and fast now and it was getting tricky to take the men upstairs before the next one came in. The running around was manic, but they managed. They were now waiting on four more to arrive and then they would have the twelve. There was a break of ten minutes, which was welcomed, and Boomer reassessed where everyone was. The men upstairs had to have their feet tied as well because they were trying to run around and make a noise to alert the next person arriving. They were all laid on the floor in the two bedrooms, quiet now. Boomer's team were still psyched up and raring to go. The next four would use up a lot of their energy.

For some reason Paula felt jittery, and she didn't know what was causing it. She wasn't used to working undercover and thought that must be it. The cloaks and cowls were strange and a little eerie; she didn't know why they dressed like that, apart from not wanting to be recognised, but it was so weird. Surely anyone seeing them would think them odd, and that must draw attention to themselves? She asked herself these questions but there were no answers yet.

Gary, sitting at the table, asked what was troubling her. He had watched her pacing a little and thinking. She turned to him and asked if he had ever seen the men coming into the mansion in their cloaks. Gary nodded and said he had. Paula looked at him, incredulous.

"So why didn't you think there was something strange going on here, then? Men in cloaks coming and going, how odd is that?"

Gary, now comfortable and in his element, said, "No, my darlin', not strange at all. You ain't from around here, are you?"

Paula shook her head.

"Well, we have things going on here that would turn your pretty hair grey. We thought they might be monks because Bateman was kinda close to the church in Canewdon." He paused to ensure Paula was listening, and she was listening intently.

"There again, we thought they could be a new coven in Paglesham. Canewdon has a coven of witches and we thought Paglesham might now have a coven. You can only have thirteen witches in a coven, and with Bateman the twelve that came here would make thirteen. We don't mess with witches in Paglesham. We keep our distance from them." He could see Paula gulp at the thought.

"So you think the men we have got here are witches?" asked Paula, a little out of her depth now.

Gary was bored, and a little playful, but he could see he had scared the lass and that wasn't fair. "Could be, but they is paedophiles and they is scum. Witches are white witches around here and they wouldn't be part of this."

Paula was thinking now. "Perhaps they pretend to be witches to keep the locals away, what do you think?"

Gary thought and nodded. "You could be right,

but they wear their cloaks and cowls inside – why do they do that?"

Just then the back door opened and in walked Ash. He had been running and was out of breath. Paula nearly jumped out of her skin. She felt seriously spooked. She was out in the middle of nowhere in a place that had witches, and she didn't know what the hell was going on.

Ash looked at her and wondered why she was so jumpy. By way of explanation he said, "I thought I had better come in the back way in case I bumped into any of them. Any more to arrive?"

Paula nodded and said, "Four more to come." Just then, the intercom buzzed again.

Jazz stood in the middle of the room and looked around. Mad Pete had said something about a secret cupboard. *What the fuck did that mean*? he asked himself. One wall was full of filing cabinets and they didn't seem to have anything interesting in them. The wall behind the desk was wood-panelled and had nothing on it, not even a picture.

He started to tap the panels on this wall, not knowing why, but he had seen it done in films. He tapped and pushed firmly on the panels. The first one didn't do anything but the second panel moved when pushed hard. Jazz pushed harder and the panel sprung open. The hinges had been cleverly hidden, and it was a surprise when the panel turned into a door. Behind the door was a filing cabinet with shelves above. He nearly did a jig. This had to be it. You just don't hide stuff unless it is secret stuff.

The cabinet had names and dossiers on various people. He recognised the names on some of the files as those of people who were here tonight. There were other files in there that were for people who were not here tonight and not on the list. There looked to be at least one hundred files in the cabinet, each one on a different person, and all seemed to be men. He skimmed the odd file to get a flavour of what they were about, and they listed the men's predilections for sexual pleasure. Most of those he looked at liked children – some just boys, some just girls; some both. He didn't have time to look at too many, but he had found what he was looking for. He laughed to himself – he had them, he had them all. This was the evidence to keep them banged up while everything was gone through.

On the shelves above were books on child pornography, obviously from abroad; some were not in English but they had pictures. He thought that surely the internet was used these days, but there again, it was not as secure as it used to be. This was a very secretive group of paedophiles.

He rummaged around as quickly as he could. Further down the room was another panel that opened when pushed hard. Behind this was a treasure trove of sadistic and barbaric sights. There were pictures catalogued with the age and sex of the child and what had been done to that poor child. Jazz felt a sadness he was not used to feeling. He also found videos and DVDs, which had been meticulously catalogued and stickers put on them. He knew they were of children, and they had been killed. The sadness turned, darkly and deeply, into anger.

He was ready to go and find Boomer when he heard a shot fired in the hallway outside his door.

The man on the end of the intercom said he was here with three other members and gave their names. They were the last to arrive. Boomer said he wanted all his men in the lounge; he would need six of them for the four men. Ash was asked to go upstairs and watch over the eight who were tied up and lying quietly on the floor. He ran upstairs quickly to get out of the way and Boomer's men ran down the stairs and into the lounge in readiness for the final three members of the circle entering the mansion. With a deep breath, Boomer looked around at his men. Now they were ready.

Paula had her role as housekeeper off pat and opened the door with a welcoming smile. The four men quickly entered the hall, their cloaks and cowls hiding their faces.

Paula expected them to make their way to the anteroom to disrobe, but one of the men stopped and turned and looked at Paula and asked abruptly. "Who are you and where is Betty?"

No one else had asked about Betty. It threw Paula for a moment, and then she said, quite airily, that she was helping Betty. Betty was in the lounge with Mr

Bateman and he had something exquisite to show them. It had worked before, so she hoped it satisfied the four of them.

She wasn't prepared for what happened next. The fist came at her in a blink of an eye and with such force that it threw her across the hallway. Her head hit the marble floor, knocking her out. A trickle of blood worked its way from her mouth to the floor. No one saw what had happened except the four men standing there. The four whispered together and each went in a different direction. One opened the kitchen door and swiftly noted it was empty. Gary was sitting on the back step with another fag and a cup of tea. He saw nothing.

The second hooded man went up the stairs quietly and quickly. He opened the first bedroom door and it was empty. Ash, in the other bedroom, heard the door open and close quietly, far too quietly to be Boomer's men with the latest paedophiles. Thinking quickly, Ash hid behind the door and withdrew his asp from the holder around his waist; he waited expectantly for the door to be opened.

It all happened in the blink of an eye. The door opened, and the hooded man stood for a second, surveying the sight of eight men tied up and lying on the floor. That split second of indecision was his mistake. They all made noises, trying to warn him of Ash behind the door, but before he understood what was going on, Ash brought his asp down heavily on the head of the hooded man and he fell unconcious to the floor with a thump.

Ash, shaken but feeling good, turned and smirked with satisfaction at the eight on the floor, who were now silent. Quickly he tied up this man and put masking tape across his mouth. He pushed off the cowl to take a look at this paedophile, and figured he was about thirty years old. With a blonde crew cut and a chiselled, square chin, he had a look of Dolph Lundgren, the actor; the one in *Rocky IV* who was built like a brick shithouse. This one was certainly a big bugger and Ash was glad he didn't think about that before he hit him. He looked again at the man he had felled. His cloak had parted, and Ash saw a rippling six-pack of a stomach and a neck the width of a tree trunk. With a shiver he thought, *Given half a chance this huge, vicious fucker could have killed me with just a look.* Ash's bowels growled pathetically in blind panic. He tugged on the ropes binding the man again, just to make sure they were tight.

Calming a little, Ash took a deep breath and then that prickly sense that something was very wrong came over him. This man was up here – why? What was going on downstairs? He felt sick, that awful feeling of trepidation overtook him and the hairs started to rise on his arms. *Oh my good God*, he thought, *I think I've got to go and see what is happening downstairs.* The cold sweat of fear rose up from his stomach and nearly choked him; he was barely breathing now. He spent a few indecisive minutes arguing with himself. *I should stay put. I might put those downstairs in danger if I make an appearance. I should stay with the nine*

I've got now in case they get away. I feel sick – I can't go downstairs like this. When he had finished arguing with himself, there was no contest: he had to check what was happening.

With a deep breath, feeling as ready as he ever would be, he checked his asp and got ready to quietly go out on to the landing and look over the banister. It was as his hand touched the door handle that he heard the gunshot which froze him to the spot.

Hearing the gunshot, everyone on the floor became manically animated, struggling to thump the floor with their tied legs and arms and making muffled noises as loudly as they could through the masking tape, sensing they could be saved. They all knew who the four men were; they would always arrive together for these events. They sensed it wouldn't be long before they were rescued and able to get away.

Ash watched with dismay as they rolled and lashed out as best they could in an excited frenzy. He hoped they were too far up the stairs for anyone to hear. The gunshot made this a whole new ball game for Ash, and he wasn't sure what to do now. The atmosphere in the bedroom had changed from fear to elation and it didn't sit well with Ash. His bowels growled again.

CHAPTER 34

Trouble Afoot

The three hooded men had watched as the fourth went up the stairs. They each had their roles: one would check the bedrooms, one would check the kitchen, then the three of them would tackle the lounge. They knew they would have opposition in there. The woman was still out cold on the floor. They didn't know what had happened here but each was professional and streetwise and knew how to deal with any situation. They waited as one checked the kitchen and on his return informed the others that it was empty. They had swept the surrounding area in seconds with a quiet efficiency that was slick and smart.

They looked to the lounge door and together they rushed into the room to surprise whoever was in there. They must have had military training from the way they moved, each knowing what the other was doing. The gun was fired at the biggest one in the room, and that was Boomer. He fell to the ground with a grunt of pain.

Boomer's detectives, taken by surprise, stood

rooted to the spot for the moment in shock, their response time nil, and then seeing Boomer fall to the floor as the gun fired caused panic and confusion. The three hooded men didn't stop; they rushed all six detectives and after a melee of scuffles and shouts it only took two minutes for the hooded three to have Boomer and the six detectives tied up and kicked to the floor. Boomer's men didn't have time to reach for their guns, to shout or retaliate as trained; most were knocked down with one blow.

The hooded man in front, the one who seemed to have taken control, pushed his cowl off his head. "Who the hell are you and what the fuck are you doing here?" he asked menacingly in an accent that had an educated Scottish lilt to it. The other three hooded men took off their cowls. Each detective observing realised they would not get out of this situation to tell the tale. It was the only logical reason why these three would show their faces.

Boomer lay still. He was winded but still alive, *A bloody miracle*, he thought, although he figured, with a sarcasm he didn't have time for, that the bulletproof jacket he had on might have helped. He wasn't going to move for the time being. He lay there thinking on his next move. He wasn't fast; it would take him all of five minutes just to stand up – his stomach, weighing the most, would have held him down. He had his gun though, and he would wait for an opportunity to get it out of his holster, as long as they didn't frisk him in the meantime. He continued to play dead and listened for his opportunity to get these fuckers.

The eldest of the detectives, Andrew Thorn, was singled out to answer the question. Thorn looked down at Boomer and saw no signs of life. Forlorn, scared and not sure what to say, he stammered, "We, well, we, that is, all of us here…" He swept his arm around the other detectives on the floor. He was stalling for time, not sure what to say. He knew Jazz and Ash were somewhere, although why that didn't make him feel confident he couldn't say. "Well, we were told to come here and assist. We don't know why, it has just all kicked off."

The lead hooded man was having none of that, and punched Thorn in the stomach. He looked at Thorn on the floor, doubled up and winded, and urgently and fiercely told him, "You had better start again, sunshine, and make it clear and true, otherwise one of your friends is going to be the next one for a body bag."

Thorn knew it to be true. He had been with Boomer for the past three years and knew a thing or two, but this was outside of anything he had dealt with before. There was nothing for it; he would have to tell the truth. Stalling didn't work and he knew they would all be killed at the end of the day. *Please, God, let Jazz and Ash do something interesting.*

Before he started, the lead hooded man nodded to another. "Go check out upstairs, he should have come down by now." Without another word one of the men left the room, leaving just two to guard them. Again with menace, the lead man grabbed Thorn by his lapels and pulled him to his feet. With his face so close, Thorn could smell his stale cigarette breath.

"Now let's start again – where are Bateman and Simmonds?"

Just to reinforce this question, the hooded one punched Thorn in the stomach again. Thorn yelped in pain but was still standing.

He saw an opportunity and said, "They are tied up and locked in one of the cottages outside."

He hoped the third hooded one would go and take a look. They might stand a chance of doing something if they had only one to contend with. The hooded one was having none of that. He just nodded. They weren't stupid enough to leave just one with this lot.

"So," he continued, looking at what he had before him with utter contempt, "who the fuck are you and why are you here?"

Thorn, sweating now, frightened and in pain and with nowhere to go, was going to have to tell the truth. "We are all Metropolitan Police officers and we have to report in soon, otherwise our station will come looking for us."

The hooded one laughed. "Nice try," he said, and punched Thorn again in the stomach. This time he reeled and fell down. The hooded one grabbed his lapels and roughly pulled him up. He took hold of Thorn's face and squeezed his cheeks until Thorn thought his teeth would break.

"Let's start again, shall we?" the hooded one said rather pleasantly, but added, "But if you want to keep your fucking teeth, tell me – why are you here?"

He gave Thorn's face a final hard squeeze that

pushed something out of place, just to emphasise that he wasn't going to be messed around any more.

Thorn, hurting like hell and unable to straighten his face for a moment, mumbled and coughed. It gave him a few moments to think, but he could think of nothing except to tell the truth.

Feeling defeated now, Thorn quietly said, "We are Met Police, and most of us are DCs. We were asked by our boss – the one you killed, you bastard – to come here to sort out and apprehend a paedophile ring."

This earned Thorn another punch. He was seriously feeling sick and ill now. He had nowhere to go with this story except to say that Bateman and Simmonds said they were going to tell all. It was a lie but he hoped it might make them a little edgy. If Boomer had taught them nothing else, it was evasion tactics. Mainly for keeping their bosses off their backs, but it might work here too.

Those tied up and bundled in a sitting position, propped up against the wall, watched closely what was going on. They winced at the punches delivered to Thorn, and when all eyes seemed to be on him, one of them saw Boomer move a finger. This was relayed to all five sitting there through looks – not a word was said. The relief was hidden but all thought about what they could do to manipulate this tense and deadly situation. The two fuckers had guns trained on them and they knew it was only a matter of time before they were finished off.

CHAPTER 35

Deliver us from Evil

On hearing the gunfire, Jazz, like a coiled spring, leapt into action. He headed for the door and checked to see if he had his asp with him; he didn't.

He quietly cursed himself – "Fucking idiot!" – and looked around urgently for something he could use as a weapon. He picked up a hole punch from the desk which might do. It had a handle and if he smacked it into someone's face, it should take him off guard, he thought optimistically. He opened the door just a crack to see what was out there.

He spotted Paula laid out on the floor. Opening the door a little wider, he checked the hall was empty and tiptoed to Paula. She was still out cold. He spotted a can hanging out of her pocket: it was the CS gas spray. *Bloody lucky they didn't spot that*, he thought, and took it. *No contest between a CS gas spray and a fucking hole punch*. He would have laughed if it weren't all so serious. He dropped the hole punch by Paula and left her there for the moment. She was breathing, he had checked and that would have to do for now; there was no time for any first aid.

It was all done in the blink of an eye. He had to do something quick. He went back to the study door for the moment whilst he looked around. Where was everybody?

The lounge door handle turned, Jazz heard it, and in an instant he was back to the study and just closed the door as one of the hooded men quickly made his way through the lobby and up the stairs. Jazz now knew where everyone was; they were all in the lounge. He thought Ash was upstairs guarding the paedophiles and was torn between going into the lounge or up the stairs. On second thought, he decided to go upstairs. Only one man to take on and he needed Ash to help him with whatever was going on in the lounge. If there was bloody gunfire and all he had was a CS gas spray, he didn't fancy his chances.

It was worrying. What the hell was Ash to do now? He opened the door a crack and listened. The decision was taken out of his hands with the sound of a door being opened and closed and footsteps running up the stairs. He closed the door quietly and stood behind it once again. He tried to control his breathing, but he was panic-stricken. It worked last time, but could he do it again, he asked himself?

He held his asp in readiness. Last time he was fearless; this time he was a bag of nerves. The paedophiles tied up on the floor were looking towards the door, ready to move and shout and alert an ally if he entered. It took only a minute or two but it felt like a lifetime and Ash could feel the tremor in his legs. He held the wall, not sure his legs would hold him as he waited.

The door opened suddenly and dramatically; this one wasn't so easily fooled and he was on the alert for any trouble. Fortunately one of the paedophiles on the floor made a supreme effort to struggle to get his attention. He wanted to warn him of Ash standing behind the door. While he looked for a split second at this thrashing man on the floor, Ash stepped forward; the hooded man was ahead of him with his back to him. Ash, with asp raised high and held in both hands, brought it down on the head of the hooded man.

For a second he thought he had killed him. The asp, unforgiving, crushed the side of the man's head and he fell to the floor with a thump Ash felt sure could be heard around the house.

Nervous now but needing to know what was going on, Ash again crept forward and out on to the landing to peer over the banisters to the lobby below; he hoped he could see what was going on. He saw Jazz coming up the stairs quickly but silently. He waved to him, not wanting to make a noise, and in a second Jazz was on the landing. Ash whispered what he had done. He allowed himself a smug smile.

"I've bloody well knocked out two of the paedophiles, and they were carrying guns," he added triumphantly.

"Fucking marvellous, Ash, you will get a medal for

that," Jazz told him as he walked into the bedroom with the floor full of paedophiles.

"We need guns, Ash, have you got their guns?" he asked, pointing towards the two hooded ones.

"Do you mean these?" said a very smug Ash as he held up two handguns for Jazz to inspect.

Jazz looked at them and said, "Bloody hell, they are Glock 17 semi-automatic pistols, and the latest standard issue for the British Army. I reckon they are fucking army personnel. If they are, what in hell's name have we uncovered here?" It was a rhetorical question and he didn't wait for a response. "You are up for another medal, my son, for sorting these out. OK, Ash, you and me are gonna go down there and relieve them of their guns and see what's going on. One shot fired, please God, no one killed."

He looked over all the bodies on the floor and swiftly assessed that all were tied up and no bother. The latest hooded one had the side of his head caved in and was out cold so he wasn't going anywhere. With that he quickly made his way to the stairs.

With everything happening in split seconds and Jazz talking at the speed of light, Ash was still standing, shocked at the speed of everything and at what Jazz was asking him to do.

"Move your arse, Ash, remember the medals and your children. Make them proud."

With that resounding speech done, he ran quietly down the stairs. Ash followed, reluctantly at first but gaining speed, and by the time they reached the lounge door they were together. Jazz looked and saw Paula still out cold, but for the moment she would have to wait. Slightly out of breath, they stood outside the lounge door. Jazz put his ear to the door but could hear nothing. It was very quiet. He whispered to Ash that they would burst in and look immediately for the two hooded men.

"Shoot the bastards first and ask questions later," were Jazz's instructions.

Ash nodded fervently. He knew it was either them or the paedophiles, and no way was he going home in a body bag. For a second his bowels growled again, but he ignored the problem. There were seven colleagues in there and they had to be rescued.

Just as Jazz was about to say, 'On the count of three, we go in', a voice shouted from the kitchen door. "What the bloody 'ell are you doing? That lass is on the floor, fainted!"

Fuck, it was that bastard Gary, thought Jazz. He waved furiously at him to get back in the kitchen and gestured to him to be quiet. Gary hovered for a moment and then, muttering to himself, went back into the kitchen. But it was all too late: the lounge door opened suddenly and one of the hooded men stood there menacingly, pointing a gun straight at Ash. Ash dropped his gun and stood rooted to the spot in blind panic.

It all happened in a flash: Ash first saw the man's resolute and cruel face, then he became transfixed by the gun pointed straight at him. He swore he saw the trigger being pulled back, and in the next second he was on the floor, sliding towards the wall. Jazz had pushed him to the side with a brute force that only someone like the Hulk could possess. At the same time, Jazz fired his gun three times at the man in the doorway and threw himself to the side, sliding towards Ash and bashing into him.

Like a man possessed, Jazz was up and running towards the lounge door; he knew another man was in there and he had to assume they all had guns. A shot was fired as Jazz ran up to the lounge door. For a second, with a heavy heart, he thought he was too late. It was the cheer that rang out from Boomer's lads that gave him hope.

"I fucking did something to my shoulder, going down like that. Where is the other fucking bastard?" was the welcome from Boomer.

Jazz ran over to the last hooded man on the floor. He felt his pulse and pronounced him dead. Now he swiftly untied all six of Boomer's men. Jazz asked them to check on Paula, and two confirmed she was knocked out but breathing. Boomer's men went off to search the house, check the paedophiles upstairs and call for backup.

Jazz relaxed for a second against the wall. His body suddenly felt like it had turned to jelly, and he slid down on to the floor. The Action Man stunt of sliding across the floor had done something to his shoulder too.

Boomer told him, "Your bleeding flying leap,

doing a James Bond and shooting the bastard who shot me, made the other fucker more interested in you than me, so I shot him, 'nuff said. Except you took your fucking time to get here."

Jazz just raised his eyebrows at Boomer in answer to that. Still sitting on the floor, he told the detectives not to touch the study room. "It's got everything we need to put the lot of them away. It's stuffed full of names, videos, pictures and the predilections of the bastards. We have got the lot of them. Someone call an ambulance for Paula, pronto." Jazz slumped some more and said to no one in particular, "I could do with a fucking drink."

Boomer saw a table with bottles of whisky, brandy and other stuff on it. He went and got a bottle of brandy and handed it to Jazz.

"You will fucking need it when Radley gets hold of you," he said, laughing. He got a couple of glasses and sat down beside Jazz, and poured a couple of generous measures of brandy.

"Cheers, bastard," said Boomer as he clinked glasses with Jazz. They finished it in a few minutes. Refreshed and with lots of moans, they stiffly got up and checked what was happening in the house.

Ash by now was in the lounge and had called an ambulance for Paula. He asked if anyone else was injured and they all looked at each other and said that apart from two dead men, they were fine.

Jazz, aching but pleased, wandered about, thinking how great this was, until Ash came up to him. He said that

DCI Radley was at Southend Police Station, pacifying the Essex Police who were spitting nails at so many of their cells being taken and their car park full of Barking Police vans, and further, no respect had been shown for them undertaking such a big operation without their knowledge, on their turf! Ash told him it was two in the morning and DCI Radley was still up, and he was coming to the mansion in one of the police vans.

"Bugger me, no bleeding peace for the soddin' wicked. Boomer, we are in trouble and I need another drink."

Boomer filled the glasses and they sat back down, relaxed and let the men finish looking around. Paula was sitting up, a bit worse for wear but the ambulance came quickly and took her off, to shouts from Jazz of, "See you later, Paula, take care and well done, girl." They finished their glasses of brandy with a cigarette. Boomer commented that Paula had done good, and was now an honorary man in his books.

Jazz laughed, nearly choking on his brandy, and with as much sarcasm as he could muster in the circumstances said, "She's gonna be pleased with that, Boomer."

Boomer grunted and said, "That's a typical woman for you. How can you find fault with such praise?"

It was a smooth moment, and Jazz in particular savoured the warmth of the brandy. He knew it could be his last quiet moment for a long time.

Again he held up his glass, and with a crack of emotion in his tired voice he said, "Cheers, Kevin, we got them all for you. You rest in peace, little fella."

CHAPTER 36

So You Think its All Over

DCI Radley appeared far too soon with the three police vans from Barking nick. He looked very worried, but not his usual nitpicking, angry self, as he normally did when things had happened out of his control. Jazz reckoned he was tired and just didn't have the energy, and he was grateful for that. Another ambulance had been called for him and Boomer, who had both been injured from throwing themselves down on the floor.

Jazz protested he couldn't go in an ambulance yet. There was much to explain and show to DCI Radley. The men upstairs and those at Southend Police Station would be under the PACE clock so it was imperative that evidence was presented to ensure they were charged. These were all high-ranking men who could wheedle their way out of things and there was no way Jazz was going to have that. They were all going down and he would ensure that happened.

The ambulance men gave up on Jazz and turned to Boomer. They had been told that he had been shot at, and although he wore a bulletproof vest, there could be some injury from the impact. Boomer laughed at them, and held his chest – it was a bit sore but he told them he had been on pheasant shoots that were more dangerous than today.

With contempt he added, "Fucking city gents shoot at anything that moves, including me."

One of Boomer's men heard the comment and shouted, "Guv, they knew what they were doing."

The laughter got more raucous as Boomer retaliated with an update on what he would do with his gun if his officer came closer.

Jazz smiled; it was a bit of light relief after the long day. It didn't last; he had DCI Radley to contend with now. First, he needed to prove to him that this operation had been successful. DCI 'I want to rise in the ranks and be the commissioner of police before I hit forty years of age' Radley would be very worried indeed by these arrests. He had already been upstairs and seen how eminent men, faces he recognised, were tied up on the floor with duct tape across their mouths. The sight was shocking enough, and the implications of what Jazz and Boomer had done were catastrophic in his view. He was withholding judgement on this but only just, and beads of sweat were forming on his forehead.

With another brandy poured into his glass, Jazz, past caring what DCI Radley would think of him drinking on duty, went to find his superior. He took him into the study and showed him what he had found.

An hour passed quickly. The files of names were impressive. Some Jazz knew, but most were out of his league. Radley knew more, and the beads of sweat were now dripping down his face into his collar. He took out a pristine white handkerchief and mopped his brow.

They had to sit down for the next bit. One door opened to row upon row of DVDs. They were named and dated. The first was dated October 1999, with the name David on it. It was put in the DVD player by the television and they sat and watched. It took only a minute to realise they were watching a child being raped and tortured; the screams were unbearable. It was too much to watch and listen to. Radley turned the DVD off swiftly and slumped back down into his chair.

"In the name of all the gods, what have we found here?" he muttered, almost to himself. The shock was palpable – Radley, never at a loss for words, just sat and shook his head. Jazz and Boomer watched in silence. The brandy and the DVD had got to Jazz, and he felt the tears welling. He scrambled in his pocket for a tissue or something to wipe his eyes. The three of them were locked in a hell of knowledge no decent human being should know.

The polite knock on the door brought them all to their senses, and they stood to see who was there. DCI Radley, now fully back in control, listened to the officer telling him that all twelve suspects were being taken to Fresh Wharf in Barking.

Radley nodded and ordered, "Ring ahead and tell Fresh Wharf how many are being brought in, and I will ring Southend and get one of their vans to help us take the other four being held there. Now get a bloody move on!"

The officer could tell DCI Radley was not himself. He had never heard him swear before, or sound so jittery. He would tell the lads to watch themselves. Experience told him a DCI rattled was not someone you crossed swords with. With a nod he disappeared to get on with moving the paedophiles.

The room fell silent and they could hear the shouting, scuffles and running footsteps in the hall outside, but for the moment they were locked in silence.

With a heavy sigh, Radley stated the obvious. "It is necessary to get moving. Nothing in this room is to be disturbed. I will pack up the DVDs, the named files, the lists, but tomorrow I will have this room fingertip-searched for more hidden areas." Boomer and Jazz nodded.

Now fired up, DCI Radley stood, and with shoulders back, he surveyed the room. With all the authority and presence that a detective chief inspector could muster, he phoned Southend Police Station and ordered twenty empty boxes for highly confidential exhibits to be sent to them immediately. Someone, stupidly, seemed to be arguing on the other end of the phone.

Radley was in no mood to be argued with, and in

a voice not even Jazz had been subjected to, he told the custody sergeant on the phone, "I am Detective Chief Inspector Radley from the Metropolitan Police, Barking. Get those fucking boxes to me within fifteen minutes otherwise I will ensure you never, and I mean never, see your police pension. In fact, I will have you thrown into the fucking cells and you know what a villain will do to you, arsehole! So get a fucking move on. I am counting down the time from now!"

With that Radley put the phone down and tried to calm his temper; this was so not like him. Jazz quite liked the new DCI Radley, he was getting things done and for the moment the temper was not directed at him. His time would come; he knew that.

The boxes arrived in twenty minutes. Pretty good going; Southend Police Station was nearly that distance away and they had to find all the boxes, so someone moved fast to get this done. Radley only wanted the three of them to fill the boxes. He didn't want anything contaminated by too many hands.

"Right," he said, "I want us to take all the DVDs and the other boxes are for the files, particularly the named files. I want to take the majority back with us, but it will be tomorrow by the time this room is gone through with a fine-toothed comb and we might find more. I need to take as much as we can, and we keep it with us." Radley emphasised that, and Jazz wasn't sure what he meant. But before he could ask Radley continued busily, "I need officers to stand guard at the house overnight. Southend Police will do that for us. I will ring their superintendent."

Radley looked at his watch and told them it was three in the morning and they needed to get back, get some sleep and sort this out later. This was the most businesslike and forceful Jazz had seen DCI Radley, and he wondered what was behind it.

"I want out of here by 3.30am, so let's get moving," were DCI Radley's final words. Jazz and Boomer started to pack whilst Radley made his phone call.

Boomer's men had gone in the vans with the prisoners. Two had gone to Southend Police Station to pick up the four there. Fresh Wharf was big but they hoped it was a quiet night. They would need sixteen cells. It felt good.

They were packed up by 3.30am as Radley said. Two Essex Police officers arrived and were told to stand guard at the house. They were told they could wait inside but the study was not to be touched. Tired now, Jazz, Boomer and Radley took the police car in the garage and made their way back to Barking.

DCI Radley had something to say that was only for Jazz's and Boomer's ears. He was adamant they listen and adhere to this. All the boxes had to be put somewhere safe, and no one was to know their whereabouts until the morning, when they would decide what to do. It was very odd but Radley was firm and clear. They knew something was going on, but what?

Radley was dropped off in the police yard, where

he got into his BMW. His final comments were to hide the boxes safely and to be in his office by 9am that morning. They watched his nice piece of machinery gliding quietly out of the car park.

Jazz wondered where he could put all the boxes until the morning. He needed to bury them. He had the perfect place. The stationery room was full of boxes of stationery. He would hide the boxes in there until the morning. No one would come for stationery at night, and he knew where the key was.

After Boomer had helped hide the boxes underneath the pile in the stationery room, he wished Jazz a good night and took himself off home. It was five in the morning – not much time for sleep, he grumbled.

All the prisoners were being processed through custody and charged. It was very odd; Jazz had never known all the cells emptied for any operation, let alone an operation that had sixteen prisoners. He was told that all thirty cells had been vacated for them. Cells already being used were emptied and those prisoners were taken to Ilford, Plaistow, and Chadwell Heath Police Stations.

Jazz decided to take one of the empty cells for himself. He didn't have time to go home. He just needed a couple of hours' sleep and then he would be ready for the next day. He didn't know it, but it was going to be a day that would take all his energy and wits to survive.

The prisoners, cocky and demanding earlier, were too tired now to make a fuss. They were told they could make their phone calls in the morning and they accepted this. Jazz smiled ruefully. *Wait till the world hears what scum they give positions of authority to*, he thought. It would all start tomorrow.

CHAPTER 37

Storm Clouds

It was the kick in the back that woke him.

"Jesus fucking Christ, what did you do that for?" he screamed as he tried to rub his back. He glanced at his watch – it was only 8pm and he had another hour's sleep yet to come. He turned over and looked up at one of the ugliest mugs he had ever seen.

"Who the fuck are you, you bastard?! That hurt."

The ugly one wasn't going to start talking. He just pulled Jazz to his feet and frogmarched him to one of the interview rooms. Jazz, disorientated, tired and confused, looked around for the custody sergeant – this wasn't right. He was an officer and he was being treated like a prisoner. There was a mistake here, he wanted to say, but he was busy trying to keep himself upright as he was dragged along.

Jazz was pushed into the interview room and told to sit. Two more men arrived and took a seat. The three of them sat for a few moments and just looked at him. Jazz was still disorientated, after all, this was his nick, it was his place, and he was usually in charge in a situation like this. The three men had a pile of papers in front of them, and they glanced at whatever was written on the pages. He could see they were armed with holsters under their left armpits; he saw the bulges. An uncomfortable feeling that he really didn't like washed over him. Jazz knew it was stone-cold fear.

In a situation like this perhaps tact, maybe courtesy, or even professionalism might have been the correct approach.

"Who the fuck are you bastards? You come into my nick and act like the fucking CIA. You'd better start talking before I call for backup."

Jazz got a slap for that. They were not interested in talking to him or giving him explanations. Their total disinterest in and lack of emotion regarding anything remotely human was the most frightening part of them. They looked like they could shoot him without a thought or a care. He was irrelevant. They wanted, at this time, only one thing. They looked at him with deadpan eyes. One of them asked just one question.

"Where are the boxes you brought from Paglesham?"

Jazz feigned confusion, not too difficult in this situation, whilst he thought. Something big was happening here and he didn't know what. He suspected DCI Radley had an idea, though. He had been told to hide the boxes.

"Boxes?" he said, trying to gain some time whilst

he thought. Another slap came his way for being so stupid.

"Where are the boxes?" asked the robot sitting opposite him once again.

"They're in the car where I left them last night. In the boot and back of the car, go look for yourself. Now can I go? I need to go to the toilet."

They ignored his request. One of them went off, Jazz presumed to look in the car. When they saw they were not there, he figured there was going to be trouble.

"I really need to take a piss. Someone can come with me. I can't think straight. I need the toilet," Jazz pleaded.

The ugly one got a nod from the man who had spoken and got up, grabbed Jazz and took him out of the interview room. Jazz figured they didn't know where the toilets were and he directed him towards the other interview rooms – he wanted to know if they were in use too. It was too early for interviews of prisoners; they had their human rights and had to have their fucking breakfast before being interviewed.

He passed three with the *engaged* sign on the doors, and he heard Boomer's voice coming from one of the rooms. He sure wasn't happy, judging by the shouting and profanities filling the air. *What the fuck is going on?* Jazz thought.

In the gents', he stood at the urinal, thinking. What the fuck was he going to do now? He had an idea, but not a good one. He washed his hands and allowed the ugly one to escort him back. As they passed the interview rooms he made a dash for one of the doors and burst in. There he saw Boomer and two men sitting opposite him. All were taken by surprise, but Jazz rushed up to Boomer and stood behind him.

"OK, what's going on here?" Jazz asked.

The ugly one, in two bounds, grabbed Jazz and pulled his arms behind him, ready to put on handcuffs.

"Is this what the British services have come to?" asked Jazz, not sure what British service they came from, but knowing they must be pretty important to have the run of a Metropolitan Police station.

One of the seated men waved a hand at the ugly one and he let go of Jazz.

"Take a seat beside your companion."

Jazz nodded and sat down. He looked at Boomer; neither said anything but Jazz saw the same look of disorientation and fear he felt.

"Can we see our detective chief inspector, sir?" asked Jazz courteously.

"Later," was the reply. "Tell us where the boxes you took from the mansion are, and no more messing around."

Boomer looked at Jazz. Obviously they had asked him the same question. Jazz answered airily, "I told the others that the boxes are in the car where I left them. We got back so late last night there wasn't time to process them. Was going to do that this morning."

The ugly one confirmed he had said that and it was

being checked. Jazz felt more in control now, and with Boomer beside him, a little cocky too.

"So are you going to tell us who the fuck you are and why the fuck we are being interrogated when we have done our job?"

"Watch your mouth and we will tell you when we are ready."

Jazz asked, "Are we under arrest?"

"No, you are not under arrest, you are helping us with our enquiries."

Jazz laughed. "Oh, that old chestnut. In that case Boomer and I want to go to breakfast. We will come back later." He got up to go, and pulled Boomer with him. "You will find us in the canteen if you want to talk to us again."

The two men stared at them, and then just said they could go. They had DCI Radley and these two were not that important. They might be good at what they did, but they had no idea that releasing Jazz and Boomer would cause them more trouble than they could imagine.

Their parting words were, "Under no circumstances will you mention anything to do with this case, and don't leave the station. Hand over your mobiles."

Reluctantly Jazz and Boomer got their mobiles out of their pockets, nodded and walked out. Once in the corridor they looked at each other and quickly made their way to somewhere that was more crowded; the canteen would always be the best place.

The lovely Milly saw Jazz and ordered him to sit down. He did it without any protests and waited with Boomer for his morning tea and a 999 breakfast. Jazz whispered something to Milly and she surreptitiously got her mobile out of her pocket and handed it to him.

He whispered, "You are an angel, Milly, and a lifesaver.

"What the fuck is going on, Boomer? Did you get anything from them?" whispered Jazz. Boomer shook his head, still bemused by it all. Jazz covertly looked to see where the goon was. He couldn't hear them if they whispered.

"We need to see DCI Radley and find out what is going on, and where the fuck is Saint Ash? We could do with him to find out what's happening."

With that, Jazz took Milly's mobile out of his pocket and surreptitiously keyed in a text to Ash.

Ash, answer 'Yes' if you received this message. I need your help urgently but covertly. It's Jazz here.

He waited a few moments and thanked Milly for the cup of tea she put in front of him. She said his 999 would be along soon. She even brought Boomer a cup of tea, almost unheard of; she normally made him queue and wait for his. She had an uncanny way of knowing when the chips were down and a bit of TLC was needed.

Ash replied:

Yes, in office. What do you want, and I hope it is legal? There is a lot to do today and I have to get on with processing these files in readiness for the CPS charging advice.

Jazz, he showed Boomer the message. "Still fucking moaning, I see," was Boomer's response. Jazz composed a quick message and hoped it might make sense to 'Mr Ash Perfect'.

A team in nick from something like British service with more clout than police. Do you know who they are? They want all the files collected last night. Any idea why? Will be called back to them soon so reply ASAP.

For all the mickey-taking, Jazz knew that if anyone could find out the information, it would be Ash. He was brilliant at ferreting out information from paperwork, computers etc. There must be something somewhere that could identify who they were dealing with and just how scared they should be.

They looked around for someone in charge but the place seemed bereft of detective inspectors – no sign of DCI Radley, not even any sergeants. The officers milling around the canteen came over to ask Jazz what was going on but Jazz feigned ignorance and the officers just got on with breakfast and work. They didn't believe him, but the atmosphere in the station was weird and almost threatening. No one wanted to make a fuss and come to anyone's attention.

It was 10am by the time they had eaten their 999 breakfasts and finished their second cups of tea. Still no sign of Radley or Ash, or Boomer's team. It was getting very worrying. Boomer tried to ring his boys but no one was answering. He had no idea where they were.

At 10:10am a text message came through.

Come to ladies' toilets on first floor.

Jazz whispered to Boomer, "Bloody hell, I've had a few offers in my time but the ladies' toilets as a meeting place takes the biscuit."

Jazz could see it was from Ash, and they both got up and Jazz took out his cigarette packet and lighter and offered one to Boomer as they made their way to the exit where they could smoke. Once outside the canteen, with no one watching they made their way to the ladies' toilets down the corridor. They were on the first floor and presumed Ash would be in the toilets furthest away from the canteen, as they weren't often used.

Jazz knocked on the toilet door, and getting no reply, opened it and peered in. Ash was by the sinks, looking distinctly nervous. Boomer leaned against the door to ensure no one came in and Ash filled them in on what he knew. He was babbling; he needed to tell them quickly and he wanted to get out.

"They come from something called the Internal Domestic Service, it's part of MI5. They have been sent by someone in government. Someone saw their badge but I tried to Google the department and nothing comes up. It's bloody secret!"

Jazz knew they had to be pretty high up to commandeer a police station in the way they did. They wanted the boxes, but why? He knew the answer to that. They were going to bury this and set all those paedophiles free. It was the only explanation, otherwise they would let them be processed, charged and go to court. Boomer was thinking the same thing; they looked at each other and Jazz jumped into action.

"OK, Ash, do me a big favour. I need you to go to Mad Pete's flat and take him to Musty Mary's house and keep him hidden there. She will look after him. No one is to know where he is. I give you an hour's start and then I will be talking."

Ash nodded; he said he would go now. He didn't ask why, he didn't want to know. Jazz turned to Boomer.

"They will know now that the boxes are not in the car. I will give them another story. Just back me up, OK – you don't know nothing."

Boomer nodded. This was all looking very bad, and neither wanted to give up the paedophiles.

"Boomer, can you wait outside the door and check who is around? I need to make an important phone call and it's not for your ears at the moment. Soon we can make a fuss and get this team's attention."

Boomer knew Jazz was up to something, but at the moment he didn't want to know what. This lot were tough buggers and if they got caught messing around, they would be bloody shot as traitors if this was indeed MI5. *You don't mess with those fuckers*, he told himself.

CHAPTER 38

Hide and Seek

He had been in that toilet for over half an hour and Boomer was getting leg-ache. Suddenly the door opened wide and Jazz leapt out. Energised now and feeling in control, he told Boomer that it was time to do a little messing around, but first he wanted one of those tape thingies that you can have on your person and it activates automatically when there is noise.

"Why the bloody hell do you want a contraption for, Singh?" Boomer asked, fed up now with all these games.

"Come on, I know this is a bollocking nuisance but if I can catch one of these fuckers on tape saying something I can use, I will use it."

Boomer just gave a wry smile. Even when up against it, Jazz still wanted to play James Bond. They had no power and no authority with this lot. Still, the dissident in Boomer told Jazz to go find Alex in CID. He had lots of gizmos and could help him.

Alex was huddled around a desk with others,

gossiping about the team that had taken over their custody suite and how no one could enter it. They wondered what was going on. He knew Boomer and Jazz were involved, so Alex was happy to be pulled to one side to help Jazz. He was going to try and glean some information. Rumours were rife and Alex shared most of them with Jazz. They ranged from a big drugs bust to terrorists. Jazz just said it could be but he would let Alex know later what was going down. For now he needed help. He got what he wanted and put it in his pocket.

Now he was ready to cause a fuss, get MI5 interested and see what happened.

Ash found a small police car, the sort no one wanted to drive if they didn't have to. It wasn't a marked car, which was just what he wanted. He knew where Mad Pete lived, and knowing the clock was against him he drove out of the police yard at speed.

Mad Pete was still asleep. After knocking and kicking the door for what seemed an age, Ash heard movement on the other side. Mad Pete, not happy, shouted that he was asleep and Ash should fuck off. Ash shouted through the door that DS Singh had sent him urgently. After a tense few minutes whilst Mad Pete slowly opened the ten locks and bolts, Ash, stressed out and now at breaking point, exploded and threatened Mad Pete with prison and plagues, and anything else he could think of if he didn't open the sodding door.

He could hear him moving the locks and bolts quicker and the door was opened a crack, and Ash saw Mad Pete's screwed-up face and slitty eyes as he was blinded by the daylight flooding in.

In true Jazz style, Ash grabbed Mad Pete and holding him far too close (the smell was awful), told him, "If you fucking want to live past today, get whatever you need in two seconds flat and come with me. I have orders to hide you from some very nasty people."

Mad Pete took a few minutes and had all he needed – his drugs, his phones and his syringes.

They were at Musty Mary's house in Parsloes Avenue in no time at all. Jazz had rung ahead and she was ready for Mad Pete. Ash looked at the pair of them and thought they deserved each other. Both had mega hygiene problems. The cats were another thing, and Mad Pete wasn't happy with that. Ash explained he had to stay and not go out until DS Singh contacted him. He added that Jazz was trying to save his life, and that was enough for Mad Pete to happily stay, put up with the cats and not utter a word. He nodded to Ash and followed Musty Mary to what was going to be his room. Ash left, hearing Musty Mary say that the other bedroom was normally for the cats, but it was Pete's now. Ash didn't know whether to laugh or feel almost sorry for Mad Pete.

Ash didn't know what the hell was going down, but he wanted to get back to Fresh Wharf to see what unravelled. So far no one had talked to him and he was happy with that. He knew Jazz was up to something and he wanted to be there just in case. With that fucker, you just never knew what was going to happen. Ash understood Jazz, or thought he did.

If someone had told Jazz that Ash understood him, he would have laughed out loud, saying he, Jaswinder Singh, didn't even know himself. He didn't think he was complicated. He reacted as and when to each situation and this one needed some very underhanded dealings. The guns were a worry. He didn't know who he was dealing with and how easily they could use their guns. These secret agents got away with murder, it was rumoured, and Jazz didn't want to find out if this was true.

What was strange was that he hadn't heard from the secret service men since they left for breakfast. It was now lunchtime and they hadn't searched them out. He thought that really odd. They must know by now that the car hadn't got the boxes in it, and he expected them to be spitting nails and looking for them to get the truth. It was odd and very uncomfortable.

Jazz grabbed Boomer and said he wanted to go downstairs to the custody suite and see what was going on.

Boomer asked, "Why, when the wasps are settled, do you have to go and poke a fucking stick in their nest and upset them all?"

Jazz laughed. His answer was quite succinct: "Because I can."

With a shrug and a rueful smile, Boomer followed Jazz down the stairs to the custody suite.

All the interview rooms appeared to be in use. There was no one in the custody suite area, which made it very easy for Jazz and Boomer to select which room they would go into. Listening, Boomer recognised one of his boys' voices – so they were being interviewed. That explained why he couldn't get hold of them.

One of the rooms had DCI Radley in it; Jazz spotted him by looking through the spyhole in the door. That was the room Jazz wanted to enter. Cocky as he was, he felt the fear of not knowing what he was walking into. These men were not to be messed with. Jazz took a deep breath, nodded to Boomer and walked into the room.

The two men sitting opposite DCI Radley looked up as Jazz walked in. DCI Radley frowned. He had already told these two men that Singh and Black were nothing but a pain in the neck in his department. They caused more trouble than they solved. He needed to take their minds off the two of them. If anyone was going to do something here, it was going to be Singh. Normally this would be a worry, but today he hoped they would come up with something. But why had they come into the interview room? He didn't want them in here with him; he wanted them out there doing something. *Bloody idiots*, he thought.

"What the fuck do you think you are doing?" asked one of the two men, not happy at all at this interruption. Jazz feigned ignorance, confusion and a lot of deference.

"Sorry, sir, I thought you wanted to see us again

after we had breakfast and cleaned up a bit; had a wash, you know," he said amiably. "We waited but no one came for us, so we thought we ought to report to you. Can we speak to our DCI, sir?"

That got Jazz nothing but contempt. This DS standing there stupidly with the DI behind him looking like a nodding dog. Their arrogance didn't allow the men to see that Jazz and Boomer were putting on a show of sweetness and innocence that certainly wasn't them.

They told them they were about to look for them. The car didn't contain the boxes of DVDs and paperwork from the house as Singh had told them. It appeared that the car had been taken out early and it was an hour before they found out it was empty. They were not worried. They had DCI Radley, who was going to organise finding the boxes. Jazz was told that DCI Radley was fully aware of the situation and a search was being organised.

DCI Radley watched Jazz; he was acting very out of character. This compliant and respectful idiot certainly wasn't the DS Jaswinder Singh that he knew. He hoped that was a good sign.

"Sir," Jazz addressed the two men sitting there looking at this idiot before them, "I have a confession to make, sir. I didn't have the boxes in the car as I told you. You have to understand, sir, I didn't know who you were this morning. I got woken up with a kick in my back and no explanation, just you asking me where the boxes were. I lied. I didn't know what else to do."

Jazz was almost pleading for understanding now. Radley was impressed.

"So you know who we are now, do you?" asked one of the men menacingly.

"Well, I know you have more clout than the police, otherwise you wouldn't be able to commandeer the custody suite like you have. No one here knows who you are – they think it's to do with terrorism but they know nothing. You have DCI Radley here and he doesn't take shit from no one, so you must be important."

This last comment was Jazz's final salvo, which he thought was a neat thing to throw in; it nearly made him smile but he hid it well. The two men could see that this idiot had some sense – not much, but they wanted the boxes now.

"To be quite honest, sir, it was the early hours this morning and I was pretty tired when I got back and wasn't thinking straight. I got Mad Pete, my snout, to take the boxes to his flat. I didn't know what else to do with them. I hadn't the energy to move them myself and Mad Pete said he would take them and bring them back to the custody suite today."

Jazz had their attention, and he added innocently, "Have they arrived yet?"

Of course they hadn't arrived, but Jazz quickly gave Mad Pete's address to them and one of them went off to organise a search. It would stop them searching the police station for the time being. In the meantime, Jazz, conscious of the PACE clock, wanted to know when the sixteen prisoners could be charged.

DCI Radley shifted uncomfortably in his seat and asked if he could talk with DS Singh and DI Tom Black to explain the situation. It was a long time since Boomer had been called by his proper name: DI Tom Black. He had kept quiet and let Jazz do what he was good at. Personally, he wanted to shoot these fucking bastards, who he knew wanted to let the sixteen miserable fucking paedophiles go free. Nothing had happened with the prisoners, but the officers who had arrested them were seemingly being held and interrogated. It didn't bode well.

A nod of the head gave DCI Radley permission to talk with Jazz and Boomer. Jazz could see the concern in Radley's eyes and knew he would tell the story as required by the intelligence officer sitting there.

It was a very sorry story, but nothing Jazz or Boomer hadn't expected. As for the men here, apparently it was of no consequence and not necessary to mention what department they were from; their authority came from very high up. Radley nodded and looked intently at Jazz. Jazz got the point. This was sanctioned directly by someone in a high government position. It made him sick, but he listened intently and tried to look compliant.

The upshot of it all was, there were not going to be any charges. The police would forget all about this case; it would be suitably dealt with by this department with no name. All the paperwork and DVDs were now their property and the police were to hand over everything and sign a secrecy clause stating that this was to go no further. All information pertaining to this case was to be erased from computers and hard copies incinerated.

Something clicked and Jazz asked if they were responsible for erasing everything to do with the case on the AWARE system. The intelligence chap looked quizzical and Jazz said that everything had been erased over the past couple of days and the hard-copy file had been taken. The intelligence chap shook his head. He gave a little information that perhaps he should not have.

"Our attention was only brought to this situation last night when a call was made asking for help at the mansion address in Paglesham, and by Southend Police contacting the Met Police in Barking. That was our first alert, and then of course they went through the charging system on AWARE early this morning and that confirmed to us what we needed to know."

Bloody 'ell, thought Jazz, *they monitor all police calls*. This was very scary. He wasn't poking a stick at a wasps' nest any more; he was in the middle of it. At the same time, he still didn't know who had accessed the AWARE system and erased all information on the case. He felt like he was in a madhouse; nothing made sense.

"So, sir, where are the sixteen prisoners we brought in? Are they still here?" asked Jazz, as innocently as he could.

"Yes. They are not in cells any more, we have them in your meeting room. We have sent out for lunch for them. They need to be debriefed before leaving. We have booked executive vans to be here at 4pm today. It is no longer your case and therefore not your concern, Singh!"

Well, that put me in my place, Jazz thought ruefully.

It wasn't long before the other intelligence man came back and whispered to his colleague that Mad Pete was not in his flat and there was no sign of any boxes there.

Both turned to Jazz and asked where he would go if not at home. Jazz listed all the McDonald's in Barking and Dagenham, the chicken shop in Longbridge Road, and before he listed any more he was stopped with a shout of, "For God's sake, man! Where would he be with all the boxes? Where would he hide them? Time is getting on and we need those boxes. Enough messing around, I need information now. Your job is on the line and if you want a pension, you had better think clearly and tell me."

Jazz was quite enjoying this. He looked at his watch; it was now nearly 2pm, and time was getting on.

"At this time he could be at his mother's flat in Beckton. She is a fucking bitch of a woman but she's his mother and he sees her regularly. Apart from that there is a youth club type of place on the Gascoigne Estate; he often goes there too. He has friends who own a warehouse on the Barking industrial estate, he could have taken the boxes there."

With that, one of the intelligence men got up and

left the room. Jazz figured that would keep them busy for at least another hour or so, and that should be long enough. With a bit of luck Mad Pete's mother would finish them off; she had a gob the size of Blackwall Tunnel and far dirtier. He needed to keep them away from searching the police station.

"I am parched – can I go get us all teas from the canteen? I'll come straight back." Jazz looked at the intelligence man and asked nicely, "Can I get you a tea?"

With orders of five teas, Boomer said he would help carry them. They said they would get biscuits too and walked off to the canteen.

Once out of the custody suite, Jazz looked at Boomer and said, "Is it me or are they fucking arseholes, letting us walk in and out as we wish?"

Boomer laughed. He needed to get out of that room. He was wound up tight. "Trying to look stupid was easy," he muttered, "but trying not to look like you want to throttle the insignificant little bastard was fucking hard. They can't take those paedophiles from us. I don't care if they are the Pope himself or Mother bloody Teresa, they have got to pay for what they have done. This is not going to be a fucking cover-up."

"Stick with me, kid! I have a cunning plan and we will get these bastards out of our station by teatime."

Boomer looked at Jazz ruefully. "Singh, you are a fucking fantasist – they are bigger than we can take on."

Jazz laughed, "I know we can't take them on, but I know a man who can."

Jazz wouldn't say any more at the moment and Boomer left it at that. Milly got their teas and put a selection of biscuits on the tray too. She was always pleased to see Jazz and her smile got bigger as he promised he was going to take her out for a drink one day.

Just before they went back to the custody suite, Jazz said he just needed to pop outside for a cigarette, and Boomer waited in the canteen, guarding the tray.

"Bloody thieving coppers would nick the biscuits if they could," he muttered. Jazz walked off briskly, laughing at his comment.

After making a couple of urgent, whispered telephone calls and eventually getting the right person, Jazz rang Ash.

"Listen, Ash, don't reply in case anyone is listening. Get the Kevin tape and the list of names and keep them somewhere safe. Someone is going to ring you and ask you for them. It wont be the intelligence plonkers, but someone else. They will mention my name. It is urgent that you meet them immediately and give them the two items. *Capisce*?"

Ash just replied, "Yes."

Back with Boomer, who in protecting the biscuits had managed to eat half of them and was busy brushing the crumbs off his jacket, Jazz said they needed to get back before they were missed. They headed back to the custody suite in full banter with Jazz taking the mickey out of Boomer's stomach bulging over his waistband and Boomer asking if he was going to perform that candy-arsed goody-two-shoes act again. The smiles were wiped off their faces as they saw their sixteen paedophiles grouped in the custody suite enjoying a cigarette and a glass of fucking wine. Not only were they not incarcerated, they were being wined and dined as if it was a fucking party.

One of the paedophiles, the one they thought was in the army, made a move towards Jazz but was held back by an intelligence officer beside him. It was sickening to see these creeps being treated well. Boomer couldn't help himself. He handed the tray to Jazz and stepped forward; he wasn't going to have any of that scum making a move on them.

Boomer got up close to the army paedo, raising himself to his full height, and eyeball to eyeball said, "Any similarity between yourself and a human being is purely coincidental. Scum!"

They stood for a few seconds in contemptuous silence, eyeing each other until Jazz grabbed Boomer's arm and guided him away.

"His time will come, Boomer, leave it alone for now."

Boomer moved back, growling; he didn't like this at all.

Jazz whispered to him, "I know this isn't right, but just watch this space."

Boomer hoped Singh knew what he was doing. It had taken all his energy not to punch the lights out of the cocky army bastard. He knew Jazz was up to something, he just hoped he knew what he was doing.

These intelligence guys looked like nasty pieces of work.

The tea went down well. Boomer asked if he could have a word with his lads, but he got a no to that. Jazz asked if they had found Mad Pete yet and got a no to that too. So far, so good. From what he could gather, it seemed the paedophiles were being organised to leave the police station about 4pm. The intelligence team had obviously anticipated the boxes would be found. Apparently they had hired three executive vans with blacked-out windows to take them away. *No one would know they had been here*, thought Jazz. Now that couldn't happen.

Jazz asked the intelligence man who refused to give a name if he had seen any of the DVDs these paedophiles had recorded. He got silence as an answer. With time on his hands, Jazz continued to chip away at him.

"Does your department deal with paedophiles only? Do you ever see the children they abuse? Have you got any children yourself?"

In the end, the intelligence man had had enough and told Jazz, loudly and savagely, to shut it. He leaned forward menacingly and said Jazz had no idea what he could do if he was pushed too far. Jazz saw his face and believed him, and shut up. He had no idea who they were or who had sent them, but he did know if you pushed them too far you could disappear, no questions asked.

DCI Radley had sat in the interview room for

over five hours now and he was tired. His hands were tied; he had been told there was nothing he could do. In confidence he had been told that this was an undercover operation where everyone involved was held to the Official Secrets Act. Nothing was to be said outside of the custody suite, and Radley had been told that his superiors were fully informed and aware that the intelligence team were fully in control and had to be given full cooperation. DCI Radley was a corporate man through and through, but this felt so very wrong.

The only thing he had been able to do was bite his tongue. He hoped to God Jazz had hidden the boxes well because these men were hell-bent on finding them. At present the intelligence team were in control so they could afford to be quite accommodating, but he didn't think that would last. They were going to turn at some point. To an outsider, it looked like a nice tea-drinking session with dunking biscuits and the odd pleasantry, but the atmosphere in the interview room was thick with tension.

CHAPTER 39

Time and Tide

Checking his watch surreptitiously, Jazz saw it was 3pm and only an hour before all the paedophiles would be taken away. DCI Radley was not allowed to leave the room; he had asked but been told no. Boomer's team were still held in the custody suite and even Boomer couldn't see them. Strangely, they had allowed Jazz and Boomer to wander around. Jazz wondered if their reputation was such that the intelligence men thought they would be no problem. Jazz and Boomer had captured sixteen high-ranking paedophiles and they thought they were no problem? It showed how fucking stupid the retards with one brain cell between them were. Jazz conceded that he and Boomer together could look a bit like Laurel and Hardy. It gave him an idea. He needed to get out of the room with Boomer now.

"Oh my God! Was that you, Boomer? Did you fart then?"

Boomer growled, "Bloody cheek, you fucking arsehole, it wasn't me."

"Well someone did and it ain't me. You are always doing that, it stinks. Go to the toilet like a normal person, you bloody animal."

Boomer was cottoning on. Jazz never talked like this to him. "You wanna make something of it, arsehole? It was you – typical, all those fucking curries you eat, bleeding stinking the place out."

Jazz added, "Come to think of it, I could do with a dump."

DCI Radley, tense and unbearably fed up with being stuck in this room, shouted at them. "Just go to the toilet, the pair of you, and get out of my sight. This is not the sort of talk I expect from my detectives. When this is over, there are going to be some questions answered by you two."

He turned to the intelligence men and said, "See, I told you – nothing but trouble and not a brain cell between them."

Radley looked at the intelligence man and he nodded to indicate they could leave, but added curtly they had no more than ten minutes and to come straight back. With a nod, Jazz and Boomer left the room.

Before Boomer could say anything, Jazz took a right turn into the ladies' toilet.

"What is it with you and ladies' toilets, Singh?" Boomer asked.

"Look, all these intelligence people are men, so they are not going to be in the ladies' toilets, are they? I need to make calls where I won't be overheard, so hang on a minute and just check all the toilets in here to make sure a rogue WPC hasn't come down here."

While Boomer was doing that, Jazz rang Ash. Ash confirmed he had met and passed the DVD and list to the man Jazz had spoken to. That was all Jazz needed to know. He thanked Ash and redialled.

"So, have you had a chance to look at the DVD? You can see the list. Yes, they are all in custody here and gonna be set free by some undercover, bloody dangerous department who are here on the say-so of someone high up in government. Our hands are tied here. They can't be set free. Yes, they will be leaving here at 4pm. That's good. You will owe me big time for this. Thanks."

Boomer heard it all and knew something was going down but didn't know what. He wanted to ask Jazz, but as usual, Jazz kept things tight to his chest.

Jazz, happy that things were in place, beckoned to Boomer to make their way back to the interview room and DCI Radley. On their return, Jazz made himself comfortable and waited for the sky to fall in on these bastards.

At 3.45pm precisely all hell let loose outside the custody suite. There were cameras, journalists, television cameras and their vans. The whole area was a melee of talking, shouting, cameras flashing and television reporters with their booms held high to hear anyone close by. The questions being shouted were not what the intelligence men wanted to hear or answer.

The phone rang and was answered by one of the intelligence men sitting in the room with DCI Radley, Jazz and Boomer. He said nothing into the phone; he just listened. When finished, he nodded to the second intelligence man and they both rose urgently and made their way to the door. Before they left the room, the three were told, with a menace they understood clearly, to stay in the interview room and not move.

The silence felt thick and palatable. None of them knew if they should or could speak. It was not clear, after all this time, if they were being recorded in the room. None of them wanted to say or do anything that might come back to haunt them. Was this a test? What was happening? Only Jazz was clear about what was happening, and he did his best not to smile in case the hidden camera used in interview rooms was in use.

It was only twenty minutes before the two intelligence men came back into the room. Although not happy at all, they said, with as much courtesy as they could muster, that Jazz and Boomer should wait outside; they wished to talk with DCI Radley.

Jazz and Boomer were quite happy to leave, and wanted to find out what was going on. They were warned, as they left the room, to go to the canteen and wait there for further instructions. *Further instructions? What plonkers*, thought Jazz. Disgusted by these maggots of an intelligence unit, Jazz hoped they were on their way back to the black pit they had crawled out of.

Once out of the room and away from the custody suite, Jazz allowed himself a bit of a winner's jig.

"What the fuck is that?" asked Boomer.

"I reckon we have sent this lot packing and we get to keep the prize. Those paedophiles are going nowhere. We need to get them charged super-quick though, before PACE runs out. I figure we will have to wait another hour or so and then we can get cracking. I need a drink to celebrate."

Luckily Jazz had a spare bottle of vodka in his locker. God, he needed a drink. Boomer, keen to know what the fuck was going on, pushed Jazz to tell him.

"I will let you in on everything in a while, Boomer. A drink first, then a cuppa. Let's go find a quiet spot to sit and wait, just in case anything goes tits up."

He grabbed the bottle from his locker and filled his flask that had sat empty in the inner left-hand pocket in his jacket. A quick swig from the bottle was just what he needed. Boomer watched, not happy to see such a sight.

Jazz caught his glance and said, "I needed that, it's been a long day and a stressful one at that." He offered the bottle to Boomer, but he declined. He quickly put the bottle, now half-empty, back into the locker and walked briskly towards the canteen.

"Let's find a quiet corner and I will let you in on everything." Before Boomer could reply, Jazz was halfway down the corridor leading to the canteen.

The canteen wasn't very busy at this time of day. The officers who were in there gossiping about everything going on in the station today, and now with the press baying for blood outside, tried to talk to Jazz and Boomer; they knew they were involved.

Jazz just pushed them away and said, "Later, can't talk now." The officers didn't push it; the day had been weird and the guns hidden inside the intelligence officers' jackets were noted by everyone.

Milly got their tea ahead of the queue, to much moaning from the officers who were waiting patiently. She sorted Jazz and Boomer out and told the others she would get to them soon. She made sure Jazz and Boomer were comfortable and brought a few rock cakes that had been made earlier for them.

Once she had gone back to the canteen counter and they could hear her telling off the officers for grumbling, Jazz leaned forward and told Boomer what was happening.

He had called Peter White, editor of the *Guardian* newspaper. One of the paedophiles, Charles Adams, was a big newspaper magnate and an arch-rival of the *Guardian*'s, so apart from being a good story, it would be even better if White could do down his rival. Peter White contacted Ash as Jazz told him to. Ash gave him the Kevin DVD and the list of paedophiles they had arrested. It was a coup for any newspaper. The *Guardian* had obviously done a deal with the television companies who were outside as well, so there would be hordes of bloody journalists.

"I wasn't going to let them get away from us. We worked hard to get these bastards, and the thought they could get away with it is just not on. No way can they keep this secret now. I hate the bloody press but for once, they are being useful. The bastards are going to be pleased to be locked away, they won't want to be out there in public. Some of them have fucking knighthoods."

Jazz sat back, proud of what he had done until Boomer pointed out that they had signed the Official Secrets Act and he could be shot for treason for what he had done. He hadn't thought of that.

"Bugger!"

Jazz walked off again into the corner of the canteen, saying he had a call to make. Boomer wondered why there was always such fucking secrecy involved in all his calls. He wondered if Jazz had a fancy woman, which wasn't exactly helpful at this time, he thought ironically. Women were not on Boomer's radar. His saying was, *Women are like elephants: fascinating to look at, but I wouldn't have one in the house.*

CHAPTER 40

Payback Time

Milly answered the canteen phone on the wall. She shouted a message to Jazz and Boomer. Someone said they had to get themselves down to the custody suite immediately. They looked at each other; both knew there was big trouble brewing.

Knowing they would be walking into trouble, they sat in the canteen, reluctant to leave and considering finishing their tea first. Jazz looked up and saw two determined intelligence officers heading their way. He whispered to Boomer that he had to dump Milly's mobile. Quickly Jazz slipped it under the table. By the looks on their faces, it wasn't going to be good news and he didn't want to be caught with Milly's mobile. As the two men arrived at the table, Jazz looked up and smiled.

"Can I help you, gentlemen?"

The response was rough and unnecessary. Jazz and Boomer were hoisted to their feet and frisked in full view of the police officers in the canteen. To add insult to injury, they were handcuffed and led from the canteen.

There were no discussion, requests or politeness, and this wasn't right, thought Jazz.

Boomer let rip. "Fucking bastards! Take these bleeding cuffs off us. We are a Metropolitan detective inspector and sergeant, not fucking gangsters."

This got him a shove in the back and he was told to keep quiet. Jazz was thinking ten to the dozen. What the fuck was going on? Perhaps Boomer was right. Perhaps they were being done for treason. Bloody hell! He couldn't believe that was true – surely not?

The intelligence team might have lost the war, but they were taking prisoners. They charged DS Singh and DI Boomer with breaking the Official Secrets Act, which they signed as police officers, and said they were to accompany them to their headquarters.

When back in the custody suite, they were taken to an interview room and there were read their rights. DCI Radley was allowed to see them for a moment before they left. Jazz looked at the broken DCI and wondered who was going to fight their corner.

Radley looked Jazz in the eye, and with a deep breath he mustered more feeling than Jazz thought he had in him and said, "I will take this to the highest authority and have you both back here as soon as I can. At the moment, my hands are tied and they have the jurisdiction to arrest and remand you in custody. Is there anyone I should contact?"

Jazz knew there was only one person who might

make some semblance of sense out of this. "Sir, could you inform Ashiv Kumar so he can tell my landlady? He knows her well and I am sure he will know what to say and do."

Radley nodded that this would be done.

Boomer just growled, "This is fucking unfair, sir. How can they just take us like that? It's like we've got bleeding Nazi Gestapos around here. Just look after my lads and tell them I will be back soon."

Radley nodded again and said to leave it to him.

As swiftly as they arrived, they were gone. The intelligence team, with Jazz and Boomer, climbed into the three waiting blacked-out Range Rovers and raced at speed out of the yard, avoiding the press frantically trying to take pictures.

DCI Radley stood alone in the custody suite, watching at the door as the cavalcade took off. All of a sudden, it felt strange and empty. It had left a big black hole in the station. The nauseating tension that had been like a thick fog pervading the custody suite had gone and was now replaced by silence. That was going to change very soon.

He stood for a minute, perusing the area that was usually never empty or quiet. Then, with a deep breath, he pulled himself together and leapt into action. Walking briskly down the corridor, DCI Radley was again in charge of his station. He immediately got on the phone to Ashiv Kumar and told him what had happened.

Ash listened and said, "Leave it to me, guv. Jazz

has given me a plan to work to in the event of this happening. I will be back with you within two hours."

Relieved, Radley nodded at the phone and thought, *So that bugger has an ace up his sleeve. I hope it works.* He needed Singh and Black back so he could give them the bollocking of their careers. He was not a happy man.

Now he had to populate the custody suite with staff and sort out the sixteen paedophiles who thought they were waiting to be released. Someone had to tell them the news that they were not going anywhere. For the first time today, Radley smiled to himself.

The custody suite started to bustle again and it wasn't long before everything looked fairly normal. All the questions that were being asked were put on hold for the time being. DCI Radley took the custody sergeant to one side and gave him a brief idea of what was going on. He needed him to keep control of what was happening with the sixteen paedophiles and said there would be a more in-depth meeting soon, but first, there was work to be done.

There were thirty cells in Fresh Wharf and the decision was made that they were open for business. There were still fourteen cells that could be used. The sixteen paedophiles each had a cell and were locked in. Now they knew they were not being released, all wanted their lawyers and it was going to be a very busy evening. The custody sergeant made the decision that more staff would be needed to man the area for the night. DCI Radley gave him permission to allocate four more officers to help him.

Radley had a lot to do in a very short time. He had applied for more time under PACE to hold the sixteen, and this was granted. At present there was no pressure to interview all sixteen, but legally they could not be left for too long. He would get hold of Boomer's team and ask them to start organising interviews of the paedophiles, and he also contacted Emerald, who dealt with sex offenders, and the team who dealt with such large cases. There was going to be a lot to deal with and Jazz had only scratched the surface. From sitting down all day to rushing around now, Radley was raring to go, but first there was something he needed to do.

DCI Radley left them to get on with it for the time being whilst he changed into his best uniform and prepared himself to speak to the press outside. He would give them a very dull bit of information: that they had sixteen people in custody and as yet there had been no charges. He would, of course, update the press in the near future. This was like chucking them a bone with no meat and it would keep them baying at the closed gates of Fresh Wharf for the next twenty-four hours.

The calls from Scotland Yard and the chief commissioner's office kept DCI Radley busy for the evening. Milly, seeing all the problems of the day stayed on and worked another shift; she knew she would be needed. Milly quietly entered DCI Radley's office and placed a plate of hot pie and chips with baked beans on the desk in front of him. It was only then he realised he hadn't eaten anything substantial all day and in gratitude he gave Milly a rare smile.

CHAPTER 41

Blue Funk

It was 6pm by the time they arrived at the headquarters of the intelligence team. They were still not saying who they were or who their boss was, but what they did say was chilling to hear.

Boomer and Jazz had been driven to this place in separate cars. They were not to see each other again whilst here. Jazz felt desolate; he had got his friend and working partner in crime into a lot of trouble. They put him in a grey, windowless room, bigger than a police cell but when the heavy door was slammed shut and locked behind him it suddenly felt very small. He looked around and saw he had a table and two chairs that had seen better days, and something resembling an uncomfortable bed in the corner. The obligatory toilet without seat was in another corner. It was depressingly bleak.

No one had said anything to him. He had asked for food, he had asked for a drink, he had even asked to call his lawyer (he didn't have one, but what the heck) and got no reply. Sitting alone in this cell, underneath all his cockiness and Jack-the-lad attitude, he was scared. This was big boys' stuff and he didn't understand it and didn't know what they could or couldn't do to him.

They had removed his clothes and everything he carried and put him in a type of Tyvek boiler suit. They didn't say why, in fact they hadn't said anything to him. It certainly made him feel uncomfortable with nothing that was his around him, including his flask. God, he needed a drink. He presumed it was some sort of interrogation procedure to make him feel disorientated. Well, if it was, it had worked.

After a while the door opened and in came another suited one with dead eyes that looked straight through him. He carried a tray with a steaming mug of tea and a plate of sausages and mash. It was put down on the table. There was no conversation, just a statement.

"Lights out after you have eaten. Tomorrow we start."

With no opportunity to ask a question, the man had gone, slamming the door behind him just in case Jazz was in any doubt that he was a prisoner.

He sat down and drank the tea, grateful for something warm. The sausage and mash he toyed with and then decided to eat it up. He didn't know what was in store for him here in the next twenty-four hours or more. He had barely finished when the light went out and he was in total darkness. He felt like a small child again, frightened of the dark. He fumbled his way to the bed and curled up, hoping this was a nightmare and when he woke up it would all be gone. He hoped Ash had understood what he wanted him to do, and he fervently prayed it would work.

Mrs Osei – there was no way Ash was going to call her Dionne like everyone else; very unprofessional – was still staying with Nekisha at the Richmond Centre.

She was expecting Ash to arrive; he had phoned her saying he was on his way. She found him very different from that nice Mr Jazz Singh, but she made him welcome and comfortable. The common area at the Richmond Centre had been made into a Dionne area. The tired, boring leather chairs had been grouped around a coffee table and she held all her meetings with doctors and police in her little area. There were even biscuits and she had found a flask in the kitchen to keep hot water in, and she made a fuss of pouring a cup of tea for Ash. He told her he was fine but she would have none of it. After putting a teabag in a cup and messing around with the flask to get it to pour hot water, then the milk and offering sugar, it seemed ages before they were all seated comfortably.

Dionne gave a welcoming smile to Ash, which he took to mean he could now go ahead and talk about why he was there. Just as he was about to open his mouth a plate of biscuits were shoved in his face, with Dionne nodding at the biscuits, which he took to mean he had to have one. Distracted and uncomfortable now, Ash found himself trying to remember why the hell he was here.

He took a bite of the biscuit whilst he thought about how to start the conversation. Time was of the essence and he had wasted a lot of time waiting for the bloody tea. He needed to move on quickly.

"Mrs Osei—" he started.

"Dionne, darlin', please. No one calls me Mrs Osei."

This didn't sit well with Ash, but he took a sip of the tea and started again with an embarrassed smile.

"OK, Dionne."

She smiled at this and nodded for him to continue.

"The thing is, Dionne, Jazz – erm, DS Singh – is in trouble. He needs your help, if you don't mind. The press have been informed of the paedophile ring to ensure none of the group of sixteen…" He stopped and for a second looked at Dionne, who seemed on the point of fainting. She pulled herself together and although in shock, nodded to Ash to continue. Ash, slightly distracted, was not used to Dionne's dramatic ways, but he continued with a solemn look and confirmed, "Yes, sixteen, Dionne." He could see he had her full attention. "We have got to make sure none of them get away with it. I can't tell you more, because of the Official Secrets Act. What Jazz is asking you to do is say you were the one that informed the press of what has happened to Nekisha, and the press investigated it. Can you do that?"

Dionne needed less than a nanosecond to say yes.

Of course she would. In her eyes DS Jaswinder Singh was a saint, the most wonderful of men, and she would die to help him. Ash thought she was going a bit over the top but was relieved it was so easy.

"So, Dionne, with your permission, I will ring Jeremy Banner and ask him to come and see you and talk it through, hopefully tonight."

Dionne was ecstatic; she had heard of Jeremy Banner. He was someone very important in her favourite newspaper, the *Daily Express*. Ash was surprised. He would never have thought of Dionne as an *Express* reader, but what the hell did he know about anything? He got on the phone and Jeremy said he would be there in an hour. Time was getting on and Ash rang home and told his wife he wouldn't be back tonight.

It was in both Jeremy Banner's and DS Singh's interest that the story came from a good and safe source. Banner didn't want any orders slapped on his paper or to have to account for his source of information. This way the story was even better.

Jeremy arrived and got the tea-and-biscuit treatment from an extra-smiley Dionne. They got their stories straight and Dionne said she didn't mind being quoted. Ash warned her there was a possibility that certain people from a government organisation might come and check up on her story. Jeremy Banner knew what could happen. Governments had stopped many stories from hitting the headlines and this one just had to be broadcast, especially by his newspaper.

He leaned towards Dionne, and licking his lips whilst trying to find the right words, said, "It may be helpful..." he hesitated for a second and added delicately, "if you were to start to cause a fuss over the fact that these men have not been charged yet."

Dionne was no fool, she knew what they were getting at and she was ready for action. She was now in full flow and told them, "Bring it on, darlin', I can handle any amount of men. Just tell me what you want me to say and I will say it."

Jeremy left with a smile. Dionne was his star and the headline story was safe. His paper would put in a hard-hitting interview with Dionne and take it from there. He had that bastard Miles Spring, owner of the Global Corporate News Agency, bang to rights as one of the named paedophiles in the ring. It was going to make his century.

He was anxious to get back to the newspaper to make sure that in tomorrow's edition, information was leaked with a promise of much more in the near future. So far so good, but he knew there could be trouble ahead. Too many high-ranking officials were involved in this. This was going to make him a fortune and a reputation that would set him apart from any of his rivals. He took out a panatella and lit it. Not quite a big celebration cigar, but that would come later.

CHAPTER 42

A Pressing Engagement

Radley had been pacing the floor. Yes, he had the sixteen paedophiles still in the cells, but for how much longer? The real worry was what that intelligence department was going to do. The press could still be quashed; they hadn't any information worth having yet.

He was very worried a DA Notice 5 (DA Notice 5 – United Kingdom Security & Intelligence Services and Special Services. Highly classified information that cannot be disclosed without permission) would be served and then the sixteen could be let go. Even in Radley's politically correct mind this would be a heinous crime. He knew what was being kept from the public. He had been privy to many meetings in London where this had happened, but not in this case, surely, he thought. He had no Singh, no Kumar and no Boomer around to come up with something. *By God*, he thought with a passion that didn't usually pass his firewall of correctness, he never approved of their actions, but for once, just this once, he hoped those off-the-wall detectives had come up with something. He had run out of ideas and anyone to approach.

He was very aware that he would not be able to get PACE extended again for the sixteen. Their lawyers were about to arrive and they would get them out. Not used to sweating, Radley fumbled for his pristine clean and pressed cotton handkerchief and wiped the beads forming on his forehead. He was out of his depth.

Ash arrived back at the station full of angst and trepidation. Things could go well but he didn't know what to do about Jazz and Boomer. DCI Radley was his only hope and from past experience, he didn't inspire much confidence.

Ash, not used to being at the forefront, wondered how Jazz would deal with this situation. He had to get Radley to do something that went against the grain. Time was of the essence. The PACE clock would be ticking and Jazz and Boomer were in deep trouble. He could only imagine what those Secret Service men could do, and that scared the hell out of him.

He found Radley in the custody suite and took him to one side. In urgent whispers he told him that by the morning Dionne was going to be all over the newspaper like a rash. She was going to denounce the government for their cover-up of the paedophile ring and praise the police for rescuing her daughter. It was going to be a bumpy ride. The DA Notice 5 would be hard to serve after that.

Radley pulled himself up to his full height and took a deep breath. Things were looking up.

"Kumar, this doesn't smack of your idea – where did this come from?" he asked, a little cautious. Ash was not known for his ideas, more for his processes.

"All done under instructions from DS Singh, Sir. It's gonna work, Sir – by morning they won't be able to touch us, will they?"

Radley had to think. There was much that could happen through the night that would change everything. Mrs Osei needed protection until the morning. This was out of his depth. He needed a good place to hide her. He was well aware of what the British Secret Service could do. Guantánamo Bay was the American version of Bicester, which was where Jazz would have been taken. He had seriously pissed off the Secret Service and they were going to get their pound of flesh. Time was of the essence. Without Mrs Osei the paedophiles would be released and nothing further would happen, and DS Singh would be in a very dark place. Radley didn't know exactly what they did to people at Bicester, but he knew it was not nice and not pleasant.

"OK, Kumar, it is all looking good but we have got to hide Mrs Osei somewhere until the morning – it could all go tits up overnight. I have no doubt it will be known that the press have visited Mrs Osei and things will happen." He thought for a moment and asked, "Any idea where we could hide her?"

Ash, panicking a little now, tried to think. *What would Jazz do?* And then it came to him.

"It won't be nice for her, Sir, but Musty Mary has Mad Pete staying with her and Mrs Osei could go there as well. No one knows about Musty Mary and hers would be the last place anyone would stay; it's pretty filthy, Sir, but Mary is a good soul and would do anything to help DS Singh."

Radley nodded and agreed. There was a sense of quiet panic from him that made Ash scurry for the door, and with flashing lights he raced through the streets to get Dionne. En route he rang her, and she understood and said she would be ready. It all felt tense.

It was now late and the Richmond Centre was in darkness. Ash scanned the street for any sign of movement. In the quiet of night the street lights threw sinister shadows. He peered into the black abyss, imagining a movement that wasn't there. A tree rustled in the soft breeze, making him jump. Bathed in darkness, each car parked on the road, silent and empty, held a menace that didn't make sense to him. He suddenly felt alone, vulnerable and scared. What if there were agents watching? What should he do, and what would they do to him?

He closed the car window, fairly happy that all seemed normal outside and drove the unmarked police car into a side street. He took a deep breath, and with eyes darting into the darkness, searching for signs of life, he made his way to the front door of the Richmond Centre. Standing in the porch waiting for Dionne, he stood to the side of the door, not wanting to have his back to the street. If anything was going to happen, he wanted to see it coming.

Dionne opened the door quietly and slipped out carrying a small suitcase. Normally loud and vibrant, Dionne, tense with nerves, quietly nodded; she was ready to follow Ash. Still looking at all the cars parked in the street for any sign of movement, he led her to his car.

The gods were with them. As they sat in the car, and just as Ash was about to turn the ignition, they saw a car draw up outside the Richmond Centre and two suited men got out. Both Ash and Dionne held their breath. Just as the two men looked around, Ash whispered for Dionne to duck beneath the dashboard and out of view. They anxiously waited the five minutes it took for the centre's front door to be opened, and watched as the men went inside and the door to the Richmond Centre was closed.

At this point, Ash shakily turned on the engine and moved the car. He didn't put the lights on, and he moved the car slowly and silently past the Richmond Centre. Once into another road, he put the lights on and put his foot down. After a distance had been put between themselves and the Richmond Centre, Ash put on the flashing lights and raced to Parsloes Avenue, Dagenham, and Musty Mary's house.

Dagenham was a desolate place late at night. Parsloes Avenue was busy during the day with a busy bus route and a cut-through to Barking for the many cars that congested the area, but now it was silent.

Ash, spooked beyond belief, looked at the streets of Dagenham and saw agents behind every parked car and behind every hedge. He wanted to get back to the station and some semblance of safety.

With everything that had been going on, Ash, in his panic, forgot to ring Musty Mary and check if Dionne could come and stay. Being woken up by the bell continuously being pressed was not a good thing, and Musty Mary, with a herd of unhappy cats swishing their tails around her, opened the door angrily. Ash, by now in full panic, pushed past Musty Mary and got Dionne inside. Full of apologies and shaking, Ash explained how important Musty Mary was in helping Mr Singh.

"This ain't fair or nice of Mr Singh to do this," whined Musty Mary. She was tired, and she eyed up the woman accompanying Ash. She didn't like the look of this woman, who was just standing there looking around with obvious distaste at her decor.

Without the Singh charm to smooth these troubled waters, Ash thanked Musty Mary and said an embarrassed goodbye to Dionne, cautioning them both to not answer the door again tonight and to keep their heads down until the morning when he would be back to collect Dionne for her interview. The two women eyed each other up with the same hostility he had seen in the cats. He made for the door with indecent haste. *Jeez*, he thought, *I hope they are both in one piece in the morning.*

Ash returned to the station to report to DCI Radley. Nothing was said on the radio. They both knew they could be listened in to. Both were staying the night at the station; Radley on his sofa in his office and Ash was going to find an empty cell to bed down in. They would meet in the morning for a briefing at 7am and then Dionne would be taken with haste to the ITV studios for her interview.

Jeremy Banner would have a headline in the papers today regarding Dionne and the paedophiles. If all went well, that should stop a DA Notice 5 being issued to keep the press from talking.

With so much going on, Ash had only just given a thought to Jazz and Boomer and what the hell they were going through. He had no idea what those agents could do to them, but he knew it would be bad. Again, he started to shake. *I'm not cut out for this shit*, he told himself.

Later he took off for Parsloes Avenue to collect Dionne, who he hoped was in one piece. Dagenham was very quiet at this time in the morning and Ash got there in good time.

The Musty Mary household was never up early. The only person awake was Dionne, who was ready and glammed up. The bright red lipstick and the big earrings made her look like a star, she told Ash. He looked on, nonplussed at the sight of such jewellery hanging from her neck and ears. This woman was going to make an entrance.

Anxious to get moving, Ash cut her chat about the mess and cat hair everywhere and how she hadn't even had a cup of tea in this filthy place, and got Dionne out into the car, looking around all the time for any signs of agents. It all looked clear. *Who in their right fucking minds would think that anyone would stay at Musty Mary's house?* considered Ash as he wiped his feet upon leaving – he didn't want to make the floor of the car dirty. As he started his journey to the ITV studios in London he got a call that was going to change his plan.

Jeremy Banner told Ash to turn around and go back. He said, "Security breach," and hung up. Ash knew what that meant: the agents were waiting for Dionne at the studios. So it was back to Musty Mary's house and wait for instructions. Tense, confused and very upset, Ash was out of his depth.

No phones were safe to use, so all communication with DCI Radley was out of the question and Jeremy Banner had left him in mid-air. Did Jeremy know that Dionne was with Musty Mary? Ash couldn't remember if he'd told him this. Again out of his depth, he didn't know what to do.

Back at Musty Mary's home, he hoped something good would happen to put this right. He would sit and wait.

Dionne, back in this awful woman's house, was not going to be quiet. She started a series of moans that kept Ash on tenterhooks for the next hour. Actually, she was frightened. She knew that once she had been on television, she would be safer; she understood what was being said. Now she felt vulnerable and she caught some of the conversation about 'Guantánamo Bay in England', and that scared her. For all her bluster and bravado, she knew there was the possibility they might want to get rid of her; then there wouldn't be a problem.

Dionne handled all this fear in the only way she could: she moaned about the house, the cats and the woman who lived here. She had a go at Ash for being a wimp and not getting her to a proper safe place. She cuttingly said that if she was American the police would have guns, and Ash didn't even have a pea-shooter. It all culminated in Dionne bursting into tears. Ash was seriously out of his depth and wondered what the fuck was going to be done and when!

At 8.30 in the morning a knock on the door startled Ash. He went to the door cautiously, first making Dionne hide in the kitchen, much to her disgust.

"It's filthy in here, I'm not gonna stay in that cat-infested, oil-strewn, stinking-sink, dirty-plates-and-cup place. I will get dirty, honey, and that's not who I am."

Ash urgently needed to shut her up and hide her; he grabbed her arm and pushed her, none too gently, into the kitchen and closed the door. This did indeed shut Dionne up. She knew this was serious and listened, almost holding her breath, as Ash opened the door.

Outside were Jeremy Banner and a couple of men with cameras. They pushed their way in quickly.

Jeremy didn't have a lot of time. He told Ash they were live on air in ten minutes. He looked around at the filth and asked the two cameramen to set up in an area that was as respectable as possible. A chair was found and a blanket from the back of the car was brought in to cover the chair. In a matter of minutes the lights were set up and the camera put in place. Dionne was brought in, and after a mini panic, she checked her lipstick, jewellery and adjusted her dress. She was ready for an interview.

Jeremy took Ash to one side and said the agents wouldn't be far behind. They were waiting at the studio to arrest Dionne.

"On what charge?" asked Ash, indignant at such a thought.

"Don't worry about that, they would have found something. This is going to get worse before it gets better – unless we get this broadcast out, the story will be buried and all those who had anything to do with it will be buried too."

Ash, already scared, was now in the realms of that giddy state where if he didn't keep himself in check, he was likely to start screaming. He locked the front door and ran around the house, checking back doors and windows. The final minutes until the broadcast started felt like hours.

The cameramen busied themselves checking the lighting and their equipment. Jeremy looked at himself in the mirror and put on a bit of powder to cover the shine on his nose. He looked at the brightly made-up

Dionne and commented that she didn't need any help in getting ready.

If there was any irony in his voice, Dionne didn't hear it and with a big smile replied, "Thank you, darlin', I have done my best for you."

The countdown for broadcast was underway and Dionne sat ready to be interviewed. The room was full of tension – with seconds to go, it was going to happen.

The insistent knocking at the door startled everyone, but they were on air and continued. The door to the hall was shut and Ash stood in the hallway, looking at the front door. He could see the shadows of two men and he knew who they were. He didn't know how he was going to stall them but he had to give it his best shot.

At this moment a loud and croaky voice shouted from upstairs. "What the fuck do you want, you arseholes?" These were the dulcet tones of Mad Pete. Ash slipped into the kitchen out of sight. Mad Pete, with a blanket around his shoulders, lumbered down the stairs, coughing and gagging. He was not a happy bunny. It was, after all, only eight-something-or-the-other in the morning. "This is a bleeding unsociable hour to be coming here," he shouted through the door.

The voices on the other side were now getting quite frantic and threatening to knock the bloody door down if he didn't open it.

Mad Pete had been there before. "You touch this door, sunshine, and I will call the fucking police and see what that gets you."

By now the two were kicking the door and the bolt was giving way with each blow. It took them only two minutes to kick the door in and then they faced Mad Pete, who stood in their way shouting about his rights. *Way to go, Mad Pete*, thought Ash gleefully. Mad Pete was adding valuable seconds to keep these men busy, and gave the interview a few minutes' grace, which was hopefully enough.

The two men had had enough and just as they were heading for the front room, Ash stepped out of the kitchen. He looked behind him and said to thin air, "Stay in here, all of you."

With that the two men pushed Ash out of the way and went into the kitchen. Once they were inside, Ash slammed the kitchen door closed and locked it. Why Musty Mary had a lock on her kitchen he didn't know, there was nothing to hide or steal, but it served a good purpose. Ash stood triumphant and proud. He had never done anything like that before, and he giggled self-consciously at Mad Pete, who wondered what this fucking idiot was doing.

The two men, pissed off and boiling mad, kicked the kitchen door and one put his foot through the panel. Another two minutes were used up before they got out of the kitchen, punched Ash and kneed Mad Pete before going into the front room.

The interview of Dionne had gone well, and as the two men entered the room the cameras were turned on them. Jeremy Banner, in a soothingly dangerous voice, asked the two who they were and why they had broken into the room so abruptly. He asked if they cared to explain themselves to the nation. With this, the two men turned and left the room and house quicker than a turd flushed down a toilet.

The cameramen set about collecting their equipment and putting it back in the car. They were meant to be somewhere by lunchtime to film some sort of farmyard event. They weren't bothered what it was; it was all a job to them. This had been quite interesting but they were off now.

Jeremy Banner sat down on Musty Mary's settee, exhausted, relieved and shaking. "That was a bloody close call."

He smiled at Dionne, who, given her moment in the spotlight, had clearly and with passion told the nation her version of exactly what had happened and how the police had captured sixteen paedophiles. She waxed lyrical about Barking and Dagenham Police and thanked them for what they had done for her daughter.

A full interview would be taken for tomorrow morning's newspaper. The bit that Jeremy put in the newspaper that morning was enough, together with the live interview, to stop the British Secret Service from slapping a DA Notice 5 on the press. Ash felt exhausted, and he was off to talk to DCI Radley. Someone had to get Jazz and Boomer back. They couldn't keep them now, surely?

CHAPTER 43

Adaption and Desistance

Jazz woke with a start. The noise filled the room and hurt his ears. The light blinded him. He felt like he was in hell. Disorientated and distressed, he tried to bury his head in his arms but the noise and light invaded every crevice and tormented him. The noise was like that white noise you get when the television has no picture and all you see is millions of white dots, and all you can hear is an aggravating mush which, when played at a hundred decibels, pierces your senses and causes a searing pain in your ears and head.

The noise stopped after what might have been thirty minutes but he couldn't tell – he didn't have a watch or any sense of time. Still defiant, he banged on the door and demanded to be seen, but all he got back was the frustration of silence and disregard. He was alone and he felt insignificant. A sudden burst of energy brought out the defiant Sikh.

"This isn't how I expect to be treated. I am a fucking Metropolitan Police officer, a detective sergeant, for

Christ's sake! Who are you?" he shouted through the door. He wanted to be mad at them, but with no response he just felt scared, jittery and very alone.

He sat, slumped, on the side of the hard bed he'd been provided. He had expelled more energy than necessary. He knew they were Secret Service, but not which branch they came from. The day was going to be interesting, he told himself, with a bravado that didn't sink into his psyche.

He looked up sharply as the door opened. Jazz checked out the two men in t-shirts and jeans. He reckoned they were about thirty years old. They looked like your usual hooligans but their haircuts were expensive and the glint in their eyes was too intelligent for real hooligans. What was frightening was how they looked at him. He could see by their demeanour that he was of no interest emotionally or personally to them. They looked almost bored to be there. Jazz could tell that they would do whatever they wanted to him without any concern or sense of decency. What did they want from him, he asked himself. He didn't know any state secrets, he couldn't even tell margarine from butter, let alone know any fucking secrets.

"What a little shit you are, Singh!" was the opening line from the lead man. The other one stood silently watching whilst the lead man sauntered towards Jazz.

Scared and wary, Jazz asked hesitantly, "What have I done?"

The answer was swift and painful. The lead man had

something in his hand, a short cosh which he wielded and struck Jazz across his head, arms, chest. With each blow the man emphasised what a useless lump of shit he was. The pain was sharp and harsh and Jazz's head felt cracked. When the man stopped the barrage of blows to wipe the sweat from his brow, breathing hard, he told Jazz that no one cared whether he was dead or alive; that his boss had washed his hands of him.

With more bravado than sense, Jazz spat out the blood accumulating in his mouth and told them, "You can't keep me here, what is the charge? I have done nothing wrong."

This was greeted with a smile from the tall one. "We are the Secret Service and we have a whole supermarket of charges we can put on you if we feel like it." He pushed Jazz in the chest, and looking him up and down like a piece of putrid meat, said with a sneer, "No one knows where you are and no one has asked. You are mine for as long as I can be bothered. This was just a taster."

With that, they both left the room. The noise started again, leaving Jazz holding his ears. The tears came fast and hard. He hadn't cried since his mother died. He curled up on the bed and held himself. The pain was excruciating and he thought something in his head was broken.

Boomer hadn't fared much better. The beating was violent and painful. He told his tormentors defiantly, "You can go fuck yourselves."

Their reply was to smash his teeth with a small but effective cosh. Boomer fell to the floor, choking on the blood oozing from his mouth and nose. Curled up and coughing, he promised himself he would keep quiet in future. Nothing was said about what they wanted from him and he had no idea what he had done. What frightened and worried him was the promise that when they came back, the little slap he'd just had would prove to be only a taster of much, much more exquisite pain to come. They left him, laughing.

He lay down on his hard bed, trying to stem the flow of blood dribbling liberally from his broken teeth and nose.

"Fucking bastards," was all he could mumble. He was scared, although he was never going to admit it. This felt all wrong and he shouldn't be here, he told himself.

Both Boomer and Jazz felt broken and alone. Neither was used to pain and neither knew what was going to happen to them or who would care.

The nameless men in MI5 were planning carefully what exactly they wanted to get from this. They were seriously pissed off with these two jokers, but actually, there wasn't much they could do. Wasting the Secret Service's time was an offence, but up against terrorists and spies, they weren't much; a bit like Twiglets on a gourmet buffet table – hardly worth a look at but you've just got to have a go, haven't you? Noises from above would be made soon about them being banged up in this high-security compound, but before then they were going to make them pay. They had ways to inflict pain that a normal person couldn't comprehend.

Jazz tensed as he heard the key turn and the heavy door open. *What now?* he thought. If he knew anything he would have told them, but he had no secrets to tell. They made it clear they didn't want him to confess anything. This was purely revenge.

This time two different men entered the room. They appeared, and Jazz was loath to use such a word, more civilised than the last two. His body was tightly coiled in a tense panic, wondering what was going to happen now. He watched closely as the two men sat down and offered a hand to Jazz to join them. Hesitantly, Jazz got up from his bed; no more wisecracks from him as he cautiously limped to the offered chair. Without taking his eyes off them, Jazz sat down and waited.

They offered him a cigarette and he took it. His hands shook as he tried to hold on to the cigarette as they lit it for him. The first inhale of what tasted like a Marlboro, strong and full, relaxed his body a little, and as he exhaled he coughed deeply like an old man. He folded his arms across his bruised chest, hoping to stop the pain caused by the beating. They waited patiently. When the coughing subsided and he looked calmer, they started.

"Tell us where you got these names from."

Jazz would have feigned ignorance, but they wouldn't have any of that, he knew.

"It's called police detective work," Jazz answered,

a little sarcastically. He almost winced, expecting another beating.

"What about the other names, have you got them?" they asked.

Jazz looked up. *Other names?* he thought. *What the fuck does that mean?* He tried to look non-committal whilst he thought. *There are more of them. We didn't get all the bastards!*

"Sir, I think we got all of them. I think you will find, if you check the names, they are all there. We had a list and every one of them was there and we got them."

With this, the two men got up and left the room. The door slammed behind them to remind Jazz he was in a cell and was going nowhere.

So, thought Jazz, *there are more of them. The bastards didn't think I heard that.* He was in pain, but knowing the bastards had given away a bit of information made him smile, and it helped the pain immensely. There were more of them, and he had to get out of this shithole and tell someone.

When the cell door opened again, Jazz was ready for the worst. He knew they could do what the hell they wanted with him and Boomer. He saw two of the dead eyed ones enter his cell and held his breath, expecting a beating or worse. Waterboarding had been briefly mentioned during his last encounter with these bastards. It had been almost a private conversation between the two of them, nothing was said directly to Jazz at the time, but the words had caused a terror he didn't think he would ever experience; he was petrified. He knew torture was an unspoken treatment used by government forces.

They came at him, and he tried to curl up in a ball, shouting pathetically, "No, no, leave me alone!"

Without a word spoken to him, they dragged him up from the bed and he was pushed, kicked and manhandled out of the cell. He struggled and tried to kick out at them, but a swift punch to his chin almost knocked him out. Limp and weak, they had to drag him down a windowless corridor into what looked like an almost normal room with a light, a leather sofa and a table. They threw him on to the floor and left.

What the fuck is their game? he asked himself as he rubbed his chin, grateful to have been left alone. He wondered if his jaw was broken; it hurt and he couldn't move it properly. Jazz, usually optimistic, felt a deep and black cloud descend over him. He was dead meat and there was nothing he could do.

Then the shouting started. Outside the room, somewhere, he heard a familiar voice and knew that Boomer was around. It lifted his spirits a little. Boomer was cursing their captors, their mothers and advising them on what to do with their genitals, which was not only impossible but decidedly messy. Boomer was shoved, none too gracefully, into the room. As he stumbled and fell sprawling across the floor, the cell door was shut with a resounding metallic clash.

Jazz grabbed the shaking Boomer and helped him get up. He sat him down carefully on the settee and patted him on the shoulder to comfort him. Boomer was scared beyond belief and all the bravado and shouting didn't fool Jazz one bit.

"It don't look good, Boomer. I am sorry, mate, for dragging you into this," whispered Jazz.

"Oh, bollocks to all of that," was the feisty reply from Boomer. "We are here and we have to just get on with it." He raised himself up to his full height and shouted at the door, "Go fuck yourself, you perverted, mealy-mouthed fuckers."

Almost apologetically, Boomer sat back down, looked at Jazz and said quietly, "It needed saying – what more can they do to us? They have already decided our fate."

They looked at each other and instinctively hugged in friendship. It didn't help the shaking and the deep dread of more interrogation to come, but it was good to be together.

"I could do with a fag and a drink," grumbled Jazz. Boomer grunted his agreement to that. Jazz leaned over and whispered softly in Boomer's ear, "There are more paedophiles in the ring. We only got a few. They let it drop during a conversation. How the fuck am I going to get us out of here to find the others?"

With that, exhausted and fatalistic, they both slumped back on the settee and waited.

They had been in the room for a few hours, they reckoned. Just left to stew. Jazz had thought it might have been another part of the treatment, but this room was the Ritz compared with the places they had been in before, so that didn't make sense. Jazz felt stronger and braver having Boomer by his side, but then he heard the footsteps echoing along the soulless corridor. As they got closer the dread deepened and that sudden sense of bravery melted. Both Boomer and Jazz stiffened as the door opened. *What now?*

CHAPTER 44

Media Frenzy

The media scrum was something never seen outside Ilford Police Station. The interview with Dionne had caused a media hunger that was to grab anyone and any information it could about the biggest high-profile paedophile ring to have been caught in England. After Jimmy Savile dying before being made accountable for his crimes, the press were going to make sure that didn't happen in this case. In their desperation for a new lead and story they even grabbed the unsuspecting window cleaner trying to clean the office buildings next to the police station for his comments.

Questions were being asked about the officers in the case and where they were. The commissioner of police was in contact with the Home Office. The Prime Minister was being hounded by the press and television stations asking for comments. His press office fielded all the frantic press calls coming in their direction. The high-profile names hadn't been mentioned but there were rumours and hints, and now the American press and television were in on it, as were the European television stations. It was all becoming too much for the Prime Minister's office and a statement needed to be made.

At 1pm, the Home Secretary made a statement confirming that sixteen paedophiles had been arrested, and she thanked the Metropolitan Police for their diligent work in arresting them. She said that there would be a further statement regarding the arrests after interviews had taken place.

One reporter shouted out, "Why have you arrested the Metropolitan Police officers in the case if they have been so diligent and done such a good job? Why have they been arrested by the Security Department?"

The Home Secretary looked flustered for a moment, but with a smile said she would look into this. She said clearly that she thought they had been misinformed. Jeremy smiled and hoped it would do the trick.

Within two hours the news came that Jazz and Boomer were to be released.

DCI Radley informed the station of their imminent release and added, "The commissioner took a personal hand in this after reading the report I sent him. They will be back with us later today after being processed at Scotland Yard." No one believed that their release was due to Radley, but it was good news they were to be freed.

"Thank Christ for that!" was all Ash could come up with; he was knackered and wanted to go home.

He would leave all the posturing and posing to those high up with nothing better to do. Jazz and Boomer were safe and that was his priority. The paedophiles were banged up and highly unlikely to be given bail, he hoped, but nothing surprised him these days. With that he sloped off to his desk to do his report and go home.

It took a few hours to finish the report. He liked it tidy and pored over the facts carefully. Now done, he checked his mobile. His wife and mother had sent text messages citing abandonment and plain lack of caring as their reasons for the hard time he was going to get when he got home. *No hero's welcome, then?* he thought ruefully. They had no idea of what Jazz had put him through, or the fabulous result they had got. He was too tired and drained to worry about anything. For a split second he wondered if sleeping in a cell might be a better option, but nah, he missed his wife and children and even his demanding mother. With a smile, he slung his heavy satchel over his shoulder and made his way home. *At least I will get a decent meal*, he thought, and laughed.

DCI Radley took himself off to Scotland Yard in readiness for his interview. He would see Jazz and Boomer there. It had been a difficult night but once the commissioner had been alerted to the case and the press interest, things started to buzz and move. Radley had always fancied himself as a deputy commissioner, but wondered if he was maybe getting a bit above himself. Actually he thought that it had been his guidance and leadership that had caused the case to escalate, and he knew he had cracked the biggest case this year. Of course, it wasn't his case, it was DS Singh and DI Boomer who had cracked it, but as their superior, it was, of course, his case, and he would in future refer to it as such. He gave his hair a final comb, an adjustment to his ceremonial suit for his interview and he was ready to face the press gathered outside the police station waiting for news. He had plenty to tell them, and he would relish the press release showing how he had masterminded such a high-profile case.

The sixteen in the cells were some of the most important men in the country, and it was a coup not only to have caught them, but to have managed to retain them and fight off their solicitors. This case would take at least two years to come to court and in the meantime, DCI Radley would be in the headlines. He had rung his father to tell him; he would be very proud.

CHAPTER 45

Unleashed

Two men in suits entered the room and their body language made Jazz want to cower; they were not happy. In silence Jazz and Boomer were dragged from their seats and pushed towards the door and out into the corridor. Jazz didn't protest. Last time he got kneed and nutted for his comments; he wasn't going down that route again.

Boomer, with less sense, told them to, "Fuck off" but this got him a kick in the back as he was pushed down the dark and unforgiving corridor towards yet another door.

After going through a series of doors and corridors, the final door opened and they saw a blacked-out car idling in a dirty alleyway full of bins and rubble. The car door was opened and Jazz and Boomer were hurriedly pushed into the back of it.

In a stupid moment of defiance, Jazz shouted at the men outside, "Thank you so much for your hospitality, *arseholes!*"

The car sped off at a speed that caused the tyres to screech and Jazz and Boomer to be flung back and pinned in their seats. There was a driver and a silent hulk sitting in the front. In a matter of minutes, they arrived at Scotland Yard and the car glided through the open gates into the yard, where again, they were manhandled into the building. It all happened so fast, and the driver and hulk who had brought them into the building turned and left them.

For a few seconds everything was still. There had been no words between them, the hulk and the driver, just pushing and shoving and kicking to get them to move. After all the commotion there was now stillness and silence. Jazz stood shaking, trying to pull his sleeves down a bit to cover his wrists and failing. Boomer watched Jazz trying to smooth out the scrunched-up sleeve bundled about his elbow, unable at that moment to do anything. He was also shaking and trying to catch his breath. It was as if the world had stopped; all was silent and calm. They stood swaying a little from exhaustion and fear, listening to their own urgent breathing. Now what was going to happen? Surely they were safe now they were in New Scotland Yard.

In a blink of an eye, the commotion started again. The inner door opened and in rushed four officers. Jazz and Boomer were asked to follow them, but this time they were escorted in a more welcoming manner. Blankets were found and put around their shoulders. Their shaking was perceived as a result of them being cold.

This was an interview room, a bit better than where they had been kept by the security forces, but still an interview room. Mugs of strong tea with lots of sugar were handed to them. They were asked to sit at the wooden table. Without thinking they sat and accepted the strong brews, together with the digestive biscuits found for them. Still unable to speak, Jazz and Boomer sat watching the smiling faces across the table from them.

After the tea was finished, it became embarrassing to have these officers sitting staring and smiling at them.

Jazz broke the silence and with a weary sigh asked, "Why the fuck have we been brought into an interview room?" All he got back from the grinning pair across the table was a grimace and a shrug of the shoulders.

Not to be outdone, Boomer, who was now livelier after his caffeine fix, leaned forward and asked, "Are you fucking dumb? We are detectives and we have been badly treated. I want something better to eat. I am fucking starving." Another shrug of the shoulders was all they got.

This was uncomfortable; Jazz and Boomer shifted in their chairs, not sure what to do. One of the smilers asked if they were alright, and if they needed a doctor.

Jazz shook his head and Boomer mumbled, "Not bloody likely."

To avoid the staring eyes, Jazz looked around the room. These rooms were always bleak but the big mirror taking up the end wall told him they were being watched. There was the usual camera in the room, the recording equipment – better stuff than they had at Barking nick, he noted. The red line around the room was in place to be pressed in an emergency and alert all officers in the building to trouble. He hoped that wouldn't be used. The room smelled pretty good too. Barking's interview rooms always smelled of piss, sweat and other latent, underlying smells that cleaning never seemed to get rid of.

The tea had revived Jazz and his usual self started to emerge. This was fucking strange and he was on full alert; his sixth sense had kicked in and this wasn't right. He wasn't going to say anything, just sit and see what came forth. What the fuck was this all about, he wondered. Had he jumped from the frying pan into the fire? These were supposed to be the good guys, the Metropolitan Police, for fuck's sake, so why did he feel intimidated and on his guard? He caught Boomer's eye and knew he was thinking the same thing.

It wasn't long before the door opened and in walked a fairly senior officer, judging by the way the smilers jumped up when he walked in. He introduced himself as Chief Superintendent Alex Corder, and sat himself down opposite Jazz and Boomer. He looked at the file in front of him and Jazz almost held his breath; in the silence, it seemed almost impolite to breathe.

While he was distracted by the file, Jazz took the opportunity to look at Chief Superintendent Corder. He estimated he was about five foot, nine inches tall, but he had held himself so erect when he came in he could almost pass for six feet. His suit was expensive and his shirts immaculate; this man looked after himself. Jazz looked at his hands as he thumbed through the paperwork. That type of manicure didn't come cheap and his hands had obviously never done a day's manual work; they were white, clean and unblemished – a tad feminine, he thought. Jazz watched Corder closely. This man didn't smile much but his attitude seemed quite open and relaxed.

Alex Corder was a career officer and had no passion for anything other than a rise within the ranks. That this case was huge, and that these two detectives had more information that needed to be imparted to him was all he cared about. He wouldn't trouble himself with the despair of the victims' parents or the injuries and death of children; they were of no consequence. Pleasing his seniors was important, and from that point of view, he was going to get the information needed to run this case. Jazz could see the coldness in his eyes and made his decision. He gave Boomer a quick warning look. An almost negligible nod confirmed Boomer knew what he had to do.

After looking at the file, Alex Corder looked up. The smile almost reached his eyes, but not quite. "Good work, DS Singh and DI Black."

They both nodded, and subserviently, thanked him.

"So where are the papers you took from Paglesham? We need them now to progress this case."

With a look of enthusiastic sincerity, Jazz sat up

straight and in his best excited voice answered, "Sir, we want them too. I think they will hold a lot of information that will be useful to you. The trouble is…" Jazz hesitated to put on a mournful look. "The trouble is, Sir, one of my snouts took the boxes of paperwork and was supposed to return them to the police station the next day. I need to go and find him."

Boomer nodded at every sentence and added, "The bastard has gone underground, Sir, and I think we will have to go and pull him out of one of his filthy holes."

Alex Corder was not amused. This was not what he wanted to hear. "Tell me where to look and my men will go and find him." There was a hint of exasperation in his voice, which Jazz knew could be trouble.

"Sir, we want to help. We want this case trial-ready as soon as possible. I will be looking for another list – I heard there were more paedophiles. Now we are back with our teams, we will go and find him. Trust me, Sir, we want this badly. I will bring the list straight to you when I find it."

After a moment of deliberation, Alex Corder, against his better judgement, agreed. He wanted this sorted as quickly as possible. He knew there were more paedophiles on a list somewhere and he wanted that list very badly indeed. There was a senior officer, so senior everyone knew his name, who would be most grateful to have the list given to him.

Strangely, the debriefing didn't happen. Alex Corder knew everything he needed to know. He warned Jazz and Boomer that he was watching them and they should report straight to him, no one else. Jazz and Boomer nodded their agreement and promised that by tomorrow morning they would have all the paperwork for him to look through.

The car they requested was given to them. Boomer asked for a BMW but this was refused; they got a Vauxhall and were told to be grateful for that.

Boomer smiled ruefully at Jazz and said, "It was worth a try." They took off towards Barking, stopping at the first greasy spoon well away from Scotland Yard and sat down to the biggest all-day breakfast and chips they could order with a mug of tea. Now it was time to plan.

CHAPTER 46

A Cunning Plan

"What the fuck is going on?" asked Boomer with a mouthful of bacon, egg, chips and a piece of bread all turning in his mouth, carefully avoiding the broken teeth in the front.

Jazz looked on, incredulous at how it all stayed in his mouth, and that he could talk at the same time. *Bloody marvellous*, he thought.

"Those bastards in the Secret Service let drop a bit of information. They told me there was another list with more of these paedophiles on it. I reckon they are high-powered bastards too, and I suspect the Secret Service want to make sure they don't get arrested. Chief Superintendent Corder also wants that list and I don't think he is gonna prosecute them either. They want to protect those bastards! Can you believe it?" asked Jazz, feeling sick at the thought.

"I think we are being followed," he whispered. He looked out of the café window at a familiar unmarked car sitting across the road. The driver was very busy reading a newspaper. Boomer looked across the road and then back at Jazz.

"Don't be a tit! Who the fuck is gonna follow us? They think we are good as gold. We were candy-arsed sweet to that CS Corder." Boomer looked again at the car across the road, and with a sense of foreboding murmured, "Gawd, it does look familiar, now you mention it."

He turned to Jazz and whispered, "Bugger! You've got me at it now, Singh! What are we gonna do?" He quickly looked around the café to see if anyone was listening to them. Apart from the cook who took himself off to the kitchen, he noted that the only other person in there was a guy in the corner with a big beer gut and four-day stubble. He didn't look very interested in them.

Jazz put his head down and tried to look nonchalant as he cut his bacon, in case they were being watched. "If I am right, we have to find that list before they can get hold of it. We owe it to the kids."

Boomer growled his agreement.

They sat in silence and ate the glorious fry-up; nothing was going to interfere with that. They needed it. It was going to be a long night ahead of them. Neither wanted to admit they were bloody scared. They had experienced a bit of the Secret Service treatment and they were under no illusions: they could do whatever they wanted and no one would challenge them. The Met Police were not capable of protecting them.

Boomer growled, "We are in it up to our necks and

the only way out of the shit is to flush out the turds."

Jazz nodded; Boomer had got it right!

He came up with the idea whilst he ate. It wasn't brilliant, but it would work. He would tell Boomer what was going to happen ASAP, but he wouldn't talk in the car, in case it was bugged. *I'm reading too many bloody spy novels*, he thought, then he started to laugh out loud at the idea but it caught in his throat and choked him. He had to try and relax a little; he was far too tense.

"Can you contact your lad on the team – you know, Billy Bollocks?" asked Jazz.

Boomer smiled. "You mean William Balls, I presume?"

Jazz had to smile. "OK, you know who I mean."

Boomer would ring on the phone in the café; neither was sure if their mobiles were being tapped. He rang Billy and told him precisely where to be and how to look. He joined Jazz back at the table, scared and put out.

"This is bloody ridiculous," growled Boomer. "Won't be able to take a piss in private at this rate." You could cut the tension with a knife.

They had been far too long in the café and Jazz got up and said, "We have to get going soon. I will ring Ash from the station when I get there. You know what to do, Boomer – we can't talk in the car just in case."

With a nod they made their way to the door, shouting their thanks to the café owner, and left.

Jazz whispered to Boomer, "We have very little

time to get this done before we are sussed and banged up again. In about six hours we should have everything in place, if not we are stuffed, so no pressure."

Boomer looked at him and almost smiled and nodded. With a determination that Jazz always admired, he said, "Let's do it and fuck the bastards!"

Scared, resolute and wondering what the hell they were doing and why they didn't just take the easy desk job, Jazz looked around and suggested Boomer get a move on with the car. They drove steadily down Bow Road towards Stratford, and could see the unmarked car not far behind. *Come on, bastard, keep up with us for the time being*, thought Jazz. He tapped Boomer on the shoulder and made him aware of the car. Boomer nodded; he had already seen it.

Everything felt quiet; the cars outside moved timidly without the revving, blaring of angry horns and shouting that were usual in the East End. Even the shadows of the buildings they passed seemed to try and envelop them. Jazz could feel goosebumps pricking up his arms. He tried to keep it light, his voice cracking with strain as he made conversation.

"So, Boomer, what are you going to do tonight?"

Boomer looked at Jazz with a *What the fuck are you talking about?* expression, but cottoned on quick as Jazz gave him a warning glare.

"I expect I will go down the town for a few jars and pick up a couple of prossies and take them back to my place for a right seeing-to."

Jazz stifled a giggle. The bastard was milking this

for their audience – if they had one, that is. Jazz, in the same mode, stated sanctimoniously, "I am off to the *Gudwara* to pray. I haven't been for such a long time and it is my duty."

Boomer mouthed something that looked like *Fuck you*, but Jazz wasn't sure.

That merry interlude helped a bit, but the stomach-dropping fear returned almost immediately. They were getting near to Barking and plans would start soon.

"OK, Boomer, it's time to do your *Sweeney* driving."

Boomer knew exactly what Jazz meant; he put the car into third gear, foot on the accelerator and screeched round the next bend at a speed that was pretty good for a Vauxhall. For the next two minutes he took the car following them on a roller-coaster ride around Barking town centre. They would be lucky not to attract the local police. They made a lot of noise and terrified a few locals as they used the streets like a racing track. The car following them was a few heartbeats behind, so they had to be quick.

The one-way road system had a small through alleyway with a wonderful right-angled bend. The car behind them was struggling with the unknown roads and this gave Boomer time to screech to a halt around the bend, and Jazz jumped out and into an open side door. Boomer's officer Billy jumped in beside Boomer, and Boomer hit the accelerator pedal and took off with tyres screeching. The car behind them reached the right-angled bend as they took off. Jazz held his breath in case they heard his urgent breathing as the Special Branch car passed him. In seconds there was silence in the alleyway.

Jazz wanted a minute more just in case before coming out of the darkened side door and running towards Barking town centre. He had to get to Fresh Wharf before they realised he wasn't in the car.

Boomer led the unmarked car on a merry dance, speeding up every now and again and then slowing right down. He would take the surveillance team as far from Barking as he could; he was taking them to Paglesham. He would find that old tosspot Gary, who would help him.

Billy, sitting beside Boomer, was given a look that told him not to say anything. They were on a mission that, if it went well, would see them lauded as heroes, but if it went wrong, they would have the opportunity of knowing exactly what the Secret Service could do to them. Boomer didn't let on to Billy that these were the odds. He rubbed his head; that pain in his temple was throbbing again.

CHAPTER 47

So Much to do and so Little Time

Jazz got to Fresh Wharf in record time. It wasn't far from the town centre but now, out of breath and wondering if he was cut out for all of this, he bent double to get rid of the stitch in his stomach and to catch his breath. He got into Fresh Wharf through the garage so no one saw him, and that suited him fine. He found a phone and rang Ash.

With no time for niceties, as Ash picked up the phone all he heard was, "In my office, now", and the phone was slammed down. Ash stood for a few seconds wondering what the hell was going on and who the hell had called him. It was Jazz, he recognised his voice, but which bloody office he was referring to, he didn't know. He couldn't dial 1471; no police lines were listed. He took a chance; it had to be Fresh Wharf. If Jazz had gone to Ilford, someone would have seen him and that wouldn't do. You could get into Fresh Wharf by the back door. Ash borrowed his wife's car and made his way to Fresh Wharf. He knew there would be trouble, but what, he had no idea.

Jazz furtively tiptoed to the storage room where all the boxes were hidden. He checked first that no one had seen him and no one was showing any interest in him. *Jeez*, he thought, *this is bloody awful.* Knowing he was close to the information he needed, but also to all of the bloody Metropolitan Police units that could descend on him at any time, added just that bit too much tension. His hands shook violently as he tried to get at the boxes. There were tons of boxes and tons of paperwork in them – he checked his watch; he had only six hours to get the evidence found and sorted before all hell would let loose. This room wasn't used a lot but of course, it was a storeroom and officers ventured in and out as and when things were needed. It sounded like he was on some sort of hit list, so any officer finding him in here would blow the whistle. Then it would all be over; the Paglesham boxes, with the elusive list hidden in there somewhere, would be taken and buried and the bastards would get away. This thought didn't help his shaking hands.

"Get a grip, you stupid bastard," he muttered to himself. "You have work to do."

He uncovered one box at a time, and careful that if anyone came in it wouldn't look strange, he threw a few files over the box and hoped no one would realise what he was doing. He ploughed through several boxes which contained nothing of interest – more about venues and stocks, and nothing about a list or children. Patience wasn't a virtue he possessed. He was getting fed up and more spooked at being there and not finding what he was looking for.

He jumped when his mobile rang; it was Ash in his office upstairs. Not knowing if anyone was bugging his phone, he just said, "Stay," and rang off. He rushed out and up the stairs to his office. It was getting late now and would soon be changeover time for the shifts, so the place felt empty, thank goodness. He looked around the door cautiously to scan for Ash and spotted him sitting on his desk looking pretty fed up. Seeing no one else around, Jazz called out for Ash to follow him.

With more moans of, "Bloody hell, Singh! What is going on? I was at home enjoying a bit of peace and quiet for a change, and then all this cloak-and-dagger stuff." Jazz warned him to shut up and just follow. Ash recognised danger and trouble in Jazz's tense, terse voice and quickly followed him. Spooked by that grim look on Jazz's face, he kept checking for people lurking in doorways as he tried to catch up with Jazz striding down the corridor.

It was all said in whispers that stopped and started as noises outside the room kept catching Jazz's ear. Ash listened intently and after a while, the fear of capture caught up with him as well. They had a few hours to find the list. The overriding fear was being taken off by Special Branch. Jazz was under no illusions: even his own Metropolitan Police station, a place he thought he knew well, was the least safe place they could be in. Their own superintendent was looking for Jazz and anyone associating with him, hell-bent on turning them over to Special Branch.

The list had to be found, but they had over twenty boxes to go through. Ash looked at the pile and thought, *Thank God the police have no sense of order.* Everything in the room was a mess, with files over boxes of envelopes and copying paper, all badly stacked and toppling over each other – no wonder no one had spotted the boxes of Paglesham papers. They needed to organise how they would do this. Jazz and Ash were getting in each other's way and slipping on plastic covers that had fallen out of a box onto the floor.

After ten minutes they got organised. Jazz yanked four boxes over to another corner and put them on top of an old two-drawer filing cabinet for Ash to sort through, whilst Jazz started with the pile in the corner. It took an hour for anything to be unearthed. The list wasn't that simple. It wasn't a list as such, it was dossiers that when put together, made a list. Ash found and recognised the first one. The dossier was on someone high up in the Foreign Office, who had a predilection for babies.

Ash quickly read a little of the dossier and wasn't sure if he was going to be sick, cry or go and get a gun from the armoury to kill this evil bastard. He muttered that if they didn't find anyone else in these boxes, this particular nasty bastard was worth going to jail for. What he did to the babies that he sexually abused made these two experienced officers sick. Ash vowed this man was going to jail for life and no way would he get away with this.

Now fired up, Ash moved quicker and slicker. This was, after all, his forte; reading paperwork. Jazz smiled grimly; at least now he had Ash's full attention and they would get these bastards.

It was decided quickly that Jazz was a pain in the arse and nothing would get done with him around. Ash, in his element with paperwork and systems, said, "I can go through this quicker without you fannying around and getting in my way. You need to make phone calls and I will get you the information if it is here."

Jazz was drowning in paperwork and he was a doer not a paper-pusher, so with relief he said he would find an office to make his phone calls. Night-time in police stations was a dire time. At night it was the custody suite on the ground floor that was always busy and noisy, but upstairs where all the paperwork was done was fairly empty.

He made his way to DCI Radley's office. Smiling to himself, he wondered what he could do to give him just a little dig and tell him that *Jazz woz here*. He had expected support from him, just a bit of loyalty, but no, so *Fuck you, I'm gonna use your precious, pristine office*, he decided, angry now at this turncoat. He toyed with the idea of leaving a small memento that would leave no doubt that *DS Jaswinder Singh had been here!* He conceded it was not a very professional way to act, was it? *But sod it*, he thought, he would leave one of his calling cards just placed on Radley's desk. There wasn't much to smile about today but Jazz couldn't help having a giggle at the thought of Radley knowing Jazz had used his office and he couldn't do anything about it.

DCI Radley's office was locked, but hell, Jazz had been around enough burglars to know how to pick a stupid little lock. It took him under a minute to open the door. No one would come near Radley's office at this time of night, so he had some time to get organised and find the telephone number he needed.

The phone call was urgent and the key to all of this. Whether it would stop Jazz being arrested and taken by Special Branch, MI5 or anyone else who wanted to have a go, he just didn't know. He was up to his ears in shit and there was no one to call on to help him. If nothing else, though, the world was going to know what was happening here. He would ensure this wasn't brushed under the carpet. The mixture of fear and anger was a strange one and Jazz wasn't sure how to react to all the rumbling feelings and the shakes. He sat down; his legs were turning to jelly and the shakes in his hands could have frothed a full-sized bath of bubbles in seconds. He knew where Radley kept that bottle of whisky for special occasions, and Jazz made it his business to find it first. The swig of Bell's was just what he needed and after the third his hands felt steadier.

He rang Jeremy Banner, reporter for the *Daily*

Express. They had, by now, a good understanding. This scoop was a career-making big deal for Jeremy and he would do anything necessary to protect his informants and get the story. At the moment he was the nearest Jazz had to an ally. It was an odd conversation. For some reason Jazz had lost the art of stringing two words together. There were silences as Jazz tried to remember how to make a sensible sentence. Jeremy Banner, a veteran war correspondent, told him he was in delayed shock and to just calm down and take deep breaths. Jazz told him he was a fucking wanker – the anger was coming out. He hadn't got time to sit and relax; he needed to tell Jeremy now! He knew it wouldn't be long before he was caught.

He talked in urgent whispers for ten minutes until a plan was organised. At the moment there was nothing much to tell but Jeremy confirmed his suspicion that there had to be something very big and very wrong in those boxes. He made a joke that with the police and MI5 already after Jazz, all he needed was for Al-Qaeda to join in for a full complement of trouble. Jazz promised to do something particularly nasty to Banner if he carried on talking in that way. The conversation ended with an apologetic Jeremy saying he would wait in his car in the Tesco car park. When they had something for him he would come and take it, but in the meantime he would wait by his phone for an update.

Both left the call tense and worried. Jeremy Banner knew he would only be safe when he could print the information and it was out in the public domain – until then, he was in as much danger as Jazz. Jazz made his way back to the stationery room to see what Ash had found. Feeling scared and totally spooked to be in a police station where everyone was looking for him felt surreal and totally weird. He took the bottle of whisky with him. He needed it.

He found Ash knee-deep in piles of paperwork. The sound of Jazz entering the room scared the hell out of him. He thought he had been found out and the police were here to arrest him. He was a police officer, for God's sake! How had his career come to this? He wasn't made for undercover work. This man had led him into all sorts of danger. Ash just wanted to do his job and go home and enjoy his evenings. Already he had been nearly murdered many times, and now he could be tortured by the Secret Service. He was rattled and angry that Jazz had put him in this position yet again.

Jazz knew how he felt. He had done all of this without considering what would happen to anyone working with him. He apologised profusely and told Ash that without him this case would sink; that he, Ash, was the saviour of this case and that lots of little children would forever be grateful to him. He also added that a shrine would be erected to the awesome Ash. Up until the last comment Ash was almost believing him, but the shrine thing just finished it and against his better judgement Ash laughed.

"Bugger you, Jazz. Let's get on with this and get it sorted."

Jazz gave him an impulsive, emotional hug, which surprised Ash, and thanked him again for being here.

It took the night to go through the boxes, and each had to be meticulously inspected for clues and names and any details that could be helpful. There seemed to be a code that ran through lots of the paperwork and Ash had spent valuable hours trying to decipher it. It was going to be a long night but they would need all their strength to cope with the result. Some might have thought it better to leave the boxes unopened and let them rot in a pit somewhere, but that wasn't Jazz's style. Regardless of the outcome, he would have to divulge the incredible and unforgivable truth.

CHAPTER 48

Up the Creek Without a Paddle

Boomer had driven around the Essex countryside stopping at various spots including a drive-through McDonald's; he was hungry. The outline of his companion was always visible to those watching, but he stayed in the car. The car following them stayed a reasonable distance behind but they knew they were there.

He ended up in Paglesham at the Plough & Sail pub. It was only 9pm but it looked like it was about to close. Boomer was disgruntled at this countryside practice.

"Bloody pubs closing halfway through the day is bloody ridiculous," he told Billy.

He went inside to find Gary, who was at the bar talking to some old biddy who had seen better days. He looked up and saw Boomer walking towards him. Everyone looked up. Boomer was huge and imposing, but perhaps it was his shout across the pub of, "Oi, you bastard, I need you now."

Gary looked up and retorted, "I love you too,

darlin'," which raised a raucous laugh from the full tables in the bar. Gary looked around his fellow drinkers and with a triumphant turn of the head, joined in the laughter. He wasn't going to be talked to like that by a piece of shit from London.

Normally Boomer would be up for banter but the journey around Essex had rattled him more than he would admit. Seeing the Secret Service car behind him the whole time was unnerving. He knew what they were capable of and when they found out they had been on a wild goose chase, the thoughts of what they might do made him shudder. They were evil bastards if you upset them, and he figured he and Jazz had done just that.

"No time to fanny around, you inbred, I need your help." And with a resigned sigh, he added with feeling, "God save me."

Gary pondered for a moment. He could carry on this mickey-take for hours but he saw something in this bastard's demeanour that alerted him to trouble on a big scale. Although they weren't his friends, he figured Jazz and Boomer had taken down a paedophile ring and with his help; they were sort of partners in crime. He nearly giggled at the thought. Instead, he grabbed his jacket hanging lazily over the back of his chair, got up and quickly followed Boomer out of the pub.

Gary eyed the car down the lane; it had pulled over to one side and its lights were off, but he could see the outlines of a couple of people in the car.

"Who are they? Are they with you?" he asked.

Boomer shook his head.

"No one around here pulls into the side of a narrow lane, they would have either parked in the pub car park or carried on to a parking spot."

Boomer just said, "They are following us, they are Secret Service bastards and we need to take them on a merry dance. Where is your shit-heap of a boat?"

Gary was not happy; his little darlin' was no shit-heap. Begrudgingly he muttered, "Paglesham, down the bumpy road as before." He was going to say that he would do nothing to help this oaf but before he could, Boomer pushed him into the car and before he could sit up the car was speeding down the bumpy road.

The trees hanging over the road blocked out the moon and only the headlights managed to pierce the gloom. The holes seemed larger this time and the car rocked and rolled, throwing them about like rag dolls. Shaken and stirred, they reached the sea gates at a dangerous speed; Boomer raced through the open gates and screeched to a halt by the jetty. He looked over his shoulder and saw the car was still behind them, but hesitating close to the sea gates.

"Everyone run like fuck, and Gary, get that bloody boat of yours started now." He nodded towards the idling car watching them and warned, "If they get us we are dead."

Gary raced off first, followed by Boomer and the other chap, who kept his head down so he wasn't recognised. The jetty swayed as the stillness and quiet were broken by trampling feet. They hoped those Secret Service men still thought Boomer was with Jazz.

The ropes were untied fast and thrown into the boat. The engine was gunned and they began to pull away as Boomer jumped on board. He promised himself some exercise when this was all over – he felt as unfit as fuck. He held on to his knees as he tried to get his breath.

"Where am I going?" was the question Gary asked as he set sail into the darkness.

Boomer waved a hand in the air, pointing in all directions. "That island thingy place out there, that will do. I want those bastards to think we are going there to get something."

"I presume you mean Potton Island?" was the sarcastic reply.

"Yes, you bastard, just get us there."

Muttering, "Bloody London police are all bastards," Gary, now in the deep channel, gunned the boat again, making them move dangerously fast in the dark. Secretly, he was enjoying the adventure. Being one of life's dissidents, or so he thought, this was right up his street.

They all looked back to the shore to see if the SS men were about. The moon was full and with full headlights from the SS car, the jetty could be seen clearly. Two shadows of men stood at the end of the jetty, looking out to them. Boomer, seeing they could do nothing and couldn't touch them, sighed with relief. In a moment of utter stupidity and bravado, he waved his arms and gave them the two-fingered salute over and over again until the boat rocked so dangerously he was told to sit down before they all fell overboard. Billy grabbed Boomer and sat him down. This wasn't the night he had planned with his girlfriend, but he had worked with Boomer for a few years and knew this was important stuff.

Gary broke the self-satisfied quiet that followed by asking, "So what the bloody 'ell am I supposed to do now?"

All were nonplussed. Boomer hadn't thought that far ahead. That was just about the time they heard the helicopter and saw the large, sweeping searchlight that was coming towards them.

"Fuck! They got a helicopter."

CHAPTER 49

Time and Tide Wait for No Man

Jazz couldn't believe it. It was 3am and they hadn't been discovered. *Thank God the dim squad are on duty tonight*, he thought ruefully.

Ash hadn't said a word for hours now. The latest list had seven names on it and they were well-known names including members of parliament, a well-known charity worker who had collected millions of pounds for various charities, and a high-profile newscaster. It beggared belief that he had anything to do with this group. But there was one more; they just couldn't get the name. The code was very hard to crack but all the signs were that he was the top of the tree, the prize to get. Who could be higher than the ones they already had? It was tortuous looking at the paperwork and not knowing who he was.

Jazz looked at his watch. He needed the names by 4am to get them into today's newspapers. He couldn't rush Ash, who was meticulously going through everything and analysing codes. Jazz hadn't looked, he wasn't good at paperwork and Ash had told him to butt out, but time was getting on.

Jazz, trying hard to keep his impatience hidden, nudged Ash and said, "Let me just have a look. You never know, I might see something you don't." Ash looked up and gave him one of his *Who are you kidding?* looks, but handed the piece of paper over for Jazz to look at.

After a few minutes Jazz looked up and startled, said, "I ain't no genius, Ash, but I can see something here."

Sarcasm was rife and Ash said, "I know what you see, it's the watermark on the paper. Give it back, I need to get on."

Jazz was looking closely at the paper before him, and said quietly, "No, no, Ash, I really think I have it."

Ash looked over, and interested now, asked what he saw.

"Well, you know my dad worked for the post office? There are post office codes he told me about. Special high-placed people have their own postcodes. Now this here bit of code is for Buckingham Palace." Realising what he'd said, Jazz put the paper down and sat up straight. "Fuck me, it's someone in the palace."

"Do you know who?" asked Ash.

"No, but I know it's not the Queen or Prince Philip because they have their own personal codes. But it's the palace, and someone close to the Queen. The code contains part of her code, so it's not the servants or dog-walkers or nannies.

"If we get the code deciphered by a post office worker, we will have our name. Let's do it, Ash. We have only got an hour before the papers go to press and we need to put those other names and this one together for Jeremy Banner. He is in Tesco's car park now – let's go find him and we can all go to the nearest sorting office and get this done."

Ash, just about digesting all this, scrabbled to get the paperwork together so they would leave with all the relevant papers. In doing so, he asked, "Why would the post office tell us who this person is?"

"Because we are the fucking police, remember?"

"Oh yes," Ash murmured. Embarrassed and flustered, he followed Jazz out of the storeroom and they quietly and cautiously made their way out of the police station.

No one saw them; neither could believe their luck. Looking at his watch, Jazz knew that they had a few hours before shift-change, when every night-shift officer seemed to miraculously appear, ready to go home.

Their luck ran out as they left the building. A police sergeant outside having a cigarette saw them and ran over to them. Jazz saw him coming and had to think quickly. They were so close to getting away; he had to do something. Jazz whispered to Ash to stay still and look casual.

Ash looked at him. "Casual? How can I look casual when we could be bloody dead in an few hours?"

Jazz retorted, "Think of your son – he needs you, remember?"

It did the trick and Ash stood still and did his best to lounge around with the bag in his hand containing all the names of the high-ranking paedophiles; the bag the Secret Service, the Metropolitan Police and every fucking toerag who was associated with them wanted.

In a split second, Jazz left Ash and strode purposefully up to the police sergeant. He knew him, it was Martin Something-or-the-Other, a sergeant he had seen on the custody desk a few times.

"Hi, Martin, can't stop – we have places to go and people to see. You OK?" Jazz kept it easy and conversational.

"Sorry, Jazz, I've gotta take you in. There has been a bloody hoo-ha about you and Ash and Tom." He grimaced. "I don't like to do it, but it's my job. Please come with me now."

Jazz feigned utter surprise. "Wow, wait a minute. Your orders are to help me. I have the Secret Service turning up here any minute and we have the papers they want. See, Ash has the bag of files. It's really important that we don't keep them waiting."

He looked at Martin, who was listening. Jazz took out a cigarette and offered one to Martin.

"This was organised a short while ago – have you checked your emails? There should be a note on your computer saying the Secret Service are due here and need immediate assistance. It should also say that Ash and myself are helping them. Tom is already with them."

Martin was still listening. Jazz patted him on the

back, and as a gesture of goodwill he smiled at him. "Alright then, come on, I will come with you to the custody suite and you can check your emails. I bet you have had at least a couple of fags out here, so I reckon you missed the email."

He guided Martin back towards the building and offered his commiserations on night-shift work. "God, this is a bloody awful place at night. I don't blame you for taking a long fag break."

When they reached the door and Martin had swiped his badge over the security lock and entered, Jazz asked if he could just finish his fag and join him in a second. It was said with a smile that made Martin hesitate. For good measure Jazz shouted to Ash, "Come over here and wait for Martin to come back."

Martin, stupidly confident that Jazz was going nowhere and he saw Ash was also walking towards the door, left them to go and check his computer. As soon as he had disappeared through the door Jazz gestured to Ash to turn around and run.

It was a long and lonely walk away from the police station. Jazz kept looking behind, expecting to see Martin and a posse of blue lights following them. *Jeez*, he thought, there were many places they could be trapped in. He was spooked. Ash, who was not the bravest of people, seemed to be manning up to the situation, but his silence and gritted teeth came from pure terror, not bravery.

It took ten minutes to get to Tesco's car park and they arrived breathless, knackered and scared. Jazz banged on the reporter's window urgently and woke a dozing Jeremy Banner.

Time was getting on. Jeremy had a deadline and they needed to get to the post office.

"Come on, Jeremy, you bastard, earn your money instead of dossing in your car," was the urgent call from Jazz.

Sleepy but coming to life big time, Jeremy asked, "Have you found out who's on the list yet?"

"Yes," was the nearly correct answer. Jazz opened the car door and dragged Jeremy out. "We have got to get to the post office for clarification and then you will have the biggest scoop of the year – no, the century. That's if you move your arse now and come with us, it's quicker to walk."

It took no time for Jeremy to muster himself and they almost ran through the alleyway connected to the Sorting office.

"If we don't get this published by tomorrow morning I am a dead man and so is Boomer." All three of them knew that was not an exaggeration. The Secret Service would have had enough of them messing around and would deal with them in their usual way: no publicity, no explanations, just disappearance. Jazz went stone cold at the thought, but his only hope was to get the information and get it published. "Come on," he shouted, "stop fannying about and let's get moving."

This was their area; they knew how to get in the back way to the post office sorting room. The night manager wasn't happy to see them but when Jazz flashed his badge and told him it was all to do with the Queen's security, he led the three to his office, where it was quieter, and listened.

As Jazz thought, the postcode was a royal postcode. It took some time for the night manager to look through his book of confidential information. The sorting office was based in Barking, so there wasn't much call for post to go to the Queen or her offices.

Jazz tried to contain himself as he watched the night manager finger slowly through a huge directory that seemed to contain every postcode for everyone in the country. He ventured, after five minutes, that perhaps he could go a little faster. The officious little man took umbrage at this remark, and stopped what he was doing to tell Jazz what his job was and how he had procedures etc. Ash intervened and encouraged this cretin to get on with it.

Jazz, pacing up and down now, looked at his watch. It was bloody 5am and the deadline was up for getting the story in the morning newspapers. Jazz slumped in the nearest chair he could find. They were dead meat! It seemed impossible that they could have gone through all they had just to be pipped at the post. Jazz felt all the strength and energy drain out of him. Pointless! Stupid! #uselessdumbcop! He put his face in his hands and gave up.

The night manager broke the silence with the name they wanted. He had got to the royal postcodes and found the office of the Queen's chief adviser, Dominic

Bowman-Coutts. Jeremy interrupted with excitement. He knew this name. He was sixty-five years old and had been with the Queen for the past twenty years and risen through the ranks. He had access to her most private papers, and to her family. A paedophile working so close to the royal children and grandchildren didn't bear thinking about. Jazz wondered why the Secret Service would want to protect this man. He turned to Jeremy, who was busy on a little laptop. Seeing Jeremy working away, Jazz raised himself off the chair and dared to hope.

After a few minutes of mad typing, Jeremy looked up and grinned. "It's all in now. You will see this in the morning edition."

"How? I mean, I thought we had missed the deadline?" Jazz asked, nearly daring to smile but still not sure.

"While you were stressing and hanging around and baiting that night manager, Ash gave me the files and I had already sent over the other names and had the staff at the paper on standby for a very important name. The papers were delayed in going to press."

Jazz whooped with joy and relief. "Thank God." He hugged Ash. "You are amazing and I love you."

Ash nodded and tried to think of something clever to say, but it eluded him. Instead he just smiled and relaxed. Jeremy was amazing also, he thought. Ash had truly thought they were goners.

After a few minutes, Jazz calmed down and asked, "So now what? We'd better get out and hide somewhere until it's safe." He smiled ruefully and suggested, "I wonder if we should go to Musty Mary's? It's not much but no one will look for us there."

Reluctantly, Ash agreed. Jeremy was off to the newspaper office to make sure the story got into all the papers. This was going to be billed as Britain's version of Watergate, and he'd be bigger than Bob Woodward and Carl Bernstein. His career was now forged. Jeremy went back to his car in Tesco's car park. He would drop Jazz and Ash around the corner at Musty Mary's and then make his way, at speed, to his office. He was going to be the star with the scoop of the century.

Jazz, rattled, worried and tired, told the very happy reporter to, "Move yourself and get us somewhere safe. We have saved your arse, now save ours." As they left to get in the car, Jazz quickly looked around to check if officers had found them. He should have felt good that there were no signs of police, but he didn't. The gut feeling that any minute now one of the Secret Service cars would skid in front of them and grab them wouldn't leave him. When the papers came out, they stood a chance but for the next two hours at least, they had to lie low.

CHAPTER 50

Safe House

Musty Mary, the cats and Mad Pete were still asleep when they arrived in Parsloes Avenue. The road was quiet. No one got up very early around here. The road looked like a morgue and it made Jazz shudder; so quiet and still it felt wrong. Jazz found the key to the front door under the mat on the doorstep. He had told Musty Mary for years to stop doing that, but she took no notice.

Once in, he bolted the door just in case; he couldn't shake the feeling that they were sitting ducks. He shouted up the stairs, waking Musty Mary and Mad Pete. Jazz and Ash hadn't slept all night, and sitting on the stained and hair-covered settee made Jazz realise just how tired he was. Ash had sat down and was already asleep. Every part of Jazz's body craved sleep, but he had to stay awake. It wasn't over yet.

Ignoring the moaning and snivelling as Mad Pete trudged down the stairs, Jazz wondered how Boomer was doing. He hadn't thought much about him to be honest; so much had been going on that night, but now he was sitting down in comparative safety, he hoped he was alright. He thought, but only for a split second, about ringing Boomer to check, but it wasn't safe; he knew calls could be traced so he could do nothing but sit and hope he had found somewhere to hide.

Mad Pete was in the middle of giving a whining statement about how the fucking cats had scratched his precious full-length leather coat and how everything he ate here tasted of cat fur, but he saw Jazz's face and shut up.

"Are we dead meat, Mr Singh?" asked Mad Pete. He had thought of nothing else since being left to hide out at Musty Mary's place.

"Nah, why do you say that?" asked Jazz with the energy of a gnat.

"It's just I ain't never seen you look this bad before." With a snort that was almost a laugh, he added, "And I have seen you look pretty bad in the past."

Jazz gave a deep sigh. "I hope we are OK, Pete, but we'd better just sit it out and see." With more energy than he thought he could muster he added, "Now get me a decent cup of tea, I'm gasping, and none of that gnats' piss you normally make." Then he added loudly, "Check that back door is locked while you are in the kitchen."

Mad Pete shuffled off, mumbling something about arse-wipes, but he put the kettle on and checked the back door, almost happy to be doing something and not thinking about what could happen. He didn't ask why he should check the back door was locked; he could guess. He was frightened to ask the obvious question and got on with making the tea.

The tea was good and perked Jazz up. He let Ash sleep – no point waking him up for a cup of tea. Mad Pete resumed his whining.

"I ain't saying Mary is a bad person, Mr Singh, but she don't 'alf go on. I can't stand people who don't get over things and she has moaned non-stop about the council, her work, her heating, her legs, and any other bleedin' things she could think of." Mad Pete stopped for a second. He didn't want to ask, but he had to. "Are we safe here, Mr Singh?

Jazz checked his watch for the umpteenth time. Only a short while longer and then this would be over. The pressure had built and the tension was so high his voice had gone up a few octaves. He was so scared and tired, and he wasn't sure whether to grab Mad Pete and shake him until he shut up or just sit there and cry. The whole night had come back to bite him on the bum.

Mad Pete was insisting on a reply. "Mr Singh, are we safe?" he asked again.

Jazz took a deep breath, and was about to tell Mad Pete to shut the fuck up and calm down. He lied when he told Mad Pete he had everything under control. He was controlling nothing. All his energy was taken up controlling himself and his emotions.

As he was about to answer, the front door

exploded, sending shock waves and splinters and smoke throughout the room. The noise was deafening. In total shock and unable to move, they listened and looked. Through the deafening ringing in their ears they heard the trampling of feet and shouting. Jazz's eyes were stinging from the smoke but he saw the rush of black as a herd of beefcakes dressed in black and carrying bloody great guns rushed them. The precision, the speed and the explosives were slick. He watched as the tableau unfolded, unable to move. A panic-stricken Ash was roused from a deep slumber and Mad Pete was handcuffed and pushed nose to nose with his very angry captors. In a matter of seconds Jazz was yanked up from the settee and manhandled into handcuffs. He found it hard to think as he jostled for air with the thug in his face. The Secret Service goon squad had found them.

"Got you, you fucking slimy little DC."

"DS, actually," was the defiant, haughty answer. This got Jazz a stinging slap across the face.

"We want the list – *now*!" the thug shouted, eyeball to eyeball with Jazz.

Unable to move, Jazz blinked hard as the spray of spittle hit his face. It was bloody frightening and for a moment he didn't know what to do. He heard a scream from upstairs and noted they had found Musty Mary. The chaos continued as the small room was filled with hefty, kitted-out, balaclava-clad men in black, pulling chairs apart and opening cupboards. For a split second Jazz thought wryly, *And these people are working for us?* The pushing and shoving and the goading and threatening got violent. Jazz, his ears ringing with the stinging blows, could hear Mad Pete whining loudly; he was on the verge of a druggy fit. It had to stop.

Jazz's eyes darted from one to another, trying to see and think what to do. Ash cried out in pain and it all looked impossible, and Jazz was more scared than he had ever been. These men didn't care what they did. They wanted the list. He had no choice.

Above the noise and mayhem, Jazz shouted, "*Stop! I will tell you everything.*" It took a few moments for everyone to calm down but the two men holding Jazz ordered everyone to stop and wait. They were now in a vacuum of comparative silence and Jazz wondered what the hell he was going to say now.

He looked at the clock above the fireplace and hoped to God it was correct and not fast. The time was a beautiful and miraculous 6.45am. Surely it was too late now for anything to be stopped.

It was all over in a matter of minutes. He told them that the list was now with the press and they had printed it in this morning's newspaper. He added, unwisely, "It is now all over the fucking country, you bastards!"

This got him a serious beating from one of the goons, whilst one of the thugs left the room with his phone to his ear, talking urgently to someone. Jazz lost consciousness at this point. The blow to his chin knocked him for six and with a hefty kick to finish the job, he was left, sprawled across the floor.

CHAPTER 51

The Worm has Turned

Jazz opened his eyes, and for a second wished he hadn't. The pain seem to be attacking him from all directions. His head, his eyes, his mouth, his chin, his stomach, his chest, his hands; everything was screaming in pain. He squinted, frightened to open his eyes too much, to try and control the pain in his head and see where the hell he was. The place smelled clean and he could hear footsteps echoing. He was confused, and for a few seconds tried to think what was happening, and what had already happened.

He heard a polite cough and focused on the shape standing beside him. DCI Radley was here? Why? Jazz tried to figure it out.

It was all explained to him by a polite but impatient DCI Radley, who really didn't want to be there.

"I always seem to find you in a hospital bed!" There was a sense of concern that he was obviously trying hard to disguise. After a few seconds of collecting himself, DCI Radley pulled himself together, and now fully in control, continued, "You bloody fool. You have caused no end of trouble. This time you have gone too far. The government is involved now and I have calls from Scotland Yard asking for explanations in writing and demanding accountability. You have made my job impossible and I am not sure whether you will stay here or be charged with treason."

"Why?" asked Jazz, totally perplexed by this tirade. What on earth had he done? He couldn't remember anything at the moment. He could hardly hear anything; his ears were hurting.

After a few moments, a contrite DCI Radley asked how he was feeling and suggested he get some sleep. Jazz was told he had been kicked in the head and body and he needed to rest.

Jazz, heavily sedated, slept for two days, on and off. He didn't see colleagues who had passed by to check how he was. On the third day he awoke to a lovely nurse and thought he had died and was in heaven. That soon changed when the next face he saw was Radley, impatient now after waiting for two days.

The sleep had done him good and Jazz remembered everything. It would seem there were ongoing interviews with twenty-five suspected paedophiles, all, Radley whispered, high-powered men in authority.

Jazz asked, in the same whisper, "What about the one close to the Queen? His name is Bowman-Coutts. Have you got him?"

Radley shifted awkwardly. "Er, no, we didn't get him."

Jazz, in pain and feeling weak, tried to get up but failed and fell back on the pillow. "You have got to get him, Sir!" he said urgently.

Still whispering, Radley leaned towards Jazz and said, "He was found dead this morning. Apparently he was driving at seventy miles per hour and his tyre burst. He hit a tree and the car exploded into flames."

Jazz raised his eyebrows. "Bloody lucky for the government, Sir."

Radley, feeling more awkward, just nodded.

"Who gets the case now?" asked Jazz.

"Oh that's easy – this case will go to the team who deal with serious crimes based in Scotland Yard. MI5 is keen to close it down but the press have the names and are threatening to release the list if they are not kept informed. The first list of names has been printed because they know we have those sixteen in custody, but the press held back on the second list until arrests were made. MI5 slapped a DA Notice on the press but I think it will only hold for a short while."

This was all too much for Radley. It had been a harrowing few days at his police station and questions had been asked about his competence. He bade farewell to Jazz and left him with a warning that in future he was going to be relegated to little old lady cases if he was lucky enough to stay in the force.

His passing shot was, "You are being debriefed tomorrow, so make the most of a leisurely day in bed today, because tomorrow you will be kept very busy indeed."

Jazz had done a good job and was proud of catching twenty-five high-ranking paedophiles. Any other police officer would be given a medal, have the press following him and be held in high regard by his superiors, but oh no, he got a bollocking and the threat of losing his job.

Before depression set in, a knock at the door alerted him to four members of Boomer's team standing in the doorway. In unison they shouted, "They Sikh him here, they Sikh him there, they can't find that bloody Sikh anywhere."

They thrust a brown paper bag into his hands. The grease was just coming through the bag. It made him smile, and with warmth Jazz said, "You guys! My favourite! Big Mac and fries. Thank you. I needed cheering up."

They told him Boomer was being debriefed at headquarters so couldn't come, but they were under orders to bring him some of his favourite food.

The day was getting better, and as they left, Ash arrived with arms full of paperwork.

"Jeez, Ash, don't you ever travel without a file in your hand?"

Ash ignored this and proceeded to open the files and tell Jazz about the twenty-five paedophiles and where they were kept, and how they hadn't been given bail.

"Seeing as you are awake, I thought I would let

you know what is happening. It would seem half the government is on the list. It's causing a hell of a problem for the Met to find somewhere confidential to keep them, but that's someone else's problem thank goodness."

"Way to go, Ash, you are getting belligerent. There is hope for you yet," exclaimed Jazz. "Half the government? A tad exaggerated, I suspect," he added with as much sarcasm as his headache would allow.

Ash muttered, "Yeah, OK, but one would be too many and there are more than that." Now into his file again, Ash added, "I also found more DVDs in the boxes, which are incriminating. They have been taken away by the serious crime team. I don't think they will get away with anything."

With a sigh of relief, Jazz summed it up. "So, we got the lot of them and they are all now in custody or dead, and with luck none of them will see freedom again. The goons from MI5 are back in their cages. Bloody brilliant!"

Feeling good and puffing his chest out, he added, "So, Ash, they say you are what you eat; now I don't remember eating a fucking legend."

Ash raised his eyebrows and got up to leave. With his back turned to Jazz, he smiled – what the fuck was he going to do with this legend of a man called the Jazz Singher? Try and keep the bastard alive and out of trouble was his first thought.

EPILOGUE

After a month of recuperation, Jazz returned to Ilford Police Station. There was one last piece of the puzzle to complete. It was as busy as ever and no one noticed as he climbed the stairs to the offices above. He was looking for Phyllis. For years she had been his adoring clerk. She had sorted out all his case files and he was grateful to her; he hated paperwork. When DC Ash Kumar took over his case files, Jazz had thought Phyllis would be grateful to be let off the hook, and stupidly, didn't take into account that she had an enormous crush on him.

He spotted her hunched over her computer and working away. He looked at his watch; it was only 8.30am.

"Hi, Phyllis, how are you?" he said affably.

She looked up at him and blushed. He always had that effect on her. "I am OK, Jazz, thank you," she muttered, a tad embarrassed, he thought. He smiled and sat down beside her. She looked at him so close to her and blushed again.

"So, Phyllis," he started. She looked up, wondering what he was going to say. "Why did you put pornography on my computer and cause me so much trouble?"

She shifted quickly and said, "I didn't – it wasn't me."

He smiled again. "Phyllis, you are the only one who had access to my login details. You are the only one who has that information," he said gently. "Come on, tell me, why did you do that?"

She started to cry. "I should have known you would figure it out, you are a damn good detective. How did you figure out it was me? I am so sorry."

She looked pathetic now, and he almost felt sorry for her. Now the excuses started to come from her mouth.

"I was very upset when you gave DC Kumar all the work I used to do for you. I thought we had a good working relationship." She blushed again; they both knew she fancied Jazz.

"If you do that again, it will cost you your job. I hope after all that has happened no one mentions it again, but I will not forget what you did." Jazz was shocked; he felt so upset. He didn't realise until that moment how let down he felt. "I thought I was someone you liked, and I thought I had your loyalty. That was potentially a dismissal without pension for me."

She apologised, cried and pleaded that she would never do it again. He could see the relief in her face. But he wasn't finished.

"But what is unforgivable is what you did next." Jazz, venomous now, got close up to Phyllis' face and spat out, "You were the one who took all our notes on the paedophile case off the system. There is no point in denying it. That was evil. That was wicked, and I can't forgive or overlook what you did. If another child had been murdered it would have been your fault. For that I am arresting you. You don't deserve to walk in the shadow of anyone here."

He looked behind him and saw Ash waiting. He gestured for him to come forward and take Phyllis down for charging. She was scared; Jazz had always been smiley and charming with her. Phyllis had never seen such a look of disgust on his face, and now she was going to be arrested? How could he do this to her? Hysterical now, she called out to him as he walked away, crying and pleading and telling him how sorry she was and how she loved him. She begged him not to arrest her. He didn't want to hear any of that.

Jazz turned his back on her and made for the door. He needed to get the taste of filth out of his mouth. Once he left the building he promised himself a tot from his flask, which was nestling seductively in his inside pocket. With a deep sigh, he told himself it was another loose end tied up. He wasn't sure who he could trust any more, but for now he was off to find Mad Pete and see what was going on in his town. He trusted Mad Pete to be exactly what he was. Jazz knew how treacherous and devious he could be, and how he would shop Jazz to anyone if they scared him enough. He was a snivelling coward, but he was Jazz's snivelling coward. They had a good understanding and that suited him fine.